CITY OF STORMS

KAT ROSS

For Dinky

Foreword

Just a quick note to say you can find a Glossary at the end of the book with people, places and things from the story. Fantasy worlds have a lot of moving parts, especially as the series progresses, and it's always nice to have a quick reference to jog your memory. Cheers, Kat

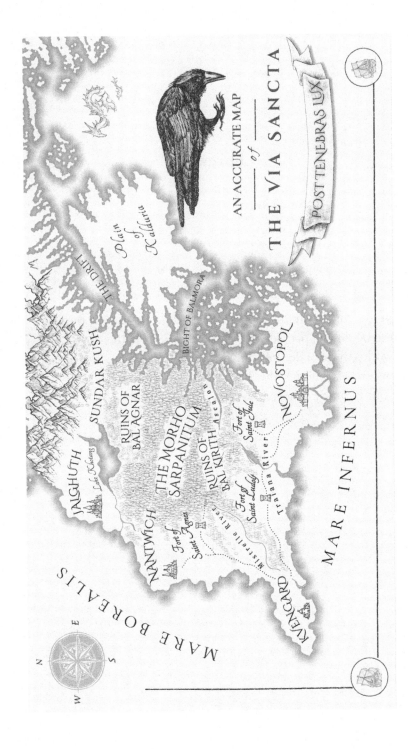

AN ACCURATE MAP
of
THE VIA SANCTA

POST TENEBRAS LUX

MARE INFERNUS

MARE BOREALIS

KVENGARD

JALGHUTH

Lake Khoung

NANTWICH

Fort of
Saint Agnes

Saint Agnes

SUNDAR KUSH

THE DRIFT

Plain
of
Kaldauria

RUINS OF
BAL AGNAR

THE MORHO
SARPANITUM

RUINS OF
BAL KIRITH

Ascalon

Misterille River

Fort of
Saint Luolof

Traiana River

BIGHT OF BALMORA

Fort of
Saint Jule

NOVOSTOPOL

N
E
S
W

Darkness cannot be vanquished with steel. If you wish to conquer darkness, you must turn on the light of reason.

— THE MELIORA, FOURTH SUTRA

Homo homini lupus. *Man is wolf to man.*

— FRAGMENT FROM THE SECOND DARK AGE, HELD IN THE TABULARIUM OF THE WESTERN CURIA AT NANTWICH

Chapter One

The baying of the Markhounds jolted the priest to wakefulness. Even after three years living next to their kennels, the eerie sound—frantic barking mingled with deep-throated howls—lifted the hairs on his neck and sent adrenaline coursing through his veins.

Fra Alexei Bryce fumbled for a match in the darkness. An instant later, a wavering flame appeared. He touched it to the stub of candle next to his armchair and leapt to his feet, knocking a fat biography of the Southern Pontifex to the floor. A quick rummage through teetering stacks of books on law and psychology unearthed a pocket notebook of supple brown leather. Alexei jotted down the hour.

11:17.

Rain lashed the narrow arched windows of the Tower of Saint Dima, though the storm was nearly inaudible over the clamor in the courtyard below. The kennels held two dozen Markhounds and they were all going off at once. Alexei rubbed his shorn skull, fighting the desperate urge to close his eyes. He rarely slept, and never for longer than three or four hours at a stretch. The doctors had given him pills, but he'd only taken them once. The sedative left him groggy and he hadn't touched them again.

Sometimes, after drifting off in the armchair, he woke with the fleeting sensation that he had dreamt, the way he did as a young child, but this was impossible. Priests of the Curia did not dream. They'd been inoculated against such folly.

The nights in Novostopol were never cold, but this one was certainly wet. He lifted a cloak from its peg and drew it on over his midnight blue cassock. The pockets held a pair of soft leather gloves and a coin-sized copper disc with a raven engraved on one side and a name on the other. Alexei absently fingered the disc before drawing on the gloves. He blew out the candle. For a moment, he stood in darkness, blue eyes searching the distant lights of the metropolis.

Somewhere beyond the walls of the citadel, someone was descending the rungs of madness.

Their Marks—intricate pictures inscribed on the skin by the psychic power called the ley—had suddenly flipped. Instead of suppressing a person's worst impulses, inverted Marks had the opposite effect, erasing all inhibitions. Alexei had seen mothers drown their children, fathers do far worse. Strangers might be the first victims if the breakdown happened in a public place. Men tended to be more violent and women more cunning, but there were always exceptions.

No one fully understood the condition, but it seemed to be triggered by extreme stress. A conflict simmering in the unconscious mind that finally erupted—often with no warning.

As an ordained brother of the Interfectorem, it was Fra Bryce's task to find and subdue these dangerous lunatics before other lives were destroyed.

He strode to the oaken door and hurried down the winding stone steps, worn smooth as sea glass from a thousand years of priestly boots. Alexei raised his cowl and stepped into the rainy courtyard. Four Markhounds stood in a semicircle, coats glistening.

They were bred from southern stock, dark brown with long, thin bodies and pointed ears, but the ley had made them into something more than hunting dogs. They could smell the moment a Mark flipped—thus the frenzied howls—and follow the trail to its source. Most people would glimpse a shadow from the corner of the eye, if they noticed the creatures at all. The thickest walls and stoutest gates would not stop a Markhound. A crevice wide enough for a tendril of fog sufficed for them to pass.

As usual, the pack had not waited for him to open the kennel door. They'd come out on their own.

The hounds fell silent the instant he appeared. Alexei had fought beside them back in the days when he was a knight in the church's war against the rebel cities. He knew they would obey his commands. Yet there was still something viscerally unnerving about the dogs, which was why the kennels were in a wooded area distant from other buildings in the Arx—especially the touristy parts.

The Markhounds watched him with alert eyes. The only sound was the steady drip of rain. Had his partner slept through the racket? Then headlights slashed the darkness. A sleek black car pulled up between Alexei and the hounds. Fra Patryk Spassov killed the engine and got out, a hand-rolled cigarette dangling from his mouth. It became instantly sodden. Spassov ground it underfoot with a grimace. He was a decade older, early forties, with a tired face that had seen its share of horrors. Like Alexei, his hair was shorn nearly to the scalp, concealing a receding hairline. His eyes were bloodshot and he smelled of cheap wine, but that was quite unremarkable.

"They always pick the filthiest weather to go crazy, don't they?" he remarked, climbing into the passenger seat.

By long agreement, Alexei drove while Spassov smoked

and provided moral support. At first glance, they made an odd pair. Alexei's views were radically different from Spassov's, who believed the insane to be better off dead. Patryk had no qualms about cracking skulls and considered himself akin to a refuse collector who was merely disposing of the trash.

This was the prevailing opinion in the Curia, not to mention society as a whole, and the reason their order was a dumping ground for defectives—priests with the brute strength to wrangle maniacs into custody but inadequate social-emotional skills to function in loftier spheres of the church. Invertido were feared and despised, making the Interfectorem equally feared and despised by association.

Alexei was a defective, no question about that, but a somewhat higher class of one. He was a war hero, after all. He was not a raging alcoholic like Spassov, the Pontifex bless his soul. And he did his best to arrest people without shedding blood. They were sick, not evil. Spassov thought he was naïve, but after years of heated arguments he had ceded some ground. At least he no longer stabbed first and asked questions later.

Alexei started the engine. The hounds arrowed forward, racing for the Dacian Gate. Circles of blue fire punctuated the night, each with a raven in the center, symbol of the Eastern Curia. The conflict had ended four years before with the defeat of the heretics, but hundreds of Wards still blazed over every window and door, a final cordon against their enemies. No mage who wielded abyssal ley could pass these walls.

Alexei floored the pedal, trying to keep the hounds in the headlights. The inner citadel was only a few square kilometers. Within a minute, they reached the broad Via Fortuna, flanked by bright yellow street lamps for its entire length. Candles and torches burned in every building despite the late hour.

The promise of his faith.

Post tenebras lux.

Light after the dark.

"I didn't see you at supper," Spassov said, rolling down the window to light another cigarette. The flame trembled in his cupped hand. "Or evening meditation."

"I was reading."

"Ah. Anything good?"

"A biography of Luk."

The Via Sancta comprised four city-states, each governed by a Pontifex. Once it had been six cities, though two now lay in ruins, their clergy dead or excommunicated. Luk was the Reverend Father of the Southern Curia, a rocky peninsula southwest of Novostopol.

Spassov gave a crooked grin. "The Wolf?"

"He made the Markhounds. Evolved them, I mean."

"I heard that somewhere." Spassov produced a silver flask and took a sip. "Ever been to Kvengard?"

"No, have you?"

"When I was younger. A delegation to commemorate Liberation Day. It's a strange place. They don't have telephones. Not even electricity. The taxis use horses! I wouldn't want to live there."

Alexei switched the wipers to high. "They probably wouldn't want to live here."

Spassov laughed. "Probably not. The weather in Novo isn't for everyone. Not unless you have gills." He tucked the flask away. "Hey, when we're done tonight, let's go to that place with the spicy noodles. They're open late."

"The one with the pretty waitress?"

"She likes me."

"Because you tip so much."

"No, no, because I make her laugh. Make a woman laugh and she's yours forever."

Alexei refrained from pointing out that women did not grant favors to priests of the Interfectorem, and most would run swiftly in the opposite direction. Patryk knew it as well as he did. But it made him happy to pretend otherwise, and who was Alexei to deprive him of his fantasies?

They sped past the Pontifex's Palace and the Tomb of the Martyrs, followed by various ministries and the gilded dome of the basilica. By the time they reached the white marble arch of the Dacian Gate, the hounds were gone. They would run until they found their prey. Then, Saints willing, they would await the arrival of their masters, although Alexei always feared the dogs might get carried away and do something stupid. Unlike Spassov, Markhounds could not be reasoned with. On the front, he had seen packs bring down Nightmages and while the nihilim heretics were his enemies, the memory made him grateful he didn't dream for he would surely have nightmares.

Alexei squinted into the rain. The hounds had vanished, but phosphorescent paw prints revealed their passage in the blue surface ley that flowed in eddies and currents along the ground. The glow would fade within minutes but it was enough to follow.

By long custom, the gates of the Arx stood wide open, embracing all who sought sanctuary inside. Alexei slowed to raise a hand to the guards, then sped up again as they entered the city proper. Raucous music spilled from cafes and bars. Taxis and trams clogged the hilly cobblestoned streets. Spassov grumbled about the traffic, as he always did. The trail led up and down through the ancient, crooked labyrinth of the city center. Alexei drove as fast as he dared, but there were people about. Most had been drinking and they staggered under umbrellas, unaware of the large Curia automobile barreling toward them. Alexei reluctantly slowed down.

"Saturday night," Spassov said in a resigned tone. "What did you expect?"

"What time is it?"

Patryk took out a battered pocket watch on a silver chain. It had belonged to his father and he carried it everywhere, just as Alexei carried the coin with the raven and name. Good luck talismans.

"11:29."

Alexei's hands tightened on the wheel. It had been twelve minutes since the alarm sounded. The Saints only knew what might have happened in the interim. Not everyone whose Marks turned became violent. Sometimes the descent was gradual.

But sometimes it was very swift indeed.

He jammed his foot down on the accelerator and took a hard left. Spassov made an unhappy noise as he was thrown against the door. The crowds thinned, then disappeared as they left the city center behind. The monotonous swish-swish of the wipers made Alexei's eyes heavy. He unrolled his window and gulped in the night air.

That was the most diabolical thing about insomnia. The acute, chronic kind that lasted for years. Exhaustion came out of nowhere, but when he tried to sleep, it would vanish. He would lie in his chamber, eyes wide in the darkness, thoughts whirling like the weathervane atop Saint Agathe's Dome.

So he'd given up trying, settling for quick catnaps here and there, usually upright in a chair, and hoping he didn't go mad himself. Not even the doctors knew how bad it was. If they did, the Curia would retire him to some mindless desk drudgery, but Alexei couldn't leave the Order until he found what he sought.

The storm grew worse. Sheets of water sprayed from beneath the tires. They entered a fashionable neighborhood of townhouses on the west side. One of the oldest parts of the city, and expensive despite the decaying infrastructure. The car rounded a corner and Alexei slammed on the brakes. Novostopol sat on top of ancient aqueducts of historic interest so it took forever to get permits to fix things. The plaza ahead was flooded, the adjacent canal having overtopped its banks. Paw prints shimmered under twenty centimeters of water, continuing up the hill on the other side of a washed-out bridge.

Alexei smacked a palm on the wheel. He turned to Spassov. "I'll go on foot, find a way across. Are you good to take the car? There's another bridge at Pavlovsk Street."

Spassov gave him a mildly offended look. "I drive drunk better than you do sober, Alyosha."

"Meet me there." His smile died. "We're close. I can feel it."

Once Spassov had mocked these sorts of claims, but they'd proven accurate so many times, he just nodded. Alexei's instincts had been honed to a fine point in seven tours of duty in the ruins of the rebel cities. A sixth sense about which burnt-out buildings held nests of mages, which blind alleys had been rigged with traps. As a result, he was still alive when most of his fellow knights were dead.

Sometimes he wished it were the other way around.

Spassov got out and walked around to the driver's side. Rain soaked them both in an instant.

"Take some steel at least," Spassov said, sliding behind the wheel. "Don't be a hero, Alyosha. Wait for me."

Alexei gripped Patryk's shoulder. "Of course."

He walked around to the trunk and popped the latch. He stared at a sword for a moment, a blade blessed by the Pontifex Feizah herself, then reached past it and grabbed an umbrella. He rapped his knuckles on the side of the car, watching Spassov drive away in spreading ripples of rainwater.

Alexei opened the umbrella and followed the fading trail toward the canal.

Chapter Two

Six blocks away, and thirty-four minutes prior to the instant Fra Bryce unfurled his umbrella, an intimate dinner party was winding down.

The host was a man named Ferran Massot. Plump and bearded with wings of white at his temples, Massot was the very picture of a respectable doctor. He wore a sober dark suit and pearl gray gloves. When he smiled, kindly crinkles webbed the corners of his eyes. Massot was smiling right now, at the young woman he had hired to read fortunes for his guests.

"I'd say it was a smashing success, my dear, wouldn't you?" he said, beaming at her.

"I hope so, Doctor Massot," she replied.

"Please." He laid a gloved hand on her arm. "Call me Ferran."

They stood in the vestibule, the last guests having just departed. The young woman, whose name was Kasia Novak, didn't care for the way his hand lingered on her sleeve, nor for his smile. But she'd been taught to always be courteous, so she coughed and used the gesture to dislodge his touch.

"Right," she said briskly. "Let's get down to business then."

Massot's grin widened. "Direct, aren't you?"

One of us has to be, she thought. "How shall we proceed?"

"Upstairs," Massot said. "In the study."

"I'll collect my cards." Heels clicked as she strode to the drawing room and scooped up her cartomancy deck from the folding table the doctor had placed near the hearth. All in all, the evening had been pleasant. She wasn't invited to eat with the guests, but the caterers fed her leftovers in the kitchen before packing up. There had been a famous actress, a semi-famous poet, and some sort of experimental glassblower who specialized in figurines of the Saints. Kasia read their fortunes, making sure to put a positive spin on things, and they had all expressed astonishment at her insights.

Like the rest of the city, Dr. Massot followed the doctrine of the Via Sancta, which taught that all things, however mundane, must be beautiful. Fresh-cut flowers sat in vases at strategic intervals. The furniture was graceful and airy. Rugs woven from fine Nantwich wool graced the blond hardwood floors. If the place seemed sterile, Kasia chalked it up to the fact that Dr. Massot was a wealthy bachelor and no doubt had hired decorators to ensure all was in impeccable taste.

She followed him up the stairs to the study on the second floor. Here, the doctor's personal stamp was more in evidence. Framed degrees adorned the walls. A large oil portrait of Massot—ten years younger and fifteen kilos lighter—hung over the fireplace. It wore the same fixed smile. Kasia stayed in the doorway while the doctor lit a fire in the hearth, then strolled to his desk. It was a hefty, sober piece of furniture. He picked up a brass cylinder, the sort used to store documents rolled around a spindle.

"You came for this, *da*? I'd expected Domina Anderle. That's what I was told by . . . ." Massot trailed off, eyes twinkling in a conspiratorial fashion, and put the cylinder down. "Well, we won't mention names, will we?"

Kasia bit back impatience. She'd already explained this when she arrived. "Natalya fell ill so I came in her stead. I hope that doesn't present a problem."

"Not at all, my dear," he murmured, staring at her. "Not at all."

"Here." Kasia dug into her jacket pocket and handed him a business card. "She asked me to give you this."

Massot scanned it and tucked it into his trouser pocket. "I'll pay you for your services, naturally. And you may have the papers for our mutual friend. But if you'd indulge me, I'd like a reading first."

Kasia frowned. "Now?"

"Is the request so peculiar?"

"You declined my offer earlier." *When the other guests were still here.*

"I changed my mind."

She glanced at the brass cylinder, then at the clock on the mantel. 11:04. "It's getting late. And the weather—"

"I'll summon a cab for you, of course." He waved a hand. "Only a few more minutes, yes? I'll double your fee."

Kasia studied him. She needed the money. "One reading."

Dr. Massot grinned. "I must confess, I find this cartomancy of yours most intriguing. Does it really use the ley?"

"Of course." *A lie.* In fact, most of the performance was pure guesswork. She was a keen observer and her clients often revealed secrets without even meaning to. But sometimes the cards did speak to her. Kasia didn't know how it could be so, only that it was.

"Fascinating." He came out from behind the desk. "Let's sit here, shall we? It's cozier by the fire."

Kasia sank into one of the sleek armchairs flanking the fireplace, Massot across from her. A low table lay between them. Lightning flashed through the windows, followed by a slow roll of thunder. She shuffled the deck. "What sort of doctor are you, Domine Massot?"

His brows rose. "You don't know?"

Kasia shook her head.

Massot chuckled. "I am a student of that convoluted maze we call the human mind, my dear."

Kasia's mouth formed a polite smile, her dislike of him deepening. The doctor managed to be both condescending and creepy. "Is there a particular question you want to pose to the ley?"

"Why, yes. I have something of a professional dilemma." He winked, but his voice sounded strained. "A very delicate matter that has troubled me for some time now. Confidential, of course."

"You needn't tell me the details. Just hold the question in your mind."

Massot opened the top button of his shirt. "It's warm in here, isn't it?"

He was sweating profusely. Kasia stared at the coffee table as she dealt a five-card spread, face down. It *was* rather hot. The fashion this season was military chic, with heavy embroidery and epaulets on the shoulders of a tight-fitting jacket, a long, layered skirt and boots with three-inch spiked heels. Not the most comfortable attire, but one had to make do.

When she looked up, Ferran Massot had discarded his jacket. Wiry gray hairs poked through the collar of his shirt.

Oh, fog it.

"Don't you have to take your gloves off?" he asked.

Ley could only be drawn through the palms of the hands. She didn't really use the power for her readings, but Massot didn't know that. As much as Kasia didn't care to expose a centimeter of flesh to this man, she had no choice. She peeled off her black lace gloves. Then she took the first card and turned it over.

The Mage. Inverted.

Which shouldn't be possible since she was certain she had dealt them all right side-up.

Massot leaned forward, eyes darkening. "What's wrong?"

Kasia forced a smile. "Nothing bad, don't worry. The Mage represents the power of the ley." And a Nightmage, when inverted. "Or it can indicate worldly power. Over other people or in the sphere of business. Just what I'd expect for a man like you. Let's look at the next one."

The Slave. Followed by the Knight. The Fool. And the Martyr.

All Major Arcana. Taken individually, they could signify a thousand things. Each contained layers upon layers of meaning. But together, in that particular order.... Nameless dread pooled in her stomach. The feeling didn't come often, and never so strongly, but something terrible would befall this man —and soon.

Massot studied the cards with bright-eyed interest. How to break the news? Should she tell him at all?

He wouldn't take it well, they never did. Fog it, she should have begged off. She'd be in a taxi on her way home by now—

Kasia glanced up just as Dr. Massot tore a glove off with his teeth and reached across the table. Clammy fingers gripped her jaw.

"Be a good girl," he growled, sweeping the cards aside. "Just relax and I'll give you what you came for. We both know you want it."

How could his hand be so cold when sweat dripped down his face?

Ungloved. He was touching her *ungloved*.

It was unthinkable. The vilest breach of custom and courtesy. Even the lovers she'd had over the years never took their gloves off. How dare he?

Kasia raked her nails down his hand. Massot yelped in surprise and jerked away, knocking the table over. She grabbed his hairy wrist. Never had she been so angry. A red film covered her vision and Massot made an animal sound low in his throat. He shoved her hard. Kasia tripped over the table and landed on her rear. She scrabbled back, heels digging furls in the carpet.

"Cardinal Falke—" she began.

"Isn't here and doesn't care what I do." Massot stood in front of the door. His pupils devoured his eyes. "You're no one."

Kasia's cheeks flamed. "Listen, we can forget any of this ever happened. Just give me the message. I won't breathe a word—"

Massot raised a pale finger. Her skin crawled looking at it. His voice was toneless. "I'm sorry, Domina Novak. You're right. I don't know what came over me." The doctor licked his lips. "You're just very pretty, my dear."

Kasia stood. The coffee table lay on its side, cards strewn across the carpet. Her best deck, but she wasn't about to bend over to collect them with the good doctor staring at her. She held out a hand and willed her voice to no-nonsense firmness. "The cardinal's papers, please."

Lightning flashed. This time, the shattering crack of thunder was instantaneous. Massot gave a strange, twitching shudder as if he was having a stroke. Then he lunged at her. He was blocking the door to the hall, so she leapt over the coffee table, wobbling in her boots, and darted behind the desk. Kasia grabbed a paperweight and threw it at his head. Massot dodged the missile, but it shattered the window behind him. A damp wind fluttered the long white curtains.

"Help!" she shouted.

The doctor feinted right, then hurled himself at the desk, teeth snapping like a rabid dog. Kasia threw herself at a door, hoping it might be another way out, and found herself in a tiny bathroom that smelled of lavender. She bolted the door and pressed her ear against the wood.

Heavy breathing. A dull thud, as if a paunchy middle-aged body had slumped down against the door. The bathroom was pitch dark except for a thin line of light coming under the door. Kasia groped along the wall for a switch.

"Domina Novak?" Dr. Massot's voice sounded eerily calm.

She hesitated, but it's not as if he didn't know she was right there behind a flimsy door. "What?"

"They'll be coming for him. They don't know who he really is, do they? No, of course they don't. They don't have the slightest inkling." A giggle. "But they'll figure it out eventually. The only question is who will use him first."

Was the doctor talking about himself or someone else?

Kasia found the switch. Light flooded the tiny bathroom. She looked around for something to defend herself, but there was only a bowl of potpourri and a bar of soap in a little ceramic dish.

"He broke six of the Wards before I got him under control. Six! My master must be told. Oh, the punishment will be dreadful if he thinks I betrayed him."

Everyone had left, even the caterers. Massot had no live-in staff. Natalya was feverish in bed at their shared flat. She might not realize Kasia had failed to come home until morning. It had never occurred to either of them that something like this could happen. If Massot had been a new client, Kasia would have taken precautions, but he was a friend of the cardinal.

"You already know all about it, don't you?" His voice took on an angry edge. "They've been listening to my thoughts. They put an imp inside me. It reports to them. Tells them everything!" The doctor giggled again. "It likes the things I do, though. They didn't expect that." More maniacal laughter. "It's a dirty little imp!"

Kasia turned on the cold tap. She bent over the sink and splashed her face, wondering how she'd get out of Dr.

Massot's house alive. He had at least thirty kilos on her. And he was fogging insane.

"Damn," she muttered, leaning into the mirror. "I thought that was supposed to be waterproof."

Flakes of mascara ringed her eyes to ghoulish effect. It didn't really matter, but Kasia used a square of toilet paper to scrub away the makeup. It gave her something to do while she waited for the doctor's next move.

"I'm too important to be trifled with in this way. They *know*. Everything is under control. *He'll* see to that. I wrote it all down." A heavy sigh. "It is no easy task to serve two masters who despise each other, Domina Novak. No easy task."

She heard Massot stand. Muffled footsteps crossed the rug toward the desk. She was about to make a run for it, but a moment later, the footsteps returned.

"Come out," he said. "I have something for you."

She pressed a palm against the door. "What is it?"

"You'll see."

How stupid did he think she was? "The thing is, I don't trust you, Dr. Massot."

Tap-tap-tap. She could picture those pale fingers creeping along the door like a spider. "As well you shouldn't, my dear."

"Listen, the cards told me something bad would happen to you, but you can still change it. The future isn't written yet."

"Oh, but it is. In fact, I can tell you exactly what will happen to you if you don't come out." He kept talking, describing in detail the things he had planned for her. Kasia tried not to listen. She yanked open the drawers under the sink, finding nothing but spare toilet paper. The soap dish was a pathetic excuse for a weapon. Could she strangle him with a hand towel? Blind him with potpourri?

"Come out, come out, Domina Novak," Dr. Massot sang, tapping the door again. It sounded different this time. Like he was holding something.

A letter opener?

She'd seen one on his desk next to the paperweight.

"*Or I'll come in, come in.*"

The scrape of metal on metal. An indistinct curse. More scraping.

Ferran Massot was digging at the lock.

Chapter Three

The rain never ceased in Novostopol.

It cascaded from the mouths of gargoyles and raced through mossy canals. It dripped from umbrellas and lapped at the cobblestone streets, eventually emptying into an ancient system of aqueducts and flowing out to sea. If the city did not sit atop a series of hills overlooking the harbor, it would have been submerged long before.

Alexei stood at the foot of a narrow bridge that had been cordoned off with sawhorses, a four-meter gap in its center. It looked like it had collapsed some time ago. The Saints only knew when it was scheduled for repairs.

The hounds must have leapt across, but Alexei couldn't follow, not that way. He gave a sharp whistle. A minute later, the four dogs came bounding back down the hill. They crouched on the opposite bank, indistinct shadows in the rain.

He'd been right. They *were* close or the hounds would have taken longer to return.

A sudden updraft seized the umbrella. Alexei struggled to close it, finally tossing the flapping thing aside and letting the wind take it. Any thought of sleep vanished. He felt the clarity of purpose that only came at these moments, when lives hung in the balance and a single minute could make all the difference.

Alexei knelt down, water soaking his cassock. He removed one leather glove and laid his left hand flat on the sodden earth. Blue ley flowed along the surface, darkening to violet at the border with the red abyssal ley—the most powerful, but forbidden by the church. He drew on the liminal stratum, watching the ley darken as it rose to meet his palm. Power burned a trail up his arm and down his back, coiling around the muscles of his legs and flaring as it met his Marks.

By the grace of the Pontifex and all the Saints, I need to cross. Find me a way.

Blood pounded in his temples, an almost sexual pressure building. He didn't choose the Marks that would answer his prayer. The ley chose for him. All that mattered was that his heart was pure, his intentions good. It raced across his flesh in lines of shimmering violet flame. On the left side of his chest, the Mark he called the Maiden opened her eyes. On his back, the Two Towers ignited. Others flared briefly, some flashing blue, others a darker indigo. Had Alexei not been swathed in layers of wool, his entire body would have given off a faint glow. Seconds later, the ley flowed out again. It sank back into the earth, joining the river of power that ran beneath the city.

The wind died, though the rain fell as hard as ever. Alexei blinked away water, his cowl falling back. Floodwater churned through the canal, spilling over the stone embankment. He pulled his glove on and waited. The footbridge did not repair itself. The flood did not miraculously subside. He did not expect either of those things to happen. The liminal ley worked in subtler ways.

The hounds paced the far bank, eager to rejoin the chase. One let out a mournful howl. Alexei had a sudden premonition that he was too late.

It wouldn't be the first time.

Movement caught his eye. A downed tree came careening

down the canal. Just as it passed, the bole was caught in an eddy. It spun sideways, jamming itself in place. Tree? More like a sapling, and barely strong enough to bear the weight of a child, but Alexei scrambled forward.

One chance.

He crawled down and tested a boot on the log. The current tugged hard, but it held his weight. Holding out his arms like a dancer, Alexei found his balance. He took one step, then another. More flotsam was already piling up against the branches. The roar of whitewater echoed in his ears. He kept his gaze straight ahead, moving as quickly as he dared. Ominous cracking sounds came from below. A thump. The log shifted. He pinwheeled his arms. *Saints, it's starting to roll—*

With an ungainly leap, he skidded onto the far bank just as the tree snapped in half and was swept downstream. The hounds ran over and gave him a desultory sniff. The largest and most intelligent, a female named Alice, nudged his palm with a damp snout. She was his favorite and she knew it. Occasionally, he found her in his room, curled up on the bed. He never told anyone for fear they'd lock her up somehow. Alice left his blankets smelling of dog, but they'd hunted mages together in the war and he thought of her as a comrade.

Alexei whistled again and they tore up the street, sleek bodies bunching and lengthening, ears laid back. He sprinted behind, trying to keep his footing on the slick cobblestones. Neat rows of townhouses with wrought-iron balconies flashed past. It was all uphill and his lungs burned by the time the dogs raced up to a well-kept house with two dormant Wards above the red-lacquered front door. Light shone from the upstairs windows. One was broken. Alexei unlatched the front gate and hurried up to the door. Locked. He pounded on it with a fist, three resounding blows.

"Open up in the name of the Pontifex!"

No answer.

The hounds could cross the threshold, but he didn't trust them inside without him present. There had been . . . accidents . . . in the past. Alexei crouched down, addressing the pack leader. Her head cocked.

"*Mane*," he commanded.

Stand guard.

Alice trotted off and sat at the gate, ears pricked.

A tight alley led to the rear of the house. The other Markhounds followed him silently, too well-trained to alert whoever was inside. Glass doors led from the first floor to a canopied terra-cotta patio with ornate iron furniture. Also locked. Alexei scanned the garden, his eye landing on a heavy planter. Seconds later, it smashed through the doors. The noise was horrifically loud, but no one came rushing out to investigate. Alexei reached through the shattered panes and jiggled the latch. He eased the handle down.

"*Sede*," he commanded softly over his shoulder.

Three sets of haunches hit the ground. Red tongues lolled.

The planter had spilled wet earth across the rug of a large drawing room. The hearth was cold, but he smelled the ashes of a recent fire. A clock ticked on the mantle.

11:39

Dirty wine glasses and empty bottles indicated a party, but there were no signs of trouble.

It'll be on the second floor. In the room with the broken window.

Alexei moved to the hall. A flight of stairs led up. The house was still quiet. He squeezed the copper coin in his pocket. Rubbed a thumb along the name engraved there. Three years he'd been searching for his quarry and time was running out at last. Could this be the night?

Alexei took the stairs two at a time, tearing his gloves off as he went.

Chapter Four

W ood splintered.

Kasia backed against the far wall. The tip of the letter opener slid through the crack, wiggling obscenely.

Doctor Massot had been hard at work for some time, but he was finally making progress.

Kasia had an exceptional memory and recalled every detail of the study. There was a poker next to the fireplace. If she could get to it before he stabbed her, she could break his arm. She could break his skull, for that matter. The bathroom door opened outward, which was good for her because it would be easier to get past him. She was bracing herself to kick the doctor in the balls when she heard a new voice. It sounded astonished.

"Dr. Massot?"

The letter opener withdrew.

"Get away from me, you filthy rook," the doctor growled.

Kasia swore softly. She was grateful to be rescued, but not by a priest of the Curia. She'd take anyone but a fogging priest.

"Step away from that door." The voice was definitely

male, measured and in control again. "Is someone in there? Hello? Are you hurt?"

Kasia kept silent.

"I won't harm you, doctor, I promise. Just drop the letter opener."

A wordless snarl.

"One of your Marks has inverted. You of all people know what that means. It's why I'm here. To help you get better."

Oh, Saints. Kasia sank down on the toilet lid. Inverted. That meant the Interfectorem. She'd be investigated.

Kasia Novak rarely thought about the past or future. She arrived late to appointments and failed to pay bills on time. If not for her talent as a cartomancer, she'd probably be digging ditches or some other menial labor. Lying came easily, which was fortunate since her whole life was a lie.

Kasia flexed her fingers, scowling at the chips in her freshly applied polish. Bruised plum was in fashion that season. She'd have to fix it when she got home.

Outside the door, the priest was still trying to persuade Dr. Massot to drop the letter opener.

"How long have we known each other? Three years? I'm not your enemy."

"Piss off, Bryce."

"Just come along with me now. We'll go to the Institute. You'll get the best care. My partner is on the way—" The priest cut off, realizing his mistake, but it was too late. Kasia heard scuffling and a loud smash. The priest let out a yelp.

For a long minute she sat on the toilet lid, staring at the door.

What if Massot knocked him out? Or killed him? Kasia had heard the stories. Inhuman strength. Men turned to savage beasts. It explained the doctor's bizarre behavior, but she didn't want to be trapped in the bathroom if he came out on top.

She definitely didn't want that.

If the priest came out on top, she'd still have to answer his questions. Maybe even go down to the Arx.

Kasia didn't want that, either.

The other priest wasn't here yet. Maybe she could still run. She cracked the door.

The two of them were rolling around on the rug. They both had their gloves off. She couldn't see the ley flowing between them, but she knew they must be using it against each other. *Not my business.* Kasia started toward the door when she saw the two brass cylinders on Massot's desk.

One contained a message for Cardinal Falke, a very powerful man in Novostopol. Her best friend and flatmate, Natalya Anderle, sometimes acted as Falke's courier. She was supposed to have been at the party tonight, but she'd been sick so Kasia went in her place. Kasia had no idea what the papers were, or why it was all so hush-hush, nor did she want to know. She steered clear of Curia business and only came as a favor. But if she returned without the papers, the cardinal would blame Natalya.

Kasia strode to the desk. The cylinders looked identical. Which one was intended for the cardinal? She hesitated, only for an instant, but the priest turned his head and saw her. He had thick dark brows and arresting blue eyes. They looked tired. Kasia stared back, challengingly. She couldn't help it. *Fogging priests.*

His gaze narrowed. Massot used the distraction to seize a handful of cassock and slam the priest's head against the carpet. The priest threw an elbow into Massot's face. They rolled away again and Kasia grabbed both cylinders. She stuffed them into her jacket and bolted for the hall, flying down the stairs. The front door loomed ahead, but she hadn't forgotten what he'd said about his partner. She ran to the parlor window to check the street. A large black automobile was pulling up in front of the house. The kind with dark windows and acres of hood and a big chrome grill with a silver raven on the bonnet.

Kasia stuck her head into the hall. The front door handle jiggled violently for about ten seconds, then stopped. She waited for a minute, then shot open the deadbolt and cracked the door. As she'd hoped, the second priest had gone around back. Rain fell in torrents. She stepped outside, gently closed the door behind her, and descended the slippery steps, the click of her heels echoing on the slate.

She almost tripped over the Markhound.

It sat at the gate, ears perked, watching the night.

Kasia cursed her luck. There was no other way out. Back through the garden maybe, but she'd seen the wall out the kitchen window. Too high to climb. Rain trickled into her collar. How long before the front door opened and they came looking? She didn't know much about Markhounds, but in theory . . . .

It can't see me.

The Markhound snuffled. Kasia studied the creature, her pulse slow and measured. Markhounds were supposed to be invisible, but this one seemed solid enough. Gleaming dark fur with a tawny muzzle. Hip-high on her—and it was sitting down. The close-set eyes looked belligerent.

Kasia stepped through the gate.

THINGS WERE NOT GOING AS PLANNED.

Alexei could feel the ley surging through his hands. He tried to use his own Marks to calm it, to make the doctor pliable, but the instant the power passed into Massot, it became wild and unruly. An ember spat from the fire and set the rug aflame, stoked by the breeze from the broken window. Somehow, he'd become tangled up in his cloak. From the corner of his eye, he saw Ferran Massot crawling for the letter opener. The doctor's nose dripped blood. A tongue crept out and licked it. He made a smacking noise.

"I'm going to cut your heart out, rook," Massot said. "Then I'll feed it to your dogs."

Alexei got a hand around his ankle. Massot kicked violently. His dress shoe came off, hitting Alexei in the forehead. An eye-watering stench came from the doctor, sweat mixed with urine and something worse. The seat of his pants was wet. He'd almost reached the letter opener.

Alexei was about to give up and whistle for the hounds when the door flew open.

Spassov burst into the study, a crossbow in his hands. His bluff face registered a look of surprise upon seeing Ferran Massot, but it didn't slow him down. He aimed the weapon and Alexei dove at his partner's knees. Spassov stumbled. The bolt flew wide, burying itself in one of the doctor's framed degrees.

"Don't!" Alexei panted. "We need him alive."

Spassov rolled his eyes, but he walked to Massot and kicked the letter opener away from the doctor's grasping fingers. Spassov planted a knee on his back. Massot writhed and spat, but he was pinned beneath ninety kilos of Curia muscle.

"Glove him," Patryk grunted.

Alexei pulled out a pair of mesh-lined gloves and forced them onto the doctor's hands, snapping thin metal circlets around the wrists to ensure they didn't come off again. Massot stopped struggling. Alexei stamped on the rug, smothering the flames.

"There was a woman," he said, pulling his own gloves back on. "Did you see her?"

Spassov shook his head. "Injured?"

"I don't think so. She was hiding in there."

They both looked at the bathroom door and the deep gouges around the knob.

"Hold on," Alexei said, sprinting for the stairs.

WALKING past the Markhound was not the most pleasant experience, but it was undeniably exciting. If she was wrong, the beast might tear her throat out. But its head never turned though it sat a meter away.

Once across the street, Kasia started running. She wasn't particularly athletic so jogging on wet cobblestones in spiked heels, at a steep downhill grade, required all her concentration. At the bottom of the hill, she caught her breath and looked back. No signs of pursuit. They must have their hands full with Dr. Massot.

Then she hit the washed-out bridge at Kopeksin Square.

It meant she would have to walk all the way through the dark, deserted campus of the Lyceum and cross the Liberation Bridge on the western bank of the Montmoray to get home. Unless she managed to find a cab . . . Kasia swore softly. Her purse was in the doctor's study. She would have driven her own car if the rear tire hadn't gone flat.

At least she had the papers. The priests would track her down, but it would take them a while. In the meantime, she had only to walk four kilometers through the pouring rain with no umbrella. Kasia jammed her hands into her pockets. She felt naked without her gloves, which were also back in the study with her best oracle deck.

A crooked smile played on her lips.

All things considered, a small price to pay.

THE FRONT DOOR of Massot's house had been left unbolted. A quick glance up and down the street confirmed that Alexei's quarry was gone. Alice trotted to his side, gazing up at him alertly. He scratched her behind the ears.

"How'd she get past you, eh?" The hound snuffled and

nosed at his crotch. Alexei pushed her head away and gave her a gentle slap on the rump. "I trusted you," he said accusingly. "Now I find you sleeping on the job."

Alice yawned.

He'd only seen the woman for an instant. Middle to late twenties with long black hair and one of those jackets with epaulets on the shoulders. Very attractive, but it was the cold look in her eye that left an impression. Not fear, which would have been expected considering her ordeal. Alexei got the feeling it was *him* she was hostile towards.

He headed back upstairs to the study. Spassov was still kneeling on the doctor.

"She's gone," Alexei said.

His partner arched an eyebrow. "We'll find her. At least we made it in time. That's a refreshing change, eh? Let's get him into the car."

Dr. Massot had gone quiet, though his eyes glittered with malice. They walked him outside. The hounds started barking savagely when they saw him.

"Sileo," Alexei snapped. The dogs shot him baleful looks but fell silent. He pushed Massot into the back seat and secured his hands to Warded rings. Spassov tugged a glove off and gripped the rings. They flared with blue fire. Massot wouldn't be touching the ley anytime soon.

"You'll be safe," Alexei said. "The dogs won't trouble you."

Massot didn't reply.

Once back inside, they performed a quick search. No one else was home. Alexei lingered in the study, collecting the cards scattered about. The pictures closely resembled Marks, painted with a skilled hand. Some of the figures he recognized. The white-robed Pontifex, for example. And the Knight. Others were inscrutable. A disembodied hand offering a gold chalice to a youth sitting cross-legged beneath a tree. A man with a bandaged head holding a stave. A nude woman pouring a jug of water into a pool beneath a black sky studded with stars. A heart pierced by three swords.

"Ironic, *da?*" Spassov said, sticking his head into the study. "He's the first one I know personally. I suppose we should be grateful it happened at home."

Alexei showed him the cards. "Ever seen this before?"

Spassov shook his head. "A game?"

"Maybe. I think they belonged to the woman."

Patryk shrugged. "Does it matter?"

"Probably not, but I'll hold onto them anyway."

He took a quick look in the bathroom. No blood or signs of a struggle. His first impression that the woman was unharmed appeared correct.

"Time?" he asked Spassov.

Patryk took out his pocket watch. "11:53."

Alexei jotted it down in his notebook. "She lasted almost an hour."

"Lucky," Spassov muttered.

"Or smart," Alexei said. "Let's go."

Once outside, he whistled for the Markhounds. Alice, who possessed both dignity and discipline, had resumed her post at the gate. The others were trotting around, peeing on Massot's shrubbery. Spassov slid into the passenger seat and unrolled the window to light a cigarette.

"Ite domum," Alexei commanded. *Go home.*

The dogs gave a final growl at the car and vanished into the rainy night.

Chapter Five

I *nvertido.*

Kasia had never expected to witness the moment a Mark turned. She didn't know a great deal about it, only that the condition was rare. The cards had warned her, but by then it was already too late.

As she hurried home through the rain, she reconsidered the cards she'd dealt for Dr. Massot. The Mage, upside-down. Well, that one was obvious. It signified forbidden impulses and secret desires. The Knight could be the priest. Half of them had fought in the war at some point. But the Martyr? It usually meant suffering for a cause, but Massot didn't seem the type. She wasn't sure about the Slave, either. Or the Fool.

This last card intrigued her the most.

The Fool was a wanderer, moving at whim between the civilized realms and the wilds of night. He liked to upset the established order, more trickster than jester. Some decks showed him with a small dog nipping at his heels. His temperament combined wisdom, madness and folly. Mixed correctly, these qualities could produce wonders. They could also lead to disaster.

She couldn't interpret more without Massot's active participation and that wouldn't be forthcoming. Kasia hoped the priest was unharmed, but his partner was only seconds away when she'd fled. She wondered what would happen to Dr. Massot. He'd seemed normal earlier in the evening. The famous actress, beautiful and with a biting wit, had been the center of attention at the party. Massot was a practiced host, affable and charming but never outshining his guests. Kasia had caught him looking at her several times but didn't think much of it. Now his attention took on a sinister cast. She remembered the way he had greeted her at the door, an odd little smile on his face.

He planned it all along.

Kasia shoved the thought away, uneasy. It wasn't entirely Massot's fault. If the Interfectorem came, it meant his Marks had reversed. He wasn't himself, was he?

She froze at swift footsteps behind her, but it was just a young couple, holding hands and laughing under a shared umbrella. The distant tolling of bells from the Arx signaled midnight. A few blocks later, she reached the busier section of town, where the cafes stayed open until two and merry voices spilled from the open windows.

Her flat was at the top of a six-story walk-up above a popular curry restaurant. By the time she reached her door, Kasia's feet were begging for mercy. She knocked until she heard footsteps. Tumblers clicked and Natalya opened the door.

"Kiska, you're soaked!" Her bleach-blond hair was rumpled from sleep, though she looked a bit better. "What happened to your key?"

"I forgot my purse."

"You walked the whole way?"

Kasia nodded.

"Why didn't he call you a taxi? Never mind, I'll get a towel." Natalya headed for the bathroom.

Kasia sank down on the couch. She unlaced her boots and

rubbed some life back into her toes. Then she took the brass cylinders from her jacket and stuffed them under a pillow. She hadn't the least desire to examine their contents, not even to figure out which was the right one. She wanted nothing to do with cardinals or priests ever again. Nor psychiatrists, either. But they had to be hidden. She was looking around the tiny, cluttered flat for potential places when Natalya reappeared.

"Come on," she said. "I'm drawing you a hot bath."

Another person would have asked about the papers first, but Natalya wasn't like that. Kasia followed her friend into the bathroom and stood while Natalya toweled her hair.

"How are you feeling?" Kasia asked.

"The fever broke." Natalya studied her in the mirror. "But you look awful."

"I know, my makeup ran—"

"Saints, I don't mean your makeup. Did something happen?"

"Massot attacked me."

The brisk rubbing ceased at once. "*What?*"

"His Marks turned. When we were alone together."

"I can't believe it!" Natalya held her at arm's length, eyes wide. "Did he. . .?"

"No. I locked myself in a bathroom." Kasia stared into the mirror. She could still smell the cloying lavender potpourri. "And then the Interfectorem came—"

"Flay me! They rescued you?"

"Just before the doctor broke the door down."

"I'm so sorry." Natalya looked stricken. "This is all my fault."

"Of course it isn't." Kasia leaned on the edge of the sink. "I got the papers, Nashka."

"Oh, Kiska. I don't care about that!" But her friend briefly closed her eyes, face flooding with relief, and Kasia was glad she'd stopped for them even though it meant the priest saw her.

"How soon can we get rid of them?" she asked. "I'm afraid they'll come looking for me."

Natalya hung up the towel. "Why would they do that?"

"Because I ran."

Now that she was thinking more clearly, she realized just how stupid her actions had been. It made her look guilty. If she had stayed and answered their questions, leaving out Cardinal Falke, they would have let her go. She had a legitimate reason for being there. The other guests would confirm it. She could have said she went up to the study to get paid for her work that evening. The priests might even have called a taxi for her. But instinct was a powerful thing, especially when one had so much to lose.

"Ah." Natalya drew a steadying breath. "Well, you were scared. It's quite natural to run."

"I wasn't scared. I just didn't want to be there anymore, so I left."

Natalya shook her head. "Well, you'll say you were scared. They'll understand when we explain it the right way. Now, how soon do you think they'll come here?"

"Massot could tell them my name, I suppose. He could tell them everything. But even if he doesn't . . . ." She sighed. "I gave him your business card. And I left the deck you made for me."

"Soon, then." She tested the water in the bath and shut off the faucet. "Was Dr. Massot coherent?"

"Not really. They were fighting over a letter opener when I left."

"Saints!" Nashka bit her lip. "The cardinal said he would send a driver around in the morning to pick up the papers. We have only to keep them safe until then. Where are they?"

Kasia led her back to the living room and showed her the two brass cylinders. "I'm sure it's one of them because he showed it to me before he went mad, but he must have taken out another when I was hiding in the bathroom. We'll just give the cardinal both and let him sort it out."

Natalya held them up. Each was about ten centimeters long and cunningly made, with etched vines and the Raven emblem of the Eastern Curia.

"Don't!" Kasia said sharply when Natalya tried to unscrew the top.

"Why not?"

"Because they're trouble. We should stay out of it."

"Too late for that, kitten."

Kasia laid a hand on her wrist. "I'm serious. Massot said things. They made no sense, but I think they had to do with whatever the cardinal is involved in."

Nashka ignored her, fiddling with the tube, but it wouldn't open.

"Leave it," Kasia urged. "We'll hide them for now."

Her friend scowled, but gave a reluctant nod. "Where?"

The flat had two small bedrooms, each with a closet already jammed to bursting. Nashka proposed putting them in a shoe box, which Kasia rejected. The living room was similarly bereft of hiding places that wouldn't be discovered immediately. Kasia finally wedged the tubes into a crack behind the refrigerator. Then she took a bath and changed into a robe.

"We have to tell Tessaria," she said.

Natalya winced. "Do we really?"

"She'll find out. She always does. Better it comes from me."

Natalya dropped to the couch and propped her feet on a stack of fashion magazines. "You're brave."

"She means well, she's just overprotective. I've had plenty of tongue-lashings from Tessaria Foy. They sting like hell, but they don't leave a permanent scar."

"She has no right to be angry with *you*."

Kasia gave a mirthless laugh. "I'm supposed to keep her

informed of our schedules, which I suppose is only fair since she refers most of our clients and doesn't even take a cut."

"Don't worry, I intend to take all the blame. But let's put it off until morning. It's too late to telephone now." She gave Kasia a searching look. "Are you sure you're all right? I'd be fogging mad if I were you. *Bastard.*" Natalya shivered and rubbed the Mark on her forearm. Kasia couldn't see the ley, but she knew it was tamping down her friend's anger.

"It was an accident," Kasia said wearily. "We mustn't hate him for it. Hatred only harms—"

"Oneself." Natalya sighed. "Yes, I know."

Nonviolence was the foundation of the Via Sancta. And for those who forgot this principle—well, their Marks would ensure they never acted on it.

Kasia dug out a fresh deck of cards. She sat in an armchair they'd bought second-hand at a rummage sale. The upholstery was stained, but Nashka had draped it with a colorful shawl.

"We must both be more careful in the future, though I don't see how anyone could have predicted it." Kasia shuffled the cards. "What do you know about Invertido? I mean, could I have triggered it somehow—"

"Don't you dare!" Natalya sat up. "This is not your fault. It was just bad timing."

"I gave him a reading right before he turned."

Natalya leaned forward. "What did the cards say?"

Kasia recited the spread. Nashka gave a low whistle. "They really do work for you, don't they?"

"Not always," Kasia conceded. "But often enough."

"Next time you see anything like that, just run. Don't stop to think." Her friend gave an uneasy laugh. "I never believed in psychic powers before I met you, Kiska."

"You read the cards, too," Kasia pointed out.

"Yes, and I make everything up wholesale." She grinned. "Fortunately, I have an active imagination. But you're something else." Natalya gestured to the cards. "What do they say?"

Kasia gave a last shuffle. "Just one, for now. I'm too tired to interpret a full spread."

She closed her eyes and fanned the cards, letting her fingertips dance over the edges. Sometimes a card would practically leap out at her. Other times, she asked a question and made a deliberate choice. Now her fingers slid across the cards, touching and rejecting each in turn. Kasia realized she was uneasy. Perhaps even a little afraid.

She started at the beginning again, letting her mind float free.

This one.

Kasia drew the card and set it aside. She opened her eyes.

The back of this particular deck had a circular mandala with a border of flowering vines. There was no way to tell if the card was reversed, yet a chill trickled down her spine.

"Turn it over," Nashka said.

Kasia flipped the card.

A man and a woman embraced beneath a full moon. The woman had long dark hair and was only visible in profile over the man's shoulder. Intricate Marks covered his back, though his face was in shadow.

The Lovers.

"What the fog?" she muttered.

Natalya hooted. "I think your luck is changing, kitten."

Chapter Six

The Batavia Institute occupied a hilltop estate owned by an infamous baron named Von Oppermann until an angry mob tried to set it on fire. Owing to the wet climate, the blaze never caught and the limestone heap sat empty for centuries before falling into the hands of the Curia, which deemed the isolated location ideal for housing Invertido. Extensive renovations brought modern plumbing and electricity, soft lighting and inoffensive pastel watercolors. The outdoor theater where the baron had staged lewd performances was turned into a parking lot.

Yet the exterior still looked like a gothic monstrosity, especially when viewed in the middle of the night through pouring rain.

Alexei slowed at a gated arch set into a high stone wall. Active Wards shone blue the entire length of the wall, slowing the ley to a bare trickle within the grounds. He rolled down his window to wave at the guard inside the booth. The Interfectorem was a familiar presence and the guard buzzed them through without bothering to look in the back seat, which was obscured by tinted glass. Alexei felt relieved. Word would spread soon enough, but he wanted to keep it quiet for as long as possible.

A drive cut through several acres of manicured lawn. He followed a curve to the rear and parked underneath a portico.

"The doctor could have saved us the trip if he'd flipped on a weekday," Spassov remarked, flicking his smoldering butt out the window.

Alexei shot him a warning look. "This won't be good for morale. We need to be sensitive. No jokes."

Ferran Massot was the head doctor at the Institute. Normally, he would be the one greeting them at Admissions to evaluate a new patient. It was all too surreal.

"Please, Alyosha." Spassov spread his hands. "What do you take me for?"

Alexei glanced at the back seat. Some people raged and spat. Some tried to bargain. Others became catatonic once they were cut off from the ley. Massot was different. He sat quietly, a slight smile on his face. Like he was enjoying himself.

"Are you ready, Domine Massot?" Alexei asked.

Massot lifted an eyebrow at the demotion from *Doctor* to *Mister*, but he inclined his head, which Alexei took for assent. They got out of the car. Spassov unlocked the manacles and they escorted Massot to the double doors. More Wards were carved above the lintel. In the event of an emergency, they could shut off the ley completely within the building, although to Alexei's knowledge, they'd never been activated.

The guard at the gate had telephoned ahead and it was only a moment before an attendant appeared. He had a mop of unruly chestnut hair and a pleasant, boyish face. His mouth fell open when he saw Massot. "Is that . . . .?"

"Yes," Alexei replied curtly. "Who's on duty tonight?"

"Dr. Pagwe."

"Find him, please."

The attendant was still staring at Massot. Dried blood

caked the doctor's face. His crooked half-smile did nothing to make him look less sinister.

"Now," Spassov barked.

"Sorry," the attendant stammered. He was young and fairly new. "Fra Spassov, Fra Bryce. Come inside, I'll be right back."

He swung the doors wide. They entered the Admitting area, which held a long desk with two chairs, both empty. Stacks of forms sat waiting to be filled out. It made Alexei think of the report he'd have to write later. As the senior priest, Spassov always signed them, but he left the paperwork to Alexei. And Alexei couldn't file anything until he'd tracked down the mystery woman. Their boss at the Office of the General Directorate would not appreciate such a lapse.

The attendant hurried off down a narrow, twisting corridor, his footsteps muffled by stain-resistant beige carpeting. The Batavia Institute was a peculiar mélange of old and new. The bones of the place were undeniably a pre-Dark Age castle, but the décor always reminded Alexei of his mother's law offices in the city center.

"Domine Massot," Alexei said, addressing him politely as if he were still a man of authority. "I wonder if you might save us some trouble. There was a woman at your house."

Massot slowly turned his head.

"If you could give me her name, I'd appreciate it."

Massot laughed contemptuously. "Stupid rooks. Go peck at some other corpse." He bared his teeth. "This one might bite back."

They all turned as Dr. Pagwe strode down the corridor with the attendant and the duty nurse. Pagwe was a tall, lanky man and walked with a brisk, bouncing step the others struggled to match. He'd already absorbed the news and made no comment except to signal that they should follow. Spassov prodded the doctor into motion.

"Pagwe," Massot said imperiously. "Order them to remove these manacles or I'll fire you on the instant!"

Pagwe did not acknowledge this request except to share a quick look with Nurse Jeyna. She turned to Alexei and beckoned him to catch up.

"Where did it happen?" she asked quietly.

"At his home. Do either of you know anything about a party he was throwing tonight?"

Both Dr. Pagwe and Nurse Jeyna shook their heads. "He never spoke of his life outside work," Pagwe clarified. "He was a private man."

"Did you hear me?" Massot roared from behind them. "This is an outrage. I won't have it!" He'd gone red in the face. "I'll see you whipped! Flayed to a hair of your lives. I—"

Spassov cuffed the side of his head, which only enraged the doctor further. Alexei dropped back to grab an arm. The two of them should have handled Massot with ease, but he fought hard enough to slam Alexei against the wall. In most cases, patients grew calmer when they reached the Institute. The absence of ley meant there was nothing to fuel their deviant Marks.

But Massot was getting worse.

"Right up here," Dr. Pagwe called over his shoulder, steps quickening. "We have an examining room prepared."

Alexei and Spassov dragged the doctor through the door, still shouting obscenities. A gurney waited, equipped with leather restraints. When Massot saw it, he gave a guttural howl.

"Sedative," Dr. Pagwe said in a clipped tone.

Nurse Jeyna took a hypodermic from a steel tray. Alexei got Massot in a headlock while Spassov immobilized his legs. With a steady hand born of long experience, the nurse jabbed Massot in the rump and depressed the plunger.

Ten seconds later, Massot fell limp in Alexei's arms. Dr.

Pagwe lifted each of his eyelids. "He's out. Let's see what we've got."

Massot was stripped to his smallclothes while Alexei and Patryk watched. Alexei took his notebook out. The doctor's chest was covered with grizzled gray hairs. He looked pathetic and small lying there nearly naked. A humiliation, and not the last he would suffer, but it had to be done.

"Turn him over," Spassov said.

Dr. Pagwe and Nurse Jeyna rolled him to one side.

Alexei froze, pencil poised above the paper. Blood thundered in his ears.

"Saints," Jeyna whispered. "Is that a Nightmark?"

Alexei cleared his throat. "It appears to be," he said, amazed at how calm he sounded.

Dr. Pagwe's composure finally cracked. He blinked rapidly, as if he could dispel the sight by sheer force of will. "Are you sure?"

There was a Mark on Massot's calf of a youth holding a golden key beneath a bower of roses, but no one was looking at that one. All eyes fixed on the Mark between his shoulder blades. A woman cupped a heart wrapped in thorns, her gaze harsh and accusing. Blood ran down her naked thighs. The Mark had flipped upside down, placing her head just above Massot's fleshy buttocks. In the lower right was an arcane symbol cunningly woven into the border. Alexei did not need to consult his notebook to find its match, but pretenses had to be maintained. He flipped through the pages to the section where he recorded every Nightmage's signature. Most of them were dead so it was a short list.

"Of course it's a Nightmark," Spassov snapped. "Look at it! How could this happen?"

"I . . . I have no idea," Dr. Pagwe said faintly.

"Well, you'd better find out," Spassov growled. "What a disaster." He turned to Alexei. "Who gave him the Mark?"

Alexei ran a finger to the bottom of the page. He needed to think. Needed to find that woman. "A Nightmage named Malach."

The name tasted like acid on his tongue. It was the signature he'd been hunting for three years now. The mage he'd nearly given up hope of ever finding again.

He looked Spassov in the eye, praying his partner didn't see his agitation, but Spassov was too preoccupied with what it meant for the Institute.

"You're his deputy, are you not?" Patryk asked.

Dr. Pagwe swallowed and nodded.

"You've just been promoted to acting chief. There's a strong possibility the whole staff will be required to submit to physical examinations, but that order is above my authority. I'm just warning you now."

"I have no objection," Dr. Pagwe said defensively. "I'm as shocked as you are."

"I want a list of all his patients. And I want to see the visitor logs for the last six months."

"Right away, Fra Spassov." The doctor let Massot slump back down to the examining table and rushed from the room. Alexei stepped forward to secure the restraints at wrists and ankles. Then he covered the doctor with a sheet to the chin. Massot's face was peaceful, his breath calm and even.

"We have to keep this quiet for now," Spassov said to the nurse. "Understand?"

"Of course, Fra Spassov." She glanced at the unconscious doctor, then away. Her hands knit together.

"I need to make some calls," Spassov said to Alexei. "Stay with him."

Nurse Jeyna started to follow his partner from the room.

"Wait a moment," Alexei called.

She turned.

"I need to ask you some questions."

She came back, but didn't look him in the eye. "How can I help, Fra Bryce?"

"Tell me about Dr. Massot."

She licked her full lips. "What do you wish to know?"

Alexei had an unpleasant suspicion. The form of a Mark was significant. It revealed something about a person's deepest character. Except for the Raven given to every ordained member of the Curia, no two Marks were ever the same. In court, a precise description of one was deemed as reliable for the purposes of identification as a fingerprint.

And Dr. Massot's inverted Nightmark spoke of disturbing sexual fantasies, particularly regarding women.

"Did he ever behave inappropriately with you?"

"No, Fra Bryce."

The reply came quickly, but he felt sure it was a lie. Or a partial truth.

"Listen," he said, lowering his voice. "It's not your fault. I don't blame you. I'll keep it out of my report if that's what you're worried about. But I need to know."

Jeyna finally met his gaze. He could see she was nervous. His boss, the one Spassov was telephoning right now, would be very unhappy to learn that the head doctor at the Batavia Institute was a servant of the church's enemies and had been for the Saints only knew how long. But Alexei had finally caught Malach's trail and he'd follow wherever it led.

"He attacked a woman at his home," Alexei said.

Jeyna pressed a gloved hand over her mouth. "Oh, no."

"At first I assumed it was simply because his Mark had turned."

Jeyna understood. The vast majority of patients at the Institute were not Nightmarked. They had Civil Marks bestowed by the clergy, usually a cardinal or bishop. The Marks let them use the ley, but only for good works. The purpose was twofold: to fan innate sparks of talent and to suppress negative traits.

Massot was different. Nightmarks could not be forced upon an unwilling victim. They were chosen. An unholy pact. Alexei needed to learn all he could about the nature of this particular bargain if he had any hope of finding the one who had given it to Massot.

"But the doctor had a hidden life, didn't he?" Alexei persisted. "I can't help but wonder if he didn't harass the women on staff. Perhaps threaten them if they tried to report it."

Jeyna stared at Massot's still form. A strand of silvery blond hair had come loose from her cap and she tucked it behind an ear. Her hand trembled. A flash of guilt crossed her face.

"Not me," she whispered, glancing at the door. "But possibly his patients."

"BISHOP KAROLO GAVE Massot his other Mark," Spassov announced. "She's out of the city at a conference in Kvengard, but she'll be livid when they tell her what he's done."

Alexei found his partner smoking in Dr. Massot's office. Stacks of patient files sat on the desk, next to a green-shaded lamp and a telephone. The file drawers were all pulled open, but it would take hours to read through Massot's case notes and Alexei doubted they'd find anything. The doctor was too careful.

"Bishop Karolo leads the Conservatives, doesn't she?" Alexei said.

Spassov nodded glumly. "Saints know what they'll do with this. Heads will roll, brother. Let's try to keep ours intact."

"What else did Kireyev say?"

He was their boss.

"I gave him Malach's name. He'll put men on it."

Alexei scanned one of the files. The binder was identified

only as Patient 63. "*Persistent delusions of grandeur. . . exhibits gener-alized rage at authority figures . . . lack of self-control in the context of impulsive urges. . .*"

Massot might have been describing himself.

"If this mage sets off any Wards, the brothers will kill him on sight," Spassov said.

Alexei expected as much, but the news did not make him happy. He needed Malach alive.

"Bold bastard to come inside the city." Spassov stared out the window at the rain-soaked grounds. "You think he's still here?"

Nightmarks were assumed to be rare, although without regularly strip-searching every adult citizen, which would be a clear violation of their civil rights, no one knew exactly *how* rare. This was for two reasons, the chief one being that most of the mages had been killed in the war. The second reason was that Nightmarks didn't seem to spontaneously invert like regular Marks. They were more stable, which made sense. Nightmarks unchained the psychic beast, while Marks tamed it.

But a mage could invert any Mark with a single touch of the abyssal ley, making it likely that Malach had been inside Massot's house tonight.

"Not unless he's stupid," Alexei said. "And I don't think he is."

Spassov exhaled a stream of smoke. "Mages know all about Markhounds. He knew they'd start to howl the instant he turned his victim. Maybe he wanted Massot to be found quickly."

"So he flipped him as punishment for some misstep," Alexei said, far more casually than he felt. "What could be worse than to be locked up at the Institute he used to run?"

"Malach must have been one of the party guests. Kireyev's boys will round them up. At least we'll get a description."

"And here I thought you'd missed that about the party."

Spassov laughed. "I miss nothing, Alyosha." His face grew wistful. "The doctor had a nice life. What did he throw it all away for?"

Alexei said nothing. He'd promised to keep what Jeyna said to himself, but the man she'd described was nothing like the cheerful, efficient bureaucrat Alexei had met on his many visits to the Institute. Massot was temperamental at best, dictatorial at worst. And he'd been spending a great deal of time alone with some of his patients. He said it was an experimental new therapeutic technique, but Nurse Jeyna had seen fading bruises on some of the women.

Self-injury wasn't uncommon. It hadn't been enough to report Massot, especially when the women denied that he'd done anything wrong. Jeyna didn't believe them. Not when closer examination revealed needle tracks, as well. She was anguished over it now.

"If I'd known about the Nightmark, I never would have approved the sedative," Spassov said dourly. "We need to question him. How long will he be under?"

"The nurse said a few more hours." Alexei paused. "I think we should focus on finding the woman. She must have seen something."

"Kireyev is working on it."

"And time's wasting," Alexei snapped, more harshly than he intended.

Spassov took it in stride. "Look, he can't get past the city walls now. They've tripled the watch. It's impossible. So either he's already gone, or he's here. If he's here, he's not leaving again." He pushed a stack of files across the desk. "Make yourself useful."

Alexei sighed and pulled up a chair. Framed photographs hung on the wall behind the desk. Massot shaking hands with Bishop Maria Karolo. A group photo of the staff assembled on the front lawn. Massot speaking on a dais, his hands animated. A formal shot of the doctor appearing much younger, clad in the black gown of the Lyceum. The obligatory portrait of the Pontifex, found in cafés and drinking establishments across the city. And an autographed photo of Cardinal Dmitry Falke. Alexei leaned forward, trying to decipher the scrawled note at the bottom.

Medicus est timendum magis quam morbo. –C.

The doctor could be worse than the disease.

Meant in jest, obviously, but a strange omen nonetheless.

He started to plow through the case files, looking for anything unusual. It was a sad catalogue of pathological deviance, the magnetic poles between ego and id suddenly swapping places. There was no cure, only heavy sedation until the end, which usually came within months. The madness took a subtly different course in each person, but there were certain constants.

Narcissism. Paranoia. Zero tolerance for delayed gratification. Lack of remorse. Severely impaired empathy.

Alexei's chin drooped. Rain beat a gentle tempo against the glass. He blinked, trying to focus, but the letters swam away . . . .

"Fra Spassov?"

His head jerked up as the young chestnut-haired orderly entered. He sounded out of breath, like he'd been running. Alexei jumped to his feet, the file spilling to the floor.

"What is it?" he demanded. "Is Massot awake?"

"No, Fra Bryce. But I went through his clothes before sending them to the laundry. I found this in his pocket." The attendant handed him a small card.

Alexei studied it, adrenaline pumping. It was heavy stock, glossy black with constellations of gilded stars in the corners. The gold lettering was ornate. *Love, Fate, Destiny. What does the ley hold for YOU?*

"Well?" Spassov demanded.

"Her name is Natalya Anderle. Number 44 Malaya Sadovaya Ulitsa."

"Malaya Sadovaya," Spassov mused. "Isn't that near Kebab House? I used to go there all the time. They have an all-you-can-eat lunch buffet."

Alexei jingled the car keys. "Fancy some curry?"

Chapter Seven

K asia saw them arrive. She was sitting in the window
seat filing a chipped nail and watching the street with
half an eye. The rain hadn't let up and even the diehard
revelers had gone home. Traffic was nonexistent so the slow-
moving headlights caught her attention.

She'd wondered who would come first—the cardinal's
bagman or the Interfectorem—but either way, she didn't
really expect them to turn up at three o'clock in the fogging
morning.

She leaned out over the fire escape, hoping the long black
automobile would keep going. But it stopped in front of the
curry shop, parking illegally at the curb in a no-standing zone.
The doors opened and two priests got out. From six stories up,
in the rainy darkness, they all looked the same, but she knew.

"Nashka!" she hissed. "They're here."

Natalya muttered something. She was sleeping on the
couch.

"Wake up!"

Kasia shoved the stack of fashion glossies under the couch
with one foot. She threw her boots into the closet and was
searching for a pair of gloves when the buzzer rang. Kasia

waited until it rang again, two sharp peals. She hit the intercom with an unsteady hand. "Yes?"

"Curia," a male voice said.

"I didn't order any curry," she said.

The buzzer sounded for a third time. Natalya sat up, blinking.

What do we do? Kasia mouthed.

"Let them in."

Kasia made a face.

"You have to!"

With a sinking heart, she pressed the button.

The priests had six flights to climb. For the first time, she was glad the building didn't have an elevator.

"Lipstick?" she muttered. "No, they'd expect me to be sleeping. Only guilty people stay up watching the street."

"Here." Natalya pressed a pair of long lace-trimmed gloves into her hands.

"Why are they here in the middle of the night? That can't be good."

"Just stick to the story. I was hired to do readings at the party, but I was sick so you went instead. Massot attacked you. You were terrified so you ran for your life at the first chance. You weren't thinking straight. In fact, you planned to telephone the Curia in the morning. But of course you'll give them your full cooperation."

"Right."

"I'll confirm every word. They'll be gone before you know it."

Natalya sounded so confident. But then, she had nothing to hide, did she?

"And if they ask about the reading?"

"Don't muddy the waters. Say it was nothing unusual."

Kasia knotted her robe and pulled the gloves on just as a knock sounded.

"Look sleepy," Natalya whispered.

Kasia lowered her lids to half-mast. Gave her hair a quick muss and trudged to the door. She left the chain on, opening it a crack. The priests stood in the hall, dripping. The one she remembered from the study wasn't breathing hard at all, but his partner looked on the verge of fainting.

"May I see some identification?" she asked politely.

The younger one hooked a finger into his cassock and turned so she could see the Raven Mark on his neck. The other, older and even bigger, just stared at her coldly. "Open the door, Domina Anderle," he said.

"Certainly, Father. One can't be too careful." Kasia closed the door, unhooked the chain, and opened it again. "I'm sorry, I was sleeping."

"You don't have to apologize." That was the younger one. She remembered the gentle way he'd spoken to Massot. He was using the same voice on her now. It would be easy to let her guard down, but she couldn't afford any more mistakes.

She moved back to allow them inside. The small space felt even smaller.

"And I'm not Domina Anderle." Kasia looked at her friend, who sat with her feet curled underneath her on the couch. "She is."

Natalya gracefully unfolded herself and stood. "Can I get you anything? Coffee? Tea?"

"No, thank you. My name is Fra Bryce. This is Fra Spassov."

"And Fra Spassov is confused," the huge one said. "Which one of you was at the home of Ferran Massot earlier?"

"That would be me," Kasia said. "Massot went mad and trapped me in the bathroom. I was terrified so I ran for my life at the first chance." Tears welled in her eyes. "I'm so sorry, Fathers, I wasn't thinking straight. In fact, I planned to telephone the Curia first thing in the morning." She lowered her lashes, voice catching. "But of course I'll give you my full cooperation now."

The priests exchanged a look. "And your name, Domina?" Spassov asked.

She dried her face with a sleeve. "Kasia Novak."

Bryce jotted this down in a notebook.

"It was supposed to be me," Natalya said. "I feel terrible, knowing what almost happened." She cast a tender look at her friend. "Poor Kasia. We're just grateful you arrived when you did."

"Are you all right?" Fra Bryce looked at Kasia.

Her first impression had been accurate. He looked tired. But also perceptive, which did not bode well.

"I'm fine. Just, you know . . . ." She heaved a watery sigh. "Shaken up."

"We need to ask you some questions about what happened," Bryce said.

"Right, of course you do. I'm so sorry I ran off. I wasn't—"

"Thinking straight," Spassov finished dryly. "You already told us."

Bryce shot his partner a quelling look. "Who else was there?

Kasia met his direct gaze. Nothing to hide here, Fra Bryce. "Well, the caterers. They left right after supper."

"What time was that?"

"I'd say about eight or nine."

"What was the name of the catering company?"

"I'm sorry, I have no idea." She sat next to Natalya, one foot tapping a rhythm on the carpet.

"How many people were there, excluding you and Massot?"

"Only three. It was a small affair."

"Names?"

Kasia recited the list. Bryce wrote them down. "And you were invited by Dr. Massot?" He posed this question to Natalya.

"Not exactly." She crossed her legs, giving them a flash of smooth brown ankle. "Won't you sit down?"

"No, thank you," Spassov said. "What does *not exactly* mean, Domina Anderle?"

"It means that I wasn't a guest. I was hired to be there." She gave her answer to Bryce, who either didn't notice or didn't care. He was still looking at Kasia.

"In what capacity?" Spassov asked.

"I'm a cartomancer. So is Domina Novak. Surely, you've heard of it."

"No."

"Well, it's all the rage. We use oracle cards to tell fortunes. I make the decks, but Kasia does most of the readings. She's better at that part."

Bryce took a pack of cards from his pocket. "These?"

The sight of her beloved cards in the priest's hand . . . well, it was like watching an escaped monkey root through her underwear drawer. They'd be contaminated with his aura now. She'd have to sage the whole house and each individual card.

Kasia shot to her feet. "May I have them back? They're my best deck."

"No," Spassov replied. "Tell us exactly what happened. Every detail."

Kasia scowled and earned a sharp elbow from Natalya. "I'll make you another deck, Kiska," she said soothingly. "Go ahead and tell them."

So Kasia did, leaving out the bizarre things Massot had said and of course, the brass cylinders she had stolen from his desk.

"Then Fra Bryce came and I was afraid that if Massot overpowered him, he'd come back for me. So I ran."

"How did you leave?"

"Through the front door. I—" Kasia fell silent. Oh, *fog it!*

"There was a Markhound at the gate," Fra Bryce said softly. "How did you pass it?"

"I climbed over the fence, down by the end of the flowerbeds."

"In spiked heels?"

He *was* perceptive. Kasia eyed him with a spark of interest. He'd only seen her for an instant, yet he'd noticed what she was wearing down to her shoes. Of course, she had perfect recall of the encounter, too. Hyperthymesia, the doctors called it. The condition was similar to eidetic memory, except hers applied to events rather than static images.

"I'm quite athletic," she said. "Just ask Domina Anderle."

"Oh, she is," Natalya added wickedly. "She does *everything* in heels."

Bryce jotted something in his notebook. His face was impossible to read.

"Let's back up for a moment," Spassov rumbled. "We know Massot's Mark inverted at exactly 11:17 p.m."

Kasia nodded, unsure what they were after.

"Were the guests still there?"

"I don't know. I wasn't keeping track of the time."

"Approximately."

She thought back, replaying the evening moment by moment. They'd stood in the hall, watching Massot's guests get into their chauffered cars. Then she and the doctor had gone upstairs. He'd asked for a reading and Kasia had hesitated because it was getting late. Also because she didn't like him and wanted to get out of there.

"I did look at the clock," she said. "The one on the mantel in his study. It was just after eleven when we sat down to do his reading."

"And you were alone at that point?"

"Yes."

They stared at her impassively. No one leapt up and shouted *aha!* But the tension in the room ramped up a notch and Kasia felt a glimmer of unease. I just boxed myself in. *But to what?*

Bryce lowered his notepad. "You're doing very well, Domina Novak. Now, in the course of the next quarter of an hour, did Dr. Massot leave you at all? Did anyone else come to the house? Maybe just for a minute or two?"

The quiet urgency in his voice worried her. She didn't understand what he was getting at, but she knew she needed to lie.

"Now that you mention it, Dr. Massot excused himself. I'm not sure where he went. It wasn't long. But when he came back he was different."

"That's when he attacked you?"

"Yes," she said firmly.

"But you didn't see anyone else?" Spassov prompted. "Did you hear voices?"

Keep it simple.

"I'm afraid not." She pretended to think. "It's possible I heard the front door close. But I was shuffling the cards. Mentally preparing myself for the reading. I just wanted to get home."

"Are we done here?" Natalya asked. "She's been through a terrible ordeal."

Spassov glanced at Bryce, who gave a slight nod.

"We're done," Fra Spassov said. "For now." He gave them both a stern look. "You're not to speak of this incident, Dominas. To anyone."

"I wish it never happened," Kasia said. "And thank you. I owe you both my life."

"Telephone the Curia if you remember anything else," Fra Bryce said. "Give my name to the switchboard and they'll put you through."

"Certainly. Oh, I left my purse at his house. And my raincoat. Will they be returned?"

"We'll convey your request," Spassov said in a noncommittal tone.

The priests left.

Kasia stood at the window, watching until she saw them emerge from the building and get into their car. "Do you think they believed us?"

"Of course they did." Natalya slung an arm around her shoulders. "You were very credible." She frowned. "Did Massot meet someone? You never mentioned that part."

"No, but I thought I should say so." Kasia disliked loose ends. One hard tug and they could unravel a whole story. "The exact time his Mark turned was obviously important to them, though I don't know why it matters. Unless they think something set him off. Fog it, I wish I knew."

Natalya yawned. "Fra Bryce was rather delicious though."

"He's too young," Kasia muttered.

"He can't be less than thirty." Nashka laughed. "I suppose the big scruffy one is more to your taste."

"Normally, yes. But since I was thinking with my *brain*, I can't say either of them appeals."

"You just don't like priests."

"I don't dislike them," Kasia clarified. "Not on principle. I just don't want them poking into my affairs."

Nashka wound a strand of Kasia's hair around her finger, then made it into a mustache. "All the pretty ones get snapped up by the Pontifex, did you ever notice that?"

"You're a terrible person."

"It's true." She tickled Kasia's ear with the hair until Kasia batted her hand away. "Well, now that I'm up, I may as well do some work." Natalya took her robe off and tossed it over a chair. She only had one Mark, an amber-maned dragon that wrapped around her left biceps and wound all the way down to her wrist. The scales shimmered in shades of red and green like burnished metal.

Natalya settled down at the worktable and removed her

left glove. She had immense artistic talent, inborn, and the ley took that spark and stoked it to a hot blaze. Now she took up a fine horsehair brush, lips pursed in concentration as she consulted a sketchpad. Her latest commission was a cartomancy deck for a wealthy client. The Major Arcana were variations of the saints and the four suits represented the Curia cities: Wolves for Kvengard, Flames for Jalghuth, Ravens for Novostopol and Crossed Keys for Nantwich. Each card took a full day to paint, the colors as rich and vibrant as a garden in bloom. When it was done, the deck would cover Nashka's share of the rent for the next two months.

Kasia watched her work with the melancholy she always had in the presence of her friend's genius. Envy wasn't the right word. More like regret. She rarely fretted over the past, there seemed to be no point, but now she saw the branching paths of her own life, the choices made or not made, the turns left rather than right, and wondered. She earned her keep from the idea of destiny, but she wasn't sure she believed it anymore. The Lovers? *That* was unlikely. Kasia trusted no one except for Nashka and Tessaria Foy. *Could* trust no one.

She curled up on the couch and fell asleep to Natalya's humming and the ceaseless sound of rain.

Chapter Eight

✦✦✦

"Do you believe them?" Alexei asked as he drove back to the Arx.

Spassov shrugged. "We'll find out soon enough if the story checks out."

He squinted through the torrents of rain battering the windscreen. "It seemed rehearsed to me."

In fact, he knew it was rehearsed. Spassov was very good at wrestling people to the ground, but he lacked finesse when it came to questioning witnesses. Domina Novak was a skilled actress, but she was hiding something. The foot tapping. The veering between defiance and avoidance. She had magnetism in spades, though. As tired as he was, Alexei's mouth had gone a little dry when she answered the door.

"Forget about the woman," Spassov covered a yawn. "It's Massot we need to focus on."

"Do me a favor," Alexei said. "Keep Novak's name out of it. Just for now."

Patryk shot him a look. "You have to put both their statements in the report. We do this one by the book, Alyosha, or they'll hang us out to dry."

"Of course," Alexei said reasonably. "I just want to look

into her before Kireyev's legions come swarming down on our case."

"Why?"

"A hunch."

Patryk sighed and leaned back against the headrest. "It's the middle of the night anyway. I'm going to bed until we hear from Pagwe."

The streets were deserted. Alexei slowed for the red lights but didn't bother stopping, and ten minutes later they drove through the gates of the Arx. Spassov stumbled up the stairs to his quarters, but Alexei was wide awake. He splashed water on his face and changed into a fresh cassock. Then he went to the kennels to look in on the Markhounds.

They were kept in a stone building behind the Tower of Saint Dima that had once been used for storing casks of wine. The vaulted interior smelled strongly of wet dog, but he noted with approval that clean straw covered the floor and the water bowls were full. Alexei held the novices to high standards when it came to care of the hounds. They might be creatures of the ley, but they were also living, breathing animals who deserved humane treatment. He checked on them at least twice a day, and woe if he discovered neglect. He also performed a head count after they'd been loose.

As always, Alice was the first to greet him at the door. Her brown eyes looked apologetic like she knew she'd been outfoxed. Alexei took a glove off and rubbed her flank, hand lingering on an old scar transecting the haunch. It gave her a slight limp, though she ran just as swiftly as the others. His gaze blanked out for a moment. Violet fire traced his Marks, surging up from the liminal ley. Alexei's eyes cleared.

"Never mind," he said. "You did your best."

A quick survey of the kennel showed the rest accounted for. There were six packs altogether, housed in adjoining chambers. When someone's Marks turned, they all started barking, but only a single pack would appear in the courtyard. It was one of the mysteries Alexei pondered when he couldn't sleep. Did the dogs decide who would take the duty? Or did the ley? The Pontifex Luk would surely know the answer, though Alexei doubted he'd ever have a chance to ask.

Satisfied that his charges were settled in for the night, he grabbed the car keys and drove to the Tabularium. It was just after four a.m. when he parked in front of the neoclassical building next to the Pontifex's Palace. It housed kilometers of shelving with records dating back more than a millennium to the Second Dark Age. The one in Nantwich was even larger, with fragments from the time before. Clavis, the Pontifex of the Western Curia, had made it her life's work to gather old knowledge—some of which, it was whispered in certain quarters, would be better forgotten. Alexei wasn't sure he agreed, though he understood the perils. Before the discovery that Marks could channel the ley, society had nearly doomed itself to oblivion. An age of wonders—and horrors beyond imagining.

Some of that knowledge had been revived during the war against the rebel Nightmages. Explosive shells, for example. Poison gas. After heated debate, the Curia had banned such weapons again. They joined a technology blacklist encompassing everything except for cars and basic telephone and electrical service. Kvengard rejected even those conveniences, but in Novo the conservatives were overruled by the more liberal Neoteric faction headed by Cardinal Falke. Alexei had been relieved. Horses feared Markhounds and he couldn't imagine hauling an Invertido to the Institute draped over the back of a saddle.

He climbed the steps and rang the bell. There was no overhang and he huddled in the rain for more than a minute before pressing the buzzer again, a long, sustained peal. At last, shuffling footsteps approached. The bolt was thrown back. A priest peered through the door, chin thrust forward.

He was in his early forties, but his face had the pinched, sunken aspect of a much older man.

"Do you know what time it is, Bryce?" he demanded.

"I apologize, but I need access to the archives, Fra Bendixon," Alexei said, inwardly cursing his luck.

Most people who joined the church fell into two broad categories. The first were naturally generous souls who wanted to make the world a better place. The second were troubled and lonely and had difficulty relating to others. Fra Bendixon was one of the latter.

The priest stared at him in annoyance. "Just because you keep ludicrous hours, you seem to expect the rest of us ought to, as well. Come back in the morning." He started to close the door. Alexei jammed his foot in the crack.

"I have the authority," he said mildly. "As the on-duty archivist, you cannot refuse me. And if I'm forced to wake my superiors in the middle of the night, who do you think they'll be more upset with?"

Fra Bendixon viewed the Interfectorem as a bunch of savages, and Alexei in particular as a thorn in his side. As far as Alexei knew, he was the only one to regularly demand admittance outside of regular hours, but his work necessitated it. Night duty rotated among the roster of archivists so at least he didn't wake the same priest each time. None were exactly happy to see his face, but Fra Bendixon took it as a personal assault to be roused from his blankets.

They had the same exchange each time, an obligatory joust that always ended with threats from Alexei and ill-humored concession by Bendixon.

"What's so important anyway?" the priest muttered.

"We have a delicate situation, you understand? It can't wait. If I don't file my preliminary report in the next few hours—"

"*Da, da*," Bendixon said sourly. "But make it quick or I'll be the one to lodge a complaint." He stabbed a finger at Alexei's sodden exorason. "And leave that in the cloakroom. I won't have you dripping all over the wood floors. They were just waxed!"

Alexei refrained from pointing out that he was only so wet because Bendixon had left him standing out in the rain. "Of course," he said. "Thank you for the indulgence, brother."

Alexei's stubborn courtesy only annoyed the archivist more. He sniffed loudly but stepped back and opened the door. Once the offending garment was stowed in the cloakroom, Bendixon escorted Alexei past the reception desk, flipping on overhead lights as he went. By ancient tradition, the records repositories were the only buildings inside the walls of the Arx to have electricity. The risk of fire was simply too great to permit candles or torches.

"Civil register, I assume?" Bendixon asked briskly.

"Yes."

The Eastern Curia kept files on every citizen of Novostopol, and a separate register for members of the clergy. Access to the latter was restricted, but anyone had the right to examine the first. If you wished to know how many Marks someone had, and who had given them, you had only to fill out a request at the reception desk—during regular business hours, of course.

The records Alexei sought were in a vast gallery lined with row upon row of file drawers. Bendixon unlocked the door, then hovered with arms crossed as Alexei took out his notebook.

"The subject of my report is confidential," Alexei reminded him. "I'll have to request that you wait elsewhere."

Another loud sniff, but the priest retreated. "You have twenty minutes," he called over his shoulder.

Alexei didn't waste time responding. He strode swiftly down the center of the gallery, pausing at M. Ferran Massot's file was already gone—pulled by Kireyev's agents at the Office of the General Directorate, no doubt—but he located Kasia

Novak's within minutes. Alexei wrote down the pertinent details in his notebook.

Twenty-eight years old. A Novo native. Parents killed in a car wreck, no siblings. Marked by a retired vestal named Tessaria Foy. Public school through age eighteen, but she never went on to the Lyceum. Occupation listed as self-employed. Unless she lied massively on her tax returns, Domina Novak didn't earn much as a cartomancer. The extent of her criminal activity was a slew of parking tickets. Her address matched the flat on Malaya Sadovaya Ulitsa. Alexei jotted down the license plate of her car and replaced the file. He rubbed his eyes. Another dead end.

It would be a very long day tomorrow. Or was it already today? Time had grown fuzzy of late. He should try to sleep, but Alexei knew it would be useless. Once he got into bed, he'd lie there staring at the ceiling. If he took the pills, he'd be foggy when they questioned Massot, and he couldn't afford that . . . .

"Fra Bryce!"

Bendixon's petulant voice snapped him out of oblivion. Alexei realized he'd slumped against the filing cabinet. The notebook lay at his feet. He didn't remember dropping it.

"Are you deaf? I've been calling your name for five minutes!"

Alexei scooped up the notebook. He stood too fast and the gallery lengthened like a hall of mirrors, file cabinets marching to infinity. Trembling fingers scrabbled for the pocket of his cassock. He found the copper coin, squeezing it hard in his palm. The world righted itself.

"I'm finished here," he said, brushing past Bendixon.

"You can see yourself out, Bryce. Twice in one night is quite enough. I'll never know why they don't just give you people a key!"

Twice? Alexei thought blurrily, steering for the cloakroom. Oh. The Massot file. That explained why Bendixon was even grumpier than usual. But they didn't know about Domina Novak when Spassov called from the Institute, did they?

No, not yet, or her file would have been gone, too.

Alexei stumbled down the steps, but instead of returning to the Tower of Saint Dima he crossed the muddy green to the Iveron Chapel. The doors were always left open, the candles kept burning, though it was deserted now. He knelt before the stained glass windows of the clerestory.

There was no God in the Via Sancta. No Heaven or Hell. The doctrine of his Church taught individual responsibility. Seeking the highest expression of humanity here on earth, in this lifetime. The five virtues were compassion, courage, fidelity, honesty, and forgiveness. Purity had been dropped from the list after the Ninth Pontifical Council. It was impossible to enforce and frankly, a species that denied its lustful urges wouldn't last long. Not even priests and vestals were expected to be celibate anymore. The prohibition on alcohol had been even more short-lived.

In general, the Church took a progressive stance on personal freedoms, even mild vices, but it drew a hard line on violence for self-gratification. Hatred had no place, nor revenge.

Saints, help me.

Alexei gazed up at the triptych, a fevered flush cresting his sharp cheekbones.

The first showed Lezarius defending the walls of Nantwich. His forces had swept down from the north to break a siege of the city. A crucial, bloody battle.

The second, his captivity in Bal Agnar. The heretic Nightmage Balaur stood over a chained Lezarius, whip in hand. Blood leaked from a hundred cuts.

In the last triptych, blue light streamed from the martyr's palms and eyes. Nihilim cowered as loyal knights drove spears into their bodies. The creation of the Void. In his agony, Lezarius had shifted the course of the ley away from Bal

Agnar and Bal Kirith, the rebel cities at the heart of the continent, stripping the mages of their power. This single act decisively turned the tide of the war. Despite the chaos around him, Lezarius appeared serene.

Through a veil of exhaustion, Alexei saw another face, but this one was contorted in psychic agony, the eyes wide, the mouth a yawning hole.

Alexei's bile rose. He tore a glove off, pulling ley into his Marks. They flared with blue light, then went icy cold. It wasn't the memory itself they fought to suppress. Memories were simply a record of past events, necessary to self-identity and orientation in the world. No, the problem arose in the emotional state they triggered. The Dark Wound.

His stomach cramped, pain gripping his head in a vise.

Saints, help me . . . .

ALEXEI SMELLED SMOKE.

Sweat soaked the tunic beneath his chain mail. Midsummer in the ruins of Bal Kirith and the jungle humidity made each breath feel like drowning. His company of twenty knights occupied the former Arx, setting up camp in the shelled ruins. The ley had flooded and the stelae needed to be inspected. Most of it had already seeped back into the earth, following veins too deep to access. The tidal force imposed by the grid would pull the ley back to the Curia cities within a few days, but he could sense a weak residue.

Two knights were tinkering with a field radio, trying to find a signal. Alexei sat on a scorched wooden pew, sharpening his sword and watching barn swallows dive through holes in the chapel dome. They were feasting on swarms of mosquitoes that hovered in visible clouds, undeterred by torches soaked in eucalyptus oil. He slapped his neck and examined the smear of blood on his glove with weary resignation. Mosquitoes avoided Marks, but any bit of exposed flesh was fair game. Two of the knights already shivered in their bedrolls, down with fever. Malaria, most likely. Or dengue.

Alexei silently cheered on the swallows and ran a cloth down his blade, drawing off excess oil from the whetstone. It didn't need sharpening, but he wanted something to take his mind off the oppressive heat. Torrential rains came early each morning in Bal Kirith, forming the stagnant pools that bred pestilence. By eleven or so, when a fierce sun broke the tree-tops, the mercury soared into the triple-digits and stayed there until nightfall. Then it would be feeding time in earnest. Thank the Saints they slept under netting, which helped as long as you weren't on sentry duty. But the humidity never relented and between the blood loss and constant sweating, Alexei estimated he'd lost five kilos since they arrived.

"Sir!" A knight strode up, a pair of Markhounds trotting at her heels.

The captain turned. "Yes, Vilmos?"

"We found the residue of a campfire inside the basilica." Only her green eyes were visible through the helm. "Looks fairly fresh."

Alexei tensed. Nine days without a single skirmish. It seemed too good to be true, though they hadn't let their guard down. Not for an instant. The newspapers back home trumpeted the Curia's victory, but Alexei knew better. As long as a single nihilim lived, there would never be true peace. Alexei glanced at the captain, tall and resplendent in his gilded armor. He was poring over a map of the Arx and didn't seem surprised. Alexei realized then that the mission to inspect the Wards was in fact a search-and-annihilate.

Well, of course it was. He felt a surge of betrayal at the subterfuge, but it faded as quickly as it came. Their captain was only following orders. He'd never put his knights at risk without a good reason.

Unlike the rest of them, he never seemed tired or afraid. He was everything a leader ought to be. Decisive, strategic, rational. He knew when to force engagement, and on what terrain, and which fights could not be won without maximum bloodshed. He taught them that each contact with the enemy was an equation to be manipulated for advantage. Emotion had no place on the battlefield.

Yet he was also a man of boundless humanity, their captain. Every one of them would have died for him.

"Bryce, you're with me," he said.

Alexei stood, sheathing his blade. He picked up his own helm but didn't put it on yet. Too fogging hot. He suspected Vilmos wore hers more to repel the bugs than the mages.

"Parsa and Degermark, leave the radio for now. Lieutenant Serikev, you're in charge until we return."

The captain's second was a slightly built woman with a mild demeanor that masked utter fearlessness. "Yes, sir." She went back to studying the map, which was marked by a series of X's representing the stelae. Two teams of four were inspecting them. The rest manned a perimeter line around the camp.

In three more weeks, the knights would withdraw from the Void, never to return. The Tenth Pontifical Council would deem the expense of maintaining garrisons far outside the Blue Zone to be profligate in both lives and treasure, and not worth the effort. But none of them knew that yet, and it would change nothing in terms of what was about to happen.

"How old was the fire?" the captain asked as they left the chapel and crossed the quad. The dogs took point, noses to the ground.

"Hard to say," Vilmos replied, flipping her visor up. "The spot is sheltered from the rain. But it wasn't there when we first came through, I'm sure of it. Kortier and Tann stayed behind to keep watch."

"Could it be Perditae?"

"It's possible." She sounded doubtful. "But you know as well as I do that they avoid the ruins."

Perditae were a byproduct of the civil war, humans grown corrupted by the psychic degradation of the ley in the Morho Sarpanitum, the jungle at the heart of the continent where the twin cities of Bal Agnar and Bal Kirith once stood. The word meant degenerate or morally depraved, but also abandoned, hopeless, lost. Alexei had heard the mages hunted them for sport but didn't know if it was true. He'd only encountered a band once. It was enough to hope he never did again.

"They fear the nihilim," the captain agreed. "Perditae are bloodthirsty but not stupid."

Alexei raised a hand to block out the slanting late afternoon sun. The shattered dome of the basilica gleamed in the distance. It was inside the cordon, which troubled him. How did they get through? Markhounds had combed every meter of the Arx a week ago.

"Care to guess how many?" the captain asked.

"Judging from the animal bones, no more than two or three, which also argues against Perditae. Their bands are usually larger. At least a dozen."

They passed the scorched skeleton of a Curia automobile. Moss colonized the wreckage, carpeting the interior in a thick green sponge. The raven had been sawed from the bonnet and dangled upside-down from the rearview mirror, a wire noose twisted around its feet. Alexei tore his gaze away.

"Most of the Wards are back," the captain said. "If it was nihilim, they're probably outside the perimeter by now, but we'll tighten it up."

Alexei shared a quick look with Parsa and Degermark. *Probably outside the perimeter?* There was a reason they had the lowest casualty rate of any company. Every risk was calculated and their captain never, ever assumed the mages would behave rationally. The opposite, in fact.

But in the last year, he had changed. On the surface, he was the same confident, calm leader, but Alexei sensed darkness lurking beneath. A detached coldness that saw his knights as game pieces and didn't really care if they lived or died. This was so far from the man he had been that it was hard to comprehend.

A pair of sentries stood on the steps of the brick post office.

"Lux, Veritas, Virtus," one shouted, saluting.

The captain waved a hand in greeting. "Helms on and gloves off," he ordered the rest of them.

Alexei pulled his helm on, but left the visor raised. It was a relief to discard the leather gloves. He sank down and pressed a palm to the scraggly grass, testing the ley. His Marks barely flickered—yet it wasn't entirely gone, a fact that heightened his uneasiness. He looked at the hounds trotting twenty paces ahead. No raised hackles, no barking. The dogs were the first and best defense. Now he wondered how the ebbing ley might affect their instincts.

He hurried to catch up with the others, who were almost at the edge of the quad. The basilica lay just ahead. Even the bright sunlight failed to illuminate the interior.

"Captain?" Alexei said. "May I have a quick word?"

"Of course."

The other knights stepped aside, taking the opportunity to test the ley themselves. Alexei lowered his voice. Neither of them acknowledged their blood ties, not in the field, and he'd never had cause to question orders before, but he'd rather speak up than regret it later.

"This feels like a trap," he said. "And we're walking straight into it."

"It's an old campfire," his brother said dryly. "Are you suggesting we don't investigate?"

"No. But it might be better to go in with reinforcements."

"There's five of us, plus Kortier and Tann. I can't pull the sentries off duty."

"We could take one of the units inspecting the stelae."

Misha stared back, untroubled. "The Wards are our first priority."

"Are they?" The words were out before Alexei could take them back. He knew he skated dangerously close to insubordination, yet Mikhail didn't take offense.

He clapped Alexei's shoulder. They had the same light eyes and dark hair, though Misha was a little taller. No one bothered shaving in the Void and both men wore scruffy beards. "Trust me on this, brother."

"You know I do. That's not it."

"If it was a trap, do you think they would have let Vilmos walk out?"

"Maybe it isn't Vilmos they want," Alexei said.

His brother glanced at the hounds, who'd flopped down to wait in the shade of an orange tree, tongues panting. "The dogs would have warned us by now if mages were near."

"Not if the ley is too weak."

Mikhail laughed, white teeth flashing. "Then it's weak for the mages, too. And they're not stupid. My guess is that they baited us so I'll do exactly what you're suggesting. Concentrate resources on the basilica, thus wasting time."

"For what purpose?" Alexei wondered.

"Sow confusion. Create a dilemma." He paused. "Now, why do you think they'd do that, Alyosha?"

Mikhail had often posed such questions to him when they were half-feral boys left to run wild on a sprawling forested estate. Their father paid for tutors, but the most important lessons came from Misha, who'd devoured philosophy and strategy from the moment he learned to read. Alexei had worshipped his brother, and still did. Misha never imparted knowledge by rote, preferring to ask questions and force him to think it through for himself.

"To buy time?"

"Good." His brother nodded. "Time for what?"

Only one possibility made sense. "Their own reinforcements to come?"

The spark of pride in Misha's eyes warmed him, though it felt false somehow, as if his brother was simulating an emotion he didn't truly feel.

"You perceive the correct question then. Which is the greater risk? To finish our mission and withdraw as planned, with the slim chance of an ambush, or to delay out of caution and potentially face superior forces in the future?"

He wants to get us out of here, Alexei realized. Quickly.

"The second," Alexei said. "I'm sorry, I shouldn't have doubted you."

"Never be sorry for doing what you think is right, Alyosha," his brother said seriously. "As long as you don't disobey a direct order in the midst of a fight."

Misha's lips quirked and for a brief instant, he looked like the eleven-year-old boy who'd climbed up to the roof to pee down the chimney one memorable evening when their father had his banker friends over for dinner. Misha had been whipped for it, but that act of rebellion cemented his godlike status in Alexei's eyes. They still laughed about it sometimes.

Alexei forced himself to grin back. "Let's have a look before it gets dark."

Their captain whistled and the Markhounds leapt up. Misha put his helm on, dropping the visor. It would be the last time Alexei saw his brother smile.

The doors to the basilica had been torn from their hinges decades before, leaving a gaping black hole. Vines clung to the stonework, slowly prising it apart, though the structure still stood. Alexei could see a little way inside, but the rest was lost to shadows. He drew his sword. So did the others. The hounds loped ahead. A hot breeze riffled the stalks of high grass, bearing the loamy, animal smell of the forest.

Once there had been an Arx in each of the six cities of the Via Sancta. They were known as the Arxes Invicta, the

Unconquered Citadels, built after the Second Dark Age to be beacons of sanity in a world gone mad. For nearly a millennium, they'd lived up to this promise. Then the slow decline began.

Bal Kirith and Bal Agnar became cesspools of sin and greed, necessitating the collective excommunication of their inhabitants. Then, the war. The creation of the Void and the bloody mop-up that followed. The "unconquered" part was dropped. Keeping it seemed an insult to the dead. The inner cities of the Curia were now known simply as the Arx.

Bal Kirith and Bal Agnar were outside the ley lines and thus had been left to rot and ruin.

After being massively shelled, of course.

Through the bars of his visor, Alexei saw the Markhounds vanish into the basilica. His breath echoed in the confines of the helm. It smelled sour, but then he hadn't been clean for weeks.

They approached in a line, Captain Bryce leading. As he neared the doors, Kortier appeared. His sword was in its scabbard and Alexei relaxed a little.

"We searched the ground floor," he said. "One of them desecrated the altar with his own filth, fogging savages."

"None of that," the captain snapped. "The enemy is to be respected, if only so we never underestimate them. It was a message, intended to provoke. Will you give them what they want?"

"No, sir." Kortier's helm was tucked under one arm and his ruddy face flushed deeper at the reprimand.

"Good." The captain's tone softened. "Where's Tann?"

"Inside. We searched the upper choir, but it looked undisturbed."

They entered at the west end of the nave. It enclosed a soaring space, with buttresses supporting the arched roof. The stained glass windows were long gone and the last rays of the sun angled inside, pooling on the stone floor. Alexei caught a foul odor, faint but unmistakable. Anger tightened his jaw. He knew his brother was right, but the sheer childish ugliness of the act was hard to dismiss. We have to be better than they are, he reminded himself. We *are* better.

But he saw the others felt the same. Sickened and vengeful. That was the problem with deployment to the Void. Their Marks stopped working. Worse, the ley itself was tainted, like a river passing through a toxic dump. Misha was the only one who never seemed affected. Never lost his head. Which was why, Alexei thought ruefully, they'd put him in charge.

"Keep a sharp watch," Captain Bryce told the radio operators who'd been conscripted. The two men saluted and took up posts at the entrance.

"The fire's over here," Vilmos said, leading Alexei and Mikhail to the transept where Tann stood with the two Markhounds. They were circling the ashes, whining low in their throats. The captain studied the scattering of bones and greasy charcoal.

"Looks like rabbit," Tann said, just before an arrow pierced his right eye.

A second arrow bounced off Alexei's gorget, centimeters from the juncture with his helm. The force of it knocked him back, the world narrowing to a blurred slit as he crashed into the wall.

"Fall back!" the captain shouted.

Forms rappelled down ropes dropped from the dome above. Alexei got his sword up just in time to parry an overhand blow from a woman with gray-streaked hair and arms corded with muscle. She pivoted away, stabbing at someone just out of sight. He heard the hounds snarling. A very human scream. Blood sprayed his eyes, blinding him. Not his own. Misha's? Saints, no. . . .

Alexei tore his helm off. Vilmos lay on her back, green eyes staring sightless. The two knights at the door were also down, open helms fletched with arrows. He had witnessed violent death many times, yet it never got easier. He'd served two tours with Vilmos. Laughed and ate with her. She had kids back home. And now, in the space of four heartbeats, she was dead.

In the opposite transept, Kortier and his brother flanked a mage with short black hair. The man wore no mail or armor. In fact, he was stripped to the waist. Sweat glistened on his Marks, but he moved with assurance.

Alexei absorbed all this in the instant before the woman turned back to him. Her sword had been taken from a knight. He recognized the double Raven hilt. With a wordless roar, Alexei leapt forward. Their blades joined. She couldn't have been less than sixty, but Alexei found himself giving ground.

Were there only two? Or more? He risked a glance around and nearly lost his head for it. But he saw no more nihilim. They must be mad to take on an entire company alone.

Parry. Feint. Thrust.

Maybe his brother was right. They were waiting for more to arrive. But why tip their hand early?

Lunge. Parry. Counter attack.

Their blades rang in the silence. Ley shimmered where her palms met the hilt. Whatever happened, Alexei couldn't let her touch him. He retreated. Then his boot heel hit something slippery. A patch of moss. Alexei felt his center of gravity shift. He pivoted, desperately seeking a foothold, but it was too late. Stone slammed into his back. His sword skidded away. The mage quickly adjusted her grip for a downward stroke. Alexei knew he was about to die. That his luck had finally run out. He felt no fear, only shame that he'd let his brother down.

Then a dark blur hit her from behind. The Markhound sank its teeth into her calf, jaws scissoring the flesh. She twisted away and stabbed the hound in its haunch. It whimpered and fell over, sides heaving.

Alexei tried to regain his feet. She slammed the hilt into his temple. The world swam out of focus. He raised a mailed arm to ward off the inevitable killing blow. That's when Alexei saw his brother in the opposite transept. Mikhail had disarmed the mage and driven him into a corner. Blood streaked the nihilim's chest from a dozen shallow slashes.

"Beleth!" the mage cried.

The woman limped toward them, spitting on Kortier's body as she passed. Alexei shouted a slurred warning. Mikhail never turned. He was speaking to the mage, his face contorted in anger, but the words were lost to the buzzing in Alexei's ears.

The next part happened fast. The woman caught Mikhail's forearm as he raised his sword to deliver the *coup de grace*. The bare-chested mage's Marks lit with red fire. He hurled himself at Mikhail, his weight bearing them both to the ground. Abyssal ley flickered between them, dimming and pulsing. Misha screamed. Alexei had never heard such a sound, before or since. His brother stiffened, heels drumming, back arched, and then he stopped, though his eyes remained open. Alexei tried to crawl to him, but only made it a few meters before he turned his head to vomit. Surf pounded in his ears, a hissing roar. The hound lay in a pool of blood not far off. He reached out a hand, half mad with grief. She whined and crept closer, dragging her useless hind leg, until he felt fur under his fingers. A rough tongue licked his face.

Later, when the other knights said she had to be put down, that she was too badly hurt, Alexei raged and fought until they gave up and let him carry her back to his tent. He expected her to die on the journey back to Novostopol, but she didn't. Over the long, dark days that followed, he nursed her back to health, changing the pus-soaked dressing on her wound twice a day and coaxing her to take antibiotic pills pressed into a wedge of soft cheese. He thought she would never walk, but again, she proved everyone wrong. The afternoon he returned her to the kennels, he told her she was a good dog, and then he wept while she sat there, looking grateful but faintly embarrassed for him.

Time passed, but he never forgot, and neither did she.

He named her Alice.

"FRA BRYCE?"

A face peered down at him. It was the chapel's archpriest. He wore a midnight blue cassock, thinning hair combed over to conceal a bald spot. A small concession to vanity that Alexei had always found endearing in such an otherwise kind and selfless man.

"I came to light the candles and found you on the floor." He frowned, the riverine network of lines on his face deepening. "Could it have been a seizure? Your eyes were rolled back. You were shaking, brother."

Alexei sat up, drained and faintly nauseous. He'd been kneeling in contemplation but couldn't recall what happened after.

"Just a touch of flu," Alexei said, climbing to his feet. One of his gloves was off. He hurriedly retrieved it. "It's going around."

"You must see the doctor," the archpriest said. "If you have a fever, you ought to be in bed."

"I will," Alexei called over his shoulder.

"Fra Bryce——"

"I promise!"

Alexei strode for the door. The rain felt good on his face. Cool and soothing. He fetched the car from outside the Tabularium and drove to the Tower of Saint Dima, parking in the small lot next to the kennels. When he reached his rooms, he sat down at his desk, rolled a sheet of blank paper into the typewriter, and started pecking at the keys.

It was just a fainting spell. He had them sometimes. They came and went quickly, and he often managed to catch some sleep afterward. But he could get a head start on the report in the meantime. He checked his notebook, entering Massot's address and pertinent details.

"The Markhounds sounded the alarm at 11:17 p.m. Fra Patryk Spassov and Fra Alexei Bryce responded. Due to flooding conditions at the Kopeksin Square Bridge, Bryce was first to arrive at the residence, owned by Dr. Ferran Massot (see biographical note attached). The front door was locked, necessitating a forced entry through the rear garden at approximately 11:39 p.m. Bryce encountered Massot in his study." Alexei paused, replaying the scene. The insectile jerk of the doctor's head as he stepped through the door. The darkness in his eyes.

Get away from me, you filthy rook.

"Subject was taken into custody after a brief struggle. A female witness fled the premises and was later questioned at her residence (see interview notes attached). Subsequent examination of the subject by Dr. Dheerhaj Pagwe established that the Mark in question was given by a Nightmage. Comparison of the signature led to positive identification of a nihilim known as Malach. Age unknown. Whereabouts unknown."

Alexei stared at the words, fingers poised over the typewriter. He composed the next sentence in his head, choosing the words carefully. *Fra Bryce requests approval to be appointed as primary investigator . . . .* No, something stronger. *In light of his unblemished record of military service . . . .* Too arrogant. *In light of his extensive experience in the field, Fra Bryce requests approval to be appointed . . .* humbly *requests approval . . . .*

A hand gripped his shoulder. Alexei's eyes flew open. He was cheek down on the typewriter.

"Alyosha."

Alexei looked up blearily. Spassov stood there, jingling the car keys. It was still dark outside. "Dr. Pagwe just called. Massot's awake."

Chapter Nine

❧❧❧

A hundred thousand souls inhabited the port city of Novostopol, each and every one of them yearning for something they didn't have. Most would never admit it, not even to themselves, but this need was like a starving rat gnawing away at their happiness. It didn't matter how many Marks they had, or how rich and successful and brilliant and beautiful they were, it was never enough.

That's just human nature.

The interesting thing wasn't the desire but the seduction. And the harder they resisted, the sweeter the inevitable surrender.

Malach stood in the rain, watching the gates of the Arx. The walls blazed with Wards, a tide of cold, shimmering light like stars fallen to earth. He couldn't go closer without agonizing consequences, but it filled him with terrible rage and envy to be within a stone's throw of the church's stronghold.

"All is not lost," he said softly. "One day, you will bend knee to me. Every one of you."

In the last hour, only a single car had entered the citadel.

Malach moved to the shelter of the columned entrance of the Banco Barondesi, horn-rimmed glasses fogging in the humidity. He could see perfectly well without them, but they suited this evening's persona, a tax auditor named Stavros Hosikos. A briefcase stuffed with papers sat at his feet in case an Oprichniki patrol came along. Malach pretended to study a tourist map, but he wouldn't be there long. Her shift had ended ten minutes ago.

A sally gate opened. A woman in a gray cloak stepped through, holding an umbrella. She hurried across the plaza and entered the warren of side streets. Malach flipped his collar up and followed. He'd tailed her before and knew which route she always took. Eddies of ley swirled around her galoshes. He was still half drunk on it. Although he'd been inside the walls of Novostopol many times, the first few hours always left him raw and wonderstruck as a newborn. So much ley. An ocean of it.

The church had violated natural law by hoarding the power beneath its cities. Twice a year it surged into the Void, the flooding heralded by weeks of incessant storms. But the rest of the time, his home in the Morho Sarpanitum, called the Black Zone by the knights, had no ley at all.

Malach cut through an alley to get ahead of her, then lurked in a doorway. Within a minute, footsteps approached. Malach removed the glasses and slipped them into his breast pocket, heart beating wildly. She held the umbrella angled down against the wind. The instant she passed, he crept up behind and pressed a hand over her mouth.

She struggled. Malach let go immediately. He stepped back.

She spun around, more furious than scared. "*You*."

Malach jammed his hands in his pockets and gave her a saucy grin. "I told you I'd be back." He leaned against the wall of the building, careful not to crowd her. Throw them off balance, then retreat. Sow confusion.

"It's been four months." The note of accusation pleased him.

"I didn't say when. But I always keep my promises."

She studied him. Her hair was bound up in a scrap of cloth. Her cloak was threadbare at the sleeves. She held the umbrella with hands roughened from scrubbing Curia floors. But Nikola Thorn was still a beautiful woman, with high cheekbones, skin the color of melted caramel and full, sharply defined lips. When she spoke, silver flashed on her left incisor. It made her look like a pirate.

"I suppose you want my answer," she said.

"Only if you have one." He shrugged. "I can always come back again, some other time—"

"I have your answer." She lifted her chin. "No."

Malach tipped his hat. "So be it, Domina Thorn. I'll be on my way then—"

"Wait," she said.

"Do you wish me to escort you home first? I'd be happy to."

Her gaze was intent. "I have a counteroffer."

"Do you?" This was getting interesting. "I'm all ears."

"The last time we met, you asked me what my heart's desire was. If I could have anything, anything at all, what it would be."

The standard question. Very few people managed to lie when Malach finally got around to asking it, which came after he'd penetrated their defenses with a sustained onslaught of expert manipulation. He was only thirty-four, but he'd heard every conceivable reply. He didn't judge them. The only true sin was self-deceit.

"And you never answered me," Malach pointed out.

"Because I needed to think on it."

He wondered what she would ask for now. Revenge against some member of the Curia, perhaps. He'd be happy to grant that wish. Or power. Wealth. Status. All the things they'd denied her.

"I'll tell you," she said. "But I want to know what yours is first."

Malach felt a flicker of interest. He was careful to hide it. Some women liked to be fawned over, but aloofness was key with this one. His heart's desire? Nikola Thorn couldn't give him that. But she might still be of use.

"I want a child," he said curtly.

She hesitated. "Is there nothing else?"

"No."

"Then I'll give you one." Her eyes flashed. "If you take me away from this place. But I won't be Marked!"

And there it was. The exquisite moment when they convinced themselves it was all *their* idea. When they realized they needed him desperately and that life without whatever he could give them was intolerable.

"Take you away?" Malach said in puzzlement. "To where? I don't live in a fairytale castle."

She made a noise of scorn. "I never believed in fairytales, Nightmage. And I don't care if you live in a hovel. I don't expect you to make me your wife." Her gaze turned toward the Arx, hot with loathing. "Just to get me away from them."

"You say that now," he pointed out in a reasonable tone. "But you've never been to the Void."

"It can't be worse than here."

He smiled. "Oh, Domina Thorn, it most certainly can."

"You live there."

"I have no choice."

"And you think I do?"

"Your life is harder than most, better than some. It can always be worse."

"Not to me." She stared at him challengingly. "But I have no intention of playing house with you in the forest, Malach.

Part two of this bargain is that you help me secure passage to Dur-Athaara."

"The witches?" He laughed in disbelief. "Out of the frying pan, into the cauldron."

Nikola didn't smile. "Rumor says they take in Unmarked."

"They trade in slaves."

"If you're a man. Luckily, I'm not. You told me your terms and I accepted them. What more is there to discuss?"

He hesitated. "This is all very unorthodox. Well beyond the bounds of the standard bargain."

"What do you usually ask for in return?"

Malach shrugged. "Nothing."

She looked angry. "I don't believe you."

"It's true. My Marks are given freely." He seized her wrist, tugging her forward just as a taxi sped past, flinging a wave of water over the curb. The action conveniently brought him beneath her umbrella. Malach lowered his voice. "Of course, if at some point in the future, I require a favor, I assume the gesture will be reciprocated."

Nikola took a half step back. "What if you wanted something vile?" she whispered.

"By the time I asked, Domina Thorn, you'd be so entirely liberated from moral constraints that you wouldn't care."

"Well, your honesty is refreshing. I think I'll stick to my original offer." She gazed at him steadily and Malach realized she was serious. His heart beat faster. "In that case," he said, bowing at the waist, "done and done."

"Wait. How do I know you won't leave me here?" She gripped her umbrella. "Once you get what you want?"

"You'll have to trust me."

"You're a Nightmage."

"Exactly. I don't lie. Not out of principle, of course. I just don't need to."

That was a lie, every word of it. He couldn't tell if she believed him.

"Will you hurt me?" The question was asked in a direct tone.

"You mean on purpose?" Malach laughed. "Not if I can help it."

"What does that mean?"

"Some of us do feed on pain," he admitted. "But I've always been more . . . flexible. It's not the act itself I'm interested in. Just the result."

Another lie—Malach wasn't made of stone—but it seemed to reassure her.

"When?" she asked.

"No time like the present," he said cheerfully.

She stared at the Arx for a long minute. "My flat's a mess," she said at last.

"You should see mine," he replied with a straight face.

"All right," Nikola said. "I warned you."

He retrieved his briefcase. They walked in silence. The Curia kept its pariahs close and she lived a few blocks away, right at the fraying seam where the grandeur of the Arx gave way to rundown concrete blocks. As promised, her room was a mess. Not filthy, just littered with clothes and magazines. A few empty bottles.

Nikola lit a candle—no electric lights around here—and excused herself. Malach heard water running. He shook the rain from his hat and hung it on the neck of a bottle. Then he nudged a damp towel off the bed and sat down. When Nikola came out, she was wearing a bathrobe. Her hair sprang out in all directions. She smelled like soap.

"I was thinking of taking my clothes off," he said. "It seemed the logical next step."

She arched an eyebrow. "Go ahead."

Malach undressed and stood before her in the candlelight. Nikola stared at the Marks covering his body. All of them were bestowed by his aunt Beleth, but the ley chose the symbol, not the mage.

"You can touch them if you like," he said.

She wasn't so bold, but she walked around him in a circle, examining each one with interest as if she'd never seen a Mark before—which, he realized, she probably hadn't. The entire Via Sancta embraced prudery as an art form, but Novostopol was the worst.

"They're rather beautiful," she said at last. "But disturbing."

"I suppose to you they are."

"Could you cut them off if you wanted to?"

"No. When the skin grew back, it would still hold the Mark."

She looked at his hands. "You're not wearing gloves. What happens when you touch me?"

"Nothing, unless I want it to."

"But—"

"Forget what you think you know about the ley," he said impatiently. "It doesn't apply to me."

"Why not?"

"Because I am wholly myself. I have no shadow side to repress." How he despised that label. "I am the Shadow."

She studied him curiously. "But you seem so . . . I don't know. Civilized."

"You're afraid of all the wrong things, Domina Thorn."

"I'm not afraid of anything." Nikola's silver incisor gleamed wolfishly. "And certainly not you. What does that Mark do?"

She pointed at a crouching woman with raven feathers for hair. A demi-masque covered the upper half of her face and a chain with a blood-red jewel dangled from pale, taloned fingers. The Mark started on the upper left side of his chest and ended just below the ribcage.

"All sorts of things." His tone hardened. "But I'm not here to give you a lesson in how nihilim use the ley."

She shrugged. "Just asking. *Your worship.*"

Malach scowled to hide a smile. "I could still give you one of your own."

"I told you, I'll never be Marked. Not by you or anyone else."

Her stubbornness intrigued him. "What if I agreed to trade the Mark for my protection?" he asked silkily. "You wouldn't have to suffer through an unwanted sexual encounter, not to mention the agonies of birthing a mage. I'll still bring you with me when I leave."

She bit her lip. "When you put it like that . . . ."

Malach stood very still, hardly daring to breathe, as she reached out a hand. Nikola gave him a pat on the cheek. "No, thanks," she said.

"Just making sure," he said softly.

She ruffled his dark hair as if he were a small boy. "You're cute, you know that?"

Malach's eyes narrowed.

"Especially when you're offended."

She discarded the robe in a brisk fashion. Her figure was as lovely as her face—and a blank slate. Nikola Thorn was one of the Curia's castoffs. A moral degenerate unworthy of receiving Marks. Now she was condemned to the lowest caste of society with no hope of escape. Malach didn't court the Unmarked for the simple reason that it was too easy. He preferred corrupting the virtuous. The true believers.

But Nikola Thorn was different from the other outcasts in Ash Court. He'd sensed it right away when he saw her drinking alone at a posh café in the financial district. First of all, she wasn't wearing gloves. He'd never seen someone flaunt their lack of Marks. The waiter didn't refuse her service—there were laws against discrimination—but she attracted uneasy stares from the other clientele. She ignored them. Malach had taken the next table and buried his nose in a newspaper. He timed his exit to match hers, made an innocuous remark about the weather, and left.

The second and third times at the same café, he didn't speak to her at all. But he made a point of discarding his own gloves and knew she was aware of him.

The fourth time, he rose as she was paying her check and pretended to be searching for a taxi when she emerged.

"No one will stop for you like that," she said, glancing at his hands.

Malach brandished his tourist map. "I'll walk then. Maybe you can point the way to my hotel."

"Not from around here?"

"No. I'm nihilim."

Nikola laughed. "And I'm the Pontifex," she said.

Malach shrugged and turned away to study the map.

"I thought you're all supposed to be dead," she said dryly.

"Is that what they say?"

She took a step toward the curb, then stopped. "Would you like to get a drink with me?"

He'd never seen her with another soul, but she didn't strike him as lonely. Just bored. And he'd sparked her curiosity.

"I might. What's your name?"

"Nikola Thorn." She held out a hand. Malach shook it. In that simple act, palm touching palm, they'd conspired to piss on the most fundamental tenet of societal decorum.

"I'm Malach," he said.

"No last name? Oh, of course, nihilim don't use patronyms."

"You're not afraid?" he asked lightly.

"Should I be?" she countered.

"No. Lead the way, Domina Thorn."

They went to a dim place around the corner and ordered a bottle of cheap red.

"You look rather like a knight," she said, eyeing his broad shoulders over the rim of her glass. "But you're no priest."

He liked the way she said "priest." With the faintest trace of contempt.

"I told you what I am."

Her eyes darkened a shade. The jest was wearing thin. "Prove it then."

"How?"

"Make something happen."

"Like what?"

She looked out the window. A trellis of withered, neglected vines enclosed the outdoor seating area. "Those flowers. Make them bloom."

Malach thought about it. The abyssal ley pooling around his feet remained calm and indifferent. "It has to be something selfish. I don't care about the flowers."

Nikola leaned forward. She looked sympathetic. "I think you're like me, Malach. And you're ashamed to admit it."

That made him laugh aloud. Her eyes narrowed.

"I'm not mocking you," he said. "Really."

"Sure seems like it." Nikola's chair scraped back. "I think I'll go now."

"Wait." He didn't want her to leave. An idea came to him. "How about this?"

Malach flattened his palm on the table. This time the ley surged eagerly, ready to play. Goosebumps prickled his arms as he delved through the icy surface current, reaching for the true power beneath. It always reminded him of scum floating on a pond. Mildly unpleasant, but tolerable if one wanted to go swimming. The violet liminal ley came next, a very thin strata, and then the turbulent abyssal ley, crimson like fresh blood. It was the deepest layer by many orders of magnitude, extending down to the very core of the continent. None of his Marks were visible, but he filled with heat and light and aching want.

Malach's eyes unfocused. It was like rising from the dead. Like becoming a god.

Priests approached the ley on their knees like beggars. They left the desired outcome unspoken, hoping the ley would come to their aid. He knew this because he'd caught one once and tortured him until he explained it to Malach's satisfaction. The technique seemed bizarre, but then he couldn't work the first two currents at all. They wouldn't respond to his mind.

The abyssal ley coursing through his blood changed course, imbued with purpose. It flowed outward from his palm. An instant later, a draft swept through the window. It ruffled Malach's hair and passed by, sending aloft the smoldering contents of an ashtray two tables over. A single glowing ember floated towards an image of the Pontifex Feizah hanging over the bar. The portrait was printed on cheap paper, taped to the wall next to the chalkboard listing the house specials, and the edges curled to ash in seconds, tongues of flame licking at her stern face. The barman cursed and slapped at it with a rag. A few of the less drunk patrons stumbled over to help.

Nikola stared for a moment. "I stand corrected. Why are you here?"

"To do business."

She eyed him over the rim of her glass. "Not with me you aren't."

"I didn't say it was with you."

She took a sip, wincing at the cheap vintage. "Well, you're definitely not here for the wine."

Malach loosened his tie and undid the top two buttons of his shirt. He spread the starched plackets. Her eyes traced the thick black chain etched into the skin of his throat. At the juncture of his collarbone, the links were broken. The Mark of Bal Kirith.

"We're both outcasts," Malach said in a low voice. "But better to reign in the Void than serve the Via Sancta."

Nikola gave a slow, thoughtful nod and Malach knew he'd guessed right. She didn't hate herself. She hated them.

They'd become acquaintances after that. Now they would be . . . not lovers. That implied romance. This was purely a business arrangement. If he failed to produce an offspring, the Cold Truce would end and the shells would start falling on his home again. Malach would never relinquish his immortal hate for the Curia, never submit to its authority, but he was also a realist. Sometimes you had to play for time while you waited for a better hand to be dealt. Cardinal Falke called it the Inner Front strategy.

Malach let Nikola Thorn come to him. He expected she'd want to get it over with, quick and impersonal, but she surprised him with a kiss. His glasses fogged. She took them off and tossed them onto a pile of clothes.

"You look like an accountant," she said. "That haircut."

"I just got it. For you."

"Liar."

"No, really."

"What makes you think I like accountants?" Nikola mussed his neat side part. "That's better. Now you look like a proper Nightmage."

"Do I?"

She grinned. "Dark and evil."

Malach grinned back lazily. "Do you know where the word comes from?"

"I thought you called yourselves that."

He could feel the heat of her body, though they weren't touching. "It's the invention of an anonymous author writing as the Countess De Fonblanque. Twenty-odd years ago, she penned an erotic memoir called *Ninety Days in the Abyss*. It was filthy. I blush just mentioning it, Domina Thorn."

"I suppose you may call me Nikola. Since we're both naked."

"Nikola." Malach liked the sound of it. A bit prickly, just like her. "Well, in this reprehensible volume, she coined the word Nightmage. The Curia banned it immediately and ordered all the copies destroyed, which naturally made the book an instant bestseller. The publisher was arrested and then acquitted after a very public trial. Countess De Fonblanque spawned an entire genre with that book, which continues to thrive today." He bent his head and kissed her neck. "Or so I hear."

"Oh yeah, they're at every newsstand. The library has a whole wall."

His lips found the tender place behind her earlobe. "In a final irony," Malach whispered, "the term Nightmage eventually surpassed nihilim in common parlance. Even the priests use it now."

Her breath quickened. "What do you prefer?"

"I don't mind it. I prefer it to nihilim, since it's inaccurate to say we believe in nothing."

"What *do* you believe in?"

Her pulse beat against his mouth. Malach cupped the silky weight of her breast. "Getting what we both want."

Afterward, he laid a hand on her belly and let the ley flow through her while she slept. He felt his seed take root in her womb, a spark of new life spring into existence. Malach stroked her stomach until she woke. "It's done," he whispered.

She was silent for a long moment. "How do you know?"

"I just do."

Nikola leaned on an elbow. "How soon can we leave?"

"I have some meetings to deal with first."

In fact, he was supposed to meet Ferran Massot at the doctor's home earlier that evening. He'd almost gone, but then he'd thought of Nikola Thorn and decided her company would be infinitely preferable. Massot talked far too much and said far too little. But he was a useful contact and Malach couldn't leave without seeing him.

"I've saved up money," she said. "It should be enough to buy myself passage. I just need someone to get me safely through the Black Zone."

Nikola's eyes were bright with hope. She'd been planning this for years, working up the nerve to make a run for it.

Maybe she drank alone in the cafés hoping to cross paths with someone like him. Most likely she would lose the child like all the others, but half-bloods had power. If this one survived, he would take it home and forge it into a weapon against the Curia.

"I can manage that," he said.

"So when do we leave?"

"As soon as I finish my business here. There are islands off the coast. Smugglers drop anchor there and come ashore to barter. I know a few of them."

"What do you trade?"

"There's only one thing we have of value to the witches."

"Slaves?"

Malach shrugged. "If they're stupid enough to get captured, it's not my fault."

Nikola shook her head. "That's charming, Malach. So people still live in the forest?"

"Some."

"What's it like?"

How to describe the world without ley? His face went bleak.

"Empty," he said coldly, rolling away.

Chapter Ten

A gray dawn broke as Alexei drove back to the Batavia Institute. The rain beat down relentlessly, turning the gutters to rushing streams. He had the wipers set on high and could still barely see through the windscreen.

"Did Kireyev's men find—*futuere!*" he swore, yanking the wheel to avoid a line of sawhorses placed strategically in the middle of the street. The office of the Curia devoted to the preservation of historic sites was infamous for digging holes in busy thoroughfares, fencing them off, and then failing to return for weeks.

The car skidded, clipping one of the barriers before the tires gripped pavement again. They hurtled through a red light, but it was early Sunday morning and traffic was sparse.

"You'd better slow down," Spassov advised, blowing smoke out the cracked window.

Alexei tapped the brake at a roundabout, then gunned the engine for the long straightaway down the Admiral Karachay Embankment. The adjacent canal churned with whitewater, but it hadn't flooded yet. In the distance, he could just make out the fog-wreathed masts of merchant ships anchored at

Novoport. The traffic picked up, mostly trucks ferrying luxury cargo to and from the docks.

"Did they turn up any leads on the mage?" Alexei asked.

Spassov shook his head. "The other guests confirmed Domina Novak's account of the evening. They all left a little before eleven."

Alexei accelerated through a yellow signal and turned left on Barracks Square, heading north into the hills. Fish stalls under brightly colored awnings jammed the plaza. Not even Spassov's cigarette masked the pungent smell, though the catch was freshly packed on ice. The market already bustled with restaurant buyers selecting the choicest cuts for their chefs.

"The catering company checked out, as well," Spassov said. "No one saw a stranger at the house. Either the mage wasn't there or he came later, as the witness said."

Alexei shot him a look. "I have trouble with that part."

Spassov rested a meaty hand on the dashboard. "Okay."

"If they were meeting, why didn't Malach wait for her to leave first?"

"Maybe he didn't know she was still there."

"So what? He knocks on the door. Massot answers. He inverts Massot's Mark and just walks away?"

His partner shrugged. "Why not?"

"It feels weird."

Spassov sighed. "Well, you can ask the doctor yourself."

"The neighbors heard nothing?"

"The weather. Everyone had their windows closed."

The car climbed higher and higher, the city center giving way to quiet, leafy suburbs where only a few lights shone in the windows. Eventually, the houses themselves receded down long gated drives. They weren't far from the sea. Alexei rolled down his window and inhaled the clean tang of salt air.

"I checked Domina Novak's file. She's apparently a model

citizen." He turned down the elm-lined road that led to the Institute's gatehouse.

"Because she has nothing to do with it. Wrong place, wrong time." Spassov glanced over. "We handle Massot like a newborn, eh? No mistakes."

Alexei caught the edge in his voice. If he hadn't been so fogging tired, he would have asked the question earlier. "Why is Kireyev letting us take first crack anyway? His boys are pulling all the paperwork. I couldn't even get Massot's file from the Tabularium. They're taking the case away from us, Patryk."

Spassov looked innocent. "Dr. Pagwe called me. We need Massot's testimony to complete our report."

"So Kireyev doesn't know we're here." Alexei grinned.

"What?" Spassov cupped his ear. "Did you say something?"

"Only that I could kiss you."

"Wait until I shave." He stroked his jaw with a mournful expression. "I'm a little rough, Alyosha."

Alexei slowed at the stone wall of the Institute, composing himself for the interview. They'd have one shot at the doctor before the Office of the General Directorate took over the case. He intended to make it count.

This time the guard abandoned the shelter of the gatehouse, jogging out with rain streaming from his cap to inspect them both before waving the car through. A new shift had come on and they were met at Admissions by an orderly with short ginger hair and a bland face. Alexei disliked him, though not for any reason he could adequately explain. Oto Valek had worked at the Institute for eight years without incident. He was always courteous and knew the patients as well as any of the doctors or nurses. It was something in his eyes, Alexei thought. A cold, calculating quality.

"Massot attacked Dr. Pagwe," Valek said. "He's in restraints."

"You didn't sedate him again?" Spassov said with a frown.

"No, he's awake."

"How's Dr. Pagwe?" Alexei asked.

"A bloody nose. He's lying down in his office with an icepack."

"Were you there?"

"Me and another orderly." He shook his head and sighed, though Alexei sensed no genuine remorse. "Massot moved so fast. We never should have let him out of the restraints."

"Why did you?" Spassov asked.

The tone was mild, but Valek hunched his shoulders defensively. "He said he had to use the bathroom. I mean, he used a crude term for it, but he seemed calm. Dr. Pagwe approved it." The orderly shook his head. "I never heard the doctor swear once, not in all the years I've worked here. But the things he's been saying, Fathers . . . . We're all in a state of shock."

"I'm sure you are," Spassov said, shooting a look at Alexei. "Has anyone else come from the Arx?"

Something flickered in Valek's eyes, so fleeting Alexei might have imagined it. "No one, Father."

Spassov took out his watch and checked the time. "Then let's proceed."

They found the doctor strapped to a chair in one of the "quiet rooms" set aside for difficult patients. He'd been cleaned up and given a white cotton shirt and pants with an elastic band. Gloved fingers gripped the armrest. Valek tried to hang about, but Spassov closed the door in his face.

Alexei no longer felt anything but revulsion for Massot. He might not be accountable for what he'd done after his Marks inverted, but the man's crimes had begun long before, starting with the day he took Malach's bargain. The Nightmark would have corrupted him further, led him deeper down the rabbit hole of his own dark impulses, yet he'd chosen that path of his own free will, not caring how many lives he destroyed. Alexei's hands clenched, the leather creaking. He forced them open.

The room was empty except for the single chair, which was bolted to the floor.

"Domine Massot," Spassov said. "We know you met your master last night. Where is he?"

Massot started laughing.

"Something funny?"

"It doesn't matter. I won't be here long."

"Is he coming for you?"

"Bring me that girl and I'll tell you. Just a few minutes alone with her. That's all I want." His voice took on a wheedling tone. "A fair trade, Fra Spassov. Come now, she's no one. Just another stupid whore."

Alexei's head started to pound. He needed coffee.

"You know there isn't the remotest chance of that happening," Spassov said reasonably.

"Why not? I *want* her." The whine of a petulant child.

"Tell me about Malach. When did you take the Nightmark? How long ago?"

This was a critical question. Massot had access to a great deal of privileged information, although Alexei couldn't fathom what a Nightmage might want with Invertido. It was always possible their deal had nothing to do with the Institute. But it was far more likely Malach had some involvement in the abuse, which would be a horrendous breach of trust. What if it had going on for years under their very noses?

A spear of ice stabbed Alexei's spine. His head felt like it was floating above his body. *Maybe I do have the flu.*

Massot glared. "I'm an important man doing important work. You'll regret interfering with me!"

"What work?" Spassov demanded.

Like quicksilver, the imperious, steely-eyed doctor transformed to an overgrown child. Massot cackled. He bumped his hips against the chair in a crude pantomime, an erection poking against the cotton pants. Spassov shook his head in disgust. The doctor laughed harder.

Rain beat against the barred window. The incessant noise made it hard to think. Alexei pushed off the wall and walked over to Massot. "Answer him."

"I forgot the question, rook."

Alexei's skin felt too tight against his skull. "What," he said in a low voice, "have you been doing to your patients?"

A tiny, smug smile. "Nothing they didn't enjoy."

The edges of his vision dimmed to red. Without quite realizing what he was doing, Alexei grabbed Massot by the neck, digging his fingers into the rolls of fat. "*Filius canis,*" he snarled. *Son of a bitch.* "Where is he?"

Massot's eyes bulged. He wheezed and thrashed against the restraints. Alexei squeezed tighter. He drew a gloved fist back, picturing Massot's face as he punched his teeth straight down his throat.

"Where's Malach, you piece of—"

A heavy hand seized Alexei's cassock, hauling him back.

"Alyosha," Spassov said calmly. "I think we'll take a break now."

Alexei almost hit his partner for interfering, but some spark of sanity stopped him. He drew a deep breath, exhaling it through his nose. The fury ebbed like a lanced boil.

Massot spat on the floor. He glanced at the small viewing window set into the door. "Touch me again and I'll file a complaint."

Alexei turned. No one was there, but he wondered if the orderly had been watching and cursed himself for losing control.

"What was that?" Spassov asked once they were back out in the hall with the door closed.

"He got under my skin." Alexei met his partner's steady gaze. "I'm sorry, it won't happen again."

"I don't care about Massot." The tone was mild, but

Spassov looked annoyed. "I'm supposed to be the one who beats the shit out of people, and you're the one who drags me off. So what gives?"

"Right, I know."

"If Kireyev finds out, we're both screwed. You know better, but you still played into Massot's hands." Brown eyes narrowed. "There's something you're not telling me."

Alexei felt a twinge of guilt. He wanted to trust Spassov. Did trust him. Patryk waited expectantly. He didn't look angry anymore, just concerned.

"I know Malach," Alexei admitted.

Spassov would assume it was from the war, which was true, but only a part of the truth.

"Ah. So it's personal."

"Yes."

"Why didn't you tell me before?"

"I only realized it when I was writing my report and double-checked the Mark. I've never spoken to him." *True.* "But he killed five members of my company in an ambush a few years ago."

Like most of the Interfectorum, Spassov had served in the Black Zone. He knew what those final years were like. "The one that got away, eh? Then we'll find the bastard." Spassov clapped him on the shoulder. He dug into a pocket and produced a foil packet of tobacco. "I'm going out for a smoke. We'll question the doctor again in ten minutes." A hard look. "Don't go back inside without me."

Alexei touched his Raven Mark. "I promise."

Once Spassov turned the corner, Alexei stood still for a moment. Physical violence was the last recourse, tolerated only when there was no other choice to preserve the common good, but it had to be committed without anger. Savagery was for their enemies.

He believed that, believed in his faith with all his heart, yet his own soul fell far short of the church's ideals. No matter how many Marks he had, the shadow inside him never went away. If anything, it was growing stronger.

The halls were quiet as Alexei left the secure wing and passed through a series of Warded oak doors to the section where patients enjoyed greater liberties. The wet season made the place feel dank (inevitable for an ancient castle), but the rough stone walls had been whitewashed and the arrow slits widened to give a view of lush parkland beyond. Residents weren't locked into their rooms here, but the hour was early yet and most were still sleeping.

Alexei paused at the dayroom. A man sat near the window, tall and dark-haired. He'd been handsome once, but now he was cadaverously thin. He argued silently with himself, hands gesturing.

Alexei's thumb ran across the name engraved on the copper coin in his pocket.

Mikhail Semyon Bryce.

Most patients at the Institute died within six months. When the ley was taken from them, they lost the will to live and wasted away. Alexei's older brother had already beaten the odds, but he'd never see his thirty-sixth birthday unless the Nightmage who reversed his Marks somehow undid the damage.

Misha's hands were the only animated part of him. His lips moved in a whisper too soft to hear, eyes lost in another world. Alexei wondered who he was talking to.

But the hands . . . yes, he remembered Misha gesturing like that when he would go over the day's strategy. Their father was a northerner, cold and self-contained, but their mother had southern blood. She used her hands, too—

"Fra Bryce?"

Alexei turned, startled. The old man gazed up at Alexei with sharp green eyes set into deep sockets. Most of his teeth were gone. A red carnation poked from the buttonhole of a jacket that smelled of mothballs.

"Good morning, Uncle," he said politely.

"Got a smoke?"

The old man asked this same question every time they met.

"No, but my partner does. I'll ask him when he comes back."

Alexei didn't know the old man's name. When people arrived at the Institute, their identities were erased and they became a number. It was this practice that kept his relationship to Misha a secret. The higher-ups at the Curia knew, of course, but not Spassov.

Captain Mikhail Semyon Bryce was simply Patient 26. It was intended to protect the families from shame, but Alexei refused to think of human beings as numbers so he devised his own nicknames. Even the patients who hated everyone tolerated the old man. He never caused trouble.

"How is Fra Spassov?"

"Well, thank you." Alexei admired the tweed jacket. "Is that new?"

The old man smoothed a sleeve. "Nurse Jeyna gave it to me. It was her father's."

"That was kind of her."

The old man's face grew sly. "You brought the doctor in."

"Which doctor?" Alexei asked innocently.

"You know which. Massot." He spoke with the accent of the north, lilting but harsh on the consonants.

"Who told you that?"

"I have ears."

"Uncle," Alexei said firmly. "You know I'm not allowed to talk about it."

"He gave me a kitten." The old man's eyes moved to Misha, who had not turned from his silent reverie. "I let Mikhail pet it. I trust him. Some of the others, not so much."

The old man ignored the no-names rule, though Alexei had never asked him for his own. An inverted flame Marked his neck with the words *Lux et lex*. Light and law. He must have been a priest in Jalghuth before he went mad.

"Did Misha . . . did he speak to you?"

"He talks only to himself."

Alexei concealed his disappointment. Mikhail never acknowledged his presence, but he refused to give up coming to see him.

"We play chess sometimes," the old man said. "He's the only one around here who beats me."

"You play chess?" That was a surprise.

"Oh, yes. We are friends."

Alexei felt a glimmer of hope. Maybe there was something left after all. "Thank you for looking after him, Uncle. It means a great deal to me."

The old man's gaze grew distant. "Mikhail is a good man. Not like the doctor."

Alexei kept his tone neutral. The old man was easily spooked. "What do you mean?"

Gloved fingers mechanically stroked the coat sleeve. "Did I tell you he gave me a kitten?"

"You did, yes." He bit back impatience. "What else?"

"I drew him a picture. Some other things." He gave a sweet gap-toothed smile. "Got a smoke?"

Alexei sighed. They might go round and round for another hour before he extracted anything useful. "I'm sorry, Uncle, you'll have to excuse me." He'd been gone too long already and didn't want Spassov looking for him. "But I'll bring you a cigarette later, *da?*"

The old man drifted over to Misha. He wore a pair of flannel pajamas under the tweed jacket. They'd been rolled up to the knees. Marks covered his bony legs, every single one inverted.

Alexei wanted to stay—to *spy*, if he were being honest. Chess! He wouldn't have thought it possible. In the early days, he'd tried everything to make Misha respond. Talked until his throat was hoarse. Brought photos of them together as boys, stacks of his favorite books. Nothing reached him. He stared straight through Alexei as if he were a ghost. But his brother had always loved strategy. Loved *winning*. Saints bless the old man for figuring that out.

He pressed his palm to the Raven carved into the heavy door dividing the violent and nonviolent wings. The ley flowed weakly inside the walls, but he gathered enough to deactivate the Ward. His steps quickened as he approached the quiet room. Happily, Spassov wasn't back yet. Alexei knew his partner would have waited in the hall for him before going inside. He leaned against the wall, thoughts still chewing over Misha and chess, when he heard an odd sound. Alexei glanced through the viewing window.

Massot was not alone. A cloaked figure hunched over him. Alexei wrenched the door open. "Hey!" he shouted.

Blood slicked the floor, splattered the walls. Massot slumped sideways in the restraints, his head tipped back, throat neatly slit. Alexei tore a glove off, though the ley was too sparse to do much more than trigger Wards. Massot made a weak choking sound. His eyes fixed on the ceiling.

The killer's cowl was raised, obscuring his face. He held a bloody dagger in his left hand. His cloak was nondescript, but his stance told Alexei the man had military training. It wasn't the way he gripped the knife—there were a dozen effective techniques—but rather the set of his feet and his composure at being caught in the act.

"Drop it," Alexei snapped. "Get on your knees."

The soft squeak of a shoe behind him saved his life. He twisted so the bruising blow landed on his back rather than his skull. Massot's killer charged, shoving past him. Two men, then. One must have kept watch in the corridor and concealed himself when he heard Alexei coming. He struggled to his feet. A pair of black cloaks swirled around the far corner. He gave chase, but by the time he reached the intersection, the men had vanished. Whoever they were, they had no trouble with the Warded doors.

He followed the trail across an inner bailey and then into a labyrinth of adjoining chambers the Baron Von Oppermann had built for the Saints only knew what purpose. Part of the wing had been converted to a laundry and he nearly ran down a gray-clad char carrying a stack of linens. She pressed into an arched doorway, eyes wide. He must have knelt in the pool of Massot's blood, for it soaked his gloves and the hem of his cassock.

"Did anyone come this way?" he panted.

She shook her head.

Alexei tore past. He knew every way out of the Institute. The windows were barred. They couldn't leave by the front, they'd almost certainly be seen. That meant one of the Warded side gates. Some were used by the patients when the weather was pleasant and they were given time outdoors. Others took deliveries. Alexei found the nearest exit, which led to the vegetable garden. Through stinging sheets of rain, he saw the men vanishing into a stand of willows.

Alexei sprinted across the lawn. The trees grew on the banks of a shallow creek, bright yellow flowers hanging in a feathery curtain. He swept them aside, sloshed through the creek and spotted his quarry. A rope hung down from the outer wall. The first man was already scurrying up it. Alexei's lungs burned as he narrowed the gap. The second followed on the heels of his accomplice, pausing at the top to reel it up. Alexei leapt for the end, but he was a few centimeters short. The rope slithered over the top of the wall and the killer turned to follow it. As he braced his legs to jump down, Alexei caught a glimpse of the Raven Mark on his neck.

He bent over, hands on knees, gasping for breath.

Not Nightmages.

Priests.

Alexei cursed softly and wiped the blood from his gloves

on the grass. The gatehouse was two kilometers away on the other side of the Institute. By the time he got there, the men would be long gone. They'd chosen the point of entry well. But how had they known the exact moment to strike? Someone must have tipped them off that he and Spassov had left the room. He immediately thought of Oto Valek, but he had no evidence against the orderly, just a sense of general dislike.

Alexei's analytical mind wanted to attack the problem from all angles, but he needed to tell his partner first. He jogged around to the covered portico at Admissions and found Spassov leaning on the car. He flicked his cigarette into a puddle with an apologetic shrug. "Sorry, I had a couple. Why are you out in the rain?"

Alexei suspected he'd also been hitting the flask, but maybe that was for the best. It would soften the blow.

"Massot's dead," he said, still catching his breath. "There were two—" He almost said priests but thought better of it. "Assassins."

"*Assassins?*" Spassov echoed in disbelief.

"They're gone." He braced a hand on the hood. "But they got to him, Patryk. They got to him."

Spassov cursed and bounded through the front door. Oto Valek and Nurse Jeyna were conferring at the desk. Alexei watched Valek's face, but he didn't look flustered or guilty, just mildly curious.

"Call the guardhouse," Spassov snapped. "Tell them to lock everything down."

"What's happened?" Jeyna asked with a frown.

Spassov didn't reply. He was already striding for Massot's room. When he saw the corpse, Spassov groaned. "Where were you when this happened?" Alexei stared and his partner grimaced. "I'm just asking!"

"Talking to the old man. I was only gone for a few minutes."

"You saw them?"

"Not clearly. I chased but they went over the wall."

"Descriptions?"

"They wore cloaks. I never saw their faces."

Spassov swore. "I'll call it in. Keep everyone away."

"Ask the old man, if it makes you feel better. He wanted a cigarette."

"Please, Alyosha, I believe you. Massot's master probably wanted to shut him up. It seems clear to me. Just wait here."

Alexei nodded. Even if he hadn't seen the Raven Mark, he knew it wasn't the mage. If Malach had wanted Massot dead, he'd be dead, not turned. The whole thing stank. Alexei regretted his outburst even more keenly. If he'd kept a cool head, they might have learned something useful. Now Massot's secrets would stay forever buried.

Alexei replayed the scene in his mind. Two priests enter the Institute, probably former knights. They either have an accomplice inside, or they observe Spassov leaving and seize their chance. One stands guard while the other enters the quiet room. Massot might have known them—or at least who sent them. He would have shouted, screamed, but the room was soundproof. Alexei could imagine his terror, strapped to the chair, as his killer took out the knife. He tried to summon a shred of pity and failed. The doctor got what was coming to him. An uncharitable thought, but Alexei didn't care. He, too, was a lost cause.

All he could do at this point was keep Patryk out of it. Beneath the cynical bluster, Spassov was a true friend. He was hoping for early retirement from the Interfectorem and Alexei wouldn't screw it up for him.

Twenty minutes later, a forensic team arrived from the Arx. Two burly investigators named Fra Gerlach and Fra Brodszky took their statements. Alexei showed them the spot where the killers had scaled the wall, although the rain had obliterated any footprints. He recounted every detail except for the Raven Mark. Until he had an inkling of how far this went, Alexei wasn't about to stick his head in the lion's mouth.

"You're free to go," Gerlach said. "But the boss wants to see you right away."

"Sure," Spassov said unhappily. "I figured he would."

Gerlach shot him a look. "Not both of you." His flat gaze fixed on Alexei. "Just him."

"SIT DOWN, FRA BRYCE."

Alexei did as ordered, taking a wing chair. Casimir Kireyev's office was on the top floor of the Office of the General Directorate, a building as nondescript as its name. The ivy-covered brick looked more like a university lecture hall than the headquarters of the Pontifex's spymaster, which is just how she liked it.

"Your report is still pending," Kireyev observed. "When do you plan to file it?"

"As soon as the case is closed, Your Grace."

Kireyev had nut-brown skin and large, tapered ears. When he smiled, as he was doing now, Alexei always thought of a wizened gnome. Kireyev removed his spectacles and wiped the lenses with a purple-edged handkerchief. "We will continue to look for these men, of course, but there's nothing more that can be done on your end."

"I respectfully disagree, Your Grace."

The smile faded. "And why is that?"

"Our primary witness is dead," Alexei said dryly. "I'll need continued access to his home and office, as well as permission to interview all known associates. Oh, and copies of his records in the Arx. Otherwise it will be impossible to complete my report in a timely fashion."

Kireyev sighed. "Alexei, I appreciate your devotion. As you'll recall, I offered you several other well-regarded positions within the Curia when your unit was decommissioned. With your education, you could have easily risen to apostolic legat within a few short years. You insisted on joining the Interfectorem, over my objections. I have granted you a great deal of latitude." He slammed a hand down on the desk. "But personal vendettas have no place here!"

Alexei blinked. "Your Grace?"

"You think I don't know?" Kireyev chuckled without a trace of amusement. "I know everything that happens in this city. You'd do well to remember that."

"Of course, Your Grace."

"The nihilim will be found and eliminated. He sealed his own death warrant when he set foot in Via Sancta territory. The Wards will trap him until he shows himself, and anyone who gave him aid or shelter will face the prescribed penalties. But that is my task, not yours."

Alexei looked away, gaze roaming over the bookshelves with their leather-bound volumes on philosophy and history. A fire crackled in the grate. His cassock was still damp from the rain and the warmth felt pleasant. Alexei's eyes grew heavy. He bit the inside of his cheek hard enough to draw blood.

One didn't doze off during an audience with the Archbishop of Novostopol.

"Continue on this path and you will find it leads to places best left alone. I think you know that already. *The Shadow is a tight passage, a narrow door, whose painful constriction no one is spared who goes down to the deep well.* Have you forgotten your vows?"

"No, Your Grace."

The tone softened. "You're a good soldier. A good priest. Maybe someday you'll come to your senses and realize the Interfectorem is a dead end. But in the meantime, you'll do as you're told." A pause. "Not all of us are lenient towards insubordination. My protection only extends so far."

Alexei knew he should bow his head and accept the reprimand, but a spark of rebellion lit at the implicit threat. "And what exactly am I being told, Your Grace?"

The archbishop stared at him for a long minute. "I want that report on my desk by morning. You are not to pursue this matter in any capacity."

Alexei bowed his head. "Your Grace."

"And get some sleep. You look terrible."

The bishop's gaze seared his back as he strode to the door.

Did Kireyev send the priests? Or did he simply know who did? Neither prospect was reassuring. If Kireyev hadn't ordered the killing himself, it must be someone high up indeed if he was covering for them. The only ranks above the archbishop were the cardinals—and of course, the Pontifex herself.

In the antechamber beyond, a woman with short blond hair, very light eyes and a diamond nose stud sat erect in one of the visitor chairs. She looked annoyed. Her cassock was dark blue silk with gold embroidery along the hem. Wolf-Marked on her neck.

"I'm sorry for the delay, Nuncio Morvana," Kireyev's secretary said smoothly. "His Grace will see you now."

The ambassador from the Southern Curia rose to her feet. She was tall enough to look Alexei in the eye. He saw guarded curiosity and consternation that she'd been left waiting for a lowly priest.

"It iz about time," she muttered in a thick Kven accent, striding through the door to the archbishop's office.

Outside, the rain fell in torrents. Alexei drew his cowl up. His mouth tasted like blood.

Sleep?

He laughed aloud, wishing the sound didn't remind him so much of Dr. Massot.

Chapter Eleven

Kasia cancelled all her appointments for the day. She put on sweatpants and prowled through the flat trailing fragrant smoke from a bundle of smoldering sage, lingering in the area the priests had occupied. Then she made herself a thick cheese sandwich with horseradish mustard on dark rye. It was so good, she made another one and ate that, too.

After lunch, she did some long-overdue laundry, trying not to dwell on the two brass cylinders wedged behind the refrigerator. Natalya worked at her desk, utterly absorbed, pausing only for coffee and pirozhki from the bakery down the street.

Kasia dug out her second-best oracle deck and did several simple three-card foretellings. The Knight appeared in every single one, as did the Fool. The suits in this deck were Storms, Serpents, Keys and Wards, and no matter how many spreads she laid out, the message was bleak. She saw temptation and lust, treachery and danger.

The Flaming Tower, positioned to the far left, meant that the source of a life-altering upheaval had already occurred and the repercussions were now spilling outward like ripples across a pond.

Well, *yes*.

The Jack of Wards, signaling an unbearable burden, moral or spiritual.

The Nine of Serpents, which demanded surrender to a battle that could never be won.

The Saint of Storms, indicating some calamity yet to come.

The Lovers popped up twice, and so did the Hierophant, which made her think of Cardinal Falke since the Hierophant was a keeper of dogma and tradition. She hoped he'd send an emissary, or at least telephone, but by late afternoon no one had appeared to collect the papers.

"We have to get rid of them," Kasia said, pacing the tiny living room. "Maybe we should throw them in a canal."

"No!" Natalya grimaced. "We can't. Falke will want them eventually. He gave me my Mark, Kiska. I can't cross him."

"I know, love. But they're incriminating."

Nashka snorted. "You haven't even read them."

Kasia gave her friend a flat look. "If they're so innocent, why didn't the cardinal get them himself? Those priests think Massot is involved in some shady business. What if they come back? With a search warrant?"

"Why would they?"

"Don't be dense. Massot could talk. Tell them everything. And when they don't find the papers at his house, they'll look here. We could both be arrested as accomplices in a scheme we know nothing about."

Perspiration slicked the back of her neck. No matter how hard it rained, the air never seemed to get any cooler. She twisted her hair into a bun and stuck one of Nashka's charcoal pencils through it. "You said I should listen to the cards and they're quite clear that something shitty is going to happen if we sit around doing nothing."

"Fog it all, why didn't you tell me that in the first place?" Natalya jabbed her paintbrush in a jar of water. "I never thought I'd say this, but it's time to call Tessaria."

The phone rang. They exchanged a startled look. Kasia pounced on it first.

"Darling." The voice was crisp and cultured. "What on earth is going on?"

It's her, Kasia mouthed. "I was just about to telephone you."

"I heard a rumor you were at Ferran Massot's house last night and that his dinner guests were all interrogated by the OGD. Care to elaborate?"

"Don't say anything on the phone," Nashka hissed. "What if they're listening?"

"You've read too many spy novels," Kasia whispered back.

"What's that, darling?"

"Nothing, Auntie. I'm sorry, I was planning to call you. Natalya caught a flu so I went in her place."

There was a lengthy silence. Kasia braced herself, but Tessaria's voice was calm. "I also heard a rumor the doctor's Marks inverted."

"True," she admitted. "I'm fine though. No harm done!"

A windy exhalation. Tessaria must really be furious if she wasn't even yelling. "You'd better come over for dinner and tell me *everything*." The emphasis on the last word signaled that she would be shown mercy, but only if she came clean, which Kasia planned to do. They were out of their depth, with sharks circling a flimsy lifeboat, and Tessaria was the only port in the proverbial storm.

"I'd love to," she said. "Two hours?"

"Don't be late." The line went dead.

"It's all sorted," she said to Natalya.

Nashka gnawed a thumbnail. "Why two hours? I thought you were dying to get out of here."

"I am. But look at me." She caught her faint reflection in the window. Sweats and a chemise with a mustard stain. Hair a fright. "I'm not going over there like this."

"Hell, no," Nashka agreed. "Do you want me to come? I will. I don't mind."

"No, it's fine. But maybe you can lend me a handbag?"

Her friend looked relieved. "Sure. And there's a spare set of keys around here somewhere. I'll dig them out."

Kasia ransacked her closet, discarding a dozen outfits before settling on a black velvet jacket, houndstooth pencil skirt, seamed stockings and faux snakeskin pumps. The two sandwiches she'd eaten made the skirt unpleasantly tight, but one did not appear on Tessaria Foy's doorstep without looking sharp, or one would never hear the end of it. Then she sat at her dressing table and carefully applied eyeliner, waterproof mascara, lipstick and a hint of blush. She brushed her hair and wove it into a severe French braid. With the humidity, it was the only option.

"Do I pass inspection?" she asked Natalya, who was eating ice cream out of the container and looked entirely too comfortable in a worn flannel shirt and boxer shorts.

"Gorgeous," Nashka mumbled through a mouthful of pistachio mocha chip.

"You always say that." Kasia blotted her lipstick.

"Because it's true."

"Tessaria will find something. She always does."

"Fog Tessaria."

Kasia shot her a look. "Don't say that. I'd be nothing without her."

"You couldn't be *nothing* if you tried," Natalya said seriously. "But I get the point." She planted a sticky kiss on Kasia's cheek. "There, I smudged you. Now she'll have something to complain about."

Kasia stuffed the cylinders into one of Natalya's giant knockoff designer handbags, along with the spare house key, lipstick and a handful of *fide* banknotes. "You stay here in case anyone comes from the Curia."

Nashka trailed her to the door. "I sort of have plans later."

"With who?" She pulled on a pair of lace-trimmed gloves.

"A party at the Café Grimaldi. Lorenzo invited me."

"The ballet dancer?"

Nashka grinned. "It's his birthday."

"How old is he? Nineteen?"

"Twenty-two!" A note of outrage.

"I suppose that makes him fair game."

"You bet it does. Have you seen his legs?"

"Well, don't stay out too late. And don't drink too much, either. You just got better."

The reminder sobered her friend instantly. "Look, I'll cancel if you want. It's not fair—"

"No, you go." Kasia smiled. "You deserve some fun."

Natalya hugged her. "Thanks. I owe you one, kitten."

"You can clean the bathroom. I think there's something living in the tub. A new organism as yet undiscovered by science."

Natalya made a face. "Yeah, okay." She blew a flurry of kisses. "Tomorrow . . . ."

When Kasia reached her car, she found a second parking ticket on the windshield. The rear left tire was still flat. She looked around. No vacant taxis. There never were when it rained, and she barely remembered the last time she'd seen the sun.

Kasia opened the trunk and took out a jack. She kept a spare tire and knew how to change it, though the procedure was a bit tricky in heels. She had just positioned the jack under the bumper and was vigorously pumping with one hand while holding her umbrella with the other when a pair of large black boots paused next to her. Men always thought women couldn't change tires on their own. She donned a polite smile and prepared to refuse an offer of help when the owner of the boots spoke.

"Domina Novak?"

Oh, fog it all!

It was the priest. The good-looking one, but still. Precisely the last person in the world she wanted to run into.

Kasia tilted her umbrella and looked up. "Fra Bryce?"

He peered down at her. "Do you want a hand with that?"

"No, thank you."

He shifted awkwardly. "I'm sorry, this is poor timing, but I need a word with you."

Kasia kept her face composed, though her pulse ticked up a notch. She wondered if the handbag looked bulky. What if he asked her to open it? Was he legally allowed to search her if she wasn't under arrest?

"I thought we already did that."

"It won't take long. Do you mind sitting in my car? It's easier than six flights of stairs."

"Oh, I don't mind," she said, cursing inwardly.

He'd double-parked down the block. The priest opened the door and Kasia slid into the passenger seat, cradling the handbag on her lap. She stared at the raven on the hood as Bryce walked around and folded himself behind the wheel. The clunk of his door sounded like a tomb sealing shut. All sound hushed save for the drumming of the rain.

"This is a very nice car," she said, the smile almost cracking her face. "I mean, mine is … well, you saw it. Always breaking down. But you can never find a taxi and the trams are sardine tins."

Bryce pushed his hood back. Stubble roughened his jaw. The thin nose and light blue eyes looked like a Kven, but his beard and brows were dark. His hair was longish for a priest, about half a centimeter and thick like a brush. Natalya was right. He couldn't have been more than thirty or so, but he had bags under his eyes. Bryce neglected himself. Yet something about him was extremely appealing—

"I pulled your file," he said, taking out a notebook.

Kasia's heart stopped.

"Marked by Tessaria Foy. A vestal. Retired. Is that correct?"

"Why, yes it is." Her left foot tapped a rhythm against the floorboards.

He studied her for an excruciating minute. "I have the authority to take you to the Arx and have your Marks examined. It would be done by a vestal, of course—"

And there it was—her worst nightmare. She should have been quaking in her heels, but Kasia was sick of being bullied by men. She wasn't going to take it anymore, not even from a priest of the Interfectorem.

"What have I done, Fra Bryce?" she asked in an acid tone. "I'm the victim, in case you've forgotten. Massot threatened to rape me. To do even worse things. You saved my life. Why are you persecuting me now?"

He looked away, pale cheeks flushing. "I didn't say I would, Domina Novak."

"What is it you're after then? I already told you everything I know."

"I don't think you have." A gloved hand gripped the wheel as he turned toward her. His cassock was open at the throat and she could see the very edge of a Mark on his collarbone. "Did you see the mage?" Fra Bryce demanded. "Did he speak to you?"

"The what?" Kasia stared at him. "Did you say mage? As in *Nightmage?*"

He watched her closely, but she didn't need to feign astonishment. She'd never even considered the possibility that Massot was Nightmarked. He was a respectable man. A follower of the Via Sancta!

"Saints!" she muttered. "No, I didn't see anyone else. I swear it." She held the priest's eyes, willing him to believe her. "You thought I might be . . . oh, no." Kasia felt ill. "I would *never*, Fra Bryce. I'm a good person. I mean, I try my best. There's nothing I want so badly . . . ." She drew a deep breath. "You've seen my flat. It's tiny and overpriced and smells of curry. And my car. Would I drive a car like that if I'd made a bargain with a Nightmage?" Kasia knew she was rambling. "Please don't take me to the Arx—"

"Why did you look at me like that?"

The question baffled her. "Like what?"

"Like I was a monster. Back at Massot's house."

"Oh." For a moment, Kasia was at a loss. Then she realized the obvious answer. "I'm sorry, but you're Interfectorem."

Bryce stared at her for a moment longer. Kasia couldn't tell if he believed her. He reached into his pocket. She tensed, half expecting a set of Warded manacles.

"These are yours," he said.

Kasia took the deck of cards. They both wore gloves, but she felt a surge of warmth, low in her belly, as their hands brushed. She quickly looked away. *I need to get out more.*

"Do they really tell the future?" he asked.

Dangerous ground, that question. Kasia gave it a wide berth.

"Most of my clients just want reassurance. Someone to talk to."

"So you lie."

"I tell them what the cards mean and offer an interpretation. I make no promises, nor do I give explicit advice. There's nothing illegal about it. My fee is quite reasonable."

The directness of his stare unnerved her. Only very young children looked at you like that, with no filter.

Or crazy people.

Her palms went clammy inside her gloves as she remembered Ferran Massot, but Bryce didn't have the same calculating, covetous quality. He seemed driven to the point of obsession, but not with her. She was just a means to an end, which fit with the character of the Knight. A man of determination and action, even to the point of recklessness. Once he set his mind on a goal, he'd do anything and everything to achieve it—

"Would you give me a reading if I asked for one?" Bryce asked.

Kasia met his gaze levelly. "You can schedule an appointment if you'd like. I believe you have Natalya's business card. The number is the same. But I'm already late for an engagement."

Tension crackled between them. The priest was a wily one. She felt tempted to switch to an unlisted number, but it would kill her business. If he *did* demand a reading, she'd give him what he expected: a passel of lies.

Fra Bryce smiled suddenly. "And that's my fault. Can I give you a lift?"

"How kind of you to offer." She returned the smile. "But the traffic police are merciless. If I don't move my car, I'll end up with a third ticket."

"At least let me help with the tire." His door opened and he was gone before she could object. Kasia stuffed the cards into her handbag, cramming the brass cylinders down to the bottom, and zipped it up. She watched in the rearview mirror as Bryce fixed the flat and tossed the jack in the trunk. The instant he finished, she opened the car door and ran over.

"Thanks." She snatched the sodden tickets from the windshield. "I'd better be going then—" She bit off an oath.

"What is it?"

"The key is in my purse." Kasia gritted her teeth. "The one that still hasn't been returned."

Bryce blinked away rain. "Do you want that ride after all?"

She didn't, but it could be a test. If she refused, he'd think she was hiding something. He already knew about Tessaria Foy. There was nothing suspicious about visiting her patron. Kasia trudged back to the Curia automobile.

"Where to?" he asked, sliding behind the wheel.

"Lesnoy Prospekt."

Bryce started the engine and slipped into the evening traffic. No one honked, even when he blatantly cut them off. He stared through the windshield, not speaking, and the silence wasn't the comfortable sort, as between friends, but brittle and charged. She tried to think of a conversational opener that didn't involve Massot or Nightmages and came up empty.

Tell me, Fra Bryce, how did you end up at the Interfectorem? Does the name really mean *killer* in the old tongue?

So, Fra Bryce, have you always been this grim and peculiar, or did the job make you this way?

Traffic thickened as they approached the four-lane drawbridge over the Montmoray River that led back to the city center. Kasia stared out the window. Water and sky blurred into a gray mist, the lights of downtown Novo twinkling on the far bank. The priest still hadn't uttered a word. Maybe he hoped she was one of those people who couldn't stand silence and would say anything to fill it up. That she'd blurt out something incriminating. Well, let him brood. She'd be damned if she uttered a single syllable.

Then Kasia realized the car was drifting slowly but steadily for the barrier. Forty meters below, the river rushed along, the heavy rains and outgoing tide churning the current to dark froth. Kasia glanced over. Bryce's eyes were closed, chin drooping towards his chest.

"Saints!" She grabbed the wheel and yanked it back. Brakes squealed behind them and someone had the temerity to sound their horn. The priest's eyes shot open. He gripped the wheel, blinking rapidly. "What happened?"

"You nodded off."

Bryce rolled down his window but didn't seem surprised or embarrassed. "Don't worry, it won't happen again."

"When's the last time you slept?" she asked with a frown.

"This morning."

"For how long?"

"I've no idea. An hour or so."

"That's not—"

"Domina Anderle makes the cards, is that correct?"

His voice was cool and professional. Apparently, she was back on the witness stand.

Kasia sighed. "Yes."

"And you do most of the readings?"

"Yes."

"So why didn't Massot hire you in the first place?"

"I don't know," Kasia replied, flustered and annoyed. "Maybe he prefers blondes."

The flippant answer didn't go over well.

"Massot was a brute who hated women," he said in a low, serious voice. "You say you were there because Domina Anderle got sick. Can anyone else corroborate this story besides Massot?"

"Well, no—"

"Domina Anderle seemed fine to me."

"Her fever just broke!"

"But you can see why someone might find it strange."

They crossed the bridge and inched past the ornate marble edifices of the banking district west of the Arx. Men in fedora hats rushed along the streets, vying for the few vacant taxis. The women wore heels and long, belted raincoats. Traffic was horrid. It took all her willpower not to fling open the door and walk the rest of the way.

"No," Kasia said in a wintry tone. "I can't. Natalya does readings all the time. She's charming and sought-after. I think you're fishing for whatever you can find, but there's nothing *to* find, Fra Bryce. You're looking for a conspiracy that simply doesn't exist."

Blue eyes weighed and measured her, but Bryce said nothing. He was so damned hard to read! A minute later they reached Lesnoy Prospekt, a broad plaza shaped like a pentagon that marked the epicenter of the city's priciest real estate. The ballet, opera and Museum of Antiquities were all a brief stroll from the tall limestone apartment buildings, each with an awning and 24-hour concierge.

"What number?" he asked.

"Seven." Kasia pointed. "Over there."

The car glided up to the curb. A uniformed doorman hurried out with an umbrella and opened her door. It was like being paroled from prison after a twenty-year stretch.

"Goodnight, Fra Bryce," Kasia said acidly. "Thanks for the lift."

"Goodnight, Domina Novak." A quick, humorless smile. "I'll be in touch."

As Kasia watched his taillights vanish into the darkness, she realized she'd left her own umbrella in his car.

Fogging perfect.

Chapter Twelve

D r. Massot's townhouse was a hive of activity.

Alexei slowed at the corner but didn't turn down the street. Three Curia cars were parked out front and a pair of priests stood on the front steps, talking under umbrellas. He didn't need to see the insignia on their robes to know they were General Directorate. Kireyev's men.

Then one turned his face to the light of the streetlamp. It illuminated the shiny pate and blond beard of Fra Gerlach, who had questioned him at the Institute. The other was probably his partner, Fra Brodszky.

Alexei sped up before they noticed him.

Kasia Novak was still lying. He couldn't pinpoint exactly what she was lying about, but taking her into custody had been an empty threat. What he should do is finish his report and give it to the archbishop before they demoted him to candle-lighting duty.

Yet Alexei couldn't stop thinking about her.

She was his very last lead.

And she knew something. He could smell it.

He needed leverage and there was one other place that

would have records on her—although unlike the Tabularium, these would be under lock and key.

Alexei drove back to the Arx, speeding through red lights whenever he could get away with it. If Malach was still in the city, every Oprichnik of the City Watch would be hunting him. It made no sense. Why bring down the wrath of the Curia by turning Massot when he could have killed the doctor and quietly disposed of the body in one of the rivers? Massot would simply have been a missing person, with no one the wiser that he was Nightmarked.

Then there was the matter of who *had* murdered Massot in a public and messy way. Someone couldn't risk the doctor talking. But about what? Something that threatened the Church as a whole or merely the individuals involved?

Either way, he was running out of time. Chess matches or not, Misha was dying. Nurse Jeyna had told him so. His body was slowly wasting away. In the last few weeks, he would turn his face away when she brought the tray of food and no amount of coaxing could make him eat. If it continued, she would need Alexei's permission to insert a feeding tube down his throat. When she described the procedure, he nodded calmly and said he would have to think about it. Then he ran to the staff lavatory and threw up. She didn't ask again.

But every time the telephone rang, he half expected it to be the Institute informing him that his brother had slipped away in the night. Just another number to be bagged and burned, his ashes presented in a cheap tin urn.

Someone else would become 26—perhaps an Invertido he brought in himself—until they too died and the number was recycled again.

The image haunted him and not even Alexei's Marks could dampen his grief and terror.

. . .

THE OFFICES of the Probatio were in the Tower of Saint Lieven, a six-story stone structure with narrow barred windows. The most secretive, opaque organization in the Curia, its members rarely associated with anyone beyond their own Order. The Probatio had only existed for thirty-odd years, since the defeat of the rebel nihilim cities, but it wielded immense power and was accountable only to the Pontifex.

Twice a year, agents fanned out to elementary schools across the city, where they administered a battery of psychological tests designed to weed out children who were unfit to wield the ley. Individuals with pathology, but not just any pathology—the kind of moral deficits that characterized the nihilim and their sympathizers. It was a complex calculus that no one but the Probatio fully understood, but there were certain common traits. Lack of empathy and remorse. Diminished fear response. A tendency to lie and manipulate others.

Alexei remembered taking the tests himself three years after Misha. They'd both had tutors but were required to go to Saint Clara's school a few kilometers away on the day of testing. He still remembered the palpable anxiety among the students. The questions changed every year so older siblings couldn't coach the younger ones.

A runaway tram is about to kill five people. You are standing on a footbridge next to a large stranger. Your body is too light to stop the train, but if you push the stranger onto the tracks, killing him, you will save the five people. Would you push the man?

There were others in the same vein, moral dilemmas that had seemed inexplicable at the time. Now he knew they were designed to force a truthful answer. Others were open-ended. *How do you like to waste your time? If something breaks, what is the first thing you do? If you work hard, do you deserve a reward?*

Alexei had never seen his own scores, but he was summoned to the Arx to receive his first Mark a week later.

Bells summoned the faithful for supper as he parked in the lot behind the Tower of Saint Lieven. Alexei killed the engine.

He hadn't eaten all day, yet he didn't feel hungry. His mind was clear and alert. Did passing out behind the wheel count as a nap?

Sure it did.

He waited as a dozen priests emerged, hoods raised against the rain, and set off for the dining hall. The communal meals were intended to bring the various orders together, though in reality they tended to segregate themselves by table. The exception was Patryk Spassov, who had friends everywhere. Alexei pictured him with a cup of wine in hand, amusing his companions with jokes and anecdotes related in his signature deadpan style. For some reason, the taint of the Interfectorem didn't touch him. Spassov was universally liked.

The tolling of the bells faded to silence. Alexei approached the tower with no plan, only the determination that he would get what he came for, one way or another. He pounded on the door until a bespectacled clerk appeared. The young man's cassock bore a trident on the breast, the symbol of all three aspects of mind. It was identical to the one on Alexei's own robes, except that the trident of the Interfectorem was inverted.

"I'm here to view a file," he said.

"I'll need prior written authorization to grant you access," the clerk replied in a bored tone.

"Written authorization from whom?"

"Archbishop Kireyev."

That wouldn't be happening. "I'm the primary investigator in a sensitive case. I need those records tonight."

"I still need written authorization. Or he can telephone it in."

"The archbishop is a very busy man."

The clerk gave him a condescending smile. "Surely you're aware these records are highly confidential. I can't simply hand them over to anyone who asks."

"I understand." Alexei turned away. He slipped his gloves

off as the clerk started to close the door. "Oh, one last thing, brother."

The man sighed. "I already told you—"

Alexei slammed a palm against the wooden door, pulling ley into his Marks. He drew deep, reaching through the blue surface current to the violet liminal power beneath. And then deeper still to the abyssal ley.

He'd never touched it before. He hadn't been sure it was even possible. Abyssal ley was forbidden to the clergy under pain of exile. The currents ran in the opposite direction from the surface ley, and were ten times stronger. Alexei's Marks burned with white-hot agony even though it was just the barest trickle. The muscles of his arm cramped. He gritted his teeth and drew more. Primal urges stirred in the limbic system of his brain. The frontal cortex, which governed judgment, impulse control and reasoning, packed its bags and took an extended holiday.

The priest opened his mouth to yell for help. Alexei's ungloved hand found his wrist. Scarlet light bathed the doorway like a mouth to Hell. A ragged sigh escaped the clerk's lips. His eyes were wide and staring. Ley pulsed between them.

For a moment, Alexei forgot what he was doing there. A tight, dark well opened beneath his feet and part of him wanted to see how deep it went.

Temptation. Forbidden knowledge. Both had led to the fall of the nihilim.

I am a priest of the Eastern Curia. I will not succumb so easily.

With an oath, he wrenched his palm from the door, severing the connection. Rain beat against Alexei's face as he fumbled for the copper coin in his pocket, clutching it like a lifeline.

"You already have the authorization," he said, barely recognizing his own voice. It was calm and controlled even as molten ore scoured his veins. "If you misplaced it, that's not my fault. If I'm forced to get another one, the archbishop will be quite annoyed with you. So the best thing for everyone would be to let me see the records immediately."

He released the clerk's wrist, letting the power ebb away, and pulled on his gloves with shaking hands. The man's eyes looked vacant. Alexei feared he'd hit him too hard, but then he blinked rapidly, returning to his senses like a diver surfacing from the depths.

"Don't worry," Alexei said. His own knees were weak, his stomach cramping with spears of ice. Holy Marks did not like abyssal ley. "I won't tell anyone you lost the paperwork. I'm sure it will turn up."

"I'm sure it will." The clerk cleared his throat. A drop of blood oozed from his left nostril, but he didn't seem to notice. He swung the door open and stepped back. "What year are you looking for?"

The round chamber beyond was austere. No reception desk, no waiting area. It was the first time Alexei had ever come here and, like the Batavia Institute, visitors were clearly a rarity. He double-checked his notebook for Kasia Novak's birthdate, then calculated the year she would have turned eight.

"Third floor," the clerk said with a nod. "Follow me."

They climbed up the winding tower stairs to the third-floor record room. It wasn't much larger than the Tower of Saint Dima, but the ceiling was double-height with specially fitted cabinets stretching up into the gloom.

"Kasia Novak, you say?" the clerk murmured, producing a ring of tiny keys. He hopped on a rolling ladder, unlocked a drawer, and riffled through the contents. He peered down at Alexei. "I don't see the name."

Alexei silently cursed. The OGD had beaten him again. "Is the file missing?"

"No, they're sequentially numbered. Are you sure you have the right year?"

"It could be the following one," Alexei said.

The clerk climbed down the ladder. He crossed the chamber to another file drawer, this one chest-high, and ran a practiced finger swiftly down the tabs. "Nothing, I'm afraid."

"May I see?"

The clerk hesitated. "I'm not supposed to allow visitors access to all the files, just the requested ones."

"I won't look at the scores, just the names. Surely those aren't confidential. Every citizen has a file."

The priest pushed his glasses up on his nose. "All right, have a look. But I tell you, it's not there."

Alexei started at the first cabinet, slowly flipping past each dossier and checking the numbers as he went to make sure none of the files had slipped down or stuck together. There was nothing for Kasia Novak. The clerk looked increasingly nervous. He kept glancing at the door and fiddling with his spectacles.

"Almost done," Alexei said cheerfully.

He had never used the ley to compel someone before. Did the effects wear off? But the thought of touching it again made him shudder inwardly. He wasn't sure he'd be able to let it go next time.

"This is against the rules," the clerk muttered. "I'll have to insist you stop."

Alexei was already at the second cabinet. His fingers flew over the yellowing tabs. Nothing on Kasia Novak. And nothing missing. The file identifiers were all in sequence.

"Fra Bryce—"

One of the files caught his eye. Alexei pulled it out with a rush of excitement. Once, in a different life, he had spent hours every day digging through dusty libraries. Searching for the needle in the haystack. He still remembered the feeling of satisfaction when he succeeded.

"Did you find it?" the clerk asked in surprise.

Alexei gave him a bland smile, though his pulse raced. "It's my fault. Domina Novak is married now. Foolish of me not to look for her maiden name."

The man stared at him. "What is it?"

Alexei showed him the file. "You see? The birthday matches, as well as other particulars. May I have a moment to inspect the file?"

"You can't take it out of this room. But yes, you may read it."

Alexei cracked the folder. The first thing he saw was a red stamp that said REJECTED. This was followed by four pages of test scores with half the numbers circled, also in red pen, which he assumed indicated an abnormal result.

Of course, it might be a different person altogether. If it *was* Kasia, why hadn't Kireyev destroyed this record, too? Perhaps because he didn't expect anyone to find it. Altering her record at the Tabularium might have been deemed sufficient. Whoever was protecting her, Kireyev or someone else, had no reason to expect a full-blown investigation. There was just enough of a paper trail to satisfy a casual inquiry.

Alexei slid the file back into the drawer. "The Interfectorem is grateful for your assistance in this matter," he said.

The clerk nodded uncertainly.

Alexei's couldn't meet the man's eyes. That was the nihilim way, manipulating people with no regard for the sanctity of their minds. He'd crossed a line there was no returning from.

Alexei muttered a farewell and hurried back down the winding stairs. At the bottom, two bishops were coming in the front door. They stared suspiciously as he brushed past. One shouted something as he ran to his car. He ignored it, tires spitting gravel as he circled around to the main road.

It wouldn't be long before word reached Kireyev of his disobedience. Before they discovered who the witness was and whisked her away.

Which meant he had nothing left to lose.

Chapter Thirteen

K asia strode into the mirrored lobby and waited while the doorman called upstairs. He wore a navy jacket and cap with gold braid, the buttons straining against a generous waistline.

"Domina Novak is here," he said, winking at Kasia. He'd known her since she was a teenager. "Of course, Domina Foy." He hung up the phone. "I'll take you right up."

"Oh, I can do it myself," Kasia said. "No need to let your coffee get cold." She smiled at the mug, which said *World's Greatest Dedushka*. "And congratulations. I see Yana finally had the baby."

He beamed. "A healthy girl. Seven weeks tomorrow."

He summoned the lift, which resembled an elaborate birdcage, and Kasia stepped inside, hoping no one else would come into the lobby. The instant the door closed, she started rooting through her handbag. Fortunately, No. 7 had the world's slowest elevator and Tess lived in the penthouse.

Kasia found one of the cylinders. She tried to twist off the end, but it wouldn't budge. She ran her fingers over the smooth brass, searching for a hidden catch. If Massot was Nightmarked, she wanted to know what was going on and what exactly he was telling Falke. Staying in the dark wouldn't help them if it all went to hell.

The car creaked past the third floor.

Come on, fog it!

She felt a tiny indentation and pressed it. The lid popped open. There was a spindle inside. She slid a leather cord off and unwound two documents from the spindle. They held the shape, rolling up into a tight scroll. Kasia crouched down and flattered them out on the floor of the lift.

The first was a map of the continent, with a grid imposed on the foreground. Ley lines, each junction anchored by a stela, and whorls of power to indicate the four Arxes. The Void was shaded with thick, dark lines as if the artist had pressed hard on the pen. In two places, the nib had torn through the parchment.

Sixth floor.

She unrolled the second parchment.

It was a letter written in a looping script. The f's were written in a peculiar way, more like an s, but she soon got the hang of it. Her eyes flew over the page.

M—

I trust this finds you well. These past weeks have
proven most fruitful, but also rife with frustration at my
inability to contact you directly. If you are reading this,
it means I've missed our regular rendezvous, which in
turn must mean some calamity has befallen me.
Considering the dangers involved, such an eventuality
is hardly unforeseeable. As a precaution, I have
penned this missive in the hope it will fall into your
hands. I do not trust our mutual friend and nor should
you. He uses us both and I fear he would silence me
without remorse for what I am about to tell you.

M., I have found what you sought. Even more than

that, I suspect. At the risk of sounding melodramatic
—or insane myself!—the results of my last experiment
indicate that the Original Source of all your Troubles
is a patient at the Institute. The Marks do not lie. I
cannot explain how this came to pass, but at the very
least, he would be invaluable to B. (see sketch attached
hereto). Please forgive the indiscretion of entrusting
this message to parchment, but time is of the essence. I
fear my experiments are awakening latent abilities,
placing his removal from the Institute at risk. I cannot
be the only person aware of who he is. You must act
quickly. The sign is the Lion. The number is 9.
Yours,
F.M.

The elevator passed the ninth floor. Kasia hastily rolled
the papers around the spindle and jammed them back in the
tube. Her fingers shook as she pressed the hidden catch on the
last cylinder. It held only a single sheet of paper, written in the
same hand.

Sixth round of experiments was a failure. Increased
dosages of Sublimen induced torpor and hallucina-
tions but no ability to manipulate the abyssal ley.
Results confirm the hypothesis re: genetic predisposi-
tion. There must be a work-around, though I am yet to
see it. Awaiting further instructions.

She snapped the lid back on and shoved both cylinders in
her purse just as the elevator door slid open to Tessaria Foy's
entry hall.

At seventy-six, Kasia's patron still had firm skin and military posture. She wore her hair in waist-length dreadlocks,
pure white at the roots and darker at the ends. A smudge of
shadow emphasized almond eyes.

"Auntie," Kasia said, clasping her patron's hands.

Tessaria kissed her cheeks. She smelled of a delicate but earthy perfume. Sharp black eyes swept Kasia from head to toe. She stood up straighter, though the scrutiny seemed half-hearted.

"I am relieved to see you well," Tessaria said curtly. "Now tell me what mess you've landed yourself in."

Tessaria scorned dresses, preferring elegant pantsuits. A long-sleeved silk shirt in creamy taupe with pearl buttons hung on her tall, angular frame, tucked into wide trousers and red pumps as sharp as daggers. The gloves matched the shoes.

They walked together to the living room, which could have contained Kasia's entire flat with room to spare. The Foys were old money with properties and business interests throughout Novostopol. Tessaria occupied No. 7's top two floors, a sprawling sixteen-room mansion-in-the-sky with frescoed ceilings and polished wood paneling, though her taste ran toward modernist furniture and experimental artwork. Kasia paced the immaculate white carpet, swiftly relating the events of the last two days.

"It's outrageous," Tessaria said when she was done. "Thank the Saints nothing worse happened." Her voice hardened. "However, your recklessness makes me wonder if a single lesson I've ever imparted has managed to stick in your mulish brain." Hands framed her hips. "Why didn't you tell me Natalya was sick? You should have just called it off! Did it ever occur to you that the cardinal might not wish to have you involved in his personal business?"

Kasia kept her chin up—her godmother despised weakness or cowardice. "I didn't read the messages."

"That's beside the point. You should have consulted me first."

"Forgive me, but I could hardly foresee that the doctor's Marks would invert the moment we were alone together. I was just trying to help."

Tessaria clucked in annoyance and strode to a sideboard stocked with bottles. "Would you like a drink? I have some excellent blackberry cordial from Kvengard."

"Later perhaps, thank you. Have you ever heard of a priest named Alexei Bryce?"

Tessaria's shoulders stiffened. She paused for a beat, then glanced over her shoulder with a slight frown. "I don't think so. Is he old or young?"

"Young."

Ice rattled into the glass. She poured two fingers of clear liquid and dropped in a wedge of lime. "After my time then."

Kasia's patron had retired from the church at sixty, settling into life as a grand dame of the city's elite social circles. Most vestals went off to the countryside to hoe vegetables, but Tessaria Foy made her own rules and no one had the temerity to stop her—not even the Pontifex.

"He drove me here." Kasia parted the drapes. Cars moved in the street below, but none had the distinctive shape of the Curia's fleet, like barracudas gliding through the shallows. "After threatening to drag me to the Arx and have me strip-searched," she added.

Tessaria froze with the glass halfway to her lips. "Whatever for?"

"He thought I was Nightmarked."

The older woman was silent for a long moment. "Bryce, you say? I'll look into him."

"Oh, leave it alone, Auntie." Kasia let the curtain fall. "If you warn him off, it'll just make him worse. I can handle it."

"How?"

They locked eyes. "I'm not a child anymore. I don't need you fighting my battles."

"This is not a battle. It's a matter of your civil rights being trampled upon by some lout from the Interfectorem."

"That's a stretch. He only asked me some questions. I told you, I'll handle him." She gave Tessaria the brass cylinders.

"But I'll feel better if you'd hold on to these for a few days. When Nashka hears from the cardinal, I'll let you know."

Shrewd eyes bored into her. "Are you sure you didn't take a peek? You can tell me."

"Of course not. I don't even know how to open those things."

"Did Massot say anything else?"

"Nothing that made sense. I'd rather not talk about it."

Tessaria sighed and stood up. "I'll put them in the safe and then we'll make supper." Her voice grew fainter as she walked down the hall to the master bedroom suite. "I have sweet onions and some bryndza cheese. How does a soup sound?"

"Perfect!" Kasia called back.

She stared through the window at the distant lights of the Arx, hoping Bryce made it back without crashing his car. He was a pest, but he was just doing his job. The fault lay with the vile doctor. She doubted the priest would trouble her again. If he was going to bring her in, he would have done it already.

"Was Alyona Petrova really at the party?" Tessaria asked, once they'd regrouped in the large kitchen.

That was the famous actress.

"Yes."

"They say her husband has taken a new lover, and not another woman." Tessaria mentioned a famous actor.

Kasia's eyebrows shot up. "Wasn't he her co-star in that play?"

"None other."

"She said her husband had a business meeting and couldn't come to dinner. But she did seem a bit shifty."

"What did the cards say?"

Kasia nodded slowly. "It all fits now."

Tessaria prepared the broth while Kasia chopped onions and recounted each of the readings she'd given.

"Saints, these are sharp," she said, wiping her streaming eyes. "Hand me that dish towel, would you?"

"For the Saints' sake, don't use a towel. Take my handkerchief, it's clean. How is Natalya?"

"Home resting. She sends her apologies."

"That girl," Tessaria said fondly. "How does she manage to cause so much trouble with so little effort?"

"It's a talent."

Tessaria had been the one to introduce them nearly a decade before, after she found Kasia playing with a novelty deck of cartomancy cards. Without even looking at the little guide the cards had come with, Kasia had accurately interpreted most of the meanings. Tess kept an eye on budding artists in the city and Natalya Anderle already had a name for herself. The two young women hit it off at once and, thanks to Tessaria's extensive contacts, launched a business together within a few short years.

Even people who didn't believe were open to having their fortunes read at parties just for laughs, but after a while, Kasia built up a list of regular clients, as well. It paid the bills, which was good because she had no clue what else she would be suited for. She'd been a bright but indifferent student, passing her classes with mediocre grades. The real education had been at No. 7 Lesnoy Prospekt, where Tessaria taught her how to eat, dress and speak.

It was raining too hard to eat out on the terrace, but Tess never used the formal dining room unless she was entertaining so they stayed in the kitchen, trading gossip and laughing. The onion soup made a perfect contrast to the creamy, salty sheep's milk cheese. Kasia felt more relaxed than she had in days. As much as she'd protested about fighting her own battles, it was reassuring to know she had a powerful ally.

"But seriously, darling, you must tell me next time. Let it be a lesson, *da*? At the very least, I would have had my driver take you. He's a retired Oprichnik."

"I promise, Auntie."

Tessaria clasped her hand. The scarlet leather of her

gloves looked bloody in the candlelight. "You're the daughter I never had, Kiska. The thought of what might have happened . . . ." Her gaze was intent. "Are you sure you're all right? Does anything seem different?"

"I'm fine. What do you mean, different?"

"I just worry Massot used the ley on you."

"He only touched me for a second or two."

"Of course." Tessaria smiled, but it seemed forced. "Well. How about that blackberry cordial?"

Chapter Fourteen

The cold marble of the tomb made it difficult to find a comfortable position.

Malach shifted his hips, lacing his hands behind his head. It smelled of damp but not decay—the occupants were too ancient for that. Rain beat down on a glass oculus set into the dome above. It was surrounded by a fresco of saints trailing blue ley from their hands. He had to admire the Curia's dedication to propaganda. Not even the dead were spared.

But the chill crypt was the least of his concerns. He'd gone to Ferran Massot's house only to find it crawling with rooks. And not just any rooks. General Directorate. It had been very annoying. Did the doctor forget to pay his taxes?

The distant purr of an engine was followed by slamming doors. Malach slid off the tomb just as a key turned in the lock. The drumming of rain grew louder as the door swung wide on well-oiled hinges.

"Your Eminence," he said, bowing his head.

Cardinal Dmitry Falke had a square face, clean-shaven, with a strong jaw that was just starting to get a bit jowly. Deep purple robes set off his silver hair. He wore the heavy gold ring of office on his right hand over leather gloves.

"You've made a horrific mess of things," the cardinal snapped. "And I'm still cleaning it up! At least have the courage to look me in the eye."

Malach had played the game so long he could do it in his sleep, but this was not the greeting he'd expected.

"What mess?" he asked mildly. "I just arrived."

"Ferran Massot." Falke bit off the name. "Why on earth did you invert his Marks?"

Turned? It couldn't be. Malach tilted his head. "You must be mistaken—"

"The Markhounds are never wrong."

Malach tensed at the mention of the hated dogs. "Well, it wasn't me. Where is he now?"

Falke clenched a fist. He looked regretful. "I already took care of it. Massot is dead."

Rage, hot and urgent. The doctor had been useful. "How dare you?"

"If they'd traced him back to me, learned what he was doing. . . I couldn't take that risk."

"What else?"

Falke eyed him with disdain. "There's nothing else. And they're already hunting you. I've done what I can, Malach. It's time to run back to the Void."

Malach's Marks flared, all of them at once. Violet fire lit the crypt. Falke fumbled to get a glove off, reaching desperately for the Raven ward carved into the wall behind him. Three others sat at equidistant points in the tomb, waiting to be activated. He wasn't quite quick enough. Malach caught his arm. Abyssal ley coursed from his hand. "*Tell me.*"

Most people crumbled instantly to a compulsion, but the cardinal was cunning and fanatically devoted to the Curia. His own Marks fought back. Tried to bury the truth in his psyche. Ley blazed on the painted cherubs, spinning in a whirlpool at the feet of the two men locked together. One by one, Malach smashed through his defenses. In the end, the abyssal ley was always stronger. Will seeped from the cardinal's eyes, leaving him blank as a doll.

"Massot discovered something," he said in a monotone. "He telephoned me two days ago, asking when you would be coming."

"What was it?"

"He wouldn't say. He was always secretive. Careful."

"And?"

"I told him you'd been delayed but that he could trust me to deliver any message."

Malach's fingers dug into his flesh. Falke moaned softly. "Did he believe you?" Not even Massot could be that stupid.

"I don't know. He seemed desperate. He owed me a progress report so I used a go-between. She's trustworthy. He was supposed to give her the report at a dinner party, but then he turned." A thin line of spittle leaked from the cardinal's mouth.

"Did your emissary get the message?"

"I don't know. We're still searching his house. I won't approach her directly unless I'm forced to."

"Why?"

"The Interfectorem is involved. I can't risk this blowing up."

Ah, yes. The lunatic police.

"Was the discovery connected to his experiments?" Malach asked.

"I think so."

Interesting. "You weren't going to give it to me, were you?"

"It belongs to the Curia."

Silly old goat. "What's her name?"

"Natalya Anderle."

"Address?"

The cardinal recited it.

"Describe her."

"Blond. Attractive."

Malach hardened his tone. "I don't want your opinion. I want an objective description."

"Medium height. Brown eyes, dark skin. Mid-twenties. Her Mark is a dragon."

"Where?"

"Left arm."

"Is that all you know?"

"Yes."

"You won't remember this conversation."

"No," the cardinal agreed.

"In fact, you're still very angry at me. But you'll believe me when I tell you I didn't do it. And our bargain will stand."

"Yes."

Malach let the ley recede slowly, gently, like easing a sleeping child into bed. He stepped back and raked a hand through his hair. "Run? But every gate from the city is Warded now!"

Falke blinked. His eyes cleared. "Don't be a fool. You'll go the way you came, Malach. I'll send someone to wait at the appointed spot and disable the Ward." He scowled. "Now what of Massot? Who turned him?"

"I don't know."

"And I don't believe you."

Malach itched to slam a fist into his smug face. Or perhaps to invert all his Marks. See how he enjoyed a prolonged stay at the Batavia Institute. "Your lack of faith wounds me."

"My faith is all that's keeping you alive. Let's try again. If it wasn't you, there's another mage inside Novostopol. I find that supposition to be far-fetched. You're only here because I sanction it."

"And how do you know you're the only one with a pet mage?"

The cardinal frowned.

"My guess," Malach said, "is that Massot cracked under the pressure. It does happen. But surely you can see I have no interest whatsoever in turning him. I only Marked him as a favor to you in the first place. You claimed he needed abyssal ley to carry out his research. In fact, this whole situation is an inconvenience since it cuts my visit short."

The cardinal grunted. "He was my friend. How do you think I feel? But he was mad. It's no life." Blue light glimmered at the collar of Falke's robes. A Mark had ignited. Easing his guilt, no doubt. "What about our other project? Any news to report?"

"Not yet."

The cardinal's mouth tightened. "What exactly do you spend your time here doing?"

Malach met his steely gaze. "You know I've tried. It's not my fault if the attempts keep failing."

Falke studied him. "We have an agreement. It might be distasteful to us both, but I've honored my end. You've had free rein to come and go for three years now. My patience is wearing thin."

"These things take time," Malach said reasonably.

"Do you take me for a complete idiot? No, don't answer that." Falke drew himself up. "You think I need you more than you need me, but you fail to grasp that the war is lost." He made a sharp gesture. "It was lost before you were even born. And by the grace of the Saints, it will be the last war humanity will ever have to fight!"

Malach gazed at him without expression, but hatred boiled in his heart.

I will never yield to you. Never. And one day, when your church lies in ashes, I will find you and flay you and hang your Marks from the dome of the Basilica.

"All that's left," the cardinal continued icily, "is a return to the fold. I offer you redemption and you throw it in my face, again and again. You have one more chance, Malach. The next time we meet, you'll give me what you promised or I'll set the hounds on you. And that will be just the beginning."

Malach pretended to be chastened. "I already have a willing candidate. You won't be disappointed."

"Good. Come back when the dust settles. You have six months to deliver a child. After that, you can tell Beleth to start digging graves."

Falke swept through the door, slamming it behind him. Malach sat down on the crypt. He was still a boy when the cardinal, then a humble captain, had led the Curia to victory after victory. Falke was the one who gave the knights total autonomy in the field. Without a hierarchy issuing orders from afar—and wasting time on endless debate—they gained two critical advantages: speed and adaptability. Malach had read all of the cardinal's books. He called it "calculated chaos."

The mages had responded by denying them targets. Vanishing into the Void, then nipping at their flanks. But without the ley, it became a war of attrition. The side able to absorb the most casualties would win and the nihilim were outnumbered by the Curia a hundred to one.

That guerrilla war, fought in the ruins of Bal Agnar and Bal Kirith, was the one Malach knew. The one he had lived. The glory days when the mages commanded the ley, when they *ruled*, were nothing but stories. Reality was only the Void and the knowledge that he could die at any moment.

Eventually, after whispers of atrocities on both sides, the knights were withdrawn. The Curia declared victory.

Now they thought they were safe. That it was over.

Dominate while seeming to submit. Disguise your aggression. Then hit them where it hurts the most. Find the center of gravity that holds the system together—and destroy it.

The cardinal's own words. He was a brilliant strategist.

And Malach was an avid pupil.

He didn't know who had flipped Massot's Mark, but he intended to find out.

He also intended to collect what belonged to him.

Malach unfolded his tourist map, searching for Malaya Sadovaya Ulitsa. It was time to pay a visit to Natalya Anderle.

Chapter Fifteen

꧁꧂

K asia strode along the sidewalk, spiked heels rapping
against the paving stones. Two cordials after dinner
had done wonders to improve her mood. She loved the city at
night, the way the puddles reflected the warm yellow lamps
shining through every window, and the makeshift gardens of
terra cotta planters that jammed terraces and fire escapes.

Mist shrouded the streetlights, softening their glow to
frosty haloes. Tessaria had offered to call a cab, but Kasia
preferred to walk. She'd borrowed an umbrella with an
elegant ivory handle, which she twirled in her gloved hands as
she waited for the light to change at Kronstadt Square.

Disaster had been averted, yet she kept thinking about
those cryptic letters. She recalled every word, even the exact
spots where the ink had blotted.

> "Sixth round of experiments were a failure. Increased
> dosages of Sublimen induced torpor and hallucinations, but
> no ability to manipulate the abyssal ley. Results confirm the
> hypothesis re: genetic predisposition. There must be a work-
> around, though I am yet to see it. Awaiting further
> instructions."

Sublimin was obviously a psychoactive drug and it didn't sound pleasant. She felt sure this was the message intended for Falke, which meant Dr. Massot was experimenting on his patients with the cardinal's blessing.

The second letter, addressed to M., contradicted the first. Massot claimed he'd found something important. The letter referred to "our mutual friend" and warned M. not to trust him. Massot had used the same phrase in his study when he was talking about the cardinal. But who was M.?

The sign is the Lion. The number is 9.

The Marks do not lie.

Kasia shook her head in frustration. Massot was locked away. Whatever plots he was mired in couldn't happen now, could they? It was time to pick up the pieces and move on. Let the Curia deal with it.

In the morning, she would reschedule all her clients. The rent was coming due and they couldn't be late again.

She paused in front of a cobbler's shop, eyeing a pair of shiny knee-high boots with a sign that read *100% Waterproof!* Kasia's boots had holes so she'd been borrowing Natalya's. They wore the same shoe size, though Nashka was taut and slender like an acrobat, while Kasia had generous curves. She flattened a palm against the display window, admiring the vicious stiletto heels. On second thought . . . surely they could put off the electric bill for another month.

The curry place was still doing a brisk business as she inserted her key in the lock and started up the stairs. When she reached the third landing, she saw that the hall lights on the top two floors had burned out. Typical. Their landlady was a miserly woman who owned buildings all over the city. She never fixed things until the tenants' association filed a complaint.

Kasia was fishing for the key when a shadow detached from the wall. She stepped back, but he was already right in front of her.

"Katarzynka Nowakowski?"

The key slipped from her fingers. Fra Bryce bent down to pick it up. "That is your real name, isn't it?" he said with a hint of satisfaction.

The warm glow of the blackberry cordial evaporated. Sobriety rode in on an icy wind. She stared at him with naked loathing. "How did you find out?"

"A bit of math. Will you invite me in?"

"Do I have a choice?"

He held out the key. "I just want to talk. Then I'll leave and never bother you again."

Kasia gripped the umbrella like a sword. "You're not here to arrest me?"

"No." He glanced at the burned-out bulb. "Or we could stand here in the dark until your neighbors come out."

She took the key. Her hand shook and it took three tries to get the door unlocked.

"Coffee?" she asked, jamming the umbrella into a stand and peeling off her raincoat. In fact, she would rather sever her own feet and eat them raw than make the priest coffee, but social niceties died hard, especially when they'd been instilled by Tessaria Foy.

He nodded. "Thank you."

Kasia busied herself in the kitchen, boiling water and dumping grounds into the pot while he waited in the living room. She wasn't careful when she poured it through the copper filter, allowing a fair quantity of grounds to sludge into the cup.

"Cream?" she called.

"Yes, please."

Kasia opened the refrigerator. She sniffed the container and smiled, pouring a generous dollop into the coffee.

"It expires tomorrow, but it smells fine," she said, handing him the cup.

Bryce sat down on the sofa without being invited, legs

spread in that aggressive way men had. Kasia retreated to the window seat. She was dying to take her heels off and resented the fact that she couldn't. "What do you want, Fra Bryce?"

"Alexei." He cradled the coffee. "I may not be a priest much longer."

"Why not?"

"I've been ordered off the case," he admitted. "By the Archbishop of Novostopol himself."

Kasia shot him a guarded look. "Yet here you are. Why?"

"We'll get to that later." He gazed at her levelly. Again, Kasia felt like a witness under cross-examination. "Someone created a false record for you. That's not a simple matter."

"A friend helped me to pass as Marked."

"Tessaria Foy."

Kasia gave a reluctant nod. "I know it's wrong to pass, but you've no idea what it's like."

The priest took a sip of coffee. He made a choking sound and set the cup down. "So that's how you got past the hound at the gate. They only smell Marks. I should have guessed." Blue eyes studied her. He didn't seem shocked or repelled, just
. . . .

"Now you pity me," she said, annoyed.

"I'll admit, I've never known anyone in your predicament. It must be difficult."

Kasia gave a tight smile. "Believe it or not, cartomancers with antisocial personality disorder aren't in high demand, Fra Bryce. If my clients found out, they'd drop me in a moment. Natalya would be shunned by association. We'd lose everything, though at least she has family to turn to."

"I saw your file. You're an orphan."

"Not exactly. My father died of a heart attack when I was ten. After the funeral, my mother confined me to my room. She said the stress had killed him. That she couldn't stand the sight of me."

Bryce frowned. "Your own mother?"

"I ran away. Domina Foy took me from the streets. I never want to go back to that life."

"Did she offer to Mark you?"

"She said it was too late. I was too old."

He nodded. "I was given my first Mark at nine. The rest came later, over the course of many years, but the first must be done before the age of ten."

"Why?"

The question seemed to catch him by surprise. "It has to do with the mind. The sense of self and the way the ley interacts with it. I've read books, but I'm not sure I can explain it very well. Young children are different. More open." He glanced at the coffee. Now that it had cooled, the surface was speckled with curdled cream. "Do you think I might have a glass of water?"

There was something liberating about having her worst secret out in the open. And he hadn't treated her like she was a monster, the way most people would. "If you'll let me take my shoes off."

He smiled. It was a nice smile. "I don't mind."

"I'm sorry I tried to poison you," she said with a wince.

"You should taste Spassov's coffee."

"Spassov?"

"My partner."

"Ah. I'll be right back." She kicked her heels off and went to the kitchen, filling a clean glass from the tap.

"Finish your story," he said when she returned.

"There isn't much more to tell. Tessaria had connections. She changed my name and created a false record. I told her the names were too close, but she said it would be easier to remember." Kasia looked away. "I suppose you saw my test results."

"Yes."

"I'm a sociopathic deviant. That doesn't trouble you?"

The priest barked a laugh. "From what I can tell, Domina Novak, you're more well-adjusted than I am."

She gave him a level stare. "What is it you want, Fra Bryce?"

"Alexei."

"What do you want, Alexei?"

"The truth."

He hadn't explicitly threatened her, but he didn't need to. "Why?" she snapped. "What business is it of yours anyway?"

"I have a personal interest in locating the mage."

"I can't help you with that."

Bryce leaned forward. He still had his gloves on, hands clasped loosely over his knees, but Kasia tensed. "Did he come to the house?"

Oh, how she wanted to lie. But the priest had a nose for deception. "No," she admitted. "I made that part up. We were alone the whole time."

He was silent for a long minute. "It might have been me," he said at last.

"Pardon?"

"Do you understand how the ley works?"

"Of course. Marks harness one's innate talents. They make us better." She flushed, regretting the collective pronoun, but Alexei didn't seem to notice.

"Civil Marks, yes. The Sanctified Marks given to a priest are different. Both connect to the unconscious, but mine can project the ley outward."

It was all on her final exam on Science and the Ley. "Holy Marks decrease the entropy of the system to manifest a single outcome, or a much narrower range of outcomes," Kasia recited.

Alexei looked surprised.

"I have an excellent memory," she said.

"And what's the final ingredient to achieve that single outcome?"

"Intent."

"No, intent is conscious. It matters, but there's something more powerful."

Kasia thought for a moment. "Need," she said.

"The night Massot turned, I'd taken my gloves off to read a book. I dozed off. Only for a few minutes."

Kasia frowned. She still didn't see what he was getting at.

"I might have worked the ley," Alexei said softly. "By accident."

"But you're Interfectorem. You don't want people to go mad, do you?"

"Not consciously. But there's something else I wanted, very badly, and it's all connected."

Kasia felt intrigued. It was a startling confession. "Could the ley really do that?"

"I don't know, but Nightmarks rarely invert on their own. Not like normal Marks. You're telling me you were alone with Massot at the instant he turned. So it wasn't the mage." He studied her. "What else do you remember?"

"Massot took his gloves off. He touched me."

The priest tensed. "Did he . . . ?"

"Just my face. But I'd given him a reading moments before. The first card was the Mage, upside down. Do you think the ley could have worked through the cards themselves?"

He frowned. "But they're just paper."

"And Wards are just stone."

"Those are different. They were made with the ley."

"So are the cards. Natalya is Marked. She's the artist."

Bryce looked skeptical. "A thousand everyday objects are made by people with Marks. It doesn't make those objects conduits for the power."

Kasia shrugged. "I think that's when Massot went mad though. That moment. He wasn't violent before, though I do think he planned to proposition me. He had it in mind all along."

"He has a history of abusing women," Alexei said with disgust. "I learned about it from a nurse at the Institute."

"What a vile man."

"Would you show me the cards?"

Kasia fetched her best deck, which Bryce had kindly returned in the car, and recreated the spread she'd drawn for Massot. "I understand it a little better now," she said. "First off, they're all Major Arcana, meaning they represent significant archetypes in the subject's life, not just passing events." She touched a card depicting a man in leg irons straining to reach a barred window. A chest overflowing with gold coins sat at his feet. "The Slave could be Massot himself, in thrall to the mage who Marked him."

Kasia moved on to the next card, an armored man astride a horse. "The Knight would be you, of course. A foot solider of the Church. But I'm uncertain of the Fool and the Martyr."

"What do they mean?"

Kasia found herself warming to his interest. Here, she felt on solid ground.

"The Martyr implies a loss of health and vitality through oppression by some controlling force. We suffer at the hands of our own contradictions." She touched the image of a man dangling upside-down from the bole of a tree, one knee bent. His hands had been severed at the wrist. "Thus, we hang from our former ties that defined us in the physical realm. But a fresh perspective will turn the world upside down."

"And the Fool?"

"He's a trickster." She regarded the barefoot figure in motley. He wore a traveler's knapsack slung on one shoulder and played a pipe. "There are many layers of meaning. New beginnings. The life of a vagabond, or one who travels between worlds, unconstrained by time and space. The Fool is the first card in the Major Arcana, so numerically it's considered zero. A nullity. But I wonder . . . ." She tapped a tooth with one finger.

"What?"

"If it doesn't represent the nihilim himself. I'd assumed it was the Mage, inverted, but that might simply represent Massot's ultimate fate."

Alexei stared at the cards. "They look like Marks," he said softly.

"That's deliberate. We live in a culture of symbolism. Of archetypes. My clients draw comfort from the familiar. We all want to impose some kind of order on our lives, to find meaning in what can seem like chaos."

"Do you believe they tell the future?"

Kasia thought of all the times she'd accurately predicted births and deaths, sudden windfalls and impending financial ruin. It helped to know something about her clients, but she'd seen twists of fate foretold in the cards that no one believed until they actually happened. One or two blamed her and never called again, but the vast majority refused to undertake a major decision without consulting her first.

"Yes." Kasia met his eye. "For me. Not for Domina Anderle. I don't know why that's so. There's nothing special about me." Her mouth twisted. "Excepting that I was never Marked. But it's possible. . . ." She bit her lip.

"What?"

"The ley might be sentient."

She thought the priest might scoff, or worse, accuse her of heresy, but he did neither of those things. "I've wondered the same thing," he admitted.

"Because we don't really know what it is, do we?"

"No," he agreed. "We don't."

A quiet intimacy stretched between them. He had striking eyes despite the shadows beneath—a shade of blue you noticed from across the room and alive with blazing intelligence. She had a sudden urge to feel his bare hands on her skin. To find out just what priests wore under that cassock.

A flush crept up her neck.

"Are you all right?" Bryce eyed her with concern. "You look unwell."

"I just need some water," she muttered, striding for the kitchen.

Kasia filled a glass from the cold tap and pressed it to her forehead.

How could she go from debating the physics of the ley to mentally undressing him in fifteen seconds? A *priest*? If there had been a Hell, she would surely burn in it.

It was the cards. All that talk made her think of The Lovers. But it didn't mean him. It couldn't possibly.

Kasia gulped down the water, then refilled the glass and returned to the living room. She busied herself collecting the cards, not even glancing in his direction, but now that the idea had been planted, it was hard to banish.

"Kasia?" he said.

"Hmmm?"

"Is that what you prefer? Kasia?"

She nodded and retreated to the window seat.

"If you tell me what happened that night, all of it, I'll tell you why I have to find the mage."

She'd been waiting for this. Kasia met his gaze. "It's not my secret to share," she said. "I could get others in trouble."

"I promise not to involve Natalya. Or Domina Foy."

Kasia believed him, but she had to be sure. "Swear it on the virtue of the Pontifex."

Alexei touched the Raven Mark on his neck, holding her eyes. "I swear."

"It all started with Cardinal Falke."

Bryce's face gave nothing away. "Go on."

"He holds Natalya's Mark. He told her to attend a dinner

party at Ferran Massot's house, but not only to give readings. The doctor had a message for the cardinal."

For the second time that night, Kasia told her story, leaving nothing out this time. "When I saw you, I'd just taken the papers from his desk. I was afraid of you, but more afraid of what Cardinal Falke would do if I returned without them."

Bryce leaned forward. "Do you still have them?"

"I gave them to Tessaria Foy. Just to hold until the cardinal asks for them."

"The building at Lesnoy Prospekt?"

Kasia nodded. Alexei closed his eyes and rubbed his forehead. "So you had them in your possession when I drove you there?"

She nodded again.

"Did you look at them?"

"Yes," she admitted. "In the elevator."

Alexei waited.

"There were two separate messages. One was for the cardinal. It talked about experiments with Sublimen, but said they were a failure."

Now he did look surprised.

"You've heard of it," she said. "What does it do?"

"A drug used to bestow Marks. It induces a suggestible state akin to hypnosis. What about the other message?"

"It contained a letter and a map. The map was nothing unusual, except that the Void was shaded rather violently. But the letter was addressed to someone called M."

He leaned forward, instantly alert. "What did it say?"

Kasia recited the letter word for word.

Alexei stared at her. "You memorized it in an elevator?"

"Not intentionally. It just stuck in my head."

"Would you copy it down for me?"

"Certainly." She tore a piece of paper from Nashka's sketchbook and transcribed the message in slanting script that closely resembled Massot's. "Here you are." She handed it to the priest. "Any clue what it means? The bit about *the Marks never lie* and *the number is 9?*"

He shook his head. "No, but I'm not very clever. I'll need time to think about it."

Kasia studied him. "I think you're extremely clever. You figured me out in less than forty-eight hours and no one else ever had a clue." She couldn't resist a jab. "Not even my lovers."

Heat warmed the sharp planes of his face. "How did you do this?" Bryce waved the paper.

"I have total recall of everything that happens to me."

"Everything?"

"Ask me what I was doing on this day five years ago and I can tell you exactly what I wore, what I ate, where I went. I can recite every conversation, describe every person I spoke to."

"You'd make a dream witness in court."

She shrugged. "I was a poor student, but I have a phenomenal memory for the mundane. I don't know why. It started when I was eight."

"When you were tested."

Kasia nodded. "Who is M.?"

"Malach is the Nightmage." Alexei's voice turned to ice. "Beleth is his aunt."

"Well, I've never heard of either of them. I have nothing to do with it. I just happened to be there because Nashka was sick. Look, I really have told you everything now——"

"I believe you," he said quietly. "And I swear to keep my promise. I'll tell no one of this."

She hugged a throw pillow to her chest. "Listen, you don't have to tell me your reason if it's personal." *I just want you to leave.*

"No, I'll tell you." He laughed hollowly. "Maybe you'll have some insight for me."

People often confessed things to her. Maybe they sensed

she was morally challenged and wouldn't judge them. It was good for business, but more than a little awkward. Whatever secrets Bryce was keeping, she wished he'd take them to the grave. Now he was looking at her with a wary vulnerability that was hard to resist. Kasia couldn't decide if she wanted to kiss him or run for her life.

"I'm listening," she said.

Alexei took something from his pocket, clenching it in a gloved fist. "My brother is Invertido. His name is Mikhail."

It wasn't what she'd expected. "Oh, Saints. I'm so sorry, that's awful."

"Do you think he could be the patient Dr. Massot was referring to?"

"He never mentioned a name in the letter. I really don't know."

"This Nightmage, Malach. He Marked my brother and then he turned him. I saw it happen."

"I'm very sorry."

"We served together. I don't know why he accepted Malach's Mark, but he must have done it willingly. Night-marks can't be forced."

"Did he never tell you?"

"He hasn't spoken since it happened."

"So you want revenge."

"No!"

Kasia recoiled at the vehemence in that single word. She almost apologized again, but how many times could one say they were sorry?

"Then what do you want?" she asked.

Alexei gazed out the rain-streaked window. "I've been searching for Malach for years. This is the closest I've ever come. Misha will die if the Mark isn't removed. I need the mage alive."

"I thought Inverted Marks were permanent."

"We can't fix them, but nihilim are capable of things beyond even the Pontifex. I have to try."

"So you think he's here?"

"Massot's message was meant for him. It implies that Malach is in Novostopol, or planning to come."

"Did your brother know Dr. Massot?"

"I thought of that, but I'm sure there's no connection between them. Misha and I served seven tours together before the Curia pulled out of the Void. I joined the knights because of him. If you'd known Misha . . .Well, I can promise you, he would never associate with a man like Massot."

Kasia nodded, but Alexei seemed to see doubt in her eyes. "You're thinking that maybe I didn't know my brother as well as I thought I did. And you're right. He kept secrets from me. But he was a good man, a loyal knight, right up to the end, and Malach's claim doesn't change that fact!"

"I'm sure he was," Kasia said hastily. "*Is.* I suppose people could take a Nightmark for all sorts of reasons."

Alexei shot to his feet so fast she jumped. He strode to the window and threw open the sash, gulping in the night air. Rain came in too, beading on his gloved hands, which he braced on the sill. He stood like that for a minute or so.

"I'm sorry," he said.

"Don't be."

"No, I shouldn't have shouted at you."

"You didn't shout. You only raised your voice a little."

He turned to her. "You're being kind."

"Not at all." She paused. "It's raining rather hard though."

He closed the window. "I'm better now."

"Good."

"It's hard to talk about. I never have before."

"Not even with Fra Spassov?"

"Not even with him."

"Then tell me the rest," Kasia said. "If you can."

He nodded and walked back to the couch. It sagged beneath his weight and Kasia wondered if she might forego the waterproof boots and invest in a new sofa instead. Bryce was heavier than he looked. This triggered an inappropriate mental image, which Kasia ruthlessly crushed.

"Just before our last deployment, Misha went on a diplomatic mission to Kvengard. This was about four years ago. I know he didn't have the Nightmark before he left because we'd gone home for the Liberation Day weekend. Misha had an argument with my father and went outside to chop wood. It was his way of letting off steam. I joined him. It was hot, so we both took our shirts off." Now it was the priest's turn to flush. "There was no one about. They live in Arbot Hills."

Her eyebrows climbed at the mention of the wealthy enclave on the east bank of the river. Tessaria Foy's family had an estate there and she'd taken Kasia once for a picnic. The dachas were all old and grand, with acres of lush lawns.

"You come from money," she said.

He shrugged the comment away. "My father does, yes. Anyway, I think he might have met Malach during that trip. Kvengard stayed neutral in the conflict. The mages were permitted to keep a consulate there, with a legat."

She frowned. "What's a legat?"

"A diplomatic attache. The peace talks always failed, but it was the only formal channel we had with the mages. I can't say for certain that Misha met with the legat, he wasn't allowed to talk about it, but I do know that Cardinal Falke headed the mission. He was our commanding officer."

Falke again. "Did your brother seem different when he returned?"

"Not at first. But over that last year, he grew distant. Guarded. When we were on leave, he'd disappear for days and refuse to say where he'd gone. Once, I followed him from the barracks. He went to a brothel in Ash Court. One that catered to . . . exotic tastes. I'm not a prude, but that wasn't like my brother. He'd be much more likely to attend a lecture on metaphysics or spend a weekend browsing the stacks at the Lyceum."

"He was an intellectual."

"At heart, absolutely. Mikhail always had a strong . . . physicality, I suppose you'd say. A natural athlete. The arts of war came easily. But more than anything, he liked to talk, to think, to debate. He lived in a world of ideas. That was his true passion."

"He sounds like an extraordinary person."

"When I confronted him about the brothel, he flew into a rage and told me to mind my own business. Again, it was not like Misha to lose his temper, not even over the smallest thing. He took after our father that way, priding himself on control. When he calmed down, he apologized and said the stress was wearing on him. But we saw no real engagement on our final deployments. Not until we were attacked in Bal Kirith and Malach turned his Mark." Alexei held out a small copper coin. "This was Misha's."

She squinted at the tiny print. *Mikhail Semyon Bryce.* And on the Raven side, a motto: *Foras Admonitio.* In the old tongue, the phrase meant *Without warning.* "What is it?"

"A corax. Every knight is given one before being sent to the front. They're used to identify bodies burned or mutilated beyond recognition."

The civil war had always seemed far away. Dry lectures in history class. She remembered the teacher talking about sacrifice and heroism, but only in general terms. "Did it happen often?" she asked.

Blue eyes gazed straight through her to some distant place beyond. "On my fourth tour in Bal Agnar, the field artillery unit made a mistake with the coordinates and shelled our position. Misha and I were the only survivors." Alexei sounded indifferent. "They gave us Marks for bravery, but all we did was get lucky. The commanding bishops offered us both an early discharge. Misha refused, but he pressed me to take it."

"Why didn't you?"

"I couldn't leave him."

"And then?"

"We were deployed again. They said it was to inspect the stelae." He sighed. "You have to understand, at that time we all believed the war would drag on forever. The mages were scattered, but not broken. We'd dig them out of the ruins and they'd be back as soon as we left. Cat and mouse, though sometimes I wondered which side was which. Then it happened." His face betrayed no emotion. "Three weeks later, the Curia declared victory."

She returned the corax, placing it gently in his palm and folding his fingers around it. "I'm glad you told me. I wish I could be of more help."

He looked at her strangely. "Do you dream, Kasia?"

The priest sounded so very tired.

"Sometimes. They don't often make sense though."

"I can't." He blinked. "I can't even sleep anymore. Something's wrong with me."

She glanced at the window seat, then perched next to him on the edge of the couch. "You're under stress. I'm sure—"

"I've been losing time. Just a few minutes here and there, but I can't remember what happens. I'm afraid . . . ."

"What?"

He rubbed his forehead. "That one of these days, when the Markhounds start to howl, it will be for me."

Kasia had no idea what to say.

Alexei slipped the corax into his pocket. "I should go," he said. "I've bothered you for two nights in a row. At least one of us can still get some sleep."

But he didn't stand up and neither did she.

"I'm not tired," Kasia said. "We could talk some more."

"What about Domina Anderle?"

"She's out late tonight."

Alexei cleared his throat. Silence stretched between them. His eyes flicked down to her black lace gloves. "Those are unusual."

"I only wear them for show." She smiled. "Not like yours."

He flexed his fingers—a bit nervously. Kasia crossed her legs, brushing a stockinged knee against his. "Would you like a reading?"

He looked startled. "Now?"

"Unless you have someplace to be."

Alexei hesitated. "I don't."

Kasia shuffled the deck. She fanned it on the coffee table. "You choose the first one," she said.

"Gloves on or off?"

"It doesn't matter."

Alexei fumbled to draw a card with his gloves on. Two came out at the same time, stuck together. "Oh," he said. "Shall I try again?"

"No. When that happens, it means something." Kasia turned them over.

The Lovers. And The Fool.

"Interesting," she said, heart thumping. "Let's start with the first one."

Kasia had drawn the same card herself from another deck. This image was also designed by Natalya but had subtle differences. The man's Mark, for example. It began at his hips and rose up to frame the groove between the muscles of his back. Alexei leaned forward.

"The Towers," he said in astonishment. "That's mine. Except they're burning."

Tiny flames leapt from the upper stories. And the woman . . . Well, she still had long, dark hair, but her face was sly and foxlike. Kasia had used the deck countless times. She'd never noticed that before.

Her eyes locked with Alexei's. Kasia would never know

what might have happened next because the buzzer sounded, breaking the spell.

"Are you expecting anyone?" he asked.

She shook her head.

"Answer it."

Kasia rose and went to the intercom. "Hello?"

The voice was garbled. She caught the words "curry" and "delivery."

"It's probably for Domina Federov down the hall," Kasia said. "She's always ordering in. Half the time they buzz the wrong flat."

"Maybe." Alexei rose to his feet. He looked different. Cold and lethal.

"Should I let them in?"

He nodded and pulled his gloves off, his gaze never leaving the door.

"You don't think . . . . Only Massot knew I had the papers. And the cardinal, of course."

"Massot was murdered."

"Saints!" Her eyes narrowed. "Did you just use me as bait?"

"No! Buzz him in, Kasia."

Him.

"I won't let anything happen to you," Alexei said, a naked plea in his voice. "I swear. But you said you'd help me if you could."

Kasia cursed under her breath. Then, much against her better judgment, she stabbed the button to unlock the outside door.

Chapter Sixteen

A lexei took out a set of Warded manacles. Adrenaline coursed through him. They had less than a minute before Malach was at the door—if it *was* Malach.

"Does your bedroom have a lock?" he asked.

Kasia gave a curt nod. "I didn't see your car out front."

"I parked around the corner."

She stared at him accusingly. "So you wouldn't alert the mage."

"So I wouldn't alert *you*." He stuffed the gloves in a pocket. "I didn't know about those letters until a few minutes ago. I couldn't possibly have known he'd come after you. But thank the Saints I'm here, Kasia." A shadow crossed his face. "You don't know Malach like I do. Just lock everything. Don't come out."

He moved past her and stepped into the hall. Light footsteps were coming up the stairs. They moved at a swift, steady pace with no pause for a breather on the landings. The mage was fit, but he already knew that.

Alexei surveyed the battleground. He'd hunted nihilim in a thousand buildings just like this one. The only difference is that it wasn't an abandoned husk. People lived here. He had to contain Malach before he used the ley. If it came down to which of them could wield more raw destructive power, Alexei didn't stand a chance. And he didn't want collateral damage.

To the left, the stairs continued up to the roof. With the bulbs burned out, it was dark as pitch and the only place to hide. Alexei went up five risers, holding the manacles tight so they wouldn't rattle. He pulled his cowl up, blending with the shadows, and pressed a palm to the floor. The ley was thin so high up. His Marks ignited with painful slowness.

Think only of Misha and how I want to help him. My intentions are pure. By the Grace of the Pontifex and all the Saints, help me remember that.

A man appeared, moving down the hall. His hands were empty and loose at his sides. No box of curry. He paused in front of Kasia's door, so close Alexei might have reached out and touched him. A brisk knock.

"Domina Natalya Anderle?"

The voice raised the hairs on Alexei's neck. He'd heard it before in the ruins of the basilica at Bal Kirith.

"She's not here," a voice said calmly from the other side of the door. "So fog off."

Alexei bit his lip.

"Open up." The mage's voice had a hard edge now.

"I'm calling the gendarmes."

"They won't get here in time."

Malach kicked the door. It shivered in the frame. Abyssal ley swirled at the mage's feet. A pool of chaos. Malach swung his foot back for another blow. The instant he was off balance, Alexei leapt from the shadows. He snapped a manacle around Malach's wrist. Before Alexei could activate the Ward, the mage twisted like an eel, fist connecting with Alexei's nose. Pain exploded in a white starburst. Malach slapped his free palm on the wall. It flared a fiery red.

"*You,*" he said in startled recognition.

Alexei tasted the salty warmth of his own blood. He

danced back out of reach before Malach could touch him. He didn't care to have all his Marks reversed, or to be turned into a ravening, mindless beast.

Alexei braced a hand on the stair railing. Ley burned a blue trail across his skin.

Malach laughed. "What do you plan to do with that, rook?"

He flicked a finger. Every bulb in the hall shattered, showering bits of glass. It crunched under Malach's boots as he stepped forward. The mage's eyes were bottomless wells in the darkness.

Malach's Marks blazed. All of them. Alexei could feel it, a rasp drawing across his bones. The air felt heavy and charged with potential energy. He braced himself for something nasty.

The apartment door flew open. Kasia smashed a coffee pot over Malach's head. He reeled back, blood trickling down his forehead. Alexei's ears popped as the pressure eased. He dove for the manacles, but Malach saw him coming and sprinted up the stairs.

"Are you mad? Get inside," Alexei snapped. Kasia's eyes narrowed. "And . . . thank you."

She arched a brow. "You're welcome."

Alexei hit the exit to the roof at a dead run. He kicked open the heavy metal fire door just as it swung shut. The roof was fifty paces across and covered in silicon panels that stored kinetic energy from the rain. Malach was nearing the opposite edge, head down, arms and legs pumping in an all-out sprint. Alexei pelted forward, sliding on the wet panels. He shook rain from his eyes, searching for a Raven emblem. He couldn't let the mage get away. It had taken three years to find him and Alexei knew he would never get another chance.

Malach's knees bent, poised to leap across the gap to the next building. Alexei swore and prepared to follow. Then his gaze fell on one of the cornerstones. The circle was old and weathered, barely visible. He dove forward and slammed a hand down. The symbol ignited, lines of blue fire racing to the next corner, and the next, sealing the rooftop in a shimmering square.

A magetrap. The city was full of them. They were rarely used anymore, but Kasia's building was old enough to have one. Within its boundaries, the ley ceased to exist.

Malach slowly turned. His voice could have frozen stone. "I'll say this once. Let me *out*."

It was the nihilim's only weakness, the inability to make or break Wards, nor to pass one once it ignited.

Blood pounded in Alexei's ears. "Do you remember me?"

"I don't need the ley to tear you apart, *laqueus*. But you already know that. You've been down in the mud." His face hardened. "We're not easy meat, even in the Void."

So Malach did remember.

"I want you to fix what you did," Alexei said.

"Fix it?" Malach laughed. "That bomb has already dropped. There's nothing left but a hole in the ground."

They circled each other warily.

"Please, just listen. I'll bring him to you. If you make him better, I'll take your Mark in his place. On my honor, Nightmage. It's a fair offer."

"So you'd betray your faith for me?" Malach frowned. "Maybe I chose the wrong brother. You have potential."

A car horn blared in the street. Distant music drifted up from the cafés. Alexei barely heard it over the swift drumbeat of his own heart. "You're wasting your time," he said evenly. "Nihilim mind games don't work on me."

"No?" His lip curled. "Then you hold no ill will? Not even the tiniest thirst for vengeance?"

A scream echoed in his memory. Like his brother's soul was being torn from his body.

"I feel nothing for you."

"And I think you're lying." Malach smiled. "Don't forget, I know you, laqueus. I know the things you've done. You can spout doctrine at me all night, but you're an animal like the rest of us. Marks don't change that fact. They just spare you the pain of facing the truth."

Alexei tamped down a stab of anger. "What difference does it make?"

The mage's smile broadened. "All the difference in the world."

Alexei watched his plan crumble to dust. Nihilim couldn't be reasoned with. Their very nature was incomprehensible. He realized that Malach would never accept Alexei's terms. Only his own.

"What is it you want?" he asked, expecting him to demand Massot's message.

Malach loosened his tie, the manacles dangling from his wrist like a taunt. "To admit that you loathe me. That you'd like nothing better than to spill my blood and the only thing stopping you is the knowledge that your brother would die if you killed me."

"He'll die anyway."

"Probably. But the sickness is a worse way to go."

"And if I do, you'll help him?" Alexei asked warily.

"I'll consider it."

"Not good enough. I need your oath."

"All right. But I want a full confession." He tipped his face up to the sky. "I want you to tell me about every murder you've committed in the name of civilizing the human race. I want to hear about the interrogations. The scorched earth campaigns. Curia law is suspended in the Black Zone, isn't it? No rules, no limits." His eyes gleamed in the semidark. "I want to know how you felt when your damaged mind tried to repress it all. I want to know what it cost you."

Alexei drew an unsteady breath. "After you fix my brother."

"No, the confession comes first, laqueus. Let's start with your first tour of duty in Bal Agnar. Did you know there was once a treaty called the Ostravia Conventions? It was a long time ago, before the second Dark Age, but I'll wager you've violated them all."

Alexei stared. He knew every treaty the Curia was party to, but he'd never even heard of a place called Ostravia. "What are you talking about?"

"A list of war crimes. You might have missed one or two purely by accident. Let's find out."

"And what about you?" Alexei laughed in disbelief. "Your kind is a thousand times worse. Are you actually claiming innocence?"

"Not at all. But I don't deny my atrocities." Malach studied the shimmering cage. "Traps cut both ways. You can't touch the ley either, which means your Marks won't make all that bad blood go away. In fact, judging by your expression, I'd say it's bubbling up right now." Malach waited expectantly. "Well, carry on."

Alexei's fists clenched. "You're sick."

"No, you are. Wouldn't you like to unburden yourself? You'll feel better afterward. Then I'll tell you what it feels like to turn a Mark. To unchain the beast inside—"

Alexei launched himself at Malach. His fist connected with the mage's jaw, knocking him back. Malach grinned through bloody teeth. "Now that's what I'm talking about." He braced his feet. "Come on, laqueus. Just you and me. Like the old days."

Alexei swung. Malach dodged the blow and landed a jab to the ribs. Alexei grabbed him in a bear hug. They tumbled to the ground, rolling across the rain-slick panels.

Once the nihilim had been soft. Reliant on the ley to defend themselves. But their descendants who came of age in the Black Zone weren't soft at all—not the ones who'd survived. The mage was all hard muscle and lightning reflexes. They grunted and swore, each straining for the upper hand. Alexei headbutted him, then delivered a flurry of vicious blows while Malach shielded his face with his arms. A tiny voice shouted at him to lock the second manacle in place, but he couldn't stop. He wanted to beat Malach to a red pulp first.

All that bad blood.

Alexei grabbed the mage's hair, lifting his head up. "You want a confession?" he spat. "Here it is. I do want you dead. You and all your kind. You're parasites. You're a fucking disease."

Malach kneed him in the balls, hooked a leg under his ankle, and flipped him facedown into a puddle. Alexei sucked in a mouthful of water. A hand shoved him deeper.

"Here's mine, priest," Malach hissed in his ear. "I didn't want to turn your brother that day. I wanted to kill him. Call it a favor for an enemy."

Black spots burst before Alexei's eyes. He bucked and writhed, but Malach sat astride his back and couldn't be dislodged. He tried to yell. All that came out was a burst of bubbles. Mist gnawed at the edges of his vision.

"Stop!"

A woman's voice. Alexei's lifted his head and drew a ragged breath.

"Natalya Anderle?" Malach didn't even sound winded.

"Please don't kill him. I'll give you what you want."

Fingers gripped Alexei's skull. His head lifted from the puddle, then slammed down again. Fireworks burst before his eyes, but the crushing weight disappeared. Alexei rolled to one side, dizzy and gasping.

"Where," Malach demanded, "is it?"

"Leave her alone," Alexei croaked. "She doesn't know anything."

Black shoes paused in front of his face.

"I wasn't talking to you, *laqueus*," Malach said.

The second time his head slammed against the roof, Alexei slid into darkness.

Chapter Seventeen

K asia backed away from the Nightmage.

He didn't look anything like she'd expected. Mages in the novels she'd devoured as a teenager always wore black cloaks. They had long, flowing hair and cruel mouths. Being both repellent and strangely attractive, the mages did quite a bit of ravishing before a knight came along and rescued the damsel just as she was about to be Nightmarked. Sometimes the heroic knight was a woman and the victim a man, but the mages were always vampire knockoffs.

This one looked like the clerk at the bank where Kasia cashed her checks, if rather beefier across the shoulders. He wore a nondescript tan raincoat, which had fallen open to reveal a nondescript pewter gray suit and tie. His hair was cut short. Blood stained the collar of his shirt, but the rain had washed it from his face.

Which was set in hard lines that conveyed a distinct impression of impatience.

"You're not her," he said. "Where is Natalya Anderle?"

Kasia looked past him to where the priest lay in a puddle. She couldn't tell if he was alive. The sound his head made when it struck the tiles. . . .

The mage strode forward. "*Where is she?*"

"I don't know! She went out with friends. She didn't tell me where—"

Malach closed the gap in three swift steps, lifting her up with one gloved hand. Kasia struggled wildly, fingers prying at his iron grip. A manacle engraved with a Raven dangled from his wrist, but it didn't seem to be much of a deterrent. She landed a solid kick to his kneecap. He didn't even blink.

"You have five seconds before I snap your neck. Where is she?"

From the corner of her eye, Kasia saw lines of blue light surrounding the rooftop. It was eerily beautiful. Ley? Or just a lack of oxygen to her brain?

Malach's grip tightened. How cold his eyes were. He would kill her without a shred of remorse. Blood throbbed in her temples. The light faded and suddenly the mage let go. She stumbled back, rubbing her throat.

"There go the Wards," he said briskly, tugging the glove off. The tip of a sword or long dagger Marked the back of his hand, the point ending at the knuckle of his ring finger. Dense runes covered the blade, which vanished up into his sleeve.

Kasia retreated to the waist-high wall enclosing the roof. Malach followed, implacable. Rain slicked his dark hair to his forehead.

"I don't know where Natalya went. We're just flatmates." She licked her lips. "It's impossible to afford even a *studio* on one's own anymore. But you can search her room, I'll show it to you—"

He took her wrist. She had fine bones, and his hand folded around them almost gently. She hadn't noticed his eyes before, but now they locked with hers. Green, shot with golden brown. *Like mine.*

"Trust me," he said. "This is easier."

Silence poured in, and then she heard the faint barking of dogs below. The mage glanced over the edge.

"What did the letter say?" he demanded. "I know you read it. Tell me!"

Kasia yanked her wrist free. She felt disoriented, like she'd walked into the middle of a heated argument over a subject she knew nothing about and now people were demanding her opinion. Malach reached for her again and Kasia slapped his face. He rocked back, comically surprised.

"Don't touch me," she hissed.

The frenzied barking grew louder. With a curse, he sprinted across the rooftop, leaping up to the wall and across the gap to the next building. She saw him skid, regain his footing, and then the darkness swallowed him whole.

"Saints," she muttered. "What a bastard!"

Kasia hurried over to the priest and knelt down. Blood matted his hair. His eyes were closed.

"Fra Bryce?" she whispered.

She pressed a finger to the juncture between neck and jaw, steering clear of the Raven Mark. No pulse. She bit her lip, then tugged the glove off and tried again. She was unaccustomed to touching people with her bare hands, and certainly not unconscious priests. His beard felt rough, but the skin was silky. And warm, which must be a good sign . . . .

Blue eyes flew open. Kasia snatched her hand back. She hastily pulled the glove back on. "I wasn't sure if you were alive."

"Malach?" he rasped.

"Gone."

A blistering look. "Did he touch you?"

"What?" She examined his forehead. The cut was shallow, but scalp wounds tended to bleed profusely.

"Did he touch you with his gloves off?"

The quiet urgency made her pulse quicken. "Yes, but only for a moment."

Alexei sat with a low groan. "Are you hurt?"

"Not as badly as you," she replied evenly.

"What happened?"

"He said something about the Wards failing, and I heard dogs—"

"Dogs?" Alexei's gaze sharpened. "Or Markhounds?"

"I don't know. I just heard barking and then he left." She shivered. The rain fell in a steady downpour. Was there something else? No, that was all. "Listen, your head is bleeding. You need a doctor."

He touched his forehead, regarding the blood on his hand with detachment. "That's what everyone says."

"Maybe you should listen. Can you stand up?"

"I have to," he muttered. "They can't find me here."

"Let me help." She wrapped an arm around his waist and levered him to his feet, taking most of the weight.

He took a breath and winced. "I think I cracked a rib."

"What can I do?"

"Nothing." He limped for the door. "It'll heal on its own."

She scowled at his back. "Where are you going?"

"The Institute." He glanced over his shoulder. "I have to get Mikhail out of there."

"Will they let you take him?"

"They don't have a say in it."

"Fra Bryce," she said in a level tone. "You can hardly walk."

"I'll manage." Alexei swayed on his feet. He braced a hand against the door leading down. "Come with me. You can't stay here."

"I have to find Natalya," Kasia said stubbornly. "She's in danger."

Alexei went still, his gaze turning inward. "Why did Malach address you as Domina Anderle?"

Kasia shook her head. "I've no idea."

"I haven't filed my report yet. Who else knew about the liaison?"

"Cardinal Falke, of course. He arranged it. And Tessaria

Foy, but I only told her about it tonight. Saints, could Malach have gotten to her?"

"It's possible. But why would he come after you if he already had what he wanted?" Alexei's brow notched. "If Malach touched you, there's a good chance he pried into your mind. You wouldn't even remember it."

Kasia stared into the rainy darkness. A fragment swam to the surface. Malach's face, intent and frustrated.

What did the letter say? I know you read it. Tell me!

"Fog it," she muttered. "I think he did. Bastard. But he didn't get everything."

"Then he'll be back." Alexei gazed at her earnestly. "Please, let me protect you. After we get Mikhail, I'll hide you in my chamber. No one needs to know."

Kasia hoarded her secrets like a miser with gold. The thought of Malach rifling through her head left her feeling soiled and furious. Now the priest wanted to take her to the last place on earth where she felt safe.

And the only place Malach couldn't set foot.

"What about Tessaria?" she hedged. "And Natalya?"

"We'll find them. Spassov will help. He's a good man, he won't ask questions." Alexei's voice was gentle, coaxing, like she was a half-tame cat. "Do you trust me?"

An hour ago, the answer would have been an emphatic *no*, but circumstances had changed. In some way she didn't yet understand, their fates were entwined. And frankly, he needed her help even more than she needed his.

"I did leave my umbrella in your car," she said with a bleak smile. "So I'll go—but only if you let me drive."

An answering smile tugged at his mouth. It was slow and shy and made her want to kiss him all over again. "Fair enough, Domina Novak."

Bryce opened the door. A pack of Markhounds stood on the landing. Three growled low in their throats. The fourth, a brute even larger than the rest, snapped viciously at the other dogs, moving to stand between Alexei and the rest of the pack. They whimpered in submission.

"*Sileo*," Alexei snapped, his hand dropping to caress the massive head of the leader. The dogs instantly quieted.

A dozen priests poured from the stairwell and fanned out across the roof. At a nod from Alexei, the Markhounds trotted to their heels, sniffing the perimeter. Kasia pressed into the shadows. Malach must have sensed them coming. It's why he let her go.

One of the priests approached. A Golden Bough was embroidered on the right breast of his cassock. General Directorate. Kasia watched warily, still fighting the urge to run.

"The mage escaped," Alexei said, "but he can't have gone far. With the hounds, you should have no trouble tracking him, brother."

"It is not his trail we followed," the priest replied harshly. He nodded at someone behind Kasia. A hand seized her arm.

"Let go of me." Kasia struggled to free herself. The second priest held her fast, his bearded face impassive.

"She's done nothing, Fra Talgatov," Alexei said hotly.

"Cardinal Falke will be the judge of that."

Bryce was drenched and bleeding, but his voice rang with confident authority. "Do you have a warrant? If so, I'd like to see it. If not, you have no right to detain her. The civil code requires a detailed explanation of the charges, as well as any supporting evidence. If you violate that mandate, I can promise you that a lawsuit will be filed on Domina Novak's behalf for a sum of compensatory and punitive damages that would make your eyes water."

The biggest Markhound sat down at Alexei's feet, gazing up at him. If Kasia didn't know better, she'd say the dog looked sorry.

Fra Talgatov laughed. "Oh, I have a warrant, but it's not

for her. You're welcome to read it once we're out of the rain."
His voice hardened. "Alexei Vladimir Bryce, by order of the
First Tribunal of the Apostolic Signatura, you stand charged
with the first-degree murder of Dr. Ferran Massot."

Chapter Eighteen

M alach almost had her.

He stood at the wide plaza of Lesnoy Prospekt, manacle dangling from one wrist and blood on his tie, studying No. 7.

He no longer cared about Natalya Anderle. Cardinal Falke had given him the wrong name in the crypt because he'd believed it to be true at the time. Another minute and Malach would have gotten what he needed from Kasia Novak, who confessed to reading the letter herself.

Unfortunately, the sound of barking had broken his concentration. She'd managed to break the compulsion. His cheek still smarted from her palm.

Malach didn't fear priests, but he did fear Markhounds, as any sensible person should. Using the ley only antagonized them. So he'd run, assuming the pack was sent for him, when in fact it had come for the laqueus. Malach knew this because he'd used the ley to disperse his scent, then hunkered down and watched from an adjacent rooftop, hoping to return and finish the compulsion. Kasia Novak was gone now, whisked away by his enemies, but it hardly mattered.

Tessaria Foy had the letter and Malach would get it from her, one way or another.

He stepped off the curb, waiting impatiently for the light to change. Then she saved him the trouble by emerging from her apartment building and pausing beneath the striped awning. Kasia Novak had described her in detail so Malach recognized the tall, dark-skinned woman at once.

He was about to cross the street when a Curia car pulled up to the curb. Two priests got out. Malach cursed softly and faded back into the mouth of an alleyway. He considered killing them, but then a second car arrived and he judged it too risky. The manacle around his wrist was a mere annoyance, but if one of them managed to activate the Ward and lock his other hand, he'd be screaming in agony.

A priest opened the door for Tessaria Foy and she slid into the back seat. The cars pulled away, heading for the Arx.

The cardinal had outmaneuvered him again, but it only hardened Malach's resolve. He started walking, aimlessly at first, working it through in his mind. The laqueus had his own private agenda, one that brought him into direct conflict with the cardinal. The knight didn't even know the half of it. Malach laughed softly.

Who will rid me of this meddlesome priest?

The quote could apply to either of the Bryce brothers. They placed far too much trust in men like Falke, who cloaked himself in virtue even as he plotted and scrabbled for power. The funny part was that the cardinal believed his own platitudes.

From Chapter Six of *The Last War: A Historical and Strategic Perspective*: "Always occupy the moral high ground. Make the conflict a struggle for liberation against the oppressor. This external space, lying outside the physical boundaries of engagement, is the true battlefield."

The cardinal could be insightful, brilliant even, but that bit was nonsense. Malach had no cause. No crusade. He fought for himself. His faith could never be betrayed because he had no faith.

Therein lay the schism that had ultimately splintered the Via Sancta. The purpose of life was not the greater good, but the unhindered pursuit of pleasure in all its forms. The human psyche wasn't built to deny itself. And that, Malach thought, is why they had Invertido. It was why Falke tolerated his existence, as much as he would have preferred to see the mages destroyed utterly.

Malach blinked rain away and saw he was standing before a shabby wooden building in the wrong part of town. He could have gone to a dozen different places, all of them much nicer, and the people living there would have no choice but to let him in or suffer the consequences, but his feet had brought him here so he climbed a set of rickety stairs to the second floor. He knocked on the door. Silence. Malach knocked again, more insistently. He heard muffled sounds. It finally opened a few centimeters, though she left the chain on.

"I thought you might be working," he said.

"It's my night off." Nikola Thorn scowled. "And my flat isn't a hotel, Malach."

"I'm sorry."

"No, you're not." She peered through the crack. "Is that blood?"

"Are you letting me in?"

"Why should I?"

The residual anger suggested he just kick the door open, but Malach knew it wasn't directed at her, and all his hard work to make her like him would go to waste if he behaved like a child, so he decided to lie instead.

"Because I have nowhere else to go and you're the mother of my child."

Nikola sighed. She closed the door. The chain rattled and it opened all the way. She wore a white cotton nightdress and held a candle in one hand. Her thick hair was matted from sleep, but she still looked gorgeous. Malach waded through the detritus of her life and fell into an armchair.

"What happened to you?" she asked.

"I was mugged by delinquents."

"In this town? Horseshit. Let me see." She set the candle down and unbelted his raincoat, spreading it open. "Quite a lot of blood," she said flatly. "Did you kill someone?"

"Sadly, no."

"Is any of it yours?"

"I don't know," he replied sullenly, rubbing the nape of his neck.

Her eyes narrowed. "Is that a handcuff?"

Malach studied the manacle around his wrist. "Do you have a hairpin?"

"Saints," she muttered. Nikola returned a minute later with a paperclip. "How about this?"

Malach bent it with his teeth and inserted one end into the keyhole, turning clockwise until he felt a slight give. A gentle twist and the lock bar disengaged from the ratchet arm. He threw the manacles to the floor and rubbed his wrist.

"Shall we see if you have any fatal wounds?" Nikola asked.

He stared at her. "I'm not in the mood for sympathy."

"Good, because I don't feel sorry for you at all. I'm quite certain you brought it on yourself. But I won't have you bleeding all over my chair."

Malach grumbled but stood up and allowed her to remove his shirt. Nikola gave a low whistle. Curiosity won out, and he went to the bathroom mirror to survey the damage. Livid bruises colored the skin between his Marks.

"Who did that?"

"A laqueus." He caught her puzzled look. "A priest."

"Then they know you're here." Alarm crossed her features. "What the hell, Malach? You have to leave tonight."

His jaw set. "No."

"Why not?"

"Because the Curia stole something that belongs to me and I'm getting it back first."

Nikola looked pissed. "Well, where is it?"

"The Arx."

"You're joking."

"Not at all."

She gripped his bicep and spun him to face her. "You can't go in there. First, because you physically can't. And second, because even if you manage it, you'll never get out alive."

He smiled. "You love me, don't you?"

Nikola laughed without a trace of amusement. "Listen closely, Nightmage. We have a deal. I kept my end. I can't take it back now." A finger stabbed his chest, right on one of the bruises. Malach winced. "And I will not be left alone with a child to feed. A nihilim child! I'll kill myself first."

He regarded her silently for a minute. "I think you would."

"Just try me."

"Well, I'm not leaving without it. So you can help me or you can go cut your wrists." He shrugged. "Your choice."

Brown eyes flayed him. Malach covered a yawn. "Think about it. I'm going to sleep for a few hours. You can give me your answer when I wake up."

"You're not sleeping next to me!" She stomped back to the main room, Malach following.

"Can I have the chair?"

Nikola strode to her bed, balled up a blanket and threw it at him. "You're an idiot."

"Would you care to know why I want it so much?" he asked, wrapping the blanket around his shoulders. "This thing they stole from me?"

"No." She scowled. "Maybe."

"Come over here." He held out a hand. Nikola eyed his naked palm with wariness. She couldn't see the abyssal ley shivering along his skin, but she clearly knew it was there.

"Why?"

"Because I can't explain it in words. I have to show you."

"Oh, hell no," Nikola said, her silver tooth winking.

"It won't hurt."

She shook her head, but he could see her weakening. Too curious, this one. Malach waggled his fingers.

"Going once," he said. "Going twice."

She crossed her arms. "I don't trust the ley."

"Because you've never experienced it the way I have. I could give you a taste of the forbidden fruit. Not a Mark." He smiled seductively. "Just a nibble."

Malach didn't know why he was doing this and didn't care, only that it felt right.

"What does that even mean?" she demanded. "A nibble?"

"What it's like. I can show you."

"How?"

His smile died. "No more words."

Nikola bit her lower lip. She had a mobile, expressive face, and Malach watched the debate play out. She pretended to conform to society's demands, while inside she seethed with resentment and boredom. She claimed to want nothing to do with the ley, but at the same time, she craved novelty. Risk. That was an essential part of her. Secretly, Malach thought, Nikola Thorn wanted to go places most feared to tread. And he was the only one who could lead her there.

"I'm trusting you," she said. "Because I'm an idiot."

Nikola took his hand.

RED SUN on the backs of your eyelids.

Brown, itchy grass under your back and the chirr of a billion insects in the undergrowth. It's the first time you've felt the ley in half a year and you have an erection that won't quit, but part of it is because you're fourteen and your body has a mind of its own—or more accurately, no mind at all, just endless unsated lust. If you'd been alone, you'd remedy the situation, but even nihilim have some standards and your aunt is within shouting distance, doing what she always does when the ley floods, which is to study the stelae and see if she can find a way to break them.

You rest a hand on your chest, feeling the heat in your Marks, and for once you don't hate them for reminding you of all you don't have, no, you feel *powerful*, though you know it won't last because the ley is receding, minute by minute, sinking back into the earth. Back to the grid and the Blue Zones. In another two or three days, it will be gone and your Marks won't fade, but they will mean nothing again.

The anticipated rage and frustration is almost unbearable. How you could still have a hard-on remains a profound mystery, yet there's no denying that right now you also feel wonderful, whole and capable of anything. *The Void is my oyster*, you say out loud, and you start to laugh, which draws a grin from your aunt.

"Get over here, Malach," she calls, and you don't particularly want to, but ignoring Beleth when she orders you to do something is a bad idea, so you amble over, bits of dead grass stuck to the sweat on your chest, and have a look although you know it's pointless because if stelae could be broken, you'd be drinking wine in the Arx right now while the Pontifex washed your feet, not living like an exile in the ruins.

Beleth ruffles your hair as if you're a little boy and you jerk away, irritated, which provokes a chuckle. "I suppose you think that makes you a man," she says, glancing down, which finally does the trick. Your pants deflate, but you don't feel embarrassed because everyone knows what teenaged boys are like and you can hardly be blamed for that.

Shame and remorse of any kind are foreign to you.

Beleth takes your hand. Hers is sweaty, too. She has long brown hair, mixed with gray, and wears a man's shirt and man's pants, rolled up at the bottom, over heavy boots. Sometimes, on new moon nights, she'll paint her face and curl her hair and wear ballgowns pilfered from the wreckage, but you prefer her this way because it's real and the other Beleth is just a sad imitation of who she used to be.

You would never tell her this, however, because Beleth has a temper.

"What do you see, Malach?" she asks.

The stela is ten paces tall, square and tapering to a point at the top. A raven is carved into the side facing you, and an inscription, but it's too far away to read. The whole thing glows with blue ley. It sits on a juncture of the grid that used to be inside a manicured park and is now your preferred hunting ground.

"A Wardstone," you say in a bored drawl.

"What do the words say?"

You glance at her with a shrug. You've been warned never to approach a stela. "I don't know."

"Then go find out."

A sinking feeling in your gut. "Why?"

"Because I'm telling you to, that's why." Her tone never changes, but you detect a shift in the psychic weather. You are very attuned to such changes because Beleth is a great teacher of lessons and a clever pupil learns to figure out what they are and get them over with as quickly as possible.

You walk toward the stela, squinting in the bright sun. The letters are chiseled into the stone and you make out the first one, but the other words are long and the sun is coming from behind, casting them in shadow.

"Pax?" you call over your shoulder.

"And?' A hint of impatience. "What else?"

Two more steps and your skin erupts in sweat. Not the regular sweat you live with every day. Icy sweat. You swallow, suddenly nauseous. Take another step.

"Pax int . . . intrantibus," you stammer.

"Good," she says. "Keep going, Malach."

The ley pulses in your Marks, throbbing painfully in time with your heart. A shiver wracks you. The raven stares, mocking, and you force yourself to take two more steps. Hot needles prick every centimeter of flesh. Anger wells, but not at Beleth. You understand why she is doing this. The lesson.

You want to fall down, to writhe in agony, but you will not indulge yourself. You take another step. The final words snap into focus through a red haze, as if your eyes were bleeding.

"Pax intrantibus salus exeuntibus," you say in a strong, steady voice.

"Translation?"

You spit blood. It misses the stela because you're still too far, but there's something undeniably satisfying about it. Out of sheer stubbornness, you take one more step, and now the pain closes its fist, which perversely makes you hard again because the mind works in very strange ways sometimes.

"Peace to those who enter," you say casually. "Health to those who depart."

"Come back, Malach." She sounds pleased. You have passed her test, as you knew you would because you always do.

You do not run. No, you stand there for a moment more, contemplating the abomination they've planted in your city, and then you turn and saunter back to your aunt. The fist opens, but the ghost of that agony lives in your bones now and you know that when the ley recedes, it will still be there. This is the lesson.

"Someday," Beleth says, "you will topple that stela and fuck someone on it. Or whatever else you're in the mood for. Do you believe me, Malach?"

You nod seriously. You do believe her.

"I will give you another Mark tonight," she says. "While we still have ley."

"Where?" you ask, eager.

She looks you over. You have six Marks already, each one

earned except for the first, which is given to all nihilim at birth. That one came from your mother, who is dead. The rest are from Beleth.

She touches you lightly on the left hip, where there is a swathe of tanned skin running up your side to the nipple. You haven't reached your full height and your ribs poke out because you have to catch what you eat and you tend to be lazy, but a Mark would look fine there.

"What will it be?" you ask, knowing the answer.

"The ley decides," she says with a smile.

A flock of birds erupts from the canopy above. Her head turns and then you hear it too, the high whine of an incoming shell. It lands in an explosion of earth and rocks and smoke. You fly through the air and land on your back, not far from where you started before the whole stela thing. A second shell hits moments later, this one a little distance off, and you think your hair might be singed, you're certainly bruised and bleeding, but the shells are just to soften you up, within minutes the knights will come, so you get up and you run. You don't see Beleth, but she wouldn't wait for you, a mage who can't run on their own wouldn't last long anyway, so you don't worry about her, you just run and run, and the cicadas are quiet now, everything is quiet except for the booming of the guns, and all you can think of is that she'd better be alive because you still want your Mark tonight so you can grow up and kill every single fucking one of them.

MALACH RELEASED THE LEY. Nikola's fingers gripped his own so tightly they'd gone numb. He gently disengaged his hand. The memory was an old one and held no power, but she was shaken—as he'd intended.

"Where was that?" she whispered.

"Home." He suddenly wanted her badly. Malach ran a fingertip down the side of her breast, feeling the nipple stiffen through the cotton nightgown. Nikola batted his hand away. She sat on the arm of the chair and he wanted to pull her down to his lap but restrained the impulse. *Too fast. Give her time to recover.*

"Bal Agnar?" she guessed.

"Bal Kirith."

"Did that happen? Was it true?"

He nodded.

"Saints," she muttered. "Did she survive? Your aunt?"

Malach turned to display the Mark on his left hip. "I didn't find her until the next day, but there was still enough ley."

Nikola stared at the Mark, a two-headed serpent devouring some nameless creature. "A snake doesn't exactly surprise me," she said, "given your preoccupations."

Malach laughed. "What I did is called a sweven. A vision carried by the ley from my mind to yours. In this case, it was a memory, but I could share a dream or fantasy. I have lots of those. Any special requests?"

Nikola didn't find this amusing. "Have you done it to me before?"

"Every choice you've made is your own, Domina Thorn."

"That's not an answer."

"No," he said. "I haven't."

"Does it go both ways? Could you steal memories from my head?"

"Not without your consent. If you opened your mind to me, yes."

Swevens were related to compulsion, but far more graphic and explicit. It was the difference between hearing a symphony orchestra perform live and reading the notes on a sheet. If only he could have extracted Kasia Novak's memories of the last two days, he'd know what Massot's letter said. But he couldn't force her, so he'd used the same technique as he had on Cardinal Falke. She'd been about to tell him when the damned Markhounds showed up.

Nikola let out a breath. "I thought my childhood was rough, but you win, Malach."

"It wasn't all bad." He studied her. "What about your family?"

"What about them?"

"Are they alive?"

"Yeah. They're nice people. But I don't want their charity."

"What do you want?"

"This again? I told you."

"No, you've told me what you don't want, which is to live under the boot heel of the Curia. What will you do when you reach Dur-Athaara? What makes you happy?"

She looked away. "I don't know."

Her pulse beat swiftly in the hollow of her neck. The sweven had gotten to her. Not the end of it, which was just adrenaline, but the beginning. When she felt the ley through him. Malach cupped her bare knee. Power warmed his palm, but he held it inside.

A crooked smile. "Come to bed with me."

Her eyes widened. "Has anyone ever told you that you have a perverse notion of foreplay?"

"I'll wear my glasses if you want. Give your books a thorough auditing."

"Haven't changed much, have you?"

He thought about it. "Not really."

She laughed. "And you think having sex with you will change my mind about the Mark?"

"No." He stood and wrapped the ends of the blanket around her, so they were cocooned together. She didn't resist when he lowered his head and kissed her neck. "But it would make you feel better."

"Me? Or you?"

"Both."

Nikola fingered the hair at his nape, still damp from the rain. "I don't like what you just did to me. The sweven. Don't do it again."

He could hardly think straight. The smell of her filled his nose. "Okay."

"You'll never touch me with the ley. I mean it, Malach."

He buried his face in her hair. "Only to monitor the health of the child."

She hesitated. "Only that. And you'll ask first."

His hands cupped her bottom, kneading gently.

"Say it," she growled.

"I'll ask first," he replied impatiently.

Nikola kissed him and the hunger rose up, blotting out everything but her. Malach stepped back and let the blanket fall. He pulled the shift over her head and tossed it away. He hurt, but the pain only heightened the pleasure. This time, Nikola was less inhibited. He made himself lie still as her fingers moved over his Marks, tracing the sinuous lines of the broken chain circling his neck and working their way downward.

Malach told her the names. *Dark Mirror. Lady of Masks. Blinded to Agony. The Red Warden. Summoning the Storm. Today for Tomorrow. Tiger in a Cage.*

When he finally slept, his head brimmed with wild, vivid dreams.

Chapter Nineteen

❧❀❧

B ells tolled midnight as a pair of long black automobiles
approached the Dacian Gate. The one carrying Fra
Bryce peeled off as soon as it passed into the inner precincts
of the Arx. Kasia watched taillights vanish into the rain.

"Where are they taking him?" she asked.

The priests in the front seat didn't reply.

"Am I under arrest?"

Again, not a twitch.

She had never been inside the walls before. The day her
grade visited the Arx on a field trip, Kasia had feigned illness,
knowing her classmates would whisper about her behind their
hands. Somehow, they'd learned her secret. She had been
tested and found wanting. No one laughed or mocked her to
her face, though. They were too afraid of what she might do
to them.

Now she gazed out the rain-streaked window at the
glowing Wards that stretched in every direction. For the first
time, she could see them herself. Malach had done something
to her—something to lift the veil of ley-blindness that afflicted
all Unmarked. The Wards were the unearthly blue of a very
hot flame, bright yet failing to illuminate the space around

them. If anything, they made the surrounding darkness even more impenetrable.

As the car drove beneath the motto etched above the marble archway, *Post tenebras lux*, the hair on the back of her neck stirred. The Arx was an ancient place, more than a thousand years old, and she could feel it resonating in her bones, the weight of all that devotion steeped into the stonework.

Light after the dark.

She followed the Via Sancta—everyone did—but until that moment, she had misunderstood the Church's power. It wasn't the Marks, or even the ley. It was the faithful. The true believers like Fra Bryce, who had sacrificed everything for the dream of a better world.

The last bell faded. Even the rain sank to a whisper inside the moss-covered walls.

Kasia slipped a hand into her pocket, the familiar smooth texture of the cards offering some measure of reassurance. After Alexei pursued Malach to the roof, she'd returned to the coffee table and swept them up, intending to flee down the stairs. Two had slipped from her grasp, falling directly at her feet.

The Fool, lying crosswise over the Knight.

She had known then that if she ran away, Bryce would die. Funny how the thought made her feel so cold when only a short time before he'd been her enemy.

Now she wondered what secrets he'd held back.

Alexei had caught her eye as they shoved him into the back of the lead vehicle. A warning look.

Keep silent about the letters. About everything.

Kasia expected to be taken to a cell, but the car stopped in front of a three-story brick building with a circular gravel drive. A priest opened her door and escorted her inside. Kasia stood dripping in a marble entry hall. Enormous oil portraits of men and women in purple robes hung on the walls. Elaborate plasterwork scrolls traced the high ceiling. It looked like a museum, but something told her these weren't Curia offices.

The priest led her to the end of a hallway just as richly decorated as the foyer, where tall doors stood wide, revealing a walnut-paneled library. A man with short silver hair sat reading in the glow of several large candelabra, purple robes framing broad shoulders. He closed the book as they entered. It was a copy of the *Meliora*, the foundational text of the Via Sancta written by the Praefators a thousand years before, whose title meant "ever better" in the old tongue, or, more fully, "for the pursuit of the better." Falke's face was square and smooth, the expression neutral.

"Your Eminence," Kasia said, bending a knee.

The priest withdrew, silently shutting the doors.

"Please, sit down," Cardinal Falke said. He had a rich, commanding voice, but it wasn't unfriendly.

Kasia took an armchair next to the tall diamond-paned windows and crossed her legs. She met his assured gaze with a level stare of her own.

"First, I wish to apologize on behalf of the Curia," he said. "It's unacceptable that one of our own should have placed you in such danger. Had I known of your involvement in this unfortunate affair, I would have brought you here immediately."

"Fra Bryce didn't—"

The cardinal held up a black-gloved finger and she subsided. "Worse is the fact that a nihilim somehow managed to enter the city. But I can assure you, you'll be perfectly safe here."

The way he said it made Kasia wonder how long they planned to keep her. "What about Natalya?"

"We located Domina Anderle an hour ago. She is unharmed and resting in a room at this moment."

A weight eased from Kasia's chest. "I would like to see her, Your Eminence."

"Of course." He smiled. "In the morning."

"Have you found the mage yet?"

The smile slipped a notch. "Not yet. But he cannot elude us forever. It's fortunate we found you when we did. I understand Bryce has a vendetta against this mage and used you to draw him out."

"Fra Bryce is not to blame. He tried to protect me and nearly died for it." She held the cardinal's gaze. "A serious mistake has been made, Your Eminence. I heard Bryce speak to the doctor. He's a gentle man."

"Gentle?" Cardinal Falke chuckled. "He was a Knight of Saint Jule before joining the Interfectorem."

"I know, Your Eminence. He told me."

The cardinal nodded slowly. "Did he tell you he was in the Beatus Laqueo?"

Kasia had never heard of it, but there were so many divisions within the Church. "No."

"A specialized order of the knights. The main force would put the nihilim on the run and get them cornered in the ruins. When every exit was sealed, they'd send in the Beatus Laqueo. The Holy Noose tightening around our enemies' necks. They trained in shock tactics. Fra Bryce volunteered for it."

Kasia said nothing.

"The laquei received Marks for valor in combat. Fra Bryce has nineteen. Do you know what it takes to earn that many?" He smirked. "No, of course you wouldn't. But trust me, gentle Fra Bryce is not."

Kasia misliked the patronizing tone. "That was war, Your Eminence. He only did what he was ordered to."

"You misunderstand. It's not a criticism. In fact, I have great admiration for him. It's not an easy thing to kill, even when the cause is righteous." Falke paused. "Marks are designed to reconcile emotional conflict, but the human race is still a work in progress, Domina Novak."

She looked down to hide her confusion. Did he know she was Unmarked?

"Instinct is a powerful thing," Falke continued. "Even the best of us are not yet immune to our base nature." He leaned forward, face shining with conviction. "But future generations will be, thanks to the sacrifices made by men like Fra Bryce."

"If you hold him in such high regard, why is he being punished?"

The cardinal frowned. "It's not punitive to carry out the law. We have a witness who claims he assaulted Ferran Massot minutes before the body was found—coincidentally, also by Bryce." His voice was dry. "The apostolic tribunal will decide his fate."

"What will happen if he's found guilty?"

"He'll be cast out beyond the Wards."

"Of the Arx?"

"Of the city."

"A former knight exiled to the Void?" Her voice was cold. "Why don't you just execute him? It would be a cleaner death than he'll get from the mages. Or does the Curia lack the stomach for it?"

Falke's bland expression never altered. "That is the penalty, Domina Novak. Capital punishment is banned by the *Meliora*, as you well know."

"It amounts to the same thing."

"No. His blood will be on the hands of the nihilim, not ours."

She steadied herself. If one intended to blackmail a cardinal, best to do it with a cool head. "Do you have a say in the verdict, Your Eminence?"

He gazed at her curiously. "Why do you ask?"

She must be mad. But Beatus Laqueo or not, she suspected Alexei was innocent. And she felt an odd responsibility for him.

"I have something that might interest you."

He gave her a kindly smile. "Do you?"

"When I was at Massot's house—"

"He gave you a message for me." The cardinal opened a drawer and took out a brass tube. "Don't worry, my dear, I have it right here. So you see, there is nothing more for you to worry about." He rose, eyes glittering. "A room has been prepared. You will stay within the Arx until the mage has been found."

Kasia bowed her head. "Your Eminence."

One cylinder. Did he have both messages? What had Tessaria done?

"Domina Novak?"

Kasia turned at the door.

"Don't trouble yourself over Fra Bryce. If he is innocent, it will come to light. Justice is always served here."

Kasia doubted this, coming as it did from a man who'd conspired with Ferran Massot to experiment on the mentally ill, but there was little point in arguing. "Can I see him?"

The smile never wavered. "He will need to meet with his advocate. Give another statement and prepare for trial. But I'll take your request under consideration."

In other words, not a chance. Kasia bent her knee, privately seething. "Thank you, Your Eminence."

The same priest was waiting outside the door. He drove her to a fortress-like building and turned her over to a vestal with a motherly face and brisk manner. Sor Chernov wore a cassock identical to the brothers and had a Raven Mark on her neck, though on the right side rather than the left.

Torches sputtered in ornate iron brackets as they entered the Castel Saint Agathe. Pre-Dark Age for certain, Kasia thought, eyeing the thick walls and ribbed stone vaulting. The air smelled like smoke and centuries-old wood. A few gray-clad chars moved silently through the halls, eyes cast down, but it was late and most of the sisters were sleeping.

On the top floor, Sor Chernov opened the door to a small

chamber. It held a narrow bed with a cedar chest at the foot, a table with a bowl and pitcher, and a single narrow slit that served as a window.

"The privy is at the end of the hall," she said, handing Kasia a lit candle. "You'll find a clean shift in the chest."

"Thank you."

The vestal departed. Kasia set the candle on the deep stone windowsill. She undressed, put on the cotton shift, and crawled under the blanket. The bed was hard as a stone bier, but she was too tired to care. She clutched the cards to her cheek, the precise edges and smooth, waxy surface lulling her like a cherished childhood doll.

Falke underestimates me, she thought. Just like Ferran Massot did when I . . . .

The rest was lost as the dark tide of sleep dragged her under.

Chapter Twenty

A lexei walked down a series of steep staircases and narrow passageways, escorted by four silent agents of the OGD. He lost all sense of direction except for the undeniable fact that they were heading into the deepest, oldest part of the Arx. With each step, the air grew colder and danker. Pale lichen crusted the stone walls. At last they paused in a tunnel with a low, arched-brick ceiling and rows of barred cells stretching into the gloom, all of them empty.

"Face the wall," Fra Talgatov said.

Heavy chains snapped shut around his ankles. Warded manacles already circled his wrists, blocking him from the ley.

"I have the right to an advocate," Alexei said as they pushed him inside a cell.

"You'll get one," Talgatov said curtly. "At the archbishop's pleasure."

The door clanged shut. Footsteps receded.

The cell was bare, lit only by the single torch they'd left burning in the corridor. When it went out, he'd be in darkness except for the glowing Ward above the door.

Alexei surveyed the cell. The floor was uneven and stagnant water pooled in the cavities, but he found a dry corner.

As he settled down, he saw he wasn't the first prisoner to claim this patch of higher ground. Alexei ran a finger along the letters scratched into the wall.

Mox nox.

Soon, nightfall.

The etching was old, barely a shade lighter than the surrounding stone, but a mage had been held here at some point. The Saints only knew what he or she had used to gouge the stone so deeply. Alexei shivered and turned away.

The minutes dragged by. The torch sputtered and died. His chin sank to his chest, but sleep stubbornly refused to come. How long since he'd dozed off while typing his report? They'd gone to the Institute afterward and the traffic was light so it must have been Sunday morning.

What day was it now?

Alexei hadn't the slightest idea. He rubbed his hands together, trying to produce some warmth, but he felt disembodied. The ache in his ribs seemed distant. Even the various lumps on his head belonged to someone else.

And he was starting to see things.

Phantoms hovering at the edge of sight. Alexei had experienced this before after especially bad bouts of insomnia. *The Gray.* A place where the line between past and present blurred to mist. A twilight place where ghosts walked.

Once, when he was five, he'd fallen through the rotting, leaf-camouflaged cover of an old well during a game of hide and seek. He'd screamed himself hoarse for two hours before Mikhail found him. His father had given Misha a wicked hiding later that day (as the elder, he was held accountable), but when they pulled Alexei out of the well, traumatized, with a broken arm but otherwise unharmed, his father had wept— the only time Alexei had ever seen him display emotion. Even when their mother died, he'd remained dry-eyed.

The cell reminded Alexei of the well. Deep and dark and quiet.

Except that this time, Misha would not be coming to save him.

The shadows shifted. Hot breath tickled his ear.

I didn't even plan to turn your brother that day. Call it a favor for an enemy, laqueus.

All around him, he sensed things stirring. The hair on his arms rose up as, with infinite slowness, a crouching shape resolved in the opposite corner.

Mikhail, gaunt and bloodless, feeding tubes trailing from his nose.

I did it for you, Alyosha. I did it for you and look what it cost me, you faithless bastard—

"Alyosha?"

Alexei blinked in the sudden flare of a torch. The phantoms fled. His first thought was that Spassov was another hallucination, but then he smelled food.

"Patryk?" he called hoarsely.

"I brought you a pierogi." Spassov placed the torch in a bracket. "How are you holding up?"

Alexei climbed to his feet. The pain in his side brought the world into focus again. He lurched up to the bars.

"I had him," Alexei said in anguish. "I had him and he got away."

Spassov leaned in. He looked rougher than usual. "Forget the mage, brother. You're in serious trouble."

"I didn't kill Massot!"

"I know. I told them so."

"They need to question the old man. He'll tell them he saw me."

"I'll make sure of it." Spassov hesitated. "But he's Invertido. Not the most reliable witness." He held up a foil-wrapped package and a glass bottle of water. "From that stand you like by Komsomol Fountain."

Alexei ate the pierogi in six bites, then downed the glass bottle of water. He licked the wrapper and tossed it away.

"Listen," Spassov said heavily. "They found a bloody knife hidden in your room. The blood type matches Massot's."

"What?"

His partner's bluff face registered pity. "You've made someone very upset, Alyosha. I don't know what to do."

"Nothing," Alexei muttered.

"But—"

"You'll do nothing. They'd only destroy us both."

Spassov was quiet for a moment. Then he took out his flask, offering it. Alexei had always refused, but now he took a bracing swig. Straight vodka. He coughed, eyes watering. Heat flooded his chest.

"What happened to Kasia Novak?" he asked, returning the flask.

"They took her to Cardinal Falke. That's all I know."

Alexei closed his eyes. "I ruined her life for nothing," he muttered. "She must hate me. And she has every right to."

"What are you talking about?"

"Never mind. I need to see Kireyev."

"I'll convey the message. They found some banned books in your room, too. Stuff on Nightmarks."

"Those are mine. But not the knife!"

"I'll be a character witness, okay? We both know you're the last person who would kill an Invertido." Spassov smiled awkwardly. "I mean, you've stopped me from doing it a hundred times."

"They don't care if I'm guilty or innocent. But I appreciate the offer."

Spassov blew out a breath. "This is wrong, Alyosha. It's not what we stand for. Framing innocent men." He took a long pull from the flask. "Just tell me one thing. How far does it go?"

"Far enough that you can't stop it."

"You're allowed to have family visit. Anyone I should call?"

"No."

Spassov looked away. He seemed ashamed, even though none of it was his fault. "Well, then. Try to get some sleep, eh?"

The cog holding Alexei's sanity in place slipped another notch. He gripped the bars. It took all his restraint not to reach through them and grab poor Spassov by the throat. "Please, Patryk. I want Kireyev. Tell him I'll confess. Anything! Just get him down here. Or have me brought up."

Spassov nodded vigorously. "Of course. And I'll come back as soon as I can."

The mist was closing in again. Maybe he shouldn't have drunk the vodka.

"Why did they let you in anyway?" he muttered.

"I know the guards," Spassov said. "We play dominos on Thursday nights." He laid a hand over Alexei's. "Don't give up, eh? You might get a miracle."

Phantoms capered behind him, just beyond the edge of the torchlight.

"*Kireyev*," Alexei mumbled, clinging to reality by a thread.

"Okay, okay. I'll do everything I can, Alyosha, I promise."

Spassov left. Alexei sat against the wall.

He dug the letter Kasia had copied for him out of his boot and tried to decipher the meaning behind Massot's cryptic words. Certain phrases caught his eye, but every time he felt near to a breakthrough, it slipped away.

The torchlight dimmed. And the phantoms crept ever closer.

Mox nox.

Soon, nightfall.

Alexei traced the letters. They were wrong.

Night was already here.

Chapter Twenty-One

❧❦❧

Nikola was sitting in a chair drinking coffee when Malach woke. She was also naked, which he found distracting. He wondered how he'd feel when she was visibly pregnant. If it would turn him on more, or less, or make no difference. There was no way of telling. Passions came and went, and he acted on them or didn't, depending on his mood.

The only constant was his hatred of the Via Sancta.

"I figured it out," she said, eying him over the rim of a cracked mug. "You're trying to scare me off. It won't work."

"They don't shell us anymore." Malach rolled his left shoulder, working out the stiffness. "Not since the Cold Truce. It's Beleth you should be afraid of when we get to the Void."

"*If* we get there," she said tartly.

"You think I can't come and go as I please?"

"From the city. Not from the Arx."

"I haven't been inside before, that's true. But there's always a way."

"Then why haven't you tried before?"

"It wasn't worth the price. Now it is."

Nikola gave him a defiant look. "I'll help you," she said. "On one condition."

He waited.

"I don't want to be a mother. When this child is born, you'll take it away."

"You won't even nurse it?"

"I don't know. Maybe for a little while. But I don't want to be responsible for it."

He shrugged. In truth, that suited him perfectly. "Half-blood children grow fast. I'm sure he or she will be self-sufficient in no time."

"You don't mind?"

He looked at her, puzzled. "Why would I?"

She set her coffee down and came over to the bed, perching on the edge. "Will you Mark the child?"

"Of course."

Nikola studied his chest. She reached out a hand—and snatched it back with a strangled curse. "It moved!"

"You didn't look so horrified last night," Malach said dryly.

"Not *that*. The Mark!"

"Which one?"

"Lady of Masks. She turned her head and *looked at me*."

"Oh." He closed his eyes. "The ley is rising. It makes her feisty."

"But she's you, isn't she?"

"Mmm-hmm."

"I'll never understand how any of this works," Nikola said.

Malach opened his eyes. She'd bent a knee and propped her elbow on it, resting her chin on one fist. It reminded him of a picture he'd seen in an old book, but he couldn't remember which.

"Don't be sad," he said, pulling her on top of him. "I'll show you how something else works."

Thus they idled the day away. He went for takeout noodles and they ate naked with chopsticks on the bed. He told her what he was after and who had it.

"You'll never get into the cardinal's residence," she said.

"I don't need the letter itself. Only its contents."

"Who's read it?"

"Besides Falke? Two others."

"Why don't you ask them?"

Malach fed her a slice of yellow pepper. "They're inside the Arx, too."

Nikola chewed thoughtfully. "Men or women?"

"Women."

"They'll be with the vestals then."

Malach scraped the last noodles from the paper box. "Is that easier?"

"Compared to the cardinal's residence?" Nikola laughed. "Much easier. But I still don't see how you'll get past the Wards. If a single stela did that to you, the Arx will be a thousand times worse." Her face darkened at the memory. "It might kill you, Malach."

"Doubtful." He gave a tight smile. "Not that I expect it to be pleasant."

"You don't know what will happen."

He set the box aside. "Pain is in the mind."

"You spat blood. That's not imagination."

"Well, I guess I'll find out."

"This is stupid." She glared at him. "How do you know the letter is worth dying for if you don't even know what's in it?"

Malach leaned over and lit a candle. Dusk was falling. Through the grimy window, he could see the glow of the Arx against the evening sky. The mighty citadel. A generation of mages had died inside those walls. He didn't mourn them. They'd had it easy compared to the one that followed—what was left of it—and they'd still lost because they failed to understand basic martial strategy, foremost of which was to know one's own emotional blind spots. The mages were arrogant. They couldn't fathom the idea that the ley might be taken from them. Malach, who'd lived most of his life severed from his powers, was more pragmatic. He assumed nothing and expected the worst. If he had ley, he'd use it. If not, he'd fight with whatever was at hand.

"Because Falke will do anything to keep it from me," Malach said. "And if he wants something, I oppose it."

"Your pride will be your undoing, Malach."

"It's not pride," he said, tipping his head back. The abyssal ley tugged at him like a dark tide. "It's hatred."

Nikola sighed. "Let me go in your place."

Under other circumstances, Malach would have leapt at the offer. Under other circumstances, he would have subtly planted the suggestion and let her think she'd proposed it herself. But not this time.

"No," he said.

"Why not?"

"Is Falke's residence part of your regular rounds?"

She shook her head. "But his aides know my face. I could slip inside—"

"And you'd be caught. You're not falling into his hands," Malach said harshly.

Her gaze narrowed. "So I have no say in this?"

Malach laced his hands behind his head. "What do you think they'd do to a woman who's carrying a half-breed child?"

"Why would they even know? You just knocked me up yesterday."

"Oh, they'd find out. One way or another. They'd lock you up until you gave birth, and then they'd thank you for your service to humanity and they'd cut your throat and throw your body in the river. They'd keep the child, but the mother is too dangerous because she knows what it is. So let's do it my way instead."

Nikola stared at him. "You're a bastard, you know that?"

"I'm just being honest."

"Fine," she said. "Go kill yourself. I have to get ready for work."

She pulled on a gray shift and gray cloak and tied her hair up in the scarf. It was still pouring, so she grabbed a pair of rubber boots.

"There's another way to help," he said. "The risk would be much less."

Nikola's lips pursed in the way of annoyed women everywhere. "What do you want now?"

"Can you find out which room Kasia Novak is staying in?"

"Maybe."

"She'll be with Tessaria Foy. Either one of them will do."

Nikola rounded on him. "And what happens if you do get inside and find them? Will you kill them?"

"I don't know."

Her eyes went flat. "You *don't know*."

He sensed a conversational minefield. "Does it matter?"

"Yes, it matters! Saints, Malach, they've never done you wrong. Falke used them."

"Well, I'm not planning to kill them, if that makes you feel better. It serves no purpose if I can use compulsion instead."

She yanked on her gloves. "You're a seriously messed up person."

"You don't like it when I'm honest," he observed.

"Maybe I just don't like *you*."

That stung. He gave her a lazy smile. "You don't have to like me. It's not a requirement of this alliance."

"Is that how you see the world, Malach? Enemies and allies? Well, I'm neither one. Get me to the coast and find a ship bound for Dur-Athaara. I'll give you the child and we'll never see each other again. But in the meantime, I won't enable your lack of a moral compass."

He looked pointedly at her gray cloak. "I thought your moral compass was defective, too."

"Defective isn't the same as missing completely."

"I'll take that as a compliment."

"Take it any way you want." Her gaze was ice. "But if you hurt those women, the deal is off."

"How would you know if I did or not?"

Nikola Thorn stared at him, unblinking. "I'd know."

Malach thought she just might. "Then I won't."

Nikola shook her head. She grabbed an umbrella. "Do me a favor, Malach?"

He waited.

"Since you're here anyway, could you take out the trash and wash a few dishes?" She surveyed the mound of takeout containers. "The flat's even more of a pigsty since you showed up."

"I can do that."

"And try not to assault any of my neighbors."

"Only if they play loud music," he said.

She grinned, silver tooth winking, and banged out the door.

Chapter Twenty-Two

"Thank the Saints they found you in time."

Kasia glanced over. "I was perfectly fine, Auntie."

Tessaria Foy shot her a dark look. Inside the walls of the Arx, she wore a long midnight blue cassock. It swished at her feet as they walked. "I assumed you'd be grateful for my intervention."

Natalya strolled ahead, stooping here and there to sketch a flower. She had an artist's love of nature and was always looking for inspiration. The gardens surrounding the Pontifex's Palace were lush and fragrant, but Kasia hardly noticed.

"Bryce was harassing you. I thought his superiors ought to know about it."

"I explicitly told you not to do that," Kasia snapped.

Nashka didn't turn around, but Kasia knew she heard every word. Her friend wisely steered clear when the two women argued. She'd also seemed hungover this morning, subsisting on black coffee at breakfast and wincing when Kasia offered her a bowl of honeyed rice.

Tessaria's tone grew chill. "I assumed you'd be grateful. He won't trouble you again."

"Because he's under arrest for murder!"

"That has nothing to do with me," Tessaria pointed out. "Though it makes me feel entirely justified in reporting him. Bryce is dangerous."

Kasia kicked a twig from her path. "What about the letters? You just handed those over without asking me?"

"As I recall, they belong to Cardinal Falke," Tessaria replied dryly. "I thought you were eager to be rid of them. Was I supposed to lie to a senior member of the clergy and claim I had no knowledge of them?"

Kasia lowered her voice. "Does he know about me?"

"Of course."

"Why does he tolerate the pretense?"

"A personal favor."

"I didn't know you were so close to the cardinal." Suspicion edged her voice. "You're not really retired, are you?"

Tessaria smiled. "We all serve the Via Sancta."

"That's not what I'm asking."

The older woman arched a perfectly plucked brow.

"Who," Kasia said flatly, "did you telephone?"

Tessaria sighed. "Archbishop Kireyev."

The truth dawned. "You're in his pocket, aren't you?"

There was a pregnant pause. Tessaria fiddled with her gloves.

"As are you," she finally replied in an offhand way.

Kasia ground to a halt. "*What?*"

"Come, Kiska. Did you really think it was just idle gossip?"

"Fog it all, yes!" She scowled. "Does Natalya know?"

"Know what?" Nashka asked warily. Bleached spiral curls bounced around her head as she strode over. She was still wearing her outfit from the night before, a shimmery sheathe that covered her skin but left little to the imagination. Even hung over, Nashka was a vision. Eggplant-dark gloss made her full lips appear even more lush.

"That we're fogging spies."

Nashka glanced between them. "Heh?"

"Apparently, we work for General Directorate." Angry as Kasia was, the last two words came out in a whispered hiss, and only after looking around to ensure the adjacent paths were deserted.

"Grow up, both of you," Tessaria said wearily. "Half the city reports to the archbishop in one way or another."

Nashka shot a *holy shit* look at Kasia, but held her tongue. It wasn't so bad for her. She focused on designing the cards and rarely gave readings. Kasia was the one who could recall every spread she'd ever dealt and every word her clients uttered. Tessaria had a way of drawing it all out in casual conversation, but she saw now that it was in fact a debriefing.

Kasia had known most of her clients for years. Every one was a referral from Tessaria Foy, meaning they were prominent people—bankers and judges, deans at the Lyceum, luminaries in Novo's art world. They believed the ley was speaking to them through the cards and it loosened the bonds of their own Marks, exposing intimate secrets. Sexual dysfunction. Family conflict. Petty jealousies. Hidden fears and desires.

Kasia never probed, but something about her inspired their confidence. By the second or third reading—and occasionally even the first—clients often revealed personal details they had never told anyone before. Now she'd betrayed their trust utterly.

Fury clenched her gloved hands, but it was directed mostly at herself. Tessaria was right. Some part of Kasia had suspected, but she needed the money and more than that, she needed Tessaria's protection. So she hadn't asked any of the obvious questions, such as why a retired vestal was permitted to live in opulence outside the Arx.

Kasia couldn't exactly claim the high road. It became a habit to indulge in juicy gossip whenever she went to No. 7 Lesnoy Prospect. A wicked game of kiss-and-tell. Except that she'd always believed Tessaria to be the soul of discretion.

Keeping secrets is easy. It's the people you tell who can't keep their fogging mouths shut.

"Don't take it so hard," Tessaria said with a note of sympathy. "They keep files on everyone. It's just the way things are done. I don't think the archbishop uses half the dirt he digs up."

"He just holds it as leverage," Kasia said flatly.

She fell silent as they passed a pair of knights in the blue and gold livery of the Pontifex's guard, both young, stern-faced women with swords at their hips. Tessaria nodded politely. Nashka gave the knights an appraising glance, earning a grin from the taller one. She was an incorrigible flirt and remorseless rake, with a trail of broken hearts littered across Novostopol, male and female. Kasia couldn't blame them for falling so hard. She loved Natalya madly herself, though only as a sister, thank the Saints.

The gardens spread over several acres. White-pebbled pathways meandered between clumps of arrow-wood, pepperbush and black chokeberry. When the knights turned a corner, Tessaria rounded on Kasia.

"Do you know how many refugees from Bal Kirith and Bal Agnar flooded the city during the war?" she demanded.

"I've no idea," Kasia said sullenly.

"Thousands. Most were just desperate to escape the atrocities being committed in the Morho, but some were infiltrators for the mages. Not all had Nightmarks. Our enemies were smarter than that. It was impossible to weed out every nihilim sympathizer and the Pontifex refused to turn people back at the gates."

"So?"

"They sabotaged the telephone and electric lines. Set off bombs in crowded areas. One of the hydro dams was nearly blown to bits. Thousands would have died in the flood. It was only thanks to information gathered by Archbishop Kireyev that the plot was discovered in time." Tessaria's tone softened.

"I know you don't remember any of it. You hadn't been born yet. But I do. They were dark days, Kasia. If trading in secrets helps keep us all safe, it's a small price to pay."

"I understand that." Up ahead, Nashka had her nose pressed to a bush heavy with white blooms. She disliked confrontation, preferring the jest and quick getaway. "But don't you think the net is being cast rather wide? None of my clients has any history of treason. The opposite!"

"Perhaps, but they all wield power of a sort. Look at Ferran Massot. He wore a mask of respectability, and the man beneath it was a monster who nearly . . . ." Tessaria cut off.

"Nearly what?"

The older woman gave her a level look. "You have a way with people. Can you honestly claim that if you had given Massot readings before he turned, you wouldn't have suspected anything was amiss?"

"You still should have told me. Given me a choice."

"And what would you have done? Refused to work? Or simply learned to guard your tongue?"

Kasia stared at her, silent and seething.

"Our race used to be beasts," Tessaria said softly. "Far worse, actually. Women with black eyes. Children with broken bones. Suicide and murder. Poverty and famine. Now crime is nonexistent. No mouth goes hungry. No hand is raised in anger. Nature is revered and respected. The mages forced us to fight, but it will be the Last War." Zealous passion lit her eyes. "None of us has a choice, Kiska. We serve the arch-bishop because he serves the Via Sancta. Our salvation. The sooner you accept that, the sooner you will be at peace."

Her words were nearly identical to Cardinal Falke's.

Kasia regarded her mentor. The woman she loved as a mother. The woman she would die for in a heartbeat. "You always told me I didn't need Marks. That failing the tests didn't matter because my heart was true. You taught me to listen to the voice of conscience. To use logic in determining right from wrong if the answer didn't come instinctively."

Tessaria's gloved fingers curled around Kasia's. Tears shone in her eyes. "And I meant every word, darling. You're all I ever dreamt you could be and more."

"What if my conscience won't allow me to inform on people I've grown fond of, and who have done me no wrong?"

Tessaria had the grace not to look away. "If you refuse to cooperate, your true records will be made public. There's nothing I can do about that."

Kasia was eleven when Tessaria found her sleeping under the Montmoray Bridge. She'd been living on her own for weeks, hiding during the day and creeping out at night to steal scraps from the bins behind the cafes. At first she'd been wary of the Oprichniki patrols, but she eventually realized that her mother hadn't even reported her missing.

"Will you give me time to think about it?"

"Of course, darling."

The rain began again, a steady downpour. Tessaria unfurled her umbrella. "I must go meet with some of the vestals," she said. "Old acquaintances."

Nashka hurried back down the path, ducking beneath Kasia's umbrella. She smelled like flowers. "Guess our sunny day is over," she said glumly. "Though it's not as if the sun actually came out. Will it ever again, do you think?"

Tessaria poked her with the tip of her own umbrella. "You're slouching."

Natalya sighed and stood up straight. Her hair brushed the top of the black fabric.

"I'll look in on you both later. Do stay out of trouble until then." Tessaria leaned in. "I've ordered fresh clothes from the flat. They'll be delivered to your rooms. Please change into something less suitable for a nightclub."

Natalya gave her a little salute. "Yes, general."

"And you." Tessaria's black eyes speared Kasia. "Stay away from Bryce."

Kasia feigned outrage. "What makes you think—"

"Just stay away." Each word was punctuated with a stab of the umbrella. Tessaria strode for the Castel Saint Agathe, her step swift and lithe. As soon as Tessaria was gone, Nashka looked at her. "You okay?"

"I'm mad."

"Can't blame you."

"Aren't you mad?"

"Yes, but I always kind of wondered why she set us up with all those toffs. Didn't you?"

"Tessaria wanted to make me complicit, to make me one of them, but I'm not and never will be." She sighed. "Of course, if I don't play along, we're both finished."

"A moral dilemma, eh?" Nashka said sardonically. "They should put it on their fogging test."

"I wish I had some whiskey."

Natalya glanced around. "Has to be a pub around here somewhere."

Kasia blew out a breath. The rain thickened.

"Whatever you decide, I'll support you," Nashka said.

"Thanks."

"I mean literally support you. I've been doing portraits on the side, you know? It's starting to pick up. Word of mouth." She brightened. "Hey, we could get married."

"I'd rather be your mistress. If I'm your wife, you'll get bored of me inside a month."

"Give me more credit," Nashka protested. "I'd last six weeks at least."

Kasia slung an arm around her waist. "What if we run away together? Take a tour of the north."

"I've always wanted to see Nantwich. The museums have all kinds of Dark Age stuff. Plus kilometers of catacombs you can explore. I hear the original Praefators are buried down there."

"Sounds lovely."

Natalya laughed. "You have no appreciation of history."

"I'm sorry, but the *Meliora* is one of the most tedious volumes ever written. If it isn't, let lightning strike me down right now." She gazed up at the heavy skies over the Arx. Nashka grinned and shuffled back a step or two. "See? I don't give a fig for the Praefators. But I'd go to Nantwich for the chips and beer."

The heavens burst open at that moment, sending both women dashing back to the Castel Saint Agathe, their peals of laughter attracting a stern glare of reproval from an elderly vestal that went entirely unheeded.

THE PONTIFEX. The Knight. The Martyr. The Hierophant. And the Fool.

Kasia stared at the cards. Those were the key players—they'd come up again and again—but she needed more to understand how they fit together.

She closed her eyes and drew three more cards. One by one, she turned them over.

Winged Justice.

The Hanged Man.

The High Priestess, reversed.

She sat back, studying the spread.

The first signified truth as well as justice. The Hanged Man meant sacrifice. The High Priestess governed the sacred feminine, intuition and daring. Reversed, it meant secrets.

The message was clear. Fra Bryce needed her help, though whether she would give it to him remained to be seen.

As Tessaria promised, two chars had lugged a steamer trunk to her chamber, packed with clothes and toiletries from the flat.

Kasia changed into a tightly fitted gray chalk-stripe suit with short, peaked lapels. She wound her hair into a chignon, tucked it under a fedora, and applied bright red lipstick. Then she departed the Castel Saint Agathe, heels cracking like gunshots on the stone.

No one tried to stop her. They would if she tried to pass the Dacian Gate—of that, Kasia had no doubt—but it seemed she had free rein to walk the grounds. Outside, the rain had slowed to a drizzle. She stopped a tour guide with a class of noisy schoolchildren and asked for directions to the Offices of the Interfectorem.

The Tower of Saint Dima sat apart in a lightly wooded area. It had crenellations and high, pointed windows in the style of the First Dark Age. Green moss carpeted the lower two stories. A car was parked in front. Two burly priests leaned on the hood, smoking hand-rolled cigarettes.

"Good morning, Fathers," Kasia said with a bright smile. "I'm looking for Fra Spassov. He's my uncle."

They eyed her curiously. "He's off duty, but he should be in his room. Fourth floor."

Kasia climbed the winding tower stairs. The oaken door at the third level had been sealed off with yellow tape and a notice warning that it was under the jurisdiction of the Office of the General Directorate. She tried the knob anyway. Locked. Kasia continued up another flight and knocked at the door. "Fra Spassov?"

Silence.

"It's Kasia Novak."

A thump and clatter. "Just a minute!"

It was more like five, but the door finally opened. Spassov looked scruffy and bleary-eyed though the hour was nearly eleven. Even so, he would have been precisely her type. Older and a bit battered yet still appealing, like a rescue dog that occasionally bit people but was quite sweet the rest of the time.

"Domina Novak, what are you doing here?"

"I'm sorry to intrude, but I need to talk to you."

A hastily made bed sat against one wall. The rest of the chamber was more like an office, with a desk positioned next to the window. It held a typewriter, telephone and stacks of paperwork. An overflowing ashtray. He must have hidden the bottles, but she could smell wine on his breath.

"Have you seen Fra Bryce?" she asked.

"Last night."

"How is he?"

The priest's eyes were guarded. "Alive."

Spassov did not invite her inside, so Kasia stood in the doorway, gloved hands folded in front of her. "Do you believe he's innocent?"

"I know he is."

"How?"

"Because Alexei is not capable of such an act, nor did he have any reason to want Ferran Massot dead."

"Were you there?"

He frowned. "This is an open investigation. I'm not at liberty to discuss the details with you."

"I want to help him if I can." She paused. "I think I know who's behind all this."

Spassov regarded her with a glint of hope. "Do you have proof?"

"No."

His face fell. "Then I don't see how you can help him."

"If I do nothing, he's as good as dead," she said evenly. "We both know it."

Spassov rubbed the cleft in his chin, then folded his arms in an unfriendly manner. "Why are you here, Domina Novak?"

"I want to see him."

"It's impossible."

"You've visited him," she pointed out. "So it is possible."

"What do you hope to accomplish?"

"I want him to tell me himself that he's innocent. I want to see his face."

Spassov's bloodshot eyes narrowed. "Or maybe you just want to gloat. Alexei said he ruined your life and that you must hate him for it."

"I don't hate him," she said. "And he hasn't ruined my life. But before I do that myself, I want to see him."

He produced a cigarette from his rumpled cassock. "Do you mind?"

"Not at all."

Spassov lit the cigarette and blew a stream of smoke in the direction of the window. "Let's pretend I spent the night toasting Alexei and I'm a little slow this morning. Explain it as you would to a child, eh, Domina Novak?"

"I don't have physical proof of his innocence, not yet, but I might be able to get it." She smiled. "What do you have to lose?"

He smoked, saying nothing.

"Alexei was right, by the way. I did lie to you both." She held his weary gaze. "I'm Unmarked, Fra Spassov. I passed with the help of a friend inside the Curia."

A thick eyebrow rose slightly. "So you're a con artist with antisocial personality disorder. Is that supposed to make me trust you?"

"No, but I have dirt on Cardinal Falke. Enough to merit an investigation, assuming his superiors aren't in on it, too."

"Dmitry Falke has only one superior."

The Pontifex.

"That's the gamble," Kasia said. "And I'm willing to roll the dice, but only if he tells me himself that he didn't do it. So what will it be, Fra Spassov? Will you arrest me for impersonating an upright citizen or will you take me to Alexei?"

Spassov ground the cigarette into an ashtray. "I could get in big trouble."

"Bigger than the trouble he's in now?"

"Okay." He studied her. "You're his little sister. I'll vouch for you. But if you're playing with me, I'll tear your life apart." His face hardened. "And I'm a thousand times worse than Alyosha."

THEY LEFT the Tower of Saint Dima beneath leaden skies. The rain had paused but looked ready to return in buckets at any moment. Above the dome of the Pontifex's Palace, a flock of starlings wheeled in complex patterns. Priests and vestals strode along the pathways, going about the mundane business of the Curia, while tour groups in rain ponchos consulted waterproof maps of the Arx, debating their next stop.

If there was indeed some dark conspiracy afoot, Kasia saw no sign of it.

"Where are they holding him?" she asked. "I didn't know the Arx had a prison."

"Officially, we don't," Spassov replied. "Miscreants are taken to the city jail on Uralskaya Ulitsa. But the OGD keeps a few cells for political prisoners."

She glanced at him. "Nihilim."

Spassov nodded. "They haven't been used in years."

He lumbered up the walkway to the red-brick Curia Press building, Kasia hurrying to follow. They entered through double doors and Spassov strode into a maze of offices where priests and vestals labored away in the Eastern Curia's publishing division. She was just starting to wonder if his alcoholism had induced early dementia when he opened an unmarked door. Stairs led to a basement storage area with pulpy stacks of moldering pamphlets. At the far end, yet another unmarked door gave on a narrow downward-sloping tunnel. He lit a candle. A cold draft made the flame waver.

Kasia peered into the inky darkness. "Are you serious?"

"The Arx sits atop the old city. There are many forgotten ways to the cells." Spassov gazed at her blandly. "Unless you'd prefer to walk into General Directorate and ask them for a hall pass?"

Kasia laughed. "Lead on, Father."

They walked in silence for a while, his candle bobbing in the darkness.

"Where was Massot murdered?" she asked.

"At the Batavia Institute."

"The same night you came to my house?"

"No, it was the next morning, after we took your statement. I got a call that Massot's sedative had worn off. We returned to the Institute to question him about the Nightmark. We had reason to believe the mage was still in the city."

"Malach," she said softly. "I met him."

Kasia heard the distant echo of dripping water, but no other sound besides their footsteps. She wondered how deep underground they had come. If the candle went out, would they ever find their way out again? She took her hat off and wiped sweat from her brow.

"How exactly did Massot die? Are you sure it wasn't suicide?"

Spassov glanced over his shoulder. "Someone cut his throat while he was in restraints."

"Ah."

He shook his head. "Cold-blooded. That's not Alyosha."

"Cardinal Falke told me a witness saw him assault Massot minutes before. Is it true?"

Spassov sighed. "The doctor said disgusting things about you. Alyosha lost his head."

She felt oddly touched. "Then what?"

"I pulled him off before he could do any real damage. He calmed down and apologized. I went outside for a smoke. The next thing I knew, Alexei came running around the corner. He said he'd seen the killers, caught them in the act. Two men. They climbed the wall and got away."

"I take it no one else saw them?"

"No."

"That's rather damning," she said.

He scowled. "I thought you were here to help."

"I am. How much farther?"

Spassov halted, peering down at her. His eyes were close-set like a shaved bear. And like *ursus horribilis* with a new cub, he radiated fierce protectiveness. "Are you his friend, Kasia? Alyosha has very few."

"I want to be," she answered honestly.

He glared for another moment, then subsided into a fragile grumpiness. "I am afraid for him. He isn't right in his head."

"I know."

The priest looked away. "All this has pushed him to the edge. I think not even his Marks will save him if he falls. But he's not mad. Just . . . worn out."

"Why can't he sleep?"

"I don't know. He has scars from the war. I try not to pry."

She laid a hand on his sleeve. "I swear on my life that I mean him no harm, Father. Now, are we close? If I'm gone too long, people will come looking for me. I don't want to bring you any more trouble."

He nodded. "Only a little way."

Sure enough, the next turning brought the faint glow of torchlight ahead. Two priests sat at a folding table, quietly chanting the afternoon liturgy over meditation beads. They greeted Spassov with friendly nods. He introduced her as Fra Bryce's little sister. Kasia wiped away tears as she begged for a brief visit and the guards agreed on the condition Spassov accompany her to the cell.

It was halfway down the next corridor. A blue Ward glowed above the cell. Alexei sat against the wall, head tipped back. He threw a hand up at the torch.

"Alyosha?" Spassov said gently. "I brought a visitor."

Kasia stepped forward. He regarded her with profound wariness.

And a hint of fear.

"I'm quite real," she said, curling her gloved fingers around the bars.

Alexei clambered to his feet. A line of dried blood ran from ear to jaw. Her mouth tightened in anger. They hadn't even given him medical treatment.

"Kasia?" His voice was raw.

"Yes, I'm here."

Alexei drew closer, until only the bars stood between them. "I'm so sorry," he began.

"None of that," she said briskly. "I don't understand all of it, but Cardinal Falke sits at the heart of this case like a spider in his web. You got in his way so he spun a straightjacket for you. He thinks he's beaten us both."

A flash of mordant humor crossed his face. "I rather think he has, Kasia."

"Not yet." Her voice lowered. "You kept my secrets and I'll keep yours. Tell me one thing. Are you innocent of this charge?"

Alexei held her gaze. There was no guile in it, just profound weariness. "Yes."

She found his fingers through the bars and held them tight. "I believe you."

He squeezed her fingers.

"I'm not what they say." She searched his face. "I know right from wrong."

"I know, Kasia."

Spassov cleared his throat. "I must go." Kasia withdrew her hand. "Keep the faith, Fra Bryce."

His smile was a flash of white in the darkness. "I haven't lost it yet. Just don't tell me to get some sleep."

Chapter Twenty-Three

The parchment curled black at the edges and then to white ash. Cardinal Falke tossed it into the fireplace and lit the accompanying map of the ley lines with a beeswax taper. That, too, was given to the flames.

"There will be nothing to tie us to Ferran Massot now," he said heavily. "Saints forgive us."

"Are you forgetting Kasia Novak?" Archbishop Kireyev replied. "And Bryce?"

"Novak was a courier. The cylinders were intact when Sor Foy delivered them. I'm certain the girl never read the messages." He cast a sharp glance at the gnome-like man squinting up at him through a pair of round spectacles. "She is not to be harmed."

"But—"

"Does the Curia kill innocent women now?" Falke's voice cracked like a whip. "Is that what we have become?"

Kireyev bowed his head. "Of course not, Your Eminence. I only point out—"

"Consider Domina Novak to be under my personal protection." He frowned. "Come, you've used her skills for years. Are you so eager to dispose of her?"

"I defer to your judgment on the matter," Kireyev muttered. "Bryce poses a greater problem. He has defied my authority at every turn. I cannot be sure how much he knows."

"Bryce is locked up."

"There are holes in the case."

"Then plug them," Falke growled. "Have your men finished searching Massot's residence?"

"Every scrap of paper related to his research went into the furnaces." He shifted uneasily, lips pursing in distaste. "We found journals, Your Eminence. And . . . other items. Massot was a sexual deviant. We never should have permitted Malach to Mark him in the first place. The doctor was weak in both mind and soul. It corrupted him, just as I predicted it would."

Falke stared into the flames. "We had no choice. He couldn't study the abyssal ley without touching it himself and only a Nightmark can grant that power." A pine knot popped in a shower of cinders. "Oto Valek was supposed to be monitoring him. You promised me the orderly was a reliable informant, Casimir! How could he possibly have missed such blatant misbehavior?"

"Valek will be disposed of." Kireyev began to clean his spectacles with a square of blue silk. "After he performs a last service to the Curia. What can I say? The doctor was paranoid, as you well know." He scowled. "It is a scandal for the Institute, and what have we gained? The experiments were a failure and we only averted disaster by the skin of our teeth. If Malach had seen the letter—"

"I will deal with Malach," Falke said. "He's my responsibility."

"Are you certain he will come?"

A dry chuckle. "He pretends obedience and thinks I don't know he's plotting behind my back. I expressly forbade him from contacting Massot for any reason and yet, lo and behold, the two of them conspired to . . . ." He trailed off, his face setting into grim lines.

Kireyev swallowed hard.

It was the elephant in the room, what that burned letter to Malach said. Neither man had believed it at first, yet the evidence at Massot's house supported the claim beyond any shadow of a doubt. As did the medical records of Patient 9. The Marks, as the doctor had informed his master, did not lie. If the truth got out, there would be panic in the streets—and that would be the least of it.

"Valek comes on his shift at six," Kireyev said. "We need him if the operation is to run smoothly. It will all be over in a few hours."

"After everything he has done for the Church . . . I only wish there was another way." Falke sighed. "But we do what we must, Casimir. If Massot figured out who he is, others will too. There is no safe place for a lunatic who wields that kind of power. If the mages gain control of him, we will face a Third Dark Age. Another descent into the abyss, this time with no hope of salvation."

Kireyev used the square of silk to blot sweat from his brow. "I know, Your Eminence."

"Humanity has come so far." He closed his gloved fist. "Enlightenment is nearly within our grasp. We cannot throw it all away for the sake of one man, even if he is a living saint. And do not forget, there is the matter of who put him there in the first place." For a moment, he looked every hour of his age. "I am afraid, Casimir. There is a cancer in the Via Sancta, one that has been quietly growing in the dark for years, yet its source remains nameless."

"At least we know it cannot be the nihilim. The Pontifex's Palace in Jalghuth is even more heavily Warded than ours. Which means it must be one of Lezarius's inner circle. What do the records say about how he came to the Institute?"

"Nothing. They are gone. Massot must have destroyed them."

"What about the nihilim?"

"I told you, I'll deal with him."

"Does he know?"

"Think, Casimir. He is aware of the letter's existence, but he wouldn't have gone after the Novak woman if he knew what it said. He would have gone straight to the Institute to claim his prize. He must realize by now that the message has fallen into our hands, so he will come to us. And he will never leave the Arx again."

"And Fra Bryce?"

"The Interfectorem is your problem. Just ensure he doesn't interfere."

Kireyev nodded slowly—and a little regretfully—but Falke didn't notice because he was gazing into the hearth, where the last of the letters curled to ash.

Chapter Twenty-Four

F or eleven years, since the day she turned sixteen, Nikola Thorn had been a char at the Arx. She polished the gold chalices, shook the dust from the carpets, lit the hearths and scrubbed the stone floors. Acres and acres of stone floors. At twenty-seven, she had chronic bursitis in her knees. The joints of her hands ached when it rained, and it rained more often than not.

But she was a faithful worker, always arriving on time and rarely taking sick days. The sisterhood of chars was close. All were Unmarked and they looked out for each other. They also knew more about what went on inside the Arx than anyone except Archbishop Kireyev. If the Pontifex's spymaster had any inkling that such a network existed under his very nose, he would have used it himself, but he thought of the women in gray with vague pity when he thought of them at all.

Nikola went about her rounds, greeting the other chars with a smile that felt false though no one seemed to notice. When it came time for her break, she joined a woman named Marysa in the kitchen that served the Arx's central dining hall. Kettles and skillets hung from hooks near the great wood-burning ovens where the cooks baked bread and stirred soup in enormous black cauldrons. Nikola usually found the kitchen to be a cozy, fragrant place, but tonight the smell of boiled cabbage and yeasty dough made her stomach roil.

Marysa had married an Unmarked man and they had three young children. He stayed home to care for them while Marysa worked. Nikola had always pitied her. She couldn't imagine dealing with a bunch of screaming brats when she got home from a shift. If Nikola finished work before the cafés closed, she'd go out for a quiet drink, then home to a hot bath. On her day off, she mostly slept. It was hard to reset your clock when you worked nights. But mothers didn't get days off, not ever. Marysa didn't complain, in fact she seemed happy enough, which was a mystery. Now Nikola felt an unwanted kinship.

They made mint tea and sat down at the scarred trestle table.

"How much does it hurt to give birth?" she asked. "Like, one to ten?"

"Twelve, but you don't really remember it later." Marysa smiled. "Why? You met someone special?"

"No." *Twelve?* "Just wondering."

"Well, you're still young. There's time."

Marysa opened a paper bag and offered her an almond cookie. "Homemade," she said.

Nikola took a tiny nibble. "Delicious," she said.

When Marysa looked away, she shoved the rest into her pocket. They drank tea and traded idle talk. With some subtle prompting, she learned that Sister Chernov had ordered fresh linens for three guest rooms in the east wing of the Castel Saint Agathe. Her rounds included mopping the floors in the chapel so after her break ended she went directly to the hulking headquarters of the vestals.

Another cup of tea with a friend and Nikola knew which rooms they occupied—top floor, east wing. Malach hadn't forbidden her from speaking to the women, not that Nikola gave a damn if he had. She wasn't his Marked to be ordered about. If he failed, all her plans would be for naught. Worse, she would be burdened with his child. The thought was intolerable.

Bells in the highest tower chimed the hour. She was supposed to meet Malach, but she wanted to be sure her information was correct. Nikola knocked at the door of the first guest room. There was no answer so she tried the second.

"Come in," a low female voice called.

She opened the door but stayed at the threshold. "Pardon, Domina, Sister Chernov sent me. Do you have everything you need?"

A woman stood at the window. She was of medium height with an enviable figure. Long black hair fell loose over her shoulders. She wore bright red lipstick and matching nail polish and looked like she ought to be out dancing at a music hall, not confined to this stark stone chamber of the Arx. Dark kohl lined her eyes, but it was the directness of her gaze Nikola found most interesting. She knew from the chars that Tessaria Foy was nearly eighty, and Natalya Anderle had curly blonde hair and brown skin, so this must be Kasia Novak.

"Thank you, Domina, but I lack for nothing," she said.

No one ever called Nikola by the polite form of address. The other chars used her first name and the bosses called her Thorn.

"Supper is in an hour." Nikola inclined her head. "If you think of anything, just find a woman in gray. She will assist you." She started to close the door.

"Wait," Kasia said.

Nikola paused.

"Won't you come in for a minute? If you're not too busy."

That was unexpected. Nikola stepped into the chamber. A trunk stood in the corner, the contents carelessly strewn about. Shoes and clothes and cosmetics and a deck of cards. It looked rather like her own flat.

"Have you ever met the Pontifex?" Kasia asked.

"I've seen her, but we've never spoken."

"What is she like? Surely you must hear things. Is she open-minded?"

Nikola wondered what Kasia was after. "The Reverend Mother is wise and gracious. She embodies all we aspire to."

"Of course." Her gaze searched Nikola's face as if she thought they might know each other from somewhere, though Nikola could swear they had never met before that moment. "How do they treat you here?"

"Quite well, Domina."

"And they pay you a salary?"

"Naturally. Slavery is outlawed in the Via Sancta. The *Meliora* condemns it as one of the vilest crimes against humanity."

"But you weren't given much of a choice, were you?"

Nikola lifted her chin. What business was it of this woman? "I'm afraid I must attend to other duties, Domina." Her tone was polite but chilly.

"Forgive me. I have no right to question you." The words seemed heartfelt. "It's not just idle curiosity," Kasia continued quietly. "I . . . I have a sister who is Unmarked. She ran away a long time ago, but I think of her often and hope she is well."

Nikola's heart beat faster. Despite Malach's bravado, she doubted he would walk out of the Arx in one piece. Most likely he would die before he ever reached this room. But if she could befriend this woman and discover the information he sought . . . .

"There is nothing to forgive," Nikola said with a warm smile. "What is your sister's name? Ash Court is a neighborly place. If she lives there, I might know of her."

"Natalya."

What a coincidence, Nikola thought dryly. She's lying, but why?

"Hmmm. I do know a Natalya, but she is old enough to be your grandmother."

"Never mind. Tell me one more thing, Domina. How would one gain an audience with the Reverend Mother?"

"Well, it is not a simple matter. She has aides who manage her schedule. It's booked up quite far in advance." Nikola adjusted her scarf, pretending to think. "I assume this is an urgent matter."

Kasia nodded.

"One that demands perfect discretion."

Another nod.

Nikola glanced at the open door, then furtively closed it. "If you give me some idea of what you need to speak to her about, I could convey the message myself. I lay her fire in the mornings and pour her tea."

"I thought you'd never spoken to her."

Kasia Novak looked like a socialite with her hair and makeup and fashionable clothes, but there was a cold canniness lurking beneath the surface that Nikola recognized. She resolved to watch her step.

"I haven't. Not beyond a 'Good morning, Reverend Mother.' That sort of thing. But I see her every day." Nikola hesitated. "I don't mean to offend . . . ."

"Go on."

"If you're in some sort of difficulty, I'm certain the Reverend Mother would help you. She is kind and generous. A light among us."

Nikola had never met the Pontifex and despised her as much as all the rest of them, but Kasia seemed to believe it.

"What is your name, Domina?"

"Nikola Thorn."

"I am grateful for your help, Domina Thorn. It is not myself I fear for, but someone else."

"A man?"

"A priest. It's not . . . what you think. He's a friend. But he's in deep trouble."

Nikola nodded sympathetically.

"I'm the only one who can help him. But if I'm wrong, I'll lose a great deal." Kasia gave a throaty laugh. "I'm usually the one people confess their secrets to. You must think me a fool."

"Not in the least. We all face difficult decisions. It helps to have someone to talk to." She paused. "When we don't trust our own judgment."

"Yes, that's it precisely." Kasia thought for a moment. "I suppose you'll see the Pontifex in the morning?"

Tomorrow would be too late. "Actually, I'm taking her some tea in an hour."

Kasia bit her lip. A look of reckless desperation crossed her face. "Tell her——"

She cut off at a peremptory knock on the door. It opened and an older woman entered the room. She wore a simple dark blue cassock but had the haughty demeanor of an archbishop—or even a cardinal. She stared at Nikola without expression for a long moment. "Pardon me," she said to Kasia, her accent precise and cultured. "I didn't know you were occupied."

"Not at all," Kasia said. "She just came to change the linens but I explained that it wasn't necessary."

Nikola curtsied before the hostile gaze. The woman was Raven-Marked but wore no ring. A plain vestal, then.

"I haven't seen you before and I know all the chars that serve the vestals. What is your name?"

"Nikola Thorn," she said with a curtsy. "I mop the floors in the chapel, but Sister Chernov asked me to check on her guests, Domina. Do you require anything?"

"No." The word was bitten off.

"Well, just call when you need fresh towels, Domina," she told Kasia cheerfully.

The older woman's gaze burned Nikola's back as she shut the door and hurried from the Castel Saint Agathe.

"Give me one more day. I almost have her in my confidence."

Malach stared at Nikola, trying hard not to lose his temper. She'd been twenty minutes late to the rendezvous at a deserted tram stop across from the Dacian Gate. Malach had been pacing like a caged beast when she finally showed, certain something had gone wrong.

"You shouldn't have spoken to her," he said. "I told you not to take unnecessary risks."

The gates opened. A long, black car rolled out of the Arx. Headlights swept across them and Malach pulled Nikola into his arms, lowering his face to the neck of her gray cloak. The garment smelled of incense and floor wax and damp wool. His lips found the warm skin beneath, where she smelled only of herself. For a moment, he wished they were back in her flat, eating noodles and arguing, among other things.

The car passed. Nikola pulled back.

"She invited me into her room. She was worried about some priest."

"The laqueus," Malach muttered.

"I'm sure I can find out what she knows." Nikola seized his coat sleeve. "Please, Malach. Let me try."

He shook his head. "I can't wait."

"Why not?"

"Every Oprichnik in the city is hunting me, if you hadn't noticed."

"They have no reason to search my flat," she said reasonably. "But if you try to go in there, you'll be caught for certain."

He gazed at the Wards along the high walls, the dim orange glow of torches in the towers beyond. "Are there extra guards posted tonight? Anything different from the usual?"

She sighed. "Not that I can tell, but it means nothing. Surely they might expect you to come here."

"Falke is too arrogant. He thinks his citadel is impregnable."

She gave a mirthless laugh. "*Falke* is arrogant? You really do lack a single iota of self-awareness, Malach."

"Enough." His jaw tightened. "Did you get it?"

Nikola produced a rolled-up length of black cloth from beneath her cloak. "I stole it from the dirty laundry." She shoved it against his chest. "I hope you get fleas."

Malach shook out the cassock. He pulled it over his clothes and drew the cowl up. The garment was slightly short, but it covered him well enough. As long as no one realized he lacked a Raven Mark, he should be able to walk through the grounds unnoticed.

Of course, if they saw the broken chain around his neck, he'd be done for. Nikola hadn't recognized it, but any priest or vestal would know it at once. The Mark of Bal Kirith. The Mark of unfettered will.

"Where am I going?" he asked.

"The Castel Saint Agathe," Nikola said. "Her chamber is at the very top, in the east wing. Here, I drew you a map." She pressed a folded scrap of paper into his hand but didn't let go. "You won't hurt her. Promise me again, Malach."

"Compulsion does no permanent damage."

"Promise!" Her voice was hard.

Malach studied her, this woman they had rejected as beneath their standards. "I swear."

"Good." Nikola gave a friendly nod. "And I ever discover you've lied to me, I'll cut your balls off and keep them in a pickle jar."

He smiled. "Understood, Domina Thorn."

The downpour concealed them as they followed the wall to the side of the Arx that abutted the river. Malach had chosen the spot for its seclusion and distance from the Dacian

Gate. The wall was rough stone and offered plenty of hand-holds. Scaling it would be simple if not for the Wards carved three meters apart for the entire length. They were Arx's true defense.

"I'll wait for you here," Nikola said.

"Go home."

"But—"

"There's nothing more you can do."

Malach turned away. She grabbed his arm. "You'd better come back."

Her voice was calm, but he sensed turmoil beneath the surface. Normally, Malach enjoyed provoking a strong emotional response. He'd savor the victory, find a way to heighten it to serve his own ends. But she'd risked everything and so far, he'd given her nothing in return but an unwanted life inside her.

"Death is the only thing that will keep me from you," he said.

"That's what I'm worried about."

"They haven't killed me yet." He thought about it. "And not for lack of trying."

"Don't get captured either," she said.

"I wouldn't tell them about you. No matter what they did to me."

Nikola held his gaze. "I know," she said quietly.

He grinned. "See? You do love me."

"Fool." She rolled her eyes, but he earned a tiny smile.

Malach traced her lower lip with his thumb. "Leave," he said. "I don't want you to see the next part."

Nikola opened her mouth to object and he covered it with a long, deep kiss. Even now, in the shadow of his enemy's stronghold, he wanted her. He forced himself to pull away.

"Just go. Please."

She held his gaze for a long moment. Then she turned and walked away.

She did not look back.

Rain beat against the hood of his cassock. Mud and fish filled his nose. Malach crouched down and laid a palm on the sodden earth of the riverbank. A chill wracked him as he delved through the shallows and reached the fiery abyssal ley, like a hot spring beneath a glacial pool. Lines of flame raced across his Marks. He drew deeper, blood stirring with urgent need.

Malach had answered a hundred furtively whispered prayers, but his own remained out of reach. There were limits to the power of the ley. It could not heal or stave off death. It could not be used directly against itself.

In other words, he could not simply unmake the Void, no matter how badly he craved it.

Yet under every other circumstance, abyssal was the strongest. It delivered swift results—often with unintended consequences, if the wielder was inexperienced.

Liminal ley, the threshold where the surface mingled with the abyss, was second in potency. It twisted chance, which is why the Curia restricted its use to the clergy, yet it was unreliable.

Surface ley had always been the weakest, just as the conscious mind governed a mere fraction of all brain activity. Surface ley soothed and pacified. In a fight like the one with the laqueus, the red would always overwhelm the blue.

But something in the construct of the Wards turned that rule on its head.

His aunt Beleth believed it to be faith.

The Raven was not an empty symbol. Wards were steeped in the hopes and dreams of their creators, the unshakeable conviction of moral righteousness. Falke hinted at it in his book.

"Make the conflict a struggle for liberation against the oppressor. This external space, lying outside the physical boundaries of engagement, is the true battlefield."

Malach lifted his hand. The Broken Chain ignited like molten ore against his chest, then faded. He stood and pulled on a pair of leather gloves.

Compassion. Courage. Fidelity. Honesty. Forgiveness. The Five Virtues of the Via Sancta.

Romantic sentiments, but none held any particular appeal.

He took a step toward the wall, heart pumping like a bellows.

Someday, you will topple that stela and fuck someone on it. Do you believe me, Malach?

"Yes," he said softly.

Ten meters out, the nausea kicked in. He swallowed hard and kept walking, a steady, unhurried pace. Eight meters and icy sweat trickled down his back. Five, and his Marks triggered the full defenses.

"I believe," he said through gritted teeth. "I have faith."

The climb to the top took approximately a hundred years, give or take a decade. The Wards flayed him alive, then tossed him on a rack of hot coals. Knives stabbed his abdomen. Iron spikes splintered his joints. They sucked the breath from his lungs and the strength from his muscles. Blue starbursts in the image of a Raven seared his retinas.

"I believe," he rasped, reaching for the next handhold, and the next. "I have faith."

A cramped, trembling leg thrown over the top and then he was weightless, the ground rushing to meet him. Malach lay curled on his side for a minute, vomiting dark blood. He spat and scrubbed his mouth. Fingers and toes dug furrows in the earth. Centimeter by centimeter, he crawled away from the torture chamber they had devised for him. With infinite slowness, the tide of agony receded, leaving him shaken and panting.

He found a stone chapel and huddled against it until he could walk. Twinges of pain still scraped his bones, but the Wards had failed to finish him.

"Faith," he muttered hoarsely, "is a marvelous thing."

Malach took Nikola's map from his pocket, shielding it from the rain. He looked around and took his bearings. The dome of the basilica lay just ahead, which placed the Castel Saint Agathe off to the left. Bells tolled from a distant tower. Malach counted ten peals.

In Bal Kirith, the evening debauchery would just be starting, but they led tamer lives inside the Arx. The night was quiet.

Malach's teeth gleamed in the darkness.

Inside the Arx.

How many times had he watched the citadel from afar, imagining the day he would burn it all down? The urge to do so right now was almost overwhelming, but he mastered himself. First things first.

He set out along the pathway, cowl raised and hands tucked into the sleeves of the cassock. Occasionally, the glow of headlights pierced the night, but the cars moved at a leisurely pace. Half a dozen knights stood before the Pontifex's Palace. Malach didn't come close enough to see their faces.

No one challenged him.

Wards glowed everywhere and he kept his distance, pausing now and then to consult the map. At last, the hulking stone headquarters of the vestals came into view. Its counterpart in Bal Kirith was open and airy, with wide balconies and fluted marble columns—the ones that still stood, at least. This building was squat and ugly, like a closed fist.

Malach found a window and squeezed through the deep slit. After the drubbing he'd taken at the wall, the single Ward, nearly six meters away, knotted his jaw but failed to induce the dreaded black vomit.

Perhaps they'd already bled him dry.

He started down a long vaulted corridor, listening intently. Torches sputtered along the walls, the smoke smarting his eyes. He still felt raw and tender, the way he did after leaving his cousin Dantarion's bed. She liked it rough in every sense and her partners weren't spared the pleasure.

A sliver of ice touched him.

May she never, ever meet Domina Thorn.

Malach pulled his gloves off and trailed a finger along the wall, letting the abyssal ley flow into his Marks like a rush of infused blood. It couldn't heal his hurts, but it made him feel better nonetheless.

Beneath her crown of raven feathers, the Lady of Masks smiled.

True to Nikola's map, the corridor ended at a set of spiral stairs. Malach climbed them to the very top. He was about to open the door when muffled female voices sounded on the other side, growing louder. He backed down the stairs. Tiger in a Cage lashed its tail.

Be gone.

Power surged forth, primed to alter the branching course of events as it suited him. The voices receded.

Malach left the stairwell and found the third door from the end in the east wing. He knocked softly.

No answer.

He pressed a palm against the smooth age-dark wood.

"Domina Novak?" His voice was a rough whisper, impossible to distinguish as male or female.

Still no answer.

Asleep, then. That made his task easier. He touched the lock. The tumblers clicked. Malach eased the door open, a square of light spilling across the stone floor. A figure lay in the narrow bed, facing away from him. Malach stepped inside, silent as a cat.

He would take what he needed and send her back to sleep. When she woke in the morning, he wouldn't even be a hazy dream. She would have no recollection of him whatsoever.

Malach resolved to hit her with a heavy dose of abyssal

ley. He still didn't know how she'd broken his compulsion the last time and had no desire to repeat the debacle.

He stepped forward, reaching behind to ease the door shut.

Wards burst into blue flame. Over the door. The window.

He threw an arm up, every muscle seizing.

The ley vanished.

Not just regular Wards. A mage trap.

The room filled with priests. He lashed out wildly. A fist snapped his head back. Malach tasted salty warmth on his tongue. They pushed him down to the bed, where pillows had been shoved beneath the blanket to resemble a slumbering body. A dagger at his throat discouraged further resistance.

Candles were lit. Cardinal Falke eyed his cassock with a melancholy expression.

"I wish you wore that in truth," he said. "But it was a futile hope."

"Where's my letter?" Malach rasped.

"I burned it. Would you like to know what it said?"

Malach spat a dark gob. "I would, as a matter of fact."

"I'll tell you, but only because it makes no difference now." His purple robes gleamed in the candlelight. "If you'd come a day earlier, you'd be taking home a prize right now."

"Massot?" Malach sneered, although he had no real idea of what the doctor had found. "His work was useless. I don't know why I bothered Marking him. He failed both of us."

"Did you know about the women?" An edge entered the cardinal's voice. No ley to dull his anger. A flush spread across Falke's jowls, his eyes cold.

Malach stared at him, uncomprehending. "I saw Massot once a year. What did he find? Some girl who could Mark a cat? That's your obsession, not mine."

"Oh, he found a little more than that," Falke said softly. "Try the man who forged the ley lines."

Malach stared at him. "Lezarius is in Jalghuth."

The fourth city-state of the Via Sancta was in the far north, surrounded by glacial fields with hundreds of stelae—and the frozen corpses of nihilim who had died trying to break through and capture him.

"Oh, there's a Pontifex in Jalghuth, but it's not Lezarius. Not the real one, at any rate." The cardinal sat down on the chest at the foot of the bed, resting his arms on his knees. "Here's what I think happened. Let's go back thirty years. You were about four, weren't you?"

Malach didn't answer, but the cardinal simply nodded. "Beleth's forces surround Novostopol. Nantwich is burning. Kvengard clings to neutral status, but Luk knows the end is in sight. It's time to broker the terms of a final unconditional surrender.

"The Lion refuses to concede. He marches with his forces to defend Nantwich, but is taken captive and held in Bal Agnar. Under torture, he lashes out and makes the Void. At the junctures of the ley lines, stelae rise up from the earth, fully formed. His loyal forces have been trying to fight through to free him and they do, now that the ley is gone. Bal Agnar falls, and then Bal Kirith. Balaur is taken back to Jalghuth. The stelae are copied and called Wards in the cities."

"I don't require a history lesson," Malach said coldly.

Falke tilted his head. "Lezarius alone had power over the physical course of the ley, so he created the Void and cast you out. But here's something you may not know. When it was done, he thought the nihilim should be left alone. That being deprived of the ley was sufficient punishment for your transgressions. When the other Pontifexes overruled him, Lezarius was furious. He severed ties with the rest of the Curia and retreated into the Arx at Jalghuth. He's been a recluse ever since, which would make it rather easy to replace him with someone else."

"Who?" Malach scoffed.

"I have no idea, but I intend to find out." Falke looked

grim. "His Marks must have been deliberately Inverted. Only a mage could do that."

Malach swallowed against the edge of the dagger. He locked eyes with the heavyset priest looming over him. "It's rather hard to have a conversation," he said, "with your minions on the verge of cutting my throat."

Falke made a small gesture. The blade eased back a millimeter.

Malach counted four priests in the chamber, plus the cardinal. Three of them wore blue robes with no insignia. Falke's private army? The fourth had the Golden Bough of General Directorate.

"If one of us did have Lezarius under his or her control," Malach said, "why not just make him free the ley?"

"I don't know," Falke conceded.

"So they put him in the madhouse and gave his robes to another Pontifex. One who must look exactly like him."

"Apparently so." Falke shook his head. "There's an undeniable genius to it. Even if he remembered who he was, no one would believe him."

Malach was silent for a minute. Then he started laughing. "You might have come up with something more plausible. You're as crazy as Massot."

"I know you had him looking for Invertido with the ability to manipulate the ley. Obviously, you hoped he might find someone who could reverse the binding. A long shot, but you're desperate."

Malach's smile faded.

"His letter referred to the Source of all your Troubles. Capital S, capital T. What does that tell you, Malach? He wanted you to spirit this patient from the Institute and suggested you act quickly because Massot had concerns about his quote *latent powers* unquote."

"That still doesn't mean—"

"His Marks match. Massot had to dig deep to find a

description of them. He spent the last year collecting any book that referenced the Pontifex of the Northern Curia. We found them all hidden away in his house. He finally found an obscure biography of Saint Jule, who Marked Lezarius, that gave a precise description. No two Marks are the same, but you know that already. They cannot be faked. It's him."

Falke chuckled. "Massot was so eager to tell you the news. If Beleth had Lezarius, she might force him to free the ley. He's the only one on earth who could do it." The cardinal rose to his feet. "I just wanted you to know the depth of your failure."

Malach flexed his hands. "Thanks for that. I think I'll kill you all now and go pick him up, whoever he is."

The cardinal smiled. "Oh, did I forget to mention? He's dead."

"What?"

"I didn't take the decision lightly." His face grew solemn again. "Lezarius is a true martyr. I'll personally see to it that he's canonized, but he's Invertido now. Far too dangerous to be left alive."

Perhaps it was the part about making Lezarius a saint, but Malach finally grasped that Falke was telling the truth. A bloody haze dimmed his eyes. He threw his head back and howled. If he'd had the ley, he would have flipped every Mark in the Arx. The entire city.

"I've known you a long time, Malach." Falke's eyes shone with emotion. "I never gave up hoping that some part of you could be salvaged. But you belong wholly to them."

The cardinal nodded at his knights. Four blades rasped from their scabbards. He made the sign given to the dying. "*Et lux perpetua luceat.* May your heart find peace."

Malach spat in his face.

Cardinal Falke wiped it away with a gloved finger. "The Cold Truce is over," he said wearily. "Take his hands."

Chapter Twenty-Five

Fra Gerlach and Fra Brodszky drove up to the Batavia Institute and sat in the car, wipers on high, while they waited for the gates to open.

Since the murder of Ferran Massot, the guards had been strict about protocol. One shone a torch into the backseat before walking around to the driver's side window, his free hand resting on the hilt of a sword.

He swallowed hard at the Golden Bough insignia on their robes, stammered an apology, and signaled at the guard inside the booth to buzz them through. Priests from General Directorate were given instant and full cooperation, no questions asked.

The guard had no idea they were also high-ranking members of Cardinal Falke's Praesidia ex Divina Sanguis, nor that such a society even existed. As it happened, there was a fair amount of overlap between the two organizations. Both were former Knights of Saint Jule who had served under the cardinal and been hand-picked for the Praesidia. They understood the necessity of the night's task, but being pious and ley-fearing men, did not relish it.

Gerlach parked in the lot around back and took out his corax.

"Raven or name?" he asked.

Brodszky hesitated. "Raven."

Gerlach flipped the corax, catching it on the back of his gloved left hand. They looked at each other. "Two out of three?" Gerlach proposed wryly.

Brodszky didn't smile. "I'll do it," he said.

"No." Gerlach sighed. "I was only joking."

"Are you sure?"

Gerlach met his partner's eye. "The burden is mine."

They unfurled black umbrellas and walked swiftly through the rain to the rear entrance. Wards blazed above every window and door. Oto Valek was waiting for them. He bobbed his head in deference, glancing down the empty corridor as they shook off rainwater.

"It's all arranged, Fathers," the orderly said.

"Good," Brodszky said. "We need 26 first."

"Follow me." Valek set off down the corridor. The sconces had been dimmed for bedtime, leaving the hall in partial shadow. Thick carpeting muffled their footsteps.

"Where's the rest of the staff?" Gerlach asked.

"There are six attendants on duty in B and C wings, three on each side. Nurse Jeyna is in the dispensary, preparing the sedatives for tomorrow morning. Dr. Pagwe is in his office filling out reports."

"That's all?"

"Well, the Wards are activated. The patients can't cause much trouble, can they?" Valek gave a nervous laugh. "Except for . . . you know."

Gerlach decided he didn't like this man. He already knew too much. Oto Valek would need to be handled at some point. Maybe tonight, once it was done. They were already killing two birds with one stone. Why not three?

He smiled. "Don't go far. We'll need your statement as a witness."

"Of course, Father, of course." Valek cleared his throat. "I assume there will be a reward?"

"Naturally." *Though not the one you expect.*

The orderly paused at a door. "Here he is."

"Open it."

Valek took out a ring of keys. "He shouldn't give you any trouble. You won't get a whit of sense from him, mind, but he does as told."

Tumblers clicked. Light spilled in from the corridor. The room was nicer than either of them expected. Expensive furniture, lots of books, though they looked dusty. Someone paid for amenities.

A tall black-haired man sprawled on the goosedown bed. Brodszky, who had served with him in several campaigns, felt a twinge of guilt before his Marks smoothed it over. Twenty-six had paid a high price for his loyalty. He was a martyr to the cause. But as the cardinal said, it would be a mercy for them both in the end.

Rain lashed the barred window as the priests approached the bed. "Wake up," Gerlach said. "You must come with us."

Patient 26 rolled over, raising one arm against the square of light that fell across the bed. A dark beard covered his sunken cheeks. His gaze was empty, his lips so chapped Brodzsky could see spots of dried blood.

"On your feet, *miles ignotum*," he said, putting some snap in his voice.

Gerlach frowned at the term "unknown soldier" and glanced at Oto Valek, who stood in the doorway. Twenty-six lumbered to his feet, blinking uncertainly.

"Where's 9?" Brodzsky asked.

"Down the hall," Valek replied.

They prodded 26 into motion. He shuffled along like a sleepwalker, muttering under his breath. The uniform of the

Institute, a white cotton tunic and pants, hung loose on his lanky frame. The Raven Mark on his neck seemed to stare at Gerlach with a beady, accusing eye.

"Forgive me, but I have a question, Fathers," Valek said, toying with the keys. "What about these? I could get into serious trouble. How could 26 have escaped—"

Gerlach held up a set of lock picks. "They'll be found with his body. His brother must have smuggled them in when he visited."

Valek nodded, eyes agleam with sudden cunning. "I see, I see. Implicate Bryce. Of course, he would want 9 silenced. That was his only witness. Oh, it's very clever, Fathers!"

"Be quiet," Gerlach growled. "How much farther?"

"Just here." Valek paused in front of a door, shoulders hunching. "Would it be impertinent to inquire how *much* the reward will be—"

"Keys," Brodszky snapped, holding out a hand.

The orderly flinched. "Of course, Father, of course."

"Get lost," Gerlach said. "Should anyone ask, we're here investigating the murder of Ferran Massot. You escorted us to his room and left. Utter a single word beyond that and you'll never see daylight again."

Valek blanched. "No, no," he stammered. "You can count on my discretion."

"I hope so," Gerlach said with a cold smile.

The orderly practically ran down the hall. The priests shared a look of silent commiseration. Neither doubted that the work of the Praesidia was the only path to salvation. They'd been chosen for this because they would not waver. Yet Brodszky felt relieved he'd won the corax toss.

"The grace of the ley be with you," he said, unlocking the door.

Both had secretly hoped their victim would be asleep, but he was sitting on the bed, awake and dressed in a tweed jacket. A small man with wispy white hair, bare feet and tobacco-stained teeth. Yet the priests paused at the threshold.

"I wondered when you'd come," Patient 9 said.

Twenty-six stopped muttering. It was so quiet, Brodszky heard his partner draw a breath. Gerlach was the first to break the spell. "We just want to ask you some questions," he said.

They came inside and gently closed the door. The old man's eyes narrowed. "I see. Why is Mikhail here?"

"Turn around," Brodzsky said, steering 26 to face the wall. He drew a blade and pressed it to his back. Mikhail didn't seem aware of it. His mouth worked soundlessly.

"You killed Dr. Massot, didn't you?" the old man said, an edge in his voice now.

"Your work on this earth is done," Gerlach said. "It will never be forgotten. But it's time to rejoin the ley, Reverend Father."

"Don't hurt Mikhail. He's an innocent!"

Gerlach held his palms up and began the litany. "*Kyrie, eleison. Kyrie, eleison. Sancte Jule. Sancte Dima. Sancta Agathe. Sancte Kwame. Sancta Imani. Propitius esto. Ab omne malo, libera nos. Ab omni peccato, libera nos. . . .*"

From all sin, deliver us. From all evil, deliver us.

The old man sprang to his feet, faster than Gerlach would have believed possible. He backed into a corner. "You are the evil!"

"*Oremus pro fidelibus defunctis...*"

"You must not do this! Please, brothers—"

Gerlach shut out the cries for mercy. He finished the litany but had to grope for the final words. His head throbbed like a rotten tooth. It felt wrong, all wrong. Near to panic, he tore a glove off and stooped down, drawing the faint residue of ley into his Marks. A pleasant numbness came over him, washing away any hesitation. *I act for the sake of all that is right and good. I act so the light will triumph over the darkness. I act from love, not malice.*

Brodszky glanced over. "What are you doing?"

"We owe him this much," Gerlach replied, his Marks igniting.

It would be quick and painless with the ley. Lezarius would feel nothing but bliss until the instant his heart stopped. Then they would leave Bryce with the body and go collect blood samples in Massot's cell until Valek sounded the alarm. It was lucky that agents from the OGD happened to be there working late. There would be an investigation, of course, but they'd be running it. Command and control from start to finish.

"That's not what we planned!" Brodszky grated.

The angry tone startled 26, who moaned and covered his ears. He started rocking back and forth, agitated, and Brodsky turned back to him, whispering urgent words Gerlach couldn't make out.

The old man drew himself up, facing his killer. Gerlach smiled gently as his hands closed around Lezarius's throat.

"Let me ease your fears, Reverend Father," he said.

Gerlach found the windpipe and closed it off. The saint's skin was dry and thin as old parchment. Power flowed from his hands, carrying the intention to calm. Gerlach had killed for the Praesidia before, but he had never used the ley on an Invertido and he immediately encountered the same problem Alexei did when he tried to subdue Dr. Massot. The ley did not behave as expected.

Lezarius's heels drummed against the floor. Gerlach bore down, sweat beading his forehead. Power hummed between them. Gerlach felt it building, bottlenecking, and suddenly a fist clouted his ear. "You fool," Brodszky snapped. "Have you forgotten what he is?"

The next moments were a blur. Brodszky raised his blade to finish it when large hands clamped around his head, twisting it with a snap. The blade clattered to the floor. Gerlach reached for it, but 26 got there first. The tip pressed against Gerlach's sternum. Blue eyes bored into him. Gerlach saw his own death reflected back.

"Go ahead," he said defiantly. "Others will come——"

The blade twisted sideways and thrust home, finding the gap between the fourth and fifth ribs on the left side of Gerlach's chest. He had an instant to grasp the disaster he had brought upon the world before the blade jerked in a practiced lateral sweep. Gerlach's heart muscle seized, then went into stuttering fibrillation. The blade withdrew.

Unconsciousness was immediate and death followed seconds later.

A SWIFT END, and cleaner than he deserved, Lezarius thought.

"I know who sent them," he rasped. "I remember it all now."

Mikhail tilted his head in a question.

"Thirty years they left me to rot. Thirty years!" Lezarius scrubbed a hand across his mouth. "But these walls will not hold me anymore." The old man sat up. "Justice will be served, but I cannot do it alone, Mikhail. Will you be my champion?"

Mikhail rubbed his arms. He cast his eyes down and shook his head. Lezarius cupped his chin, forcing him to look up.

"Why? Because they claim you are mad?"

Mikhail's gaze burned.

"Well, I am mad, too." He laughed. "I cannot be trusted! Will you die here, like a penned sheep, or will you help me?"

He searched the dead men's pockets. Each had a corax. He read the names and put them in the pocket of his tweed jacket. He found a set of car keys and took those as well. "Now, Mikhail," he said solemnly, "I will show you something."

Lezarius wore the Warded, mesh-lined gloves that blocked patients from touching the ley, but a residue from Gerlach still sang in his blood. He focused it and the Wards dissolved. Lezarius tore off the gloves. He stared at his fingers for a long moment. The skin was pale and damp as a mushroom. He raised a hand to his nose. It smelled bad.

Mikhail watched in silence as Lezarius washed in a bowl of water, scrubbing with soap until his hands were raw. Then he sat on the floor, letting the ley wash over him. Tears blurred his eyes. This is what they had taken from him. *This.*

He touched the deep vortex beneath the Arx, remembering the making of it. Had he desired, he could have broken the reservoir, irrevocably, but he also remembered what the mages who ruled Bal Agnar and Bal Kirith had done with the ley. The slave markets. The grinding poverty of the masses, while a handful of Nightmarked lived like emperors. They'd made their cities into jungles, with the strongest and cruelest taking the lion's share, and called it the natural order.

Lezarius knew he was mad, but he was still their foe.

He took his coat off, and his shirt. He could no longer create, but he could destroy.

The Raven blazed, so fiercely Mikhail threw an arm up to shield his face.

It began at the Arx. Channels of ley raced outward, disabling Wards as they went. The shockwave rolled through Novostopol. Within seconds, it reached the Institute. Mikhail cried out as his own Marks flared, and then the wave passed, spreading outwards toward the Void.

Mikhail breathed hard, but his eyes no longer held that terrible blankness. Lezarius put his shirt and coat back on. He took a last look around at the cell that had been his home for the last three years. He knew every crack in the plaster. Every creaky floorboard. He wondered how the world had changed in his absence. They had forgotten him, but now they would remember.

Lezarius slid a cardboard box from underneath the bed,

tucking it under one arm. "Come," he said to Mikhail. "Take the sword."

A tumult of shouts echoed through the corridor outside. Doors swung wide, patients spilling forth. A woman with fiery red hair jogged down the hall. She saw Mikhail and veered toward him. "Come on, big man," she coaxed, cupping his crotch. "Do you want me?"

Mikhail pushed her, the way you might push a tree branch out of the way if it blocked your path, and she stumbled back, falling on her bottom. "Well, fog you, too," she muttered. "Which way's out?"

Lezarius pointed.

"Thanks, Uncle," she said.

"You're welcome, Chey." He pulled her to her feet. "Be careful of the others. Just walk straight out the doors and follow the drive." He smiled. "Have yourself some fun."

"I'll do that." She grinned and took off running.

"Ah, freedom," Lezarius said. "Lead on, Mikhail."

His companion did not move. He stared after Chey like a startled doe. Lezarius had spent a good deal of time with him, playing chess or just sitting together, but the precise nature of his pain was difficult to determine because he never spoke. Lezarius had a few theories, though. Mikhail was Nightmarked. This would eliminate his inhibitions. But the Nightmark had Inverted, so the result would deviate from the reversal of a regular Mark. It might actually enhance certain inhibitions, while lifting others. Either way, Lezarius could see that the chaos was not having a salubrious effect.

"We cannot stay here," he said gently. "It will be quieter outside. Do you trust me?"

Mikhail nodded, head low.

"Then you must do as I say."

Mikhail lifted the sword, but only to point towards his own room.

He is afraid, Lezarius realized. The Institute is all he knows.

"What if we found your brother?" Lezarius said. "The priest?"

Mikhail did not answer, but Lezarius detected a glimmer of emotion in his eyes. They must have been close because the brother came twice a week faithfully and he never stopped coming even though Lezarius could see how painful the visits were for him. The priest's work brought him to the Institute, but he came on his days off, as well. He brought little gifts and ensured Mikhail received every comfort.

It saddened Lezarius to see the two of them together. The resemblance was strong, yet one was hale and the other wasting away. Lezarius had no doubt the priest would continue to come until his brother was dead.

"Mikhail?" he said. "Do you hear me? I can take you—"

A woman screamed. Mikhail's head snapped around. He took off running and Lezarius hurried after him. At the next intersection, they found Nurse Jeyna fighting off three men with a folding chair. They had her backed against a wall, but she was no easy prey. She jabbed one of them hard in the chest and he stumbled back, but the others used the chance to swarm closer and try to wrest the chair away.

Lezarius watched Mikhail wade into the fray, face set in grim lines. Mad, certainly, but still a knight. Would he dispatch the attackers with the same ruthless efficiency he had shown the priests? Or would he show mercy?

The question turned out to be moot. When Nurse Jeyna's assailants saw the hollow-cheeked giant with the blade in his hand, they turned tail and ran. Mikhail started to pursue. Lezarius seized his arm. The knight could easily have shaken him off, but he stopped, gazing down with a question in his blue eyes.

A gift from the ley, Lezarius thought, that Mikhail had been called upon to save the one person at the Institute who had treated him with kindness and courtesy. And a gift that he had not been forced to kill again. There would be enough of that later.

"You're needed here," Lezarius said. "Let them go."

Mikhail touched the Raven on his neck, which Lezarius took for assent.

Nurse Jeyna eyed them both warily. She still gripped the chair.

"Let us escort you out," Lezarius said.

She mutely shook her head.

"We won't harm you." He pointed to the sword. "The blood on that blade is from Curia assassins sent to kill me. Mikhail saved my life."

Jeyna licked her lips. Lezarius sensed that she doubted him, but she also knew he was no threat. Not to her, at least. "My car is in the lot," she said shakily, setting the chair down.

A few patients milled around the admitting area, more confused than aggressive. Lezarius greeted them all by name with friendly nods. No one troubled them as they exited the building and took the paved pathway leading around back to the parking lot. It was the first time he had been outside the Institute at night. Without the Wards, the grounds were very dark. The air smelled of wet earth, of living things rather than the stench of antiseptic cleaners. He veered off the cement, wiggling his bare toes in the grass.

"Oto left me." Jeyna wrapped her arms tight across her chest. "He pushed me right at those men and then he ran away."

"I never liked Oto Valek," Lezarius remarked. "If he crosses our path, Mikhail will deal with him."

Jeyna glanced over. "I won't try to stop you from leaving, Domine Sabran. But don't you think you'd both be safer here?" Her eyes held sympathy. "I fear the Interfectorum will handle you roughly if it is not Fra Bryce who finds you."

In private, she always called him by the name written on

his admitting file, not the number they had assigned him. But both were lies. He knew that now.

"That is not my name," he said with great dignity. "I am the Pontifex of the Northern Curia. Lezarius the Righteous."

"Of course." She smiled politely and looked down. "Forgive me."

She did not believe. "Who do you think shattered the Wards?" he snapped.

Nurse Jeyna glanced at him warily and Lezarius tamped down his anger. "It is not your fault," he muttered. "They misled you, too."

At his side, Mikhail's gaze searched the night, alert for any threat. The wooden quality to his movements was gone and he moved fluidly for such a tall man, left hand gripping the sword. Lezarius supposed it was partly because his medication was wearing off. The doctors kept Mikhail on very high doses of antipsychotics, which caused confusion and drowsiness. But he suspected that was not the only reason. Something long dormant was starting to wake.

"Where will you go?" Jeyna asked as they reached the parking lot. It was mostly empty. Only a skeleton staff stayed at the Institute overnight.

"To visit an old friend." Lezarius patted her shoulder. "Don't worry, we will find our own way. May the ley shelter and protect you, my dear."

"And you, Domine . . . Lezarius." She looked like she might say something more, but an unearthly shriek from inside the building hastened her steps. Jeyna jogged to her car, threw it into gear and burned rubber out of the lot.

There was only one vehicle with a Raven ornament on the hood. Lezarius tossed Mikhail the keys he'd taken from the assassin's body. "Do you remember how to drive?"

Mikhail caught the keys in his right hand. He slid behind the wheel. Lezarius got into the passenger seat, the shoebox resting on his lap. A soft mewing came from inside and he took the lid off, stroking the ball of fur nestled in an old towel.

Mikhail started the car, trailing Nurse Jeyna's taillights down the long drive to the gate. On both sides, patients capered across the lawn, white uniforms ghostly in the rain-soaked night.

"I wish I could help them," Lezarius said sadly. "But we have other business this night, Mikhail."

The knight stared straight ahead, seemingly mesmerized by the windshield wipers.

"You are doing well," Lezarius said. "I know it's not easy to leave this place, as much as you might despise it. They've convinced you that you are unfit to be anywhere else. That it is all your fault."

Mikhail shot him a sharp glance. So he was listening after all.

"They congratulate themselves for being so enlightened, so compassionate, and yet they cage us like laboratory animals." The edges of his mouth pulled down. "I fought for them, just as you did. And where has it gotten us? We must make our own justice." He touched the inverted flame on his neck. "Lux et lex. No, no, I need a new motto. One with some real flair. The mad shall inherit the earth! What do you think, Mikhail?"

Lezarius chuckled, but his laughter died when they found the gates locked tight. Jeyna's car was pulled off to the side, but she was nowhere to be seen. A guard stood silhouetted in the window of the gatehouse. He held a telephone to his ear and gestured frantically. Sirens wailed in the distance, growing closer with every passing moment.

"Mikhail," Lezarius said gravely. "We have trouble."

Chapter Twenty-Six

R ivulets of rainwater streamed down the diamond-paned windows of Cardinal Falke's library. A fire crackled in the hearth, though instead of bringing cheer it made the room stifling. Kasia glanced at the grandfather clock in the corner. It was a beautiful, intricate piece with a moon dial and painted background of a hilltop fort overlooking a pale blue harbor. The hands stood at just after nine o'clock.

She'd been waiting in her bedchamber, hoping Tess would leave and Nikola Thorn would return, when Cardinal Falke arrived with a posse of aides and informed them that the Castel Saint Agathe had been deemed insecure. It was too large, with too many entrances and exits. He had reason to believe Malach might find his way into the Arx.

Kasia had objected, but there was no convincing argument against it. So she'd slipped the deck of cards into a pocket and allowed them to escort her and Nashka to Falke's own residence.

"Where's our minder?" Natalya slouched in an armchair, slim legs tucked beneath her. "I expected she'd be here, poking us with her umbrella and making me recite declensions in the old tongue."

"Probably off reporting to Kireyev." Kasia shuffled the cards. "I need your advice."

"That bad, eh?"

"I saw Bryce. I think he's been framed." Her voice sank to a whisper. "Falke is covering up his ties to Dr. Massot."

"Can't really blame him. Stop looking at me like that. You only know one side of the story. The cardinal was a fogging *badass* during the war."

Kasia glanced pointedly at the closed doors to the library, where two of Falke's aides stood outside. Nashka lowered her voice. "Give him the benefit of the doubt. You have no idea what those letters mean."

"No, but don't you think it's wrong to keep them from the Pontifex?"

"I think it isn't your responsibility."

"Why not? I read them. I can't pretend ignorance."

Nashka sighed. "It's eating at you, isn't it? But you don't owe Bryce anything. You hardly know him. Maybe he did kill Massot. Will you throw yourself to the wolves for a priest?"

All valid and reasonable points.

Yet Kasia had learned that her first instincts were not to be trusted. It seemed clear that sometimes the greater good required the sacrifice of an innocent, yet most people would call such an outcome unjust. If Kasia did nothing, Bryce would likely die. If she spoke out, her secret would be revealed and people she cared about would suffer for having protected her. But the same thing might happen if she refused to continue spying for Kireyev, which was an immoral action in the sense that it harmed others for little tangible benefit.

When faced with such intractable dilemmas, Kasia generally did whatever she wanted.

She remembered the clever gleam in Bryce's blue eyes. His dry laugh. *From what I can tell, Domina Novak, you're more well-adjusted than I am.*

"He's a mess," she said, "but he's an interesting mess."

"I have a weakness for those, too."

Kasia shuffled the cards. "I suppose you'll say things are complicated enough and I oughtn't make them worse by sticking my neck out."

"No, I'd never say that." Natalya had found a pen and pad in one of the cabinets and was idly sketching. "We're screwed anyway. Might as well go out in a blaze of glory."

"Serious or joking?" She couldn't always tell with Nashka.

"Serious."

"What about the cardinal?"

Natalya looked up. "I still think he's a good man. But I promised to support you no matter what stupid thing you decided to do."

"You won't try to talk me out of it?"

"I know you. No point." She glanced at the cards. "Go ahead, ask them. It's obvious you're dying to."

With a flick of her thumb, Kasia spread the cards across a polished rosewood table. She was wearing gloves out of habit, but she wanted to feel the stiff, slightly waxy stock against her fingers. She tugged a glove off and chose a card.

The High Priestess again.

She sat on a throne, hair flowing down across her shoulders. A diadem circled her brow. As a symbol of fertility and the sacred feminine, breasts and hips were exaggerated beneath a simple white gown. The figure bore an uncanny resemblance to herself, but Nashka had painted the cards and she often based archetypes for the Major Arcana on people she knew.

Kasia drew a second card and was unsurprised to see an armored man astride a charger. Knights didn't ride horses anymore, they drove cars like everyone else, but Natalya was secretly a romantic. The Knight's helm was tucked under one arm, his gaze stern yet somehow beseeching. She touched a finger to the sword in his hand—and snatched it back as lines of blue fire traced the design.

"Nashka," she croaked, just as the pulsing light subsided.

She looked over to find Natalya staring.

"Did you see it?" Kasia asked faintly. "Am I losing my mind?"

"I saw it." Natalya leapt from the chair, the sketchpad sliding to her feet. "I saw it! Fog me, did you do that? You must have. How, Kiska?"

"I've no idea." Kasia tentatively touched the card again. Nothing happened. "But I've been seeing the ley since last night. When Malach attacked me on the roof, then again after I got here."

"And you didn't say anything?"

"I wasn't sure you'd believe it."

Natalya took her arms. "Darling," she said in her best Tessaria voice, a snooty drawl one only heard in Arbot Hills. "You know you mean the world to me. I would never, ever doubt—"

"All right," Kasia laughed giddily, prying herself free. "Point taken."

Natalya's forehead notched. "Did you try to make the ley do something? Did you make a wish?"

"No."

"Then the cards could be acting more like Wards. Protective. But if they're not, if they *are* like Marks, you mustn't ever touch the abyssal. Only the surface ley. The other is dangerous."

"I'm not sure I'd know the difference," Kasia said uneasily.

Nashka nodded at the Ward above the library windows. "What do you see?"

"Blue light."

"That's the surface ley. The other two layers are underneath."

"This is crazy," Kasia said. "It must have been you who did it."

"Don't be daft. I'm wearing gloves. And I wasn't anywhere near the cards."

"But how could you have made Marks? And how could I possibly channel ley without a patron?"

Nashka shrugged. "You handle the cards all the time. Maybe they're a part of you now."

It wasn't really an answer. She thought of the eerily similar conversation she'd had with Bryce at her flat, except that he'd been the skeptic and she'd been the one suggesting that the cards might have turned Dr. Massot.

But they're just paper, Alexei had protested.

And Wards are just stone, she'd replied.

The windows looked out on a broad expanse of lawn. Lamps illuminated the avenues beyond, leaving deep pools of shadow in the gaps between buildings. Far in the distance, pinpoints of light marked the outer wall.

"I'm going to seek an audience with the Reverend Mother," Kasia said. "I probably won't get within a hundred meters of her, but if I don't try tonight, it will be too late." She shivered and rubbed her arms. "I can feel it in the air, can't you? Something is coming."

"The mage?" Natalya asked warily.

"I don't know."

"Then I'll go with you. I'm far more charming."

"No, you must stay here." She glanced at the doors. "Keep talking and make some noise now and then, or they'll get suspicious."

"What if Falke comes back? Or Tess?" Nashka thought for a moment. "Not sure which is worse, really."

"Tell them I went stir crazy and snuck out for a walk."

"They won't believe that for an instant."

"Well," she said, "by then it won't matter."

"Do you really care about Bryce so much?" The tone was more curious than judging.

"Yes. But I'm not doing it for him, I'm doing it for me. Because I won't like myself otherwise."

"A selfish selfless act," Nashka chuckled. "If you save him from the dungeon, maybe he'll put out, you know? He ought to."

"Yeah, he really ought to," Kasia agreed.

"Too bad you don't have sensible shoes."

"Give me yours."

Natalya tugged off her ankle boots and tossed them over. "Take the cards," she advised. "I haven't a clue how it works with you, but priests can tap the liminal ley. It's the violet stuff just below the surface. It twists chance in their favor."

Kasia unhooked the latch and opened the windows. "I could use some of that," she said, "since I haven't a fogging clue where her bedchamber is."

Kasia pulled her gloves on. She swept up the cards, tucking them into her jacket pocket. Then she swung her legs across the sill and dropped down, low heels sinking into the sodden lawn. The air smelled of bitter orange blossoms, warm and floral. She encountered no one until she reached the Pontifex's Palace. Six vestal knights in blue and gold cloaks stood before the engraved bronze doors of the main entrance.

She crept around the huge domed building, searching for a darkened window. More knights patrolled the grounds around the palace. A pair came around the wing just ahead and Kasia crouched behind a stone planter until their steps faded. At last, she found a small mullioned window with no light behind it. Kasia waited for a flash of lightning. When a rumble of thunder followed, she used a rock to break one of the panes and undo the latch. The Ward above didn't flicker as she climbed inside. Just like the Markhound outside Massot's house, she was invisible to it.

Kasia closed the window, hoping the darkness would conceal the broken glass for a while. She stood in a long marble gallery. Ley flowed at her feet in a phosphorescent blue river. Like water, it swirled and eddied around obstacles, moving in a sluggish but visible current towards the end of the gallery. Curious, she took a glove off and crouched down to dip a hand into the light. The ley around her fingers darkened to violet. Kasia drew a card. Nothing happened. She tried to sense the power, but although she could see it, there was no sensation of contact or control.

How on earth did she do it before?

Or maybe she hadn't at all. In which case, it was unlikely she'd get very far.

Kasia slipped the boots off and started walking in her stocking feet. She passed chapels and libraries, vast halls and administrative offices, all lavishly decorated with frescos and tapestries and decorative plasterwork. There were Ravens everywhere, set into the marble floors and sculpted on panels in the bronze and gold doors. Huge ones two meters across and tiny ones the size of hummingbirds. Ravens in flight and Ravens in profile.

Wards shone over every door and window. No nihilim could come anywhere near the Reverend Mother.

A few times she heard soft footsteps and hid herself while a gray-clad char strode past, but most of the rooms were unoccupied and lit only by standing oil lamps. She had no idea where the Pontifical apartments were. Surely it wouldn't be long before Tessaria or Falke decided to check on her and Natalya—if they hadn't already.

She picked up the pace of her search, growing increasingly frustrated. Then she heard voices approaching, low and urgent. There was nowhere to hide. She darted down a long passageway with slender fluted columns and around the corner at the end. Three vestal knights in blue and gold strode towards her. She spun around. Two more approached at a fast jog. One raised a crossbow and aimed the bolt at her chest.

"On your knees!"

Kasia sank down, fixing her gaze on the floor.

"She's ungloved."

"An assassin?"

"How did you get in here?" Rough hands dragged her to her feet. "Perhaps the inside of a cell will loosen your tongue."

She palmed the oracle deck, trying to hide it, but the action drew the knight's attention. "What is that?"

Fingers gripped her hair, jerking her head back. A card fell from the deck, floating on the surface of the ley.

The Knight of Wards.

She lay on a bower of white flowers with glossy, dark green vines wound around her armor. The barred visor of her helm was raised. Her eyes were closed, her expression serene.

Kasia heard the metallic clink of manacles and struggled wildly.

"Let go of me," she spat. "Let go!"

The card lit with lines of blue fire, blindingly bright. There was a single shout of surprise and the hands holding her let go. Kasia stumbled back, a black afterimage floating before her eyes. Five mailed bodies thudded noisily to the ground.

Oh fog it. What had she done?

A quick examination of the women revealed that they were breathing normally and didn't seem hurt. Kasia picked up the Knight of Wards. Sometimes called The Dreamer.

She stepped over the sleeping bodies and continued on, this time following the current of ley. It led her through a second gallery and up a broad, gently curving staircase to the top floor of the palace and along a corridor with painted panels depicting the Five Virtues. When she reached the end, Kasia peeked around the corner. A white-haired woman in purple robes sat at a desk positioned next to a pair of tall, heavily carved doors, jotting notes in a ledger.

It was not the Reverend Mother. Kasia knew Feizah's face almost as well as her own since it hung in every establishment in the city. She fanned the deck, searching for the Dreamer again, and threw the card to the stone floor. Nothing happened. Kasia focused her will. *Make her sleep.*

The vestal didn't look up from her ledger.

Kasia reviewed the little she knew about the ley. Only mages could control it directly, and even then, the power was unpredictable. Intent and need—those were the key ingredients. Perhaps she was going about it wrong. The cards only gave a true reading when they were drawn randomly, and it was likely they worked the same way for the ley.

She closed her eyes and let her fingertips dance along the edge of the deck until they touched a card poking out slightly farther than the rest. Kasia tossed it down, holding firm to the idea that she did not want to cause harm, only pass by unmolested. The Six of Storms floated on the surface. An instant later, lines of violet light traced the card. She'd tapped the liminal ley. Kasia peeked around the corner.

The vestal went to dip her quill pen and sneezed violently, knocking the inkpot into her lap. Kasia heard a muffled oath. The vestal rose to her feet, brushing at her cassock, which only turned her hand black. Another oath. She lifted the telephone on her desk, paused, then laid it back in the cradle. "It'll only take a moment," she muttered.

Kasia realized the woman was about to head her way and took off running in her stocking feet. She ducked into a side corridor and pressed against the wall. Footsteps approached, then paused at the juncture of the corridor. "What's this?"

Fog it. She'd left the card lying on the floor and the woman had noticed it. Ten seconds later, the vestal strode past. When she'd gone, Kasia hurried back to the vestibule. The Six of Storms was gone. How that might affect the ley, she had no idea, but she couldn't turn back now. She drew a deep breath and knocked on the carved doors.

"Enter," a gravelly voice commanded.

The doors were broad and heavy but unlocked. She opened the one on the left and stepped into a large bedchamber, closing the door behind her. A woman in half-moon glasses and beige satin pajamas sat propped against a mountain of pillows on the largest bed Kasia had ever seen. It rested atop a platform with three steps leading up to the bed itself. Curtains could be drawn on either side, although these had been left open. Papers covered the quilt. The Pontifex's hair was white and closely shorn, her skin the color of age-darkened walnut. A gold signet ring adorned her left hand, which was not gloved.

"Don't be afraid, Reverend Mother," Kasia said. "I'm not here to harm you."

The Pontifex Feizah regarded Kasia impassively. She raised her hand. A terrible wind rose, scattering the papers. Kasia flew backwards across the room, toes dragging on the carpet, and found herself plastered against the far wall.

"How did you get inside the palace?"

"Through a window," Kasia grunted, eyeing Feizah sidelong since her cheek was also pressed to the wall.

"That's impossible."

"I'm here, aren't I?"

Feizah's white brows drew down. The force hauled Kasia upwards until her feet dangled three feet from the floor. "Show some respect, girl! What do you want?"

"To seek your help with a priest."

"If he got you with child, that is your business," the Reverend Mother said tartly. "I do not intervene in affairs of the heart."

"No, no, he's in the jail below the Arx."

Shrewd brown eyes studied her. "What is his name?"

"Fra Alexei Vladimir Bryce."

The force eased enough that Kasia's toes touched solid ground again.

"Bryce?" She seemed surprised, which Kasia took as a good sign.

"Do you know him?" There were hundreds of priests in the Eastern Curia.

"I Marked Alexei Bryce myself," Feizah said. "Eighteen times. The most Marks I've ever given to anyone below the rank of bishop."

"Cardinal Falke told me he had nineteen."

Feizah's gaze sharpened. "Falke is correct. Fra Bryce's first Mark was bestowed by Bishop Bartolomes."

Kasia recognized the name. In a rare burst of initiative, she'd gone to court to fight a parking ticket—unjustly handed down since the towaway zone sign was blocked by scaffolding—and Bartolomes presided over her case. He'd taken her side, ruling against the official from the Historic Preservation Council on the basis that the scaffolding had been erected two years prior with little or no activity at the site since, and constituted a public nuisance.

"I've heard Bishop Bartolomes is a very wise man," Kasia said.

"Never mind Bartolomes," Feizah snapped. "Why is Fra Bryce in the cells?"

"There is a plot afoot, Reverend Mother."

"A plot?" A shaggy brow lifted. "By whom?"

"Cardinal Falke conspired to falsely accuse Bryce of murder in a bid to cover up his own wrongdoing at the Batavia Institute."

"That's quite an accusation. Do you have proof?"

"No."

The Pontifex shook her head in disgust. "Then I shall summon the guards and throw you in a cell for trespassing."

"But I've seen the proof, Reverend Mother. Take it from my mind."

The Pontifex blinked. "A sweven? Do you know what you're offering, girl?"

"I've heard of them. It can be done, *da*?"

"It can. But once you let me in, I can see anything I want. All your secrets. Do you understand that?"

Kasia stared at her. "I have nothing to hide, Reverend Mother."

"Everyone has something to hide. Sometimes we conceal it even from ourselves. It's not a choice to be made lightly."

"Let me down first. I feel like a blinchiki." Both she and Nashka adored the thin pancakes rolled up with strawberry jam.

Feizah lowered her hand. The force pressing Kasia to the wall disappeared.

"How did you do that?" she asked, wiggling her toes, which had gone all pins and needles.

"A unique ability and none of your concern. Now, what is this proof you claim?"

"Letters. I no longer have them in my possession, but I recall them verbatim."

"Well, your word will not suffice, girl. So what will it be?" The tone softened slightly. "I do not believe you mean me harm. Perhaps you are just flighty and lovesick, with an over-active imagination."

Kasia's gaze narrowed.

"So if you choose not to share the sweven, I won't hold it against you. If you are charged with trespassing, I will be required to give an official statement and I haven't the time. So go, if you wish. The incident will be forgotten." She waved a hand at a silver tea service. "You may take that to the kitchens on your way out and tell them to bring me a fresh pot."

Kasia considered the offer—she'd be a fool not to—but Kireyev would reveal her secret if she didn't cooperate, which she'd already decided she wouldn't. And she did not like to think of Alexei in that dripping, clammy dungeon. She just hoped she didn't end up next to him.

"I will share the sweven," she said firmly.

"Then disrobe, girl."

"Pardon?"

"I won't have you within arm's length until I examine your Marks."

Kasia swallowed. "I'm not a nihilim."

Feizah was unmoved. "So you say."

"Must I?"

"No. You can leave."

She sighed and stripped to the skin. Her cheeks burned under Feizah's gaze. Kasia liked herself well enough, but the expanse of bare skin . . . . well, no one had seen her so since she was a child.

"Why do you not wear the gray?" Feizah demanded.

"Take the answer from my head," Kasia replied defiantly.

"Oh, I will." The Pontifex's tone was not reassuring. "You may dress."

Kasia turned her back and pulled her clothes back on.

"Come closer, girl. Take my hand."

She climbed the three steps to the massive bed and sat on the edge. A huge bouquet of flowers gave off a cloying scent from the end table. Ley swirled around them both. "Think of what you wish to show me," Feizah said. "Hold it in your mind."

Kasia wound her memories back to the night of the dinner party when she offered to take Natalya's place and stood outside her own flat, hand raised to hail a taxi.

"Do you permit me to enter your mind?" Feizah asked.

A frisson of nervous energy. "Yes."

"Answer in the old tongue." The flinty decree reminded her of Tessaria.

"Verum," she said.

Feizah's grip was firm and warm, the palm slightly rough. The bedchamber receded and she was back at Massot's house, except that this time she knew what would happen and was powerless to stop it. Scene after scene unspooled, faster and faster, like a panicked rat running through a maze. The sweven reached the end, the very moment when Feizah commanded her to disrobe, and began anew. Fragments spun through her head like shattered glass, of other places, other things. She could not escape. Could not . . . .

A choked gasp tore from her throat. Kasia opened her eyes. Tears streamed down her cheeks. Her fingers gripped the bedsheet, the knuckles white. The hands of the clock next to the flowers had not moved far, only a few minutes, though it seemed much longer.

The Pontifex was staring at her with a stunned expression. "It cannot be," she whispered. "And yet . . . ."

"What, Reverend Mother?"

"Hush! I'm thinking."

Kasia wiped her face. She felt drained.

"I've never seen memories like yours, girl," Feizah muttered hoarsely. "Always, the edges are lost to mist. Key elements remain, those things that stood out, that made a strong impression, but the finer details are lost. Not with yours." She scowled. "You are Unmarked. And yet you use the ley."

"The ability only came to me recently, Reverend Mother."

"Nonetheless, I do not like it." Each word was bit off.

"I didn't do it on purpose!" Kasia protested.

"You are devious and a liar. Still, you risked much by coming to me. I suppose that counts as a sort of courage. I only hope it's not too late."

"Too late, Reverend Mother?"

The Pontifex strode to a telephone and dialed a number. "Find Archbishop Kireyev. Bring him to me. Immediately." She listened for a moment. "No, I'll tell him myself." She slammed the phone down and stood gazing into space, one hand twisting the gold signet ring.

"Will you pardon Fra Bryce?" Kasia asked.

"Bryce is the least of my problems, girl," she snapped.

"But you *will* let him go?"

"Pushy, aren't you? We'll see." She picked up the receiver and dialed another number. It was answered within two rings. "Captain Demyov? Dispatch three units to the Batavia Institute. Keep it quiet, no sirens. There's a patient I need secured. Number 9." She listened. "Saints no, don't bring him out. Just make sure the Wards are active and bar the gates. Escort all the staff from the premises. Knights only." The Pontifex hung up.

"Who's Patient 9?" Kasia asked, curiosity burning inside her.

"That's not your concern. Make yourself useful and pour me some tea."

"I won't tell a soul, Reverend Mother."

"Of course you will. And he's no one."

"Then why—"

"Tea, girl!"

Kasia lowered her head and made a face. She was filling one of the thin porcelain cups when the tray began to vibrate. Tea splashed on her stocking feet. Something swept the room. It wasn't tangible, more a sensation of some unknowable force arising and subsiding. Distant shouts echoed in the corridor outside. The flow of the ley grew stronger and more turbulent.

"What's happening?" she asked.

The Pontifex didn't answer. She stood with one hand still resting on the telephone, her gaze distant.

"Is it the Nightmage?" Kasia pressed.

"Nihilim cannot break Wards."

"What then?"

"A surge of the ley."

"How long will it last?"

"The Wards self-repair, but it could be hours before they return. The ley has been rising for weeks. I should have opened the floodgates sooner."

"So it's a coincidence?"

"Perhaps." The Pontifex sounded unsure. "But in case it isn't, help me push this desk in front of the door."

"Don't you have guards?"

"If the nihilim comes, they will do me no good." She barked a mirthless laugh. "They will try to kill me themselves if he lays his hands on them."

Kasia hurried over. She rolled up the carpet and dragged it out of the way. They braced their hips against the short side of the desk, straining for every centimeter.

"What kind of wood is this?" she panted. "It's heavy as cast iron!"

"Lignum vitae," the Pontifex replied, pressing a fist to the small of her back. "Holy wood. This piece is more than six hundred years old."

Kasia's legs were trembling. They still had several meters to go. "I don't think—"

"Just push, girl," the Pontifex snapped. "On three!"

Kasia gritted her teeth and heaved. The telephone rang. Feizah ignored it. They were both red-faced and sweating by the time they'd maneuvered the monstrous desk in front of the door. Kasia slumped down, catching her breath. She crawled over to the teapot and poured a cup. It was cold and bitter.

A sudden pounding. "Your Eminence?"

"I'm well, Sor Dvorak," Feizah called through the door.

The phone started ringing again, a shrill buzz that made Kasia want to yank the cord from the wall.

"There's a car waiting out front," said a muffled voice that sounded like the same aide who had spilled the inkpot. "The Archbishop strongly suggests you evacuate while we determine the cause of the surge."

"Kireyev," she muttered with a scowl. Then louder: "I will not flee, and neither will the Archbishop. Gather the guards and seal the palace. No one is to pass. No one!"

The phone stopped ringing, then started again seconds later. Feizah picked it up, still a touch breathless. "How many escaped?" A pause. "*All of them?*" She exhaled through her nose. "Set every pack to hunt. And release Fra Alexei Bryce immediately. The Interfectorem will be hard-pressed as it is." A muffled voice. "I don't care what he said. Just do it!" She slammed the phone down.

"What's happened, Reverend Mother?"

"Unmitigated disaster, that's what," Feizah snapped. "You should have come to me sooner."

Kasia stared back, anger welling. "If I'd been Marked, I would have," she retorted. "But I had no reason to think you'd believe me. I was useless to you before. A stain on society, to be swept under the rug. Forgive me if I didn't expect a warm reception."

The Pontifex shot her a baleful look. "So Bryce discovered your secret. Well, he's tenacious. He would have made a decent diplomat, but he turned down my offer of a post in Nantwich."

"Diplomat? I thought he was a knight."

The Pontifex stared at the door, as if judging its sturdiness. "Before joining the priesthood, Fra Bryce was a defense attorney," she replied absently. "A good one. But like many young men of his generation, he was also a patriot. When we issued an open call for recruits, his conscience compelled him to answer."

It explained why his first Mark was from Judge Bartolomes. Kasia suspected Alexei the lawyer had no trouble sleeping at night. "Why did you give him so many Marks?"

"Because I knew he didn't want them, which made him worthy."

"Isn't that cruel?" Kasia said, adding a belated, "Reverend Mother."

"Sometimes one must be cruel to lead."

"Really?" she said innocently. "But that's precisely the sort of utilitarian logic that caused me to fail your tests."

The Pontifex scowled. "Don't bandy words with me, girl.

Fra Bryce was an exemplary knight. I needed him. Marks are an honor."

"Well, you messed him up!" The words came out angrier than she intended, but Kasia saw no reason to take them back since the statement was patently true.

"In what way?"

"You saw it yourself. He can't sleep."

The Pontifex strode to the window and closed a set of heavy shutters, sliding a bar into place. "That is none of my doing."

"I think it is."

The women traded a glare of mutual dislike.

"I don't know who you really are, girl, but I intend to find out," Feizah said at last.

"I showed you who I am."

"No. There is a block in your mind, either placed there or self-imposed, but I will break through it."

Block? "What on earth are you talking about?"

"Your memories begin at age six. Rather late, don't you think?"

"I remember things before that," Kasia objected.

"Barely. They are more like the impressions of an infant. Colors and sounds with no meaning."

"I have a peculiar memory." She frowned. "You *did* dig through my head. Well beyond the sweven!"

"I warned you I might."

Kasia eyed the desk in front of the door. "I suppose I'm your prisoner now."

"Only until the Wards come back." The Pontifex smiled unpleasantly. "But you will not be leaving the Arx anytime soon, Katarzynka Nowakowski."

"That's my thanks for warning you of the cardinal's treachery?"

Feizah was silent for a long moment. "I am not convinced it is treachery, though he will be dealt with for acting without my authorization. But you . . . I think you have been using the ley for far longer than a day." Kasia opened her mouth to protest and the Pontifex held up a hand. "Not with conscious awareness. But how else do you explain your talent of cartomancy?"

"I did suspect the ley was involved," Kasia admitted. "But I didn't understand the mechanism. I still don't."

"Nor do I. Yet it is telling that Massot turned in the very midst of his reading with you."

"I know." She met the older woman's eyes. "I thought the same, Reverend Mother."

Feizah relented, her stern demeanor softening. "I will see what can be done about Bryce. Now help me gather up these papers."

Kasia obeyed, trudging through the cavernous room to collect the scattered pieces of parchment. Like Falke's library, it was lit only by several large candelabra. The decor was stuffy and rich and had probably been exactly the same for centuries.

They'll never let me go now, she thought disconsolately. I will grow old and gray within the walls of the Arx while Feizah tries to figure out how my brain works. Kasia's eye lit on the darkened Ward above the door. Though they will have a time of it trying to keep me.

"Reverend Mother?" she said.

"What?"

"Natalya didn't mean any disrespect when she said you snapped up all the pretty ones. She says things like that all the time . . . ." Kasia trailed off when she realized that the Pontifex was paying her no attention and it had grown very quiet in the corridor.

"Guards?" the Pontifex called. "Sor Dvorak?"

No answer came.

Feizah rolled up her sleeves. Abstract geometrical designs ran from forearm to wrist, thick dark lines and whorls. She knelt and pressed a palm to the floor. The Marks flared to life.

"Hide, girl," the Pontifex snapped. "And stay silent."

Something thudded against the door hard enough to crack the oak.

Kasia ran to a tall wardrobe at the far end of the apartment and parted the white robes hanging inside. She stuffed herself into the gap just as another resounding blow shattered the lock. The door opened an inch and struck the makeshift barrier. A second later, the desk screeched across the floor like a toy kicked by a petulant child.

Kasia managed to get the wardrobe mostly shut, though it wouldn't latch and a slice of the chamber was visible through the crack. She pressed back into the darkness, pulse spiking. It had to be Malach. Who else—

An elderly man in a tweed suit stepped through the splintered doorframe. Frizzy white hair crowned a dark-skinned face with bright green eyes. The Blue Flame of the North Marked his neck, but it was inverted. He carried a shoebox. At his side loomed a bearded giant holding a sword. Both of them were barefoot and bloody, like something out of a Dark Age horror novel.

"*Feizah*," the old man rasped, his voice tight with hatred.

Chapter Twenty-Seven

A mailed fist to the kidneys brought Malach to his knees. A clout to the ear knocked him flat. Boots pinned his arms and legs to the stone floor.

"I don't doubt you would prefer death," Cardinal Falke said, "but that would be a tragic waste. There are so few of you now, I can't afford to throw any away. You can still serve the Via Sancta."

He produced a scalpel from his robes, the edge glinting in the candlelight. "I'll leave your manhood intact. Without hands, though . . . you'll never touch the ley again." He sounded weary. "Think of it as a compromise."

"You don't have to do this." Blood thundered in Malach's ears. "I already—"

Falke's eyes narrowed. "You already what?"

I'll never tell them about you. No matter what they do to me.

"I already told Beleth everything. And when I don't come home, she'll bury you all."

The cardinal gazed down at him. There was no emotion in his face. Nothing but calm conviction. "I'm afraid this will hurt. It's fortunate you enjoy pain."

A sharp whiff of antiseptic hit Malach's nose. Something

cold swabbed the skin of his wrist. Pressure, and a brief sting as skin parted beneath the scalpel. It was so sharp he barely felt it, though he would once the blade reached tendon and bone.

He could speak her name. If he kept their bargain, Falke might spare him. Malach didn't really believe what he'd told her. The Curia would not kill Nikola Thorne. They would keep her as a brood mare.

Falke seemed to sense his hesitation. The blade paused in its work. Malach drew a ragged breath. His mouth tasted of hot metal.

"A scalpel won't get you through the bone," he spat.

"Not to worry," the cardinal replied serenely. "I have other tools at my disposal. I'll do my best to make it quick, you have my word."

Malach regarded the man he hated above all others, the man who had spared his life when he was just a child and now thought to use him as a prize stallion. His memory of the time was hazy, he couldn't have been more than three or four, but he remembered that moment with perfect clarity. Both parents buried in the rubble and a tall knight standing over him with a sword. He expected to die, but the knight raised his visor, a troubled expression in his dark eyes, and sheathed the blade. *Run*, he commanded gruffly. *Run, boy!*

"I never meant to give you a child," Malach said in a venomous whisper. "I would have killed it myself first."

A muscle feathered in Falke's jaw. "That is unfortunate. But you will now, Malach. You'll give me whatever I ask for."

He bore down with the scalpel. Malach had seen the severing done to others and knew exactly how bad it would be. He gritted his teeth but refused to look away. Suddenly, the blade vibrated like a tuning fork. In the space of a single heartbeat, the room filled with ley. It surged through Malach's palms and into his Marks. They flared like a dying sun.

Falke reared back. The scalpel clattered to the floor. He

was a man hardened in combat, but his voice was not entirely steady as he ordered his knights. "Keep him restrained—"

Lines of red fire traced the Mark called Summoning the Storm. On Malach's left thigh, the Red Warden opened his pitiless eyes. On his right biceps, nightmarish scenes flickered across the surface of The Dark Mirror.

And in the skies above the Castel Saint Agathe, black clouds roiled. Lightning stabbed the spire of the basilica. The wind rose to a primal howl, spinning the weathervane atop the keep.

Death flowed from him like blood from an open wound.

He tore an arm free and seized the scalpel, jamming it into Falke's thigh. The cardinal grunted and staggered back. Malach reached for the nearest priest and clamped his hand around a hairy calf, releasing a flood of pain and hatred. The priest's eyes bulged. Blood trickled from one ear. With a snarl, the man drove his blade toward the one pinning Malach's right arm. The priest spun away and it sliced across his cheek. A pitcher shattered as the pair locked together, staggering across the chamber in ferocious combat.

The third and fourth leapt back, wary. They stood shoulder to shoulder, blocking the door. Each held a broadsword. Malach ducked under a whistling slash. Behind him, he heard a fading scream as one of the others fell from the narrow window to the courtyard below.

"Come closer," he coaxed the knights, holding out his hand. A steady drip of blood pattered like rain on the stone floor. "That's it. Just a little closer . . . ."

MALACH SURVEYED the three bodies sprawled across the chamber.

The one he wanted most had fled. No fool, Dmitry Falke. But a scarlet trail led into the corridor and Malach would find him.

A quick slice with the scalpel produced a length of cloth to bind his wrist. Falke hadn't gotten far in his work and the slash was superficial. With one foot, Malach rolled over the priest from General Directorate. He divested the corpse of its black robe, putting it on himself. Malach yanked the cowl up and strode from the chamber. A char in gray ran past him down the corridor. Malach ignored her. He had no quarrel with the Unmarked.

But their masters and mistresses . . . .

Halfway down the spiral stairs, he came face-to-face with two vestals. Before they could react, his hand shot out, lightly touching the nearest on her wrist. She rounded on her companion with teeth bared. He left them rolling on the ground, trading vicious blows.

The blood trail was thick and dark and led straight to the main doors where, to Malach's fury, it vanished in the torrential rain. He stepped outside, short dark hair whipping in the gale. Lines of cars moved towards the gates. The bells tolled and tolled. Not a single Ward shone in the night. Knights poured out of their garrison, rushing in the direction of the Pontifex's Palace.

This was not for him. So what had happened?

Ley swirled at his feet, swift and deep. It had been rising for days, yes, but enough to blow all the Wards at once? Such an event was unprecedented.

Or could it possibly have been Lezarius?

If it was indeed the man who had made the Void, Malach doubted he would die so easily.

Still, he was having second thoughts about Falke's claim. Spirit a Pontifex away to some far-flung asylum and install a puppet in his place? For what purpose? At face value, it was ridiculous.

But the very improbability almost made Malach believe it. In fact, he could think of several reasons. Lezarius might have turned and it was too much of an embarrassment to admit he'd gone mad so the Curia hid him away. Or one of his rivals could be behind it.

"Fuck," he muttered.

What he really wanted was to tear the Arx apart, stone by stone, until he found the cardinal, but revenge would have to wait. Malach pulled his hood up and ran to intercept one of the departing cars, waving his arms. It slowed. The driver's side window rolled down.

"What is it, brother?" The priest behind the wheel was young, with the milky skin and dimpled cheeks of a farmboy. When he saw the Golden Bough on Malach's cassock, he sat up straighter. "Ah, I mean *Father*."

"Where's everyone going?"

The boy cast him a strange look. "We've been called out to restore order. The Invertido are loose, Father."

"Do you know what happened?"

He shrugged. "A surge of the ley. The Wards will be back soon enough."

"How soon?"

"I don't know, Father. An hour or so."

Malach leaned down. "Get out of the car."

The boy stared at him. At the Broken Chain glowing forge-red along his collarbone. A dagger appeared from his cassock, but Malach caught his hand mid-strike. The boy's eyes dilated to black holes. A choking sob tore from his throat. A sound of utter hopelessness and despair. He twisted toward the passenger seat and drove the blade into his partner's chest, six rapid blows, then sheathed it in his own heart.

Malach dragged the bodies from their seats and rolled them into the bushes. The dagger was still inside the car. He set it neatly on the dashboard. He threw the gearshift into drive and floored the pedal, humming tunelessly.

It was a lovely night for a bloodbath.

Chapter Twenty-Eight

D eep below the Arx, the water was rising.

It sloshed around Alexei's knees as he used Kasia's hairpin to pry at the lock of his cell. He'd been scratching away for hours with no progress. The heavy chains around his legs would drag him down when the flood peaked. He'd called out for the guards, but either they couldn't hear him or they had gone.

Alexei jiggled the hairpin, but he had only a superficial understanding of locks and a prison cell would hardly be simple to crack, even with the proper tools. He gave a hard, frustrated twist and the pin slipped from his fingers. Alexei dropped to hands and knees, fingers groping across the slimy stone, but it was gone.

The last torch died. Even the phantoms had deserted him.

Someone gave a dry chuckle. It took a moment to realize it was himself.

Alexei listened to the rush of water, trying to calculate how long it would take before the level overtopped the bars. The rise had been slow at first, a few centimeters an hour, but it was faster now. Would they bother to collect his corpse, or would it be left to drift in the cold and black like the bloated cargo of a shipwreck?

The Ward on his manacles gave off a glimmer of light, though it failed to penetrate the darkness pressing in on all sides.

I will make my peace before I go.

Alexei closed his eyes. Battered as his faith might be, it was all he had left. He ran the pad of his thumb over the corax and the words engraved around the edge. *Foras admonitio.* Without warning. The motto of the Beatus Laqueo.

Saints, watch over my brother. If his end must come, make it swift and painless.

Blood thundered in his ears. The sound grew louder and he realized it was not inside his head at all. He hooked an arm around the bars, bracing for the wall of floodwater that must be racing down the corridor. The Ward above his cell winked out, followed by the Ward on the manacles. Utter darkness descended.

Something swept through him like a fresh breeze on a humid summer's day. The knot in his gut loosened. Despite his circumstances, Alexei felt pleasantly relaxed. A surge of the ley. It had to be. He'd never experienced it before because the Curia always released the excess power before it could overtop the Wards.

He smiled. Heads would roll for this. And for once, it wouldn't be his.

The dull roar receded. Alexei drew ley into his Marks as if he'd crawled across a desert to find a sparkling oasis. He did not try to touch the abyssal ley again. Never again. But he bathed in the violet light of the liminal layer, letting his need flow outward into the rushing current.

After a time, distant splashes echoed on the stone walls.

"Hello?" Alexei yelled. "Is someone there?"

The glow of a torch appeared. It was two priests he knew from General Directorate, though not well. Both were low-ranking aides. His mind had cleared enough to recall their names, Zsolt and Kelemen.

"You're being released," Zsolt said. "By order of the Pontifex."

It was what he'd prayed for, but the liminal ley rarely operated in so direct a fashion. "Why?"

They glanced at each other. "There's a problem at the Institute. You're to report to the kennels immediately."

His pulse skipped. "What problem?"

Kelemen stood against the far wall of the corridor, silently watching, while Zsolt unlocked the cell. They'd placed the torch in a bracket. Reflected flames danced across the black water.

"A mass escape when the ley surged." The priest withdrew a second, smaller set of keys. "Turn around. I'll unlock your leg irons."

Alexei hesitated. "Where's Fra Spassov?"

"Waiting for you at the Tower of Saint Dima." He made an impatient gesture. "Turn around."

Kelemen stepped into the cell, standing just behind Zsolt. His hands were hidden in the sleeves of his cassock.

The bitter taste of adrenaline flooded Alexei's mouth. "Did Archbishop Kireyev send you?"

"Just turn around. Did you not hear me? You've been released!"

Alexei started to turn his back. From the corner of his eye, he saw Kelemen's ungloved hands come up. Alexei spun, driving an elbow. The priest staggered back, blood spouting from his nose. Alexei reached for the iron bars as a thin cord fell around his neck. It tightened until blackness throbbed behind his eyes.

Zsolt's breath panted against his ear. "I have him."

The cell bars receded down a narrow tunnel. Alexei scrabbled wildly and managed to get a hand over Zsolt's. He bared his teeth, drawing ley directly from the priest's own Marks.

Zsolt screamed. His feet slipped in the water and they tumbled backward, Alexei landing on top. A snap like a twig breaking and the body beneath him went still. He tore at the noose and rolled away, coughing.

Zsolt sat against the wall. His neck was twisted at an odd angle, eyes half-closed and glassy.

A one-in-a-hundred stroke of luck.

"Demon," Kelemen spat.

Alexei leapt at the priest with savage ferocity. He got him in a hammerlock and forced his head under the water. When Kelemen began to weaken, Alexei released him. The priest sputtered while Alexei dug through Zsolt's pockets. No keys. They must have fallen. He focused on the spot he'd been standing when they entered the cell, methodically sweeping his fingers through the dark water. Just where the cell bars met the corridor, he brushed metal.

Please, don't let it be the hairpin.

The current almost had it. Alexei licked his lips, taking infinite care not to push the object out of reach. He doubted he would ever find it again.

At the edge of vision, he saw Zsolt slowly slide down the wall and come to rest on his side in the filthy water. His eyes were fixed on Alexei.

I killed a priest. It was no accident. I made it happen. Saints forgive me . . . .

Numb fingers closed around the keys. He unlocked the manacles and leg irons. Kelemen was unsteadily gaining his feet when Alexei limped from the cell and slammed the door shut. Happily, Zsolt had left *that* key sticking out of the lock.

"Pray the storm breaks soon, brother," he said coldly.

"Wait!" Kelemen reached through the bars. "Don't leave me."

Alexei stared at him for a long moment. Then he tossed the keys through the bars. They landed with a soft splash.

"You'd better start looking," he said.

Alexei left the priest on hands and knees, frantically searching the floor of the cell.

He took the torch from its bracket and followed the flow of the ley. At each intersection, he flipped Misha's corax and let it guide his choice. Name for left, Raven for right. Shadows followed, whispering in the darkness. Alexei paid them no heed. There was only the corax and the endless turnings. He knew he was on the right path when the floodwaters slowly receded.

Soon, his footsteps rang against dry stone. He passed bricked-up doors and vaulted chambers full of dust and rat droppings. Climbed spiral steps so cramped he had to turn sideways to work his way up. The torch was sputtering when he finally emerged into the Chapel of Saint Iveron.

Hundreds of candles burned in the niches, a softer light than the stark flame of the torch. He inhaled the familiar scents of incense and old wood. Rain beat against the stained glass windows. The chapel was empty. It must be the middle of the night, though he could not have said which day it was if his life depended upon it.

Alexei paused, gazing up at the triptych of Lezarius the Righteous. Humanity's savior. Sometimes called The Lion.

And they shall be cast into the Void . . . .

Ley streamed from Lezarius's hands.

Dark skin, white hair, bright green eyes. The features were different, but Alexei saw a mad priest from Jalghuth.

Got a smoke?

The idea rocked him. It couldn't be—and yet it must. Nothing else fit.

Patient 9. That was the old man's number.

Alexei ran outside. Every few seconds, webs of lightning illuminated the clouds, followed by deep rolls of thunder. His breath came in jagged bursts as he sprinted down the Via Fortuna, heading for the Dacian Gate.

Whatever conspiracy he'd stumbled across, Alexei would

not let his brother be the next victim. Misha was close to the old man, maybe too close . . . .

Headlights lit the road from behind. He turned and stepped into the car's path. Alexei waved his arms to flag the vehicle down. The driver didn't slow. At the last moment, he was forced to leap out of the way. He landed on the grassy verge, the impact jarring his cracked ribs. Alexei let out a soft groan.

Brake lights flashed. Tires squealed on the wet pavement as the car reversed and stopped next to him.

"Filius canis," Alexei muttered in disbelief, blinking through the rain.

Malach sat behind the wheel, one elbow hanging out the window. The mage got out, slamming his door but leaving the engine running.

"Laqueus." His face was grim. "You look worse than I do."

Alexei climbed to his feet. He was too tired to run and too banged up to fight. He had no weapon. No Warded manacles. If Malach decided to turn him, there was little to be done about it.

"Did you break the Wards?"

"That's a stupid question." Malach flexed his fingers. "You should run, priest. Before they decide to get rid of you, too."

Alexei gave a hollow laugh. "They already tried."

Lightning flickered over Malach's shoulder. He studied Alexei for a long moment. "Not hard enough, apparently. Does your offer still stand?"

The last words he expected to hear. "Yes."

"You'd take my Mark?"

"After you heal Mikhail." The last remnant of his pride burned to ash. "I'm begging you, Malach. Tell me the truth. Is it even possible?"

The mage nodded slowly. "I can't restore the Mark, but I can remove it."

Another lie? Probably. But he'd take the deal anyway. For the first time, Alexei understood why people agreed to a Nightmark knowing full well it was a losing bargain in the end.

They had no other choice.

"Then I give you my allegiance," he said.

A cold smile. "Done and done, laqueus. He's at the Batavia Institute, isn't he?"

Alexei nodded. He just hoped he wasn't hallucinating the entire encounter.

"You drive," Malach said. "I don't trust you."

"There's a warrant for my arrest."

"Will they know your face at the gate?"

"I don't know."

"Then let's find out."

"Give me your gloves." Alexei held a hand out.

Malach stared at him for a long moment, then tossed over a pair of gloves. "They're from the same priest who lent me his cassock," he said with an ugly smile.

Blood streaked the leather, but Alexei had done far worse than wear a dead man's gloves so he put them on without comment. He'd never get through the gates with bare hands, not if he was driving. It would cause immediate suspicion.

He walked around to the driver's side and got in. A moment later, Malach dropped into the passenger seat and slammed the door. It raised the hair on Alexei's neck to be within arm's length of him. He threw the car into gear and drove up to the gates.

"Interfectorem," he said brusquely to the guard.

The man leaned down to peer into the window at Malach. "Who's he?"

"OGD," Malach said, his eyes flicking to the dead Wards above the archway. "Open the fucking gate."

The guard blinked and Alexei nearly cursed aloud, didn't he realize a priest wouldn't talk that way to another priest, even if it was a lowly guard, but then the man stood and gestured and the Dacian Gates swung open.

He hit the accelerator and they sped into the streets beyond. Malach set something on the dashboard. A bloody knife. Alexei ignored it, but felt the mage watching him.

"Go ahead," Malach said, amusement in his voice. "Pick it up."

Alexei kept his eyes on the road. "I don't think you care about Marking me," he said. "It's not what you really want."

Malach braced a hand on the dashboard. Centimeters from the knife.

"You've got me," he said. "I want someone else at the Institute, someone very valuable, but I'm not sure who he is. It's almost funny, except that it's not." Malach watched him closely.

"Where did you come by the information?"

"Falke told me. Just before he tried to cut my hands off."

"How did you even get inside the Arx—"

"Enough questions, priest. I need your help. The Wards might be up again by the time we get there, but you can disable them. So how much does your brother mean to you?"

Alexei slowed for a red light. "Everything."

A wheezing sound escaped from Malach's lips. Alexei realized it was silent laughter. "Falke was right to get rid of you. You're both disloyal." He glanced over. "Do you know what your brother wanted in return for my Mark? To spare *you*, laqueus. No mage was to touch you."

Alexei shook his head in denial. "Just stop talking. I don't want to hear any more of your lies."

"Did you never wonder why your unit enjoyed such luck that final year? It was thanks to your brother's sacrifice." Malach frowned. "It's rare to get a selfless request. Mikhail Bryce is an extraordinary man. I would not regret restoring him to health in both mind and body."

He glanced at Alexei. Getting no reaction, he plowed on.

"First, a gesture of good faith. I could compel you, but I'll give you a chance to tell me freely first. Which patient is Lezarius? Where have they hidden him?"

The number is 9.

Malach didn't know it was the old man.

Which meant he hadn't gotten his hands on Kasia or the letter, thank the Saints. Alexei gripped the wheel. "I don't know what you're talking about."

"You're lying." He leaned closer. "I can smell it. Tell me or our deal is off."

"I'll tell you after you fix Mikhail."

"You'll tell me now." The false sympathy vanished. Red light bled from Malach's sleeves. It flickered in the depths of his eyes like a pair of burning embers. Alexei grabbed the knife and jerked the wheel hard to the right. The sudden shift threw Malach towards him. The mage caught his wrist.

End it, laqueus.

The whisper came from inside his own head, a silent command. The screech of tires skidding on wet asphalt faded. The metronomic tempo of the wipers turned to the beat of his own heart.

He saw himself kneeling in the basilica to take his vows. Saw his seven tours of duty and the things he had done in the name of the Via Sancta. He watched Vilmos die, and a hundred others, while he survived untouched. Alexei watched his brother get turned as he lay helpless on the ground. Watched his own failures, over and over.

What did you really accomplish in the Void? All that pain and death, and for what? I still won in the end, laqueus.

Their hands locked together around the hilt of the dagger. Alexei tried to wrench it away, unsure which one of them he meant to stab, when the car bounced over the curb and struck a traffic light. The impact threw him violently forward. The pressure of the seatbelt against his cracked ribs brought a wave of black pain crashing down.

. . .

ALEXEI OPENED HIS EYES. Red light flashed in his face. He groaned softly and popped his seatbelt. Not abyssal ley. Just the traffic light.

Prohibere . . . prohibere . . .

Steam poured from the crumpled hood. The car had come to rest halfway up the sidewalk in front of a shuttered nightclub called the Peppermint Lounge. Droplets of blood spattered the passenger seat. Alexei tried to open the door and found it jammed shut. He swore and banged his shoulder against the door until it flew open with a screech of metal. He half fell out of the car, scanning the rainswept street.

Malach was gone.

Chapter Twenty-Nine

K asia pressed an eye to the crack in the wardrobe.

The two men who had blasted open the doors to the Pontifex's bedchamber stood just inside the threshold facing Feizah, who stared at them calmly. Ley traced the glyphs on her forearms, dark violet with sparks of crimson in the depths.

"Captain Bryce," the Pontifex said. "Did your master send you here?"

Kasia assumed the younger man was Alexei, but when the light struck the gaunt planes of his face, she realized her mistake. The dark hair was too long, the shoulders a bit broader, though his thick brows and stubborn jaw were identical. It must be the mad brother. He gripped a bloody sword, which explained the absence of the guards.

"Mikhail does not speak," the old man said gravely. He had a peculiar accent, rather like Kven but more melodic.

"Take another step, Invertido," Feizah growled, "and you will regret it for the rest of your days—which will be very brief."

The old man gave a tight, closed-lipped smile. He carefully set the cardboard box on the floor. Then he stepped forward.

Feizah raised her hand and the whirlwind howled through the chamber. It seized the stack of papers Kasia had just collected and sent them flying again. The men jerked upward like marionettes, dangling two meters in the air.

Feizah ignored the older one, focusing on Mikhail Bryce. "Where is your master? How did you escape the Institute?"

He glowered down at her, blue eyes blazing.

"I suppose you imagine that killing me will curry his favor. You are a villainous fool, Bryce. I spared you the full penalty for treason for your brother's sake, but that mercy ends now." She closed her fist and Mikhail gasped. The sword flew from his hand and buried itself in the wood paneling.

"Leave him be," the old man cried. "He cannot answer you!"

"Be silent," Feizah thundered. Fog rolled from her mouth, billowing outward to envelop the men. The temperature plummeted. Her eyes glowed with blue light like some wrathful goddess descended to earth.

Mikhail's legs kicked. He clawed at the Raven on his throat. Ropes of mist coiled around his chest, squeezing like a monster from the depths of the Northern Ocean.

Crouched inside the wardrobe, her own breath misting white, Kasia frowned. They must have killed the guards, which was bad, but Mikhail hadn't raised a hand against the Pontifex. What if their appearance had nothing to do with Malach? Alexei said his brother was mute. He could not even speak to defend himself.

This one is clear, she decided. Feizah's actions are morally wrong. Kasia was about to intervene—though she had no idea how to stop the Pontifex—when the ley vanished.

One moment, it crackled and strobed like the blacklights on the dance floor at Club Dumas. The next, Feizah's Marks faded to simple glyphs. Not a shred of fog remained. Kasia thought of the mage trap on her roof, but she saw no ley lines and the Wards over the door and window remained dark.

The two men dropped to the carpet. Mikhail Bryce drew a ragged breath. His companion laid a hand on his shoulder and whispered something too soft for Kasia to make out. Mikhail's gaze fixed on the Pontifex. There was something implacable in his expression, as if a decision had been made and there would be no turning back from it.

"What is this?" the Pontifex muttered, looking around wildly. "What have you done?" She peered at the old man. "I do not know you, Domine."

The old man shrugged off his tweed coat and unbuttoned his shirt. Kasia could see only his back, but he must be displaying a Mark.

"Do you know me now?" he demanded softly. "First you sent Massot to test me. To probe my mind with the ley. He lifted up a rock and"—the gnarled fingers fluttered—"*things* crawled into the light. I started to remember. Just bits and pieces, but enough. And I knew it was only a matter of time before you realized your mistake. Before you decided to silence me for good."

"You are wrong!" The Pontifex shook her head. "I had nothing to do with it. You are the victim of a foul plot—"

"To deprive me of life and liberty," he interrupted. "After I saved you, all of you!"

She stared at him, wonder mingling with fear. "You *are* him," she said at last. "You have the music of the north on your tongue, and I know your voice even though it has been decades since I last heard it." She frowned. "But the rest of you . . . it is different."

"They changed my face, but they could not change my Marks. The ley would not allow it." He scowled. "Tell me who did this to me. Who is responsible?"

She held her palms out. "I don't know. I swear it, Lezarius!"

Kasia couldn't suppress a soft oath. Lezarius? But he was

the Pontifex of the Northern Curia. He couldn't be this gap-toothed lunatic standing before them!

Mikhail's gaze flicked to the wardrobe. He had the same sudden alertness she'd seen in Alexei, a predator attuned to the slightest alteration in its surroundings. *Shit*, she mouthed silently. Then Lezarius spoke again and his attention returned to the exchange between the two Pontifexes.

"This is your city, Feizah." The old man's scowl deepened. "Do you expect me to believe they hid me under your very nose without your knowledge?"

"I did not know!" Her voice rose. She touched her own Raven Mark. "I swear it on my life and virtue!"

"What about these?" The old man threw two coins at her feet. "Your assassins are dead, just as you will be soon enough."

She stooped down and picked them up, her brow furrowing. "Assassins? In the Via Sancta? Impossible! They must be forgeries."

"Look at them! Even a child could see the coraxes are authentic. Do you take me for a fool?"

Feizah's voice grew quiet. "I take you for a hero. You were always the best of us."

His eyes went flat. "That man is dead. This one cares only for justice."

"Listen to me! I did not send assassins, nor did I authorize Dr. Massot to do anything. Had I known about any of this, I would have arrested him immediately."

"So you think I'm imagining it all, is that it?"

"No, I—"

He stabbed a finger at the twin discs in her hand. "Am I imagining those? They were taken from the priests you sent to murder me in my sleep! But that wasn't enough. You had to cover your filthy tracks. So you planned to pin the blame on Mikhail. An innocent!"

"Bah!" Feizah exclaimed. "How exactly is Bryce an innocent? He took Malach's Mark of his own free will. If he displeased his master and was punished for it, he need look no further than himself to lay the blame."

"That is a callous statement," Lezarius replied. "You have no idea why he took the Mark. How can you judge him?"

"You were always soft on the nihilim," she muttered. "You made the Void and left it to the rest of us to keep them contained. The job was not finished, Lezarius. Given time, they would have gathered their strength and attacked again. What if we were the ones who ended up banished to the Void? But you could never see that. You were too compassionate." She stared at him with a mixture of anger and fondness. "If you had not retreated to Jalghuth for the last thirty years, someone might have noticed sooner that you had been replaced."

The old man's fists clenched. "You are unfit to wear the ring, Feizah. You're all unfit. And I will cleanse the Via Sancta of your foul intrigues."

Feizah ran to the far wall and drew the sword from the wood panel. Judging by her confident, wide-legged stance, she knew how to use it. "You *are* mad," she shouted. "And you will be returned to the Institute, but I will keep guards on you night and day, and Ward every meter of your chamber—"

"I will never be Patient 9 again!" A note of panic. "*Never.*"

He spun toward the wardrobe and the inverted Mark came into full view. A roaring lion covered his chest, fangs bared in a snarl. In the wavering candlelight, the tawny fur and yellow eyes were uncannily lifelike.

"You are no better than the mages," Lezarius growled. "And now you stand in the Void as they did, stripped of all authority." He pointed an accusing finger, his voice stern and resonant. "Feizah the Third of Your Name, Vicar of the Eastern Curia, Successor of the Praefators, Supreme Servant of the Ley, Living Exemplar of the Five Virtues and Protector of Novostopol, I find you guilty of crimes against the Invertido. The sentence is death."

Mikhail strode toward the Pontifex. The Raven on his neck stirred, unfurling dark wings. Each feather gleamed like pale moonlight striking water. The beak opened in a silent croak of rage. Misha's face was cloaked in shadow and Kasia was glad she couldn't see it clearly. He looked too much like his brother.

Feizah raised the sword. "I hold your Marks, Bryce," she said grimly. "Traitor or not, twelve of them are mine. Kill me and you will die."

Mikhail moved like a cat, springing away from Feizah's slashing lunge. She recovered quickly, adjusting her two-handed grip. The blade cut the air with a sharp whistling sound. Mikhail leaned back as it passed within a centimeter of his throat. She unleashed another lightning slash at his legs. He leapt over the blade and wrested it away in one brutal movement. Kasia might have looked away then, but she wanted to see what happened next.

The Pontifex turned to run. Mikhail stabbed her in the back. She fell and he stabbed her again, this time through the chest. She died without much of a fuss. It was an unpleasant sight, but in truth Kasia felt little sympathy for the Pontifex. Feizah had gambled and lost.

She hoped they would leave, but footsteps approached. The cabinet was flung open. The point of Mikhail's sword touched her throat. A spray of fresh blood crossed his white tunic.

"Make it quick," she said with a dry throat, her pulse finally spiking at the prospect of imminent death.

Up close, Misha's face was a little narrower, his lips fuller. The vast gulf between the brothers lay in the eyes. Mikhail's held not a shred of warmth. Not even anger. Just fanatical devotion to his cause.

"What have we here?" Lezarius walked up to the wardrobe. "Are you a vestal?"

"I'm no one."

Mikhail's sword lifted the braid hanging over one shoulder, exposing her Raven-less neck.

"Climb out of there," Lezarius ordered.

She did, eyeing the corpse that lay across the steps at the foot of the enormous bed. It seemed impossible that the Reverend Mother was really dead. She'd been the Pontifex for as long as Kasia could remember.

"Show me your Marks," Lezarius said.

"I don't have any."

"Prove it." The Mad Saint stared at her with profound suspicion.

"Ah." *Not again.* "You mean…?"

"Prove it. Or I must assume you are part of the plot against me."

Kasia sighed, but she was past the point of modesty.

Far, far past it.

She discarded her jacket and started to unbutton her blouse. Mikhail Bryce turned his back, resting a hand on the pommel of the sword, which he held point-down. The old man watched her closely, but there was nothing leering about it. Kasia unzipped her skirt and let it fall. She rolled her stockings down and dropped them on top of the skirt. When she got down to her bra and underwear, he held a hand up.

"You are an innocent," Lezarius declared. "Do you wish to come with us?" He smiled. "You could be a follower of the saint. I offer you my protection. Unmarked are treated almost as poorly as Invertido. It is wrong. I see that now."

"Where are you going?" she asked.

"To raise an army, of course. There is work to be done." He glanced at Bryce's broad back. "Mikhail is a valiant knight. You mustn't be afraid of him."

Oh, not in the least. "He looks ill."

"Yes," Lezarius said sadly. "Perhaps he will improve in the Void."

There was much more Kasia might have said at that point, but, standing in her underwear before two Invertido who had just killed the Pontifex of the Eastern Curia, she decided that getting the fog out of there would be the smart thing to do.

"Your offer is very kind." She smiled. "But I have a cat I'm fond of. It's not a good time to leave town. Thank you for asking though."

"I own a cat, as well." Lezarius picked up the cardboard box and took out a ball of black fluff. It mewed plaintively. "I believe it is hungry."

Kasia regarded the kitten. It was like a bizarre dream, but she still felt the point of Mikhail's sword where it had touched her throat. "There's some cream," she said, pointing at the tea service, which remained miraculously upright.

Lezarius filled a saucer and set the kitten down. It lapped at the cream. "What is your name?" he asked.

Fifteen years had passed since she'd last claimed it, but he deserved a truthful answer. "Katarzynka Nowakowski."

He pursed his lips. "Got a smoke?"

"I'm sorry, I don't."

"Too bad." The Mad Saint bowed. "Domina Nowakowski, I wish you well." The kitten began to lick its paws. Lezarius picked it up, very gently, placed it back in the box and turned to Mikhail. "It's time for us to move on."

The knight cast her a quick, intense glance. He was not soulless—she saw intelligence and emotion lurking behind those blue eyes—and Kasia wondered if she should tell him she knew his brother, maybe even entice him to free Alexei from the dungeon, but before she could regret her decision the pair were walking out the shattered doors and down the corridor. Kasia stared after them for a long moment.

The last card of the Massot spread fell into place.

The Mage, inverted, was Mikhail Bryce.

The Knight was Alexei.

The Fool was Malach.

The Slave was Massot himself.

But someone else bound them all together.

"I think," she said aloud, "I just met The Martyr."

Someone had done Lezarius a terrible wrong. How and why remained unclear, but he wanted revenge and Captain Mikhail Bryce would help him get it. There was much to think on, but more guards would arrive at any moment and she did not want to be found standing over the corpse of the Pontifex in her underwear. Kasia quickly dressed and stepped into her boots. She took a moment to scoop up the two coraxes—they'd rolled under the bed— then strode for the door.

A dozen guards sprawled in the corridor outside, swords next to their outstretched hands. She recognized the woman who had grabbed her by the hair. The Knights of Saint Agathe were as fierce as any man—fiercer, if the tales of their valor during the war were true. Bryce had killed each of them with a single thrust to the heart.

Kasia raised a hand to her throat. What had he become?

She left the palace through a service door near the kitchens. Outside, a gale shook the trees like giant hands. Not a single Ward lit the night. There was only the faint gleam of torches from within the buildings, which failed to dispel the thick darkness outside. Bells tolled in towers across the Arx and she saw the sweep of headlights, but no guards in the blue and gold.

Perhaps Captain Bryce had killed them all.

Kasia used a fallen branch to break a ground floor window of the Curia Press. She found a candle stub in one of the offices and retraced the convoluted route down to the cells. Left, then right, then right, then left again . . . . It was a long, lonely trek and although she didn't fear getting lost, she missed Patryk Spassov.

Are you his friend, Kasia? Alyosha has very few.

The Pontifex had ordered his release, but she had to make sure. That's what a friend would do. At the bottom of the fifth set of stairs, the water rose to knee-deep. Kasia took her boots off and plowed on. At last she reached the card table where the guards had sat. It lay on its side, tugged by the current. Nearer to the cells, she came upon a body floating face-down. Kasia stared at it, a steel band tightening around her chest until she could hardly breathe. She grabbed the cassock and rolled it over. It was a priest around Bryce's age, with a long, mournful face. The eyes were half-open. His neck looked broken.

The steel band loosened. "Alexei?" she called.

The low vaulted ceiling threw her own voice back. She waded into the open cell. It was empty.

Kasia went back out and searched the dead priest, careful to keep her candle dry. His pocket held a corax like the ones Lezarius had thrown at Feizah's feet. She examined the three copper coins nestled in her palm. All had a Raven on one side and a name on the other. Gerlach, Brodszky and Zsolt. Words were engraved in a semicircle beneath the Raven. Hoc ego defendam. *This I will protect.*

Kasia studied it for a moment, a slight frown on her face. She'd only looked at Mikhail's corax for a few seconds when Alexei showed it to her at the flat, but she recalled the motto, which must belong to the Beatus Laqueo.

Foras Admonitio. *Without warning.*

Two different orders—and she was willing to bet the first one had something to do with Cardinal Falke.

She slipped the coins into her jacket pocket. The candle was growing short. Wherever he had gone, Alexei was beyond her help now. It was time to get back. Even with her perfect memory, Kasia didn't relish groping her way out in pitch darkness with the water rising.

TWENTY MINUTES later she reached the lawn surrounding Falke's residence and crept around to the library. The window was still unlatched. Kasia climbed over the sill. The fire had burned low, leaving most of the room in shadow. "Nashka?" she whispered.

"Natalya has been taken to Sor Foy's country estate."

Cardinal Falke stepped into the firelight. She froze. "Your Eminence, you startled me."

He glanced at the window. "Where have you been, Domina Novak? Your friend was reticent regarding the details of your sortie."

She met his eye. "That is my own business."

He sank into a chair, moving stiffly. "Let me guess. Fra Bryce?"

It was the story she'd intended to tell if she was caught— or a version of it, at least. She gave a reluctant nod. "I was worried for him, Your Eminence. So I went to see Fra Spassov, but then the Wards broke. He was called away and I came back here."

"I'm sure Bryce is fine," Falke said wearily. "If you wish, I can arrange a visit in the morning."

The offer surprised her. "I would appreciate that."

He nodded absently. "I can't seem to find a candle, Domina Novak. Would you . . . ?"

She lit a taper from the hearth and touched it to the wicks of the nearest candelabra. "You're bleeding!" she exclaimed.

Falke glanced down. His face shone with a ghastly pallor. "So I am."

Kasia hurried to the library doors and flung them open. The two priests who had been standing guard outside were gone. "Where are your aides?"

"I sent them to look for you. I feared Malach would find you."

"Did the mage do this?" The blood had been hard to see against the cardinal's purple robes, but now she realized he was soaked in it.

Falke nodded. "He killed four of my knights."

"After the Wards went down?"

"He was already inside."

Ice touched her spine. "How did he breach the walls?"

"I don't know, but I expected an attempt. Sure enough, he came to the Castel Saint Agathe. We were waiting in your chamber. I had him secured, but then the ley surged . . . he stabbed me in the thigh."

Kasia sat down and peeled a stocking off. "Cinch this above the cut, Your Eminence."

Falke took the stocking. He wore elegant woolen trousers beneath the purple robe. "I've grown soft," he said with a wince, tightening the knot. "Too many rich dinners and tedious meetings. Once I would have stayed to fight, but Malach is young and hungry, and I'm old and tired." He sat back with a sigh. "Mors vincit omnia. Death always wins."

"You need a doctor, Your Eminence. I'll call for a car."

Falke stared through the rain-streaked windows. "Have you ever made a bad mistake, Domina Novak?"

"Plenty."

"I underestimated him." Falke coughed. "Would you be so kind as to bring me a drink? There's a bottle in that cabinet, the one with the glass doors."

Kasia found the whiskey and two heavy crystal glasses, pouring a finger into each. She handed one to the cardinal. "Malach, you mean?"

Falke downed the amber liquid in one swallow. A vicious gust of wind rattled the glass panes. "Among others," he said.

"Do you think he'll come here?"

"I don't know." The cardinal regarded her with a strange

expression she couldn't quite place. "What would you do if you were Malach?"

"I would try to kill you. If I failed, I would run to fight another day."

"Always the wisest course."

"Did he get what he came for?"

"No."

But he hesitated before answering and Kasia knew he was lying. "Your Eminence?" Falke looked up at her. His face was ashen. "We'd best get you to the infirmary now."

"Do you mind bringing me the telephone? I think the cord will stretch."

She waited while he dialed a number. Falke explained the situation, then listened for a long minute. "Saints," he said faintly. "Yes, of course. Thank you."

He replaced the phone in the cradle with a trembling hand. Then he closed his eyes, lips moving in a silent prayer. His grief did not strike Kasia as feigned. In the quiet of this stately, book-lined room, she felt the weight of what had happened that night. By morning, thousands would be weeping and covering their windows in black drapes.

"The Reverend Mother is dead," Falke said heavily. "Along with at least a dozen of her guards. No one saw a thing."

Kasia pressed a hand to her mouth. "It cannot be true."

"*Malach*," he ground out. "I will hunt him to the ends of the earth for this."

They were both silent for a time. Kasia could think of nothing more to say. Cardinal Falke appeared lost in thoughts of retribution and, judging by the hollow look in his eyes, guilt. Every now and again she sensed his Marks lighting up, though he seemed unaware of it.

"Your Eminence?" she said at last.

Falke glanced over. He'd aged ten years in the last quarter hour.

"If you have no further need for me, I'd like to go home. Once you've been tended to, of course."

"I meant to send you to Tessaria."

"I prefer my own flat."

She expected him to refuse, but to her surprise, the cardinal slowly nodded. "I only brought you here to protect you, Domina Novak. Whatever you may think of me, I've always had your best interests at heart." His tone grew bitter. "But the Arx is no safer than anywhere else, perhaps less so."

"Will Malach come after me again?"

Falke considered the question. "I very much doubt it. He only wanted you for what he thought you knew. But his interests have shifted now."

To Lezarius, she thought. Good luck to you, Malach, if you think you can take both The Lion and Captain Mikhail Bryce.

The library doors opened and four aides rushed inside bearing a stretcher. The cardinal refused to lie down on it and limped out to the car under his own steam, though one of the aides supported him.

"You will be driven home, but I'm leaving two men outside, Domina Novak," he said brusquely, easing himself into the back seat. "You cannot deny me that."

"I would never attempt it, Your Eminence."

Falke studied her through the window with a peculiar mixture of regret and tenderness. Whatever evils he had done, this man would not harm her. She had no idea why, only that it was true.

Kasia raised a gloved hand in farewell as the car drove away, then hurried to a second vehicle waiting at the curb outside his residence. The rain was no longer a steady downpour, more scattered bursts of drizzle tossed about on a fresh breeze. Still, strands of hair were damply plastered to her forehead by the time she slammed the door and sat back.

"Number 44 Malaya Sadovaya Ulitsa," she told the driver.

The car pulled out and glided towards the Dacian Gate, followed by another vehicle that Kasia presumed was carrying her shadows. Somewhere beyond the walls of the Arx, a frenzied howling rose.

The Markhounds had found another trail.

Chapter Thirty

M alach stumbled through the dark streets, one hand gripping the hilt of the knife buried in his stomach.

The blade had entered just below the navel, a few centimeters lateral of the midline—right through the neck of the two-headed serpent coiled at his hip. Suction stemmed the blood flow, but burning cold radiated from the wound.

The adrenaline that had propelled him from the car was ebbing. He didn't have much time before the comedown brought him to his knees, and the laqueus would be looking for him by now. Malach regretted leaving him alive, but he'd had other more pressing priorities.

Anger dampened the fear, though it clawed at the back of his mind. Just because he was on his feet didn't mean the wound wouldn't kill him eventually. If the knife had damaged any vital organs, he'd be dead. If it had perforated his bowels or ruptured the stomach lining, he'd be dead.

The excited baying of a pack of Markhounds urged him to a stagger. He ducked into a narrow gap between two buildings just as the lead dog streaked past, swift as a galloping horse, and vanished into the rain. Three others followed on the alpha's tail, narrow snouts pressed to the ground. They left glowing paw prints in the ley for their masters to follow. Malach leaned against the wall, waiting, even though all was perfectly silent. Sure enough, a minute later, he heard the roar of an engine and a long black car sped down the block.

The pack wasn't hunting him. If the hounds had his scent, he'd be cornered already. But it wouldn't be long before more came, the ones trained specially to track Nightmages.

Falke. The name stoked his rage to a high boil. Malach started walking again. He held the blade as straight and steady as he could, but he still felt every small movement of it —intimately.

West of the citadel, limestone mansions hugged the left fork of the river. They were set back from the street behind immaculate lawns and low wrought-iron gates. Crime being nonexistent, the gates were merely decorative. Malach lurched up to one of the homes and pounded on the front door until it was opened by a girl in the gray uniform of a char. She took one look at him and tried to close the door in his face. Malach shoved past her into a marble foyer.

"Fetch your mistress," he snapped, bracing one hand against the wall. "Now."

The girl lifted her skirts and darted up the righthand branch of a curved double staircase. Muffled voices drifted down. A minute later, a handsome woman in her middle years hurried down the stairs, belting a silk dressing gown. Her gaze took in the bloody palm print and then the knife. "I'll fetch a physician—"

"No time. I need you to handle it."

She looked worried. If he died, she died. "Please, Malach, I have no idea—"

"I'll talk you through it." A wave of dizziness swept him. "Here's what I'll need."

He reeled off a list. She took off at a run, calling for Ani. Malach made his way to the kitchen, leaving a trail of blood smears on the gilded wallpaper. It was large and sparkling clean. He pulled the cloth off the staff dining table and leaned on it until the women returned, their arms laden with bedsheets, gauze and a bottle of iodine.

He instructed them to wash their hands and disinfect the table, then gingerly lay down on his back. The cold was now a constant stinging pain that sharpened whenever he drew breath.

"I'm probably going to faint when the knife comes out," he said. "You'll need to twist it slightly to break the suction, understood?"

Domina Goyon nodded, her face pale.

"First you need to disinfect it." Malach swore as she poured iodine on the knife. "Now slit the cassock open so you can see the wound."

She picked up a pair of scissors, her hand trembling slightly.

"Disinfect them," Malach snapped. The iodine burned like liquid fire, but it was better than peritonitis or sepsis.

"You look ill, mistress," Ani said quietly. "I'll do it. I've more experience with sickness than you do."

Domina Goyon nodded in relief. "Thank you, Ani."

"Set a pot of water on the stove," the girl said briskly. "At least twenty minutes under full boil. We'll sterilize the sheets before dressing him." She gave Malach a level look. "Are you ready, Domine?"

"May I have some water first?"

She filled a glass from the tap and cupped the back of his head. Malach wet his lips, just enough to ease the parch. "No iodine directly in the wound. Flush it with saltwater."

"As you say, Domine." She set the glass aside. The girl had lovely eyes. They reminded him of the fields in Bal Kirith after the spring rains and before the full heat of summer, when everything was green and bursting with new life.

Malach stared at the ceiling, heart pounding, as she washed her hands again and took the hilt of the knife. There was no point in reaching for the ley. It wouldn't spare him. If anything, it would make it worse.

Ani twisted the knife.

A thunderbolt of agony lanced down from on high. Liquid heat spilled from him. The room went gray, but he never quite lost consciousness. Soft voices faded in and out. Hands lifted him. More pain, but nothing like the shock of the blade leaving his body. He drifted for a bit, vulnerable as a newborn. If the laqueus came for him now . . . .

Malach opened his eyes.

Domina Goyon gazed down with a worried expression that turned to a tentative smile. "You're still with us. I think the bleeding has stopped. Ani stitched you up."

He pushed to his elbows. The room tilted. "What are my chances?" he whispered.

"I'm an actress, Malach. How should I know? We closed you up, but there could be major damage inside. You really must see a surgeon."

"I need a car."

Domina Goyon shook her head. She pressed two pill bottles into his hand. "The white ones are antibiotics. The pink ones will make you high as shit so take them sparingly. Do you want money?"

"Nowhere to spend it." He checked the bandage. It was tight, but not too tight. Ani had done a good job. It would hold him together for now. Malach swallowed a white pill and pocketed both bottles. He eased himself from the table with wobbly legs, shucked off the cassock—which Ani had slit from neck to hem—and threw it to the ground, spitting on it for good measure.

His shirt was a bloody wreck. Domina Goyon helped him put on a fresh one and fussed over the buttons, holding him with her eyes the whole time.

"I won't ask what happened," she said. "But will I see you again?"

"I don't know."

"You've never asked for anything before. So if you do need me in the future, don't hesitate to come back."

"Thank you." He gave her a nod. "I'll take the car now."

Rain soaked Domina Goyon's slippers as she led him out the back door and past an oval swimming pool whose water shimmered turquoise from underwater lights to a garage the size of a second home. It held four sleek, expensive automobiles. "Which one?"

Malach pointed to a low-slung silver sports car. "That."

She gave him the keys. "It's fully charged. You'll get about six hundred kilometers before you run out of juice."

Malach sank into a womb of plush leather and varnished walnut and lashings of chrome. He turned the key. The powerful engine rumbled to life as she opened the garage doors. Malach threw it into gear and hit the accelerator. He drove straight to Ash Court and climbed the stairs like a hundred-year-old man.

"It's me," he called through the door, rapping with his knuckles.

There was no reply.

He rapped again, harder. What if Falke's men had found her? What if—

The door opened. White teeth and the flash of a silver incisor. Nikola grabbed his shirt and kissed him hard. Malach pinned her against the doorframe, tasting her, his hands tangling in her hair. Relief weakened his knees. Finally he pulled back and licked swollen lips.

"The ley flooded," he said hoarsely. "We have a chance to get past the outer Wards, but it's brief. If you still want to come with me, we have to leave right now. I may not make it back to Novostopol."

Onyx eyes weighed him. "Did you hurt Kasia?"

"I never even saw her. But there's something else you should know." He braced himself for wrath. "If Beleth discovers you're carrying my child, she'll never let you go. Once you've given birth, she might . . . get rid of you. She wouldn't want the child to have divided loyalties."

Nikola recoiled. "You're telling me this *now*?"

"Better than after you're in the Void. You can still change your mind."

"I'm already pregnant, you bastard!"

"Terminate it." The words almost broke him, but Malach kept his voice cold and detached. "You're still early enough to use herbs."

A storm broke across her face. Mainly rage, but also hurt. "Is that what you want?"

"No!" He tried to kiss her and earned a ringing slap. "I won't let them touch you, Nikola. I swear it. I'll kill them first."

"Why the hell should I believe you?"

Why indeed? For all his silver-tongued flattery, he couldn't find the words to express his feelings in a way she would find even remotely credible. He wasn't sure he understood them himself. But he intended to keep his promise to her.

"We'll give Bal Kirith a wide berth and go straight to the coast," he said. "I'll put you on a smugglers' ship. You can be gone within the fortnight."

"What about the child?"

"I'll come for it when it's born."

"How?" Nikola demanded. "The witches kill nihilim on sight. They wouldn't even put you in irons. They'd just cut your throat and toss you in the sea."

"I'll figure something out." Malach wiped blood from his mouth. She'd split his lip. "Hit me again if you need to, but I need an answer."

Nikola looked like she just might. Then she strode into the flat, grabbed a suitcase and walked past him down the stairs without a backward glance. Malach followed, leaning heavily on the rail the whole way.

The streets of Ash Court were quiet, though sirens wailed in the distance. He'd parked at a drunken angle with two tires resting on the curb. He braced a hand on the roof and opened the passenger door for her.

Nikola stared at him. "I'm forced to ask this every time we meet, but is that your blood?"

He glanced down. Red spotted through the white shirt. "Yes."

She held out a hand. "Give me the keys."

He tossed them over and maneuvered himself painfully into the low-slung car. Nikola slid into the driver's seat.

"Where am I going?" she asked, not looking at him.

"Head for the river."

She put her seatbelt on and started the engine. It purred like a large, powerful cat. "Who'd you kill for this?" she asked flatly. "It must be worth at least a hundred thousand."

"No one. I called in a favor."

"From one of your Marked?"

"Yes."

Nikola backed off the curb. He winced as the tires bumped down. She executed a smooth three-point turn and headed the wrong way down the one-way street. It was admittedly a quicker route. Malach just hoped they didn't get in another accident.

"He must be rich," Nikola said.

"She. And yes, she's wealthy, but not because of me. She already had money when we met."

"What did she want then?"

"Revenge on a man who raped her. A jury believed his claim that it was all a rough game. That she was just pretending to resist and changed her mind later out of spite."

"That's horseshit," Nikola said, speeding through a yellow light.

"He argued that his Marks would never allow him to commit such an act of violence." Malach leaned into the leather and closed his eyes. "It's the flaw in their utopia. As long as you lie to yourself, you can do whatever you want."

"What happened to him?"

Malach didn't open his eyes, but he smiled unpleasantly. "I happened to him."

"Well, that's all right, I suppose."

"Of course, he could have been innocent." Malach caught her eye. "It's not my business to care one way or the other. That's the bargain."

"You're doing it again."

"What?"

"Trying to put me off."

"I just want you to know the sort of person I am so you're not disappointed later."

"Oh, I already know the kind of person you are. Trust me, Malach, the bar is set extremely low."

The car sped toward the eastern side of the Montmoray Bridge. As it hit the approach, lights appeared along the shoulder ahead. Nikola leaned forward. A dozen uniformed men stood before a line of orange barricades.

"Malach," she said, slowing. "We have to turn around."

"If we don't cross here, we'll have to drive all the way through the city past the Arx." He swore softly. "They've probably set up roadblocks on the other bridges, as well."

Nikola glanced over at him, eyes too bright. "Then put your seatbelt on."

Before he could reply, she jammed her foot down on the accelerator. The car raced up the entrance ramp to the bridge. He touched the bandage beneath his shirt. The wound throbbed like a live coal. It was placed precisely where the belt would cinch across his waist. "But——"

"Do it!"

In the headlight beams, he saw the Oprichniki scatter like a flock of frightened geese. Malach grabbed for the buckle. It clicked into place moments before they hit the barricade.

Wood exploded. The car fishtailed on the bridge, grinding against the outer guide rail. He was aware of the darkness falling away on either side. The rush of the river below.

Then the tires gripped pavement again. Nikola laughed and slapped her palm on the wheel. They hurtled off the northbound ramp, engine roaring. There were no barricades on the other side and within seconds, the bridge dwindled to a string of lights in the rearview. Brick warehouses flashed past, then ramshackle dwellings, and finally the wide, flat paddies that fed Novostopol's appetite for spicy rice dishes.

"You're a maniac," Malach grumbled, loosening the seat-belt. The pressure on his abdomen was intolerable. He fumbled in a pocket for the pills and downed two of the pinks.

"That's rich," she said, "coming from you."

Pinpoints of light twinkled beyond the edge of the fields. The outer ring of stelae. The tall stones acted as a wall, each set precisely three meters apart. And the Wards had come back up.

Nikola shot him a worried glance. "What do we do?"

Potholes scored the road. The headlights illuminated weeds sprouting from cracks in the asphalt. The Curia had deliberately let this stretch of road fall into disrepair. It led to only one place—the Morho Sarpanitum—and no one except for armed knights in heavy transports had any business there.

"Go as fast as you can without wrecking the car," he said.

Nikola leaned forward, her face intent as she navigated through the pits in the road. They dropped into a shallow crater and Malach gritted his teeth.

"Sorry," she said, shoulders hunching over the wheel. "They're full of fogging water. I can't tell how deep they are."

The car slowed to a crawl. Nausea twisted him like a wet rag.

"A little faster," he muttered. "Please."

"I can't." Her voice was apologetic but firm. "If we break an axle, we're done. You're too big to carry, Malach."

The road was more like a causeway, elevated a few meters above the flooded paddies. Malach rolled his window down, gasping air, but couldn't fill his lungs. The stelae inched closer, crooning their song of exquisite torture. A rush of warmth soaked his pants. He feared he'd pissed himself, but it was just the wound breaking open.

"*Go,*" he rasped.

Nikola took one look at him and hit the accelerator. The car bounced hard. Searing heat turned him to ash. Blue light filled the world.

"Malach! Saints, stay with me, Malach . . . ."

Her voice faded. Night frogs chirped in the paddies. It sounded like home. Malach rested his head against the window, a peaceful heaviness taking his limbs. The last thing he saw was a spray of stars across the velvet arch of the sky.

The rain had finally stopped.

Chapter Thirty-One

Alexei flagged down a gypsy cab and showed the driver his Raven Mark. She wore platform boots and a pink slicker and barely looked old enough to have a license.

"Interfectorem," he snapped. "Give me your keys."

The young woman handed them over, her heavily lined brown eyes darting around nervously. When the Interfectorem appeared, Markhounds must be close by—even if she couldn't see them.

"Sure, Father," she said in a smoky voice that sounded like Spassov's little sister. "Uh, will I get my car back?"

"Of course," he lied. "The Curia thanks you for your service." Alexei climbed in, knees brushing against the steering column. The car smelled of clove cigarettes and hairspray. He slid the seat back, gunned the engine and sped for the tunnel to the east bank.

Malach was hurt. How badly remained undetermined.

Don't let him die. Saints, don't let the bastard die.

Gently curving brick walls flashed past. The urge to drift off—just for a few seconds—was so desperate he nearly wept. How easy to turn the wheel a few centimeters to the right. One quick jerk and he'd get all the sleep he wanted. But this night wasn't over yet. He bit down on the scar tissue inside his cheek until he tasted blood.

Then the mouth of the tunnel was looming ahead and Alexei saw pale moonlight for the first time in months. The white disk hung low on the horizon, three-quarters full. He pulled over and stared in open-mouthed wonder, having forgotten that such a thing as the moon existed, and felt a painful glimmer of hope.

I'm coming for you, he thought. *For both of you.*

Alexei wiped his damp eyes and drove on, up into the hills. When he reached the Batavia Institute, he slowed down for a look. Three cars were parked just inside the main gates. Lights burned in the guardhouse, but he couldn't see who was in there.

He drove until he reached a wide place on the shoulder two kilometers past the Institute. During the day, it was a popular parking spot with hikers, but on this windswept night, no one was attempting the steep path down to the pebbled beach below. He pulled over and weighed his options. He had no equipment to scale the wall. If the warrant had been disseminated to every Order, he'd be arrested again, but the odds were fair that Cardinal Falke wanted the affair to be kept quiet.

Alexei turned the car around and drove up to the entrance. After a minute, a vestal in the blue and gold of the Pontifex's guards approached. He rolled his window down. She was tall and sturdy, with a long braid hanging over one shoulder and a short sword buckled at her hip.

"You're late to the party," she said crisply, eying the inverted trident on his cassock.

"I had a little, uh, fender bender on the way over. Had to commandeer a taxi."

"Well, we already rounded up the patients wandering the grounds."

"How many?"

"A dozen or so. Most of them didn't linger." Her expression darkened. "The guards were killed. It was chaos when we got here."

A second vestal walked up with an electric torch, shining it in his face. Alexei held up a hand, squinting, while she swept the backseat. "You know you have a lump on your head," she said. "Looks nasty."

"It's been a busy night," he muttered. "Who's inside?"

"A couple of yours. OGD, mostly."

Bad news. "I'll go report in."

"What's your name? We need to log it."

"Alexei Bryce. With a Y."

He waited for the women to draw their swords, but the one with the braid just signaled to her sisters inside the guardhouse. The gates buzzed open. He heard a telephone start to ring and drove through before someone answered it and tried to stop him. If Keleman had found the keys to the cell, he'd be reporting to Kireyev by now.

Eight other cars occupied the staff lot, all Curia. More electric torches moved across the lawn along the perimeter of the wall. He counted six, which left ten or so inside. The OGD didn't trust the vestals to mop it up. They were mounting a search for Lezarius themselves.

Alexei rubbed his eyes. It seemed insane. How could the old man be the most revered Pontifex in the history of the Via Sancta?

Just find them. Get them out. Then he could sleep for a year.

Alexei ran through a mental list of every entrance. The OGD couldn't be watching them all, not with escaped patients to deal with. He sank to one knee and pressed his hand flat against the wet grass. The current of ley was strong but slippery. It surged around his palm but seemed reluctant to enter him. Alexei cleared his mind of everything except his desperate need. A Mark flickered weakly on his left thigh, the first he'd been given after joining the priesthood. The Maiden. A symbol of both faith and innocence. He delved through the surface to the deepest strata of liminal ley where the violet deepened to crimson.

"Help me," he whispered brokenly.

Shouts erupted near the wall. The electric torches converged. A woman's voice pierced the night, cursing the fogging rooks. After a moment, two priests with the Golden Bough on their cassocks emerged from the front doors and joined the chase.

Alexei ran up to the doors and ducked inside. The neat stacks of papers at the admitting desk were strewn across the floor. He ran down the corridor to the non-violent wing, fully alert now. All the Wards at the junctions were dead. Only once was he forced to hide in an empty office as a priest strode past.

The door to Misha's room stood ajar. Alexei pushed it wide, fear and hope warring in his heart. The bedsheets were rumpled as if his brother had been awakened from sleep. He would have heard the commotion when the ley surged. The question was what he did next—

A heavy hand fell on Alexei's shoulder. He tore a glove off, lips peeled back in a snarl, before he realized it was Spassov, unshaven and haggard but a welcome sight nonetheless.

"Alyosha!" he exclaimed. "They released you?"

"Not exactly."

Spassov winced and looked around. The corridor was empty, but he drew Alexei into the room and shut the door. "Okay, spare me the details. What are you doing here?"

Alexei met his steady gaze. "This room is my brother's."

His partner's brow twitched, which was Spassov's equivalent of a shocked gasp. "You never told me."

"I'm sorry. I should have."

"No, it's your business. I understand."

"I'm not ashamed of him, Patryk. I didn't tell you because I hoped to catch the mage who Marked him and I was afraid you might try to stop me."

There was a long silence as Spassov digested this fact. Not a regular Invertido. A Nightmarked Invertido.

"Ah," he said at last. "Is it the same mage who Marked Massot?"

Alexei nodded. Spassov blew out a breath. "Saints, Alyosha."

"His name is Mikhail. Number 26. You've probably seen him around."

"Let me guess. The big one with black hair? Sits by the windows?"

"I have to find him, Patryk."

Spassov laid a sympathetic hand on his arm. "Of course. But we've already searched the grounds. Not many places to hide. The ones who were slow are back in their rooms, safe and sound. So he must have made it out before the first knights showed up. Did he have any friends?"

"Here or in the real world?"

"Either."

Mikhail had a wide circle of acquaintances, but in that last year he'd drifted away from most of them. The Curia had kept it quiet that one of their most decorated captains was both mad and Nightmarked, but word leaked out. Alexei didn't think anyone else had ever come to visit him.

"Only one," he said. "A patient."

"What number?"

"Nine."

"The old man?"

The edge in his voice made Alexei tense. "What happened?"

"Two bodies were found in his room. I got a look at them before the OGD took over."

"Tell me, Patryk," Alexei growled.

Spassov held up a hand. "Not patients. It was those investigators, the ones we gave statements to. OGD claimed the bodies and sealed the scene. The vestals weren't happy about it, but Kireyev called and smoothed things over."

"I need to see the old man's room."

"You need to get out of here before they catch you."

"Just a quick look."

"I can tell you how they died. Gerlach was stabbed, Brod-szky had his neck snapped."

"I need to see for myself. Please, Patryk."

Spassov sighed. "By all rights, I should be bringing you in."

"For what? I'm innocent." Of Massot's murder, at least.

"Yeah, I know. Come on." He held up a finger. "One minute, Alyosha."

The bloody footprints started about ten meters from the door to the old man's room. Most were smeared by overlapping traffic after the fact, most likely other patients, but as he passed one of the sconces, Alexei found a well-preserved artifact. Two men, both barefoot. The first set was small, the second enormous. About a size thirteen double-wide. Judging by the stride and weight on the ball of the foot . . . .

"They started running," Spassov said. "The prints fade out by the admitting area."

Yellow tape stretched across the door to Number 9's room. Spassov unlocked it and Alexei ducked under the tape, but didn't go any further.

More blood stained the floor and wall, though the agents who'd removed the bodies were careful not to disturb the scene more than they had to. This was probably more out of habit than any desire to preserve the evidence, but it left a reasonably clear picture of what had occurred in the old man's room that night.

"I think Brodszky died first," Spassov said. "He was on his side with blood soaked into his cassock, but it was clean underneath him, so I figure he was already down when his partner got stabbed."

The angle of impact indicated that Gerlach had been standing when he was killed. Alexei flipped the lights on and examined the ceiling. There was none of the castoff pattern you'd see from overhead hacking with a blade, just a single arterial spray against one wall and an enormous amount of blood on the floor. The outer edges were tacky and starting to dry.

"They died around the same time the Wards broke," he said. "Maybe even before. So why were they here in the middle of the night?"

Spassov folded his massive arms, keeping a close eye on the corridor. "I don't ask those kinds of questions, Alyosha. Not anymore." He shot his partner a doleful look. "And you shouldn't either."

"They haven't found the old man?"

"Into the wind."

"What about the staff?"

"OGD is still rounding them up."

Gerlach and Brodszky. He'd never know for certain, but . . . .

"Patryk, there's something else I didn't tell you."

"Saints, what now?"

"The men who killed Massot were priests. I saw a Raven Mark just before they went over the wall."

Spassov closed his eyes for a brief moment. "I won't ask why you kept it to yourself. That's obvious. But I guess you're wondering if Gerlach and Brodzsky might have done Massot?"

It was easy to underestimate Spassov. He drank too much and looked like a bouncer at a disreputable nightclub. But Patryk was no fool.

"That's exactly what I'm wondering."

"So they were sent to investigate a crime they committed themselves." He winced. "I want to say that the Archbishop of Novostopol would never condone such blatant corruption, but after what they've done to you, the words are sticking in my throat, Alyosha."

"I think they came here to murder Patient 9."

"Something to do with the doctor?"

"Because he's the Pontifex of the Northern Curia."

Spassov eyed him warily, clearly wondering if Alexei should be issued a pair of white pajamas. "Listen, you'd better get out of here. There's at least a dozen of Kireyev's boys here already and more on the way. I presume they won't be well disposed towards your presence?"

"He tried to have me killed, too."

Spassov's brow furrowed. He dug in his robes for the silver flask and took a long sip. Then he handed it to Alexei. "Keep it. Go find your brother. You need a car?"

"I have one. But Patryk, if you get the call, don't hurt him, please?"

He touched the Raven on his neck. "I promise." Voices drifted toward them from the next corridor. "Go!" Spassov mouthed with a frantic shooing motion.

Alexei took off running in the opposite direction. He didn't encounter anyone on the way back to the parking lot. Judging by the taunting laughter across the grounds, at least one patient was still leading the OGD on a merry chase.

So Gerlach and Brodzsky had come to murder the old man and met their own ends instead. He wished he could have examined the body to confirm it, but the evidence strongly suggested that Gerlach had died from a single thrust to the heart. This was far more difficult than one might think. You had to turn the blade sideways to get it between the ribs, find exactly the right angle to the left ventricle, which is the largest chamber of the heart, and finish with a lateral sawing motion to inflict massive damage to the surrounding tissue. Even then the victim might still be alive. But once the blade was withdrawn, the contraction of the muscle would cause blood to jet from the wound. This might only last for one or two seconds, but done right it would cause such catastrophic loss of blood pressure that the victim would black out before their body touched the ground.

Setting aside an intimate knowledge of anatomy, you had to be very strong to get a blade through the tough connective tissue between the ribs. Alexei knew whose hand had wielded it, but where was Misha now?

He could think of only one place. It was a few kilometers from the Institute. Walking distance—even for a pair of Invertido. The tires spat gravel as Alexei sped down the drive.

ONE SIDE of the winding road fell away to a hundred-meter drop ending on black surf-beaten rocks. The other was punctuated by private driveways flanked with manicured hedges.

Arbot Hills. The domain of the city's wealthiest and most powerful dynasties. Most had claimed titles before the Via Sancta abolished the nobility and hoped for an eventual return to the old ways, secretly funding the Conservative wing of the Church. The Bryces had once been *dvoryane*, just below the princes, but the family line was nearing its end. There would be no new blood. No heirs.

Another of his father's many disappointments.

Alexei pulled into a long drive ending at a baroque mansion with low towers at the corners, each crowned with vast belvederes of massed stone. Clouds obscured the moon and rain drummed on the roof of the car, turning the windscreen to a dark blur.

He killed the engine. He hadn't spoken to his father in three years, since Misha was admitted to the Institute. Even before that final rupture, the relationship had not been a warm one.

He fished the flask from his pocket, silently blessing Spassov, and had a generous swig. The vodka hit his empty stomach like a fist. He cracked the car door, breathing deeply.

Lights burned on the top floor. Someone was home.

Alexei took another drink before gathering the courage to go up to the front door and ring the bell. It chimed in the recesses of the house.

The door was opened by a woman named Glaine Days, who had worked for the Bryce family for nearly three decades. She wore a dressing gown and cap, and had clearly been summoned from her bed, but she smiled warmly when she saw him. "Fra Alexei! Were you expected? Your father never mentioned it."

"I'm sorry to wake you. Is he home?"

"Yes." The smile faded. Her voice sank to a whisper. "Is it Mikhail?"

Alexei nodded.

"Oh, no." She clasped her hands at her breast. "Is he . . . ?"

"It's not that. He escaped from the Institute."

A scar crossed Glaine's right eye, a remnant from her days as a slave in Bal Agnar. When she grimaced in surprise, it looked like a wink. "Come inside. Tell me what's happened."

Alexei had no desire to step over the threshold. A quick search of the outbuildings and he'd be on his way.

"I'm sorry, I can't stay. But listen, if he does come, call Fra Patryk Spassov. No one else. Can you promise me?"

"Of course."

"I'll write his number down for you."

"Let me find a pen," she said, lowering her voice.

The entrance hall opened into a grand salon. He watched her rummage through the tiny drawers of an antique escritoire. Besides the scar on her eye, she was missing three fingers—one for each escape attempt—but the remaining digits were quite nimble and her handwriting was precise and elegant.

When he and Misha were boys, she would talk about what life had been like when mages ruled the twin cities, generally after Alexei had pestered her with incessant questions. As frightening as those stories were, he knew now that she'd been holding back the worst. After the war, Glaine had been among the waves of refugees that washed up in Novostopol. When his mother got sick and his father retreated into work and mute grief, Glaine had been hired to mind the boys.

"Who's at the door? It's an ungodly hour!"

Alexei tensed at the deep, peremptory voice.

"It's Master Alexei." Glaine straightened from the desk, an anxious smile on her face. "He has some news about Master Mikhail."

Despite the late hour, his father was dressed in a starched white shirt and wool trousers. Maybe he wasn't sleeping so well these days, either. Gray threads showed in thick, wavy hair that had once been coal black, but his eyes hadn't changed. The blue of arctic icecaps and equally warm.

"Alexei," he said in surprise. "Well, don't hover on the doorstep. Come inside."

They walked together to the drawing room, which faced acres of gardens. The smell of the house, a combination of old, polished wood and new-mown grass, always made Alexei feel like a child again.

"Can I bring you anything?" Glaine asked.

"Brandy," his father replied, even though the question had been directed at Alexei. "Two glasses."

"One," Alexei said. "I'm not drinking."

His father frowned, but nodded at Glaine. "You know how I like it."

She busied herself at a sideboard while the men sat across from each other in matching wing chairs. Alexei could have poured the drink himself. It would be the thirty-year stuff from Nantwich, two fingers, neat. About a hundred *fides* a shot.

"You look terrible," his father said.

"I was in a car accident."

His brow creased. "Do you need a doctor?"

"It was minor."

They'd come to the room most haunted by the ghost of his mother. A portrait of her hung over the enormous marble fireplace. She was sitting at a table set for tea, leaning forward with her right hand clasped around the wrist of her left, which held a burning cigarette. That his father had kept the painting was evidence of the Bryce masochism, which was apparently a hereditary affliction.

She died from lung cancer when Alexei was nine and Misha was twelve, but the painting had been commissioned when they were small and she looked clever and mysterious, dark hair swept up in a loose chignon. The cigarettes had killed her in the end, but they were inextricably linked to his memories. He never minded when Spassov smoked in the car. Alexei actually liked the smell.

Glaine handed his father the drink and left, casting a quick sympathetic glance at the younger Bryce.

"So what's your news?" his father asked.

"A surge shorted the Wards at the Institute. Everywhere, actually. The patients got loose."

"Saints," his father muttered, tipping the glass back. His sleeves were rolled to the elbow and he wore a chunky gold watch on his right wrist, over a Mark of a broken crown. "Well, I'm sure they'll catch him. Isn't that supposed to be your job?"

Don't rise to the bait. "I thought he might have come here."

"Why on earth would he do that?"

"He has nowhere else."

"Well, if he does show up, I'll notify the authorities."

All too predictably, blood started to pound in Alexei's temples. "He's still your son. You could pretend to care."

His father set the glass down. The Mark flared blue. Alexei saw his titanic rage, held tightly in check. "Mikhail made his choice. He dragged our name through the dirt. Betrayed everything he'd fought for. Brought shame and scandal on all of us. And then you—" His father bit off the sentence.

"I what?"

"The Interfectorem. Saints, Alexei! It's for dimwits and thugs. Not us."

"I did it for Misha."

"Your brother doesn't deserve that kind of sacrifice. Now I've lost both my sons!"

"We're still alive, you know," Alexei said dryly.

"I don't want to argue with you. The last few years have been difficult, to say the least." His mouth set in a line. "I honestly can't say which of you is the greater disappointment."

This sort of statement was par for the course, yet it still stung.

"You were happy enough when we were knights."

"I was happy with Misha as a knight," his father corrected. "He was bent on joining the Church from the time he could speak. I knew I'd never talk him out of it. But it's not what I wanted for you."

Alexei stayed silent. It was an old quarrel. Now he wondered if his father wasn't right. If he had never bent his knee to take the vows, Mikhail wouldn't have taken the Night-mark to protect him. And the Beatus Laqueo . . . . He wished he'd never volunteered, but it was the only way to get into Misha's unit.

"Faith and family," he muttered. "I just wanted to do the right thing."

His father sighed. "You threw away a promising career in the law, and for what? To chase down lunatics?"

"I joined the Interfectorem to help people like Misha."

"They're beyond help."

"We don't know that."

"Yes," his father growled. "We do." He stood and strode to the sideboard. "I know you think I'm a callous bastard for never going to visit him, but I can't do it, Alexei. I can't see him that way."

Just like you couldn't bear to see Mother. The words were too harsh to speak aloud. Her death had scarred them all, but his father most of all.

"You could come to work with me," he said quietly, still facing the sideboard. "Take your life back."

"I have a life."

"Not the one you deserve."

Alexei couldn't hold back a bitter laugh. "Misha was always on the pedestal. Nothing I did measured up. Now that he's gone you want to put me up there in his place, but I'll fail you. We both know it." He rose to his feet. "All I'm asking is that you treat him gently if he comes here. Show some kindness."

His father stood motionless, one hand curled around the crystal decanter.

"I may not be available, but you can call my partner. His name is Patryk Spassov. Just promise me that, Papa? Don't let the Interfectorem have him. He's so big . . . they'd take one look and go straight for the crossbows."

His father glanced over one shoulder. "Why can't I call you?"

"I may have to leave the city for a while. It's too much to explain right now."

"Wait."

Alexei paused before the fireplace. His mother stared down at them both with bemusement, a thin streamer of smoke curling up from her cigarette.

"Can I help?"

The words surprised him. "I don't think so. But thank you for offering."

"Don't thank me," his father said gruffly. "I'm sorry I haven't been there for you, Alexei. I . . . ." He trailed off and swallowed a gulp of brandy.

"You've paid for one of the private rooms at the Institute. It means a lot to me."

His father waved this away. "I have the money."

"You still could have refused."

"I won't have a Bryce living in squalor like some common criminal."

The fifteen-second ceasefire was crumbling already. "It wasn't his fault."

His father dropped into the wing chair and looked up with weary eyes. "I know you worship him, but not even you can be so naïve."

If Konrad Bryce were a different man, Alexei might have confessed everything, but it would only cause more blame and recriminations.

"Can I see Misha's room? Or did you clear it out?"

His father was silent for a long minute. "Don't be ridiculous," he said at last.

Alexei wasn't sure how to interpret this statement. "I thought I might look for his *Meliora*. If you don't mind."

His father waved a hand. "Go ahead. But don't leave without saying goodbye, Lyokha."

No one else called him that. He had a sudden memory of running out to meet the car, his father looking sharp in a pinstriped suit and hat, and the woody scent of his aftershave as he swept Alexei into a hug.

"I won't, Papa," he said.

MISHA'S ROOM on the third floor was untouched. A shrine to a boy who no longer existed.

Alexei took in the collection of birds' nests and oval sea stones, each painted with lacquer so it looked freshly plucked from the waves. Two chess sets, both missing pawns and a rook or two. They used to combine the pieces to play, even though the sets were different sizes.

Books, hundreds of them. A childish watercolor of the view from a rock wall across the main road.

Stepping into his brother's old room was like falling through a time warp into the past. His heart cracked at how innocent they'd been. Every object sparked a memory of happier times. Funny how the mind forgot the pain and sadness of youth, sanding it down to uniform smoothness and the golden glow of an endless summer.

He recognized the spot in the painting immediately. An iron staircase bolted to the cliff led down to the beach below. It was submerged at high tide, but you could go down when the sea receded. They'd spent many lazy days exploring the tidal pools and swimming out past the breakers.

Once, the morning after a big storm, the waves had been huge and glassy. Slow-rolling combers that lulled you into thinking you were safe. Alexei had floated on his back for an hour or so, but when he tried to come back to shore, he found that the current had pulled him down the beach. There was a trench just where the waves broke and he couldn't get past it.

Misha lay on his stomach in the sand, reading a book. No matter how loud Alexei shouted, the roar of the surf drowned his cries for help. Again and again, he came within a few meters of salvation, only to be dragged back by the undertow.

He finally went limp and let the waves take him. This turned out to be the solution. As soon as he stopped fighting, he was flung across the trench to shallower water. He was crawling out on his knees when a strong hand pulled him from the surf and dragged him up the shore. Misha pounded his back until the water spewed out. They never told their father, who would have forbidden them from returning to the beach. Until he was sent to war, it was the closest Alexei had ever come to death.

Alexei trailed his fingers along the bookshelf until he found the pocket-sized *Meliora* Misha was reading that day. The book was bound in blue cloth, though the pages were separating from the spine. A gift on his eleventh birthday from their mother, who died not long after. Misha read it constantly and could quote whole chapters verbatim. Alexei remembered him, head bowed over the tiny print for hours. When his brother was absorbed in a task, you could call his name ten times before he heard you. But he wasn't an introvert. He needed others to talk and debate with—even if his tendency was to dominate the conversation.

Do you know why the Eastern Curia holds the Raven in such high esteem? Why she is the primary symbol of our faith?

Alexei shook his head.

Because the Raven is Fate's messenger, connecting the material and spiritual worlds. What else does that?

Alexei thought for a moment. The ley?

His brother smiled.

Alexei slipped the *Meliora* into his pocket. When he found Misha, he would give it back. If anything could reach him, it might be this slender volume he had carried with him day and night until it was literally falling apart.

Alexei turned off the light and gently shut the door.

Downstairs, his father was waiting in the entry hall— perhaps afraid Alexei might try to sneak out.

"If you need anything, just say the word," he said quietly. "You're welcome to stay the night." Shrewd blue eyes weighed him. "Or longer."

So tempting to say yes. Let his father call the city's top criminal law firm and start pulling strings at the Curia. Glaine could make up one of the dozen guest rooms. A feather bed with the softest sheets money could buy. And by breakfast tomorrow, no matter how hard they tried, one of them would be shouting at the other.

"I have to go, papa."

His father nodded, unsurprised. "Will you come back sometime?"

"If I can." He held up the battered *Meliora*. "I found it."

The anguish in his father's eyes was hard to face for more than a few seconds. Not even the Marks could tamp it down. Alexei gave a last awkward nod and left.

As he started the car, he saw a silhouette at the window, watching from the darkness.

Chapter Thirty-Two

K asia used the spare key to let herself into the flat.

Bryce's coffee sat where he'd left it, the cream revoltingly curdled. She dumped it into the sink and rinsed the cup. There'd be no more coffee for anyone until she replaced the urn she'd broken over Malach's head, though whoever had packed the bags for her and Natalya had also been kind enough to sweep up the broken glass.

Things were missing from her room—she'd have to send to the Arx to get them back—but her silk robe was hanging in the closet, and the knitted leg warmers Nashka had given her for Caristia. She changed and left her wet clothes on the floor, then took out her oracle deck and settled down at the kitchen table.

The Six of Storms would be her undoing.

The vestal outside the Pontifex's chamber had found the card and there was no way of getting it back. By tomorrow, it would be traced to her deck. She had the three coraxes, but blackmailing Falke hadn't worked the first time around and she doubted it would the second—even if he had the authority to extricate her, which was doubtful. A Pontifex was dead. The machinery of justice would lurch into high gear.

She was an Unmarked cartomancer with ties to the Night-mage who had supposedly done the foul deed.

Kasia took a glove off and touched the top card. Blue flame traced the mandala pattern on the back. When she lifted her finger, the light died.

Love, Fate, Destiny. What does the ley hold for YOU?

She'd always thought the tagline on their business cards sounded corny, but people loved it.

Now she fanned the cards out and chose one, flipping it over.

It lit with fire, a lush, deep violet this time, then subsided.

The Lovers.

She put the ivory lace glove back on, tapping a finger idly against the table. A line of verse came to her, though for once she couldn't recall the source. *Fate shall yield to fickle chance, and chaos judge the strife.*

More blood will spill before this is done, she thought. Perhaps an ocean of it. But it needn't all be bad. Not all of it.

Kasia stood and tightened the sash of her robe. She was at the door a second before the knock came. Alexei stood in the hall, one hand braced on the wall. He was soaking wet. Her heart beat hard at the sight of him, alive and as well as might be expected.

"I'm sorry, Domina—"

Kasia grabbed his sleeve and pulled him through the door.

"Saints, Bryce, I never thought I'd see you again. Get in here before they catch you."

"I came over the rooftops."

She glanced at the soot on his cheek. "So you did."

"I was driving past and saw your light on. I didn't expect you'd be home." He seemed astonished at his good fortune.

"Well, here I am."

They eyed each other for a moment.

"I looked for you in the cells," she said. "You were already gone."

"You came back for me?" Smile lines deepened at the corners of his eyes.

"I did." She thought of the body floating facedown. "How'd the hairpin work out?"

He laughed. "Not very well, I'm afraid. But I did get free in the end."

"Want to talk about it?"

"No." He walked to the window and glanced through the curtains at the Curia car parked below. "Do you?"

Kasia knew she'd have to tell him about his brother eventually, but she didn't have the stomach for it just yet. It would wreck him.

"No." She tossed him a kitchen towel. Alexei dried his face.

"I won't stay," he said. "I just wanted to tell you I'm sorry."

"For what?"

"For involving you."

"I was already involved."

"You know what I mean."

"No," she said. "I don't. But you needn't explain. You're forgiven, Fra Bryce." She looked him over. "I'm assuming they didn't let you out voluntarily. You'll have to leave Novostopol, but not tonight. You can barely stand."

He looked vaguely alarmed. "I don't want to impose."

"You're not. You can have my room."

"But I'm filthy."

"I don't mind."

He rubbed the back of his head. "Are you sure?"

"Come on." Kasia led him to her room. It was just big enough for a narrow bed and dressing table. Alexei sat down on the coverlet, the Raven stark against the pale skin of his neck.

"It's no use," he murmured, kicking his boots off. "I won't sleep."

"Just try," she said innocently. "I'll keep you company."

He lay back, lacing his hands behind his head. "I don't do well in beds. Maybe I should try the chair in the living room."

"Take your gloves off," she suggested. "Here, I'll show you how it's done." She peeled her own off and let them fall to the floor.

"You know I can't. I might use the ley by accident."

"So what?"

Their eyes met. She saw a spark and returned it in spades. Alexei pulled his left glove off and dropped it on top of the scraps of ivory lace.

"How's that?" she asked.

"Better," he said, clearing his throat. "I'm still not tired though."

Kasia sat on the edge of the bed. "Try the other one."

Alexei took his right glove off. His hands were well-made and strong. He ran a palm along the coverlet. Kasia found the gesture indescribably erotic.

"Something is different with the ley," he muttered. "I feel strange."

"Strange how?"

Animal heat flooded his eyes. He took a fistful of robe and pulled her down to his mouth. He tasted of vodka and rain. She touched his beard. Ran her fingers through the silky brush of his hair.

"Katarzynka Nowakowski," he whispered, his breath tickling her cheek. "You're the sexiest thing I've ever seen in my life."

He sat up. She unbuttoned the front of his cassock and helped to pull it over his head. Livid bruises stitched the gaps between his Marks, though he had so many she could hardly find a centimeter of bare skin. A winged maiden strumming a lute with the Polestar above and lotus blossoms at her feet. Death holding a sword with the point down. A road winding between jagged cliffs. Three carp swimming in a circle. An armored wasp, so lifelike it cast a faint shadow against his skin.

Kasia sensed layers of meaning that went down and down, all the way to the bottom of the deep well. Bryce's unconscious mind laid bare and each Mark forming part of a larger whole she could only glimpse.

"One day," she said, "I'll study these with the consideration they deserve." She touched his cheek with the back of her hand. "But not right now."

Alexei tugged at her sash with aching slowness. The robe fell open. She wore nothing underneath but the knit stockings. His eyes moved over her body, lingering and hungry. The feel of his bare hand on her breast sent a jolt straight down to her toes.

"You're the only good thing that's happened to me in a long time," he said hoarsely. "You make me feel, Kiska."

She stroked the lean muscle of his arm. It tensed beneath her touch. He drew her closer, his lips finding the hollow beneath her ear.

"I've never had sex with my clothes off before," she admitted.

She felt him smile. "And I haven't touched a woman without gloves since before I became a knight. Too many Marks. But the ley can't enter you, can it?" His thumb ran along her inner thigh, just at the edge of the stocking. "You're safe."

"Not too safe, I hope."

He laughed softly. "From me? Not safe at all."

She shivered at a tantalizing brush of tongue. He gripped her leg and then . . . nothing. His body went still.

"Alexei?"

Kasia pulled back. His eyes were shut, lashes curling against the dark shadows above his cheekbones. His lips parted. A faint snore emerged. She chuckled and drew the blanket to his chin.

"Poor thing," she said to him. Kasia blew a tendril of hair from her face and belted her robe. Her pulse still thudded heavily at various tender points. "Fog it, this is going to be a long night . . . ."

KASIA WOKE to a ringing telephone and the vague notion that she'd been ignoring the sound for quite some time. She staggered from the couch and fumbled for the receiver.

"Darling? I've been calling for ages. You didn't pick up! I was so worried . . . No, she's here. We're all fine. But I don't like you being there alone. What if I sent a taxi to pick you up? We're about to have brunch."

"Thank you, Auntie, but I just woke up." She stifled a yawn. "Hang on a moment." Kasia strode to the window and peered through the curtains. It was late morning. The long black Curia car was still parked across the street. She returned to the couch and picked up the phone. "They're still watching me. Can't you call them off?"

"Don't you feel safer?"

"The OGD does not make me feel safe, Auntie. Quite the contrary. How is Cardinal Falke?"

"Just a few stitches. He's holed up in the Conclave now."

"They're meeting so soon?"

"The Reverend Mother would want it that way. Her murder was an act of war, darling. The Neoteric faction invoked emergency powers to override the usual mourning period. We can't afford to sit on our hands."

Saints. "So they never found Malach?"

"The mage fled back to Bal Kirith, but he'll be dealt with." The tinkling strains of a piano echoed in the background. "It goes without saying that you'll keep all this to yourself. The official press release says the Reverend Mother died from natural causes. If people knew a mage had entered the Arx and killed the Pontifex in her bedchamber, they'd be rioting in the streets."

"They wouldn't," Kasia replied. "No one riots in Novo."

"You're so literal, darling. I meant it figuratively." A pause. "Have you heard from Alexei Bryce? He's missing."

"Oh no!" Kasia moved to the doorway of her bedroom, where he slept with the sheets around his waist and one arm flung over his head. "What does that mean, missing? Do you think Malach took him?"

"It means he wasn't in his cell when his advocate went there to meet with him this morning," Tessaria said tartly. "If he approaches you, call me immediately."

No mention of any dead bodies. *Interesting.*

"I certainly will," Kasia said.

Alexei laughed softly in his sleep and she closed the bedroom door. He looked adorable tangled up in the pink coverlet. Was he actually dreaming?

"Darling, are you listening to me?"

"Of course, Auntie. I'm just making tea. I broke the coffee pot. Who's leading in the vote?"

"I've no idea. It's all secret. They won't come out until it's over."

"Any other news?"

"Not just yet." Her voice sounded normal, but Kasia thought again of the Six of Storms. "May I speak with Natalya?"

"Of course. She's right here, eating all of Cook's cloudberry jam with a soup spoon. For Saints' sake, put it on a plate, darling . . . ."

There was a clunk as Tessaria set the phone down. Then Nashka's husky voice came on the line.

"Save me," she whispered. "I'm not cut out for country life. She says she'll make me play croquet this afternoon."

"Just hit the ball as hard as you can, like it's a polo match. She hates that."

"Come here." A peremptory command.

"I can't. Understand?"

A pause. "I suppose that means I can't leave, either?"

"Just give me one more day. Remember, you said you owed me."

A long sigh. "Yeah, okay."

"And thanks for, you know."

"I wanted to wait for you, but Falke and Tess ganged up on me. Did you find Fra Spassov?"

Tessaria must have walked back into the room. "I did. He wanted to help, but you know what happened next. I think we're both lucky to be alive."

"Saints. Call me later? I miss you."

"Miss you, too."

Kasia hung up the phone. She looked at Alexei. He slept peacefully, his breathing even and deep. He ought to be woken. Told what had happened.

But she couldn't do it.

Just a few more hours wouldn't hurt, would they?

Chapter Thirty-Three

The nest was in a high fork of the willow. Alexei clung to his branch, straining to catch a glimpse of the creatures that were kicking up such a dreadful racket. They seemed to be all mouth.

"Here she comes," Misha whispered, as the mother alit at the edge of the nest. The peeping reached a fever pitch, then quieted as she poked something into the gaping beaks.

"You can never, ever touch the babies," his brother said sternly. "The mothers will abandon them if you do." He touched Alexei's arm. "We'll come back tomorrow. They're almost old enough to fly. Maybe we'll see them test their wings. Would you like that?"

Alexei nodded. They climbed down and ran back into the house. In the way of dreams, it was dark now, sometime in the middle of the night, and he was barefoot and wearing striped pajamas, his brother sleeping soundly in his own bed upstairs. Alexei padded into the conservatory and saw the red coal of his mother's cigarette burning in the darkness.

"Is that you, Alex?"

She came from Nantwich, where they called boys John and Alex instead of Ivan and Alyosha.

"Hello, mama." He snuggled against her on the settee and she rearranged the blanket to cover them both.

His mother often woke up in the night to smoke, and it was easier to talk to her in the dark because he didn't have to look at her. Her voice was strong until the end, even if it was a rough smoker's voice.

"I'm glad you came down. I don't have much time left." His mother was never one to mince words. "What did you do today?"

"Flew a kite. A red one. We got the string all the way out. Then Misha let it go free." Alexei lowered his voice, though his father never came into this room. "He said that if the ley wills it, our kite will fly all the way across the ocean to the witches. Do you think it could?"

"Sure, why not?" She rested her chin on the top of his head. "You'll have to take care of your brother when I'm gone. Will you promise me that?"

It seemed backwards. "But Misha is stronger. I'm always getting colds."

"No, you're stronger, Alex." He felt her thin chest rise as she took a drag from the cigarette. "You see the world in shades of gray. Misha sees only black and white." She exhaled. "The truth is messy. It takes work to find. It takes doubts."

His mother had been a lawyer until she got too sick to practice. He wanted to be a lawyer, too, because everyone knew he took after her and Mikhail was more like their father, not the coldness, but the brash confidence, always so sure of himself.

"Will you look after him? He'll need you someday." Inhale. Exhale. Coughing fit. "Bring that water, Alex. Thank you. No, I'm fine. You're the only one he'll listen to now. He knows I won't be here much longer. I think he's written me off. And your father . . . . Well, you're not deaf. You hear them fighting. Stubborn buggers, both of them."

Most mothers didn't talk this way to their eight-year-old sons, but Eva Copeland-Bryce was not like most mothers.

"Your brother has a fire inside him and it'll burn him down to the wick someday. You must always tell him the truth, even when he doesn't want to hear it. Especially then."

"I promise, Mama. . . ."

His eyes opened. Light came through a window framed by white curtains. A pair of high-heeled boots leaned drunkenly against the bench of a dressing table. Pigeons cooed on the fire escape and faint traffic sounds drifted up from below, but the flat was otherwise quiet.

Alexei didn't move for a while, savoring the soft linen against his skin. He still wore loose black trousers, cinched at the waist with a drawstring, but his cassock and gloves were gone. The sheets smelled faintly of Kasia. A hazy memory of a kiss came back and he found himself suddenly, painfully aroused. Alexei located the bathroom and emptied his bladder, which was near to bursting. He gulped water straight from the faucet, then checked the other rooms. The flat was empty.

He found a towel in a closet and took a shower, letting the hot water beat down on his neck and shoulders. He felt stiff but otherwise fantastic, like he was ten years old again. Alexei whistled a jaunty tune as he lathered away the sweat and grime. He dried off and came out with the towel around his waist to find Kasia drinking a cup of takeout coffee in the kitchen. A flush rose in her cheeks when she saw him, but she covered it with a smile. "I washed your cassock, but it's still in the dryer."

His heart stopped. "There was a book—"

"I found it, don't worry. It's on the dressing table with your car keys and Mikhail's corax."

Alexei cleared his throat. "What day is it?"

"Wednesday."

He stood still for a moment, counting. "What happened to Tuesday? How long did I sleep?"

She glanced at the clock over the stove. "About twenty-nine hours."

He gripped the towel. "Saints."

"I tried to wake you, but not too hard, I'll admit." She patted a chair. "You must be starving."

Alexei drew a deep breath. Bits and pieces were coming back. The silky feel of her skin. Black hair tumbling across his face. "I fell asleep on you, didn't I?"

She grinned. "I think you would have died or lost your mind if you'd gone another hour without rest so I won't hold it against you, Bryce. Have a pirozhki." She held out a box of boat-shaped pastries. "Potato or apricot?"

"Apricot." He sat down. She pushed a cardboard cup of coffee towards him. "The cream isn't curdled, I promise."

He ate in silence, marveling at the flavors. The cream tasted freshly churned, the dough so light and hot it melted on his tongue. Every sense was heightened. It felt like rising from the dead. He demolished the last pirozhki and caught Kasia staring at him. He suddenly remembered he was sitting in her kitchen completely naked except for a small towel, but instead of feeling self-conscious, as any decent citizen of Novostopol ought to, it made him horny all over again.

"Still hungry?" she asked. "I can get more."

"That's not the problem, Domina Novak," he said sternly.

She arched an eyebrow. He studied her heels and severely tailored dress, which was the color of a ripe peach.

"You're overdressed."

"Am I, Father?" Kasia asked innocently.

"Very much." He knelt down in front of her and ran his hands down the skirt, then took the hem and eased it up above her knees. She let out an uneven sigh.

"Alexei, I have to tell you something—"

"Don't." He pressed a thumb to her lower lip. "Not yet. Just let me have you first."

The last words came out thick and guttural. Kasia made a

small sound of surrender. Her legs wrapped around his hips, pulling him tight against her. He slid her stockings down, tearing one in his haste. She wore those little lace gloves and her hands moved down the Two Towers, which rose from the small of his back up to his shoulder blades. He didn't need to see them to know they were burning.

Their lips met, hot and urgent, and he tried to get her clothes off but she wouldn't let him and he was beyond caring. "At least that part of you is Unmarked," she whispered huskily. "I wasn't sure . . . ."

He made love to her on the kitchen table, then undressed her in a leisurely fashion and carried her to the bed, which ended up a good two meters from where it had started. He hadn't been with a woman since joining the Interfectorem, but Katarzynka Nowakowski wasn't any woman. She was *the* woman. He'd only known her for four days but that much was already clear.

He lay across her, panting hard, still barely able to think. She smoothed the sweat-damp hair from his brow. He propped up on an elbow and kissed her, their lashes brushing. They would never leave this bed. That was the solution. Never, ever go anywhere, pretend they were both dead—

A joyful clamor drifted through the open window. It sounded like every bell in the city was pealing at once. Kasia stiffened beneath him.

"They must have chosen a new Pontifex," she said. "I didn't think it would happen so soon."

A spear of ice touched his spine, though part of him already knew. Had known all along. "I dreamt," he whispered. "Oh, Saints, I dreamt for the first time in ten years. She's dead, isn't she?"

Kasia nodded.

"How?"

"They're blaming Malach. It's only logical. He was inside the Arx wreaking havoc when it happened."

Alexei's unease grew. "How, Kasia?"

She cupped his face, holding his gaze with a fierce intensity. "Feizah gave him no choice. He was only following the orders of a madman. No one else knows and they never will."

He closed his eyes. Outside, the bells tolled on and on. Car horns honked. The sounds washed over him. All he could think of was the pool of drying blood in the old man's room. He'd been searching for his brother, terrified of what might happen to him, but it wasn't Misha who needed protecting.

"I was there," Kasia said gently. "In her bedchamber. She didn't believe me at first so I gave her a sweven of everything. She ordered your release, but then the Wards broke. Mikhail came with an elderly gentleman, an Invertido—"

"The Pontifex Lezarius."

"You know?" She gave him a startled look.

"I figured it out." He had only seen the Reverend Mother on the occasions she Marked him, but it was an intimate procedure. A joining of two minds, if briefly. She was the most forceful person he had ever known, except for one. "How did my brother seem?"

"Very thin, but strong enough. I don't think he took any pleasure from the act. He was just carrying out a sentence he believed to be just."

"Did he speak?"

"Not a word."

"Why did they spare you?"

She sighed. "Lezarius made me strip. Your brother turned his back, he was a gentleman about it. They only wanted to see what Marks I had. When Lezarius realized I had none, he said I was an innocent and offered me his protection." Her mouth twitched. "I politely declined."

"Any idea where they went?"

"I thought you'd want to know so I asked. Lezarius said, 'To raise an army, of course. There is work to be done. Mikhail is a valiant knight. You mustn't be afraid of him.' And then I said, 'He looks ill.' And Lezarius said, 'Perhaps he will improve in the Void.'" Kasia paused to stroke the line of his brow. "I think they must have gotten out of the city in the confusion, Saints help us all."

The phone rang. She disentangled herself and went to answer it. Alexei rolled to his back, listening to her muffled voice in the living room. He wished he could believe it was impossible, that Misha could never do such a thing, but he'd always been willing to cross lines others wouldn't.

Your brother has a fire inside him . . . .

That iron will had kept him alive when he should have died years ago. Now his faith was transferred to a lunatic with unspeakable powers. The worst part was that Alexei had always liked the old man. Everybody did.

Things were fitting together, though he still couldn't see why or how. It all came back to—

"Falke is the new Pontifex," Kasia said, worry in her eyes. "I'm sorry, Alexei, I had no idea the Conclave would be so brief. I should have woken you. I should have—"

He pulled her down, burying his face in the fragrant curtain of her hair. "It's not your fault." He laughed mirthlessly. "I used to admire him greatly. Misha saw him as a father figure. The one he'd always wanted."

She pressed something into his hand. "Lezarius said these men tried to kill him. He blamed the Reverend Mother, but I'm sure it wasn't her who sent them."

Alexei stared down at the coraxes in his palm. Brodzsky and Gerlach. She turned one of the coins over. "What Order is this, Alexei?"

He studied the inscription. Hoc ego defendam. *This I will protect.*

"I've never seen it before." He gazed up at her. "Thank you."

"For what?"

"Going to the Reverend Mother on my behalf."

"It was the right thing to do."

"It would have cost you everything."

"There wasn't much to save," she said. "Except for you."

He closed his fist around the coraxes and kissed her with quiet desperation until she finally pulled away. He saw sadness in her eyes. "You're leaving, aren't you?"

"I have to."

"Why? Can't you stay and fight them?" Her jaw set. "I'll give my sweven to the court if I have to. They're accepted as evidence, aren't they?"

"Yes. But that's not the main problem. With Feizah dead, the Marks she gave me will fail, Kasia. They already are, though I don't feel it yet."

"Fail? What does that mean?"

"They won't disappear, but the ley won't work as it should. It's why I dreamed. No one understands the precise mechanism of the sickness, but my Marks must be transferred to someone else and it needs to be a high-ranking official of the Curia."

"What happens if you don't?"

He didn't answer.

"Fog it all, Alexei. What can I do to help?"

"You already have. I'll go to Kvengard. The extradition process isn't simple. They'll have to take over my Marks while it's sorted out."

"You don't sound very sure of that."

"It's the only way." He pulled his pants on. "Is that car still outside?"

"Not since early this morning."

"Malach?"

"Tessaria says he's gone back to the Void."

"Good."

She frowned. "Why good?"

He picked up the *Meliora* from her dressing table,

thumbing the threadbare cloth cover. "Because Malach is mine."

Alexei peered through a crack in the curtains to check for himself when a burst of artillery fire sent him ducking away from the open window. He threw his body over hers, pressing her to the carpet. "Don't move," he whispered, heart hammering.

It came again, a string of sharp cracks followed by honking and a few cheers. He released a ragged breath.

"Firecrackers," Kasia said quietly, stroking his back. "This town is shameless. Any excuse to drink and make noise."

She was right, but his instincts still screamed at him to stay away from that window. To get out before the building came down in an avalanche of bricks and dust.

"I'm sorry," he said, feeling stupid. "I just . . . ."

"I know." She squeezed his bottom. "If your first thought was to shield me, I think I've got myself a good one. Want your cassock back?"

He smiled, nerves still singing. "No, but I'll take it anyway."

He finished his cold coffee while she went down to the basement laundry room. Other than the bout of combat trauma, which was an old, familiar acquaintance, he didn't feel bad. But he'd read about Mark sickness in order to watch for the signs in his brother and knew it would get much, much worse.

"Still warm," Kasia said when she returned, pulling the cassock over his head.

"I should have asked you something," he said haltingly. "Before I lost my head. We didn't use anything—"

"I can't have children, Alexei, if that's what you're worried about. I'm barren."

He felt like a clumsy bastard. "I'm sorry."

"Don't be, I'm not. It's just the way it is." She didn't elaborate, but she didn't seem upset with him. In truth, he never thought about children anyway. They were part of someone else's life.

He tucked Misha's corax and book into the pocket of the robe, along with his gloves and car keys. At the door, he pulled her into his arms, silently cursing himself for sleeping so long. They could have had hours more. "I don't want to say goodbye."

She kissed his palm and his knees went a little weak.

"Come with me," he said recklessly. "We'll run somewhere they won't find us."

She gazed at him with regret. "That's not what's meant to happen, Alexei. There are things I have to deal with here. And I can't leave Natalya and Tess without a word." The flecks of gold in her eyes turned molten. "But you won't escape me so easily. We're bound together, for good or ill."

It was an odd way of putting it, but Alexei believed her. He had to, or he'd never be able to walk away.

"Don't forget about me, Katarzynka Nowakowski."

"Never, Alexei Vladimir Bryce."

He kissed her thoroughly one last time to make sure she didn't, then walked down the stairs, feeling both happier and sadder than he ever had in his life, certainly not both at the same time.

The gypsy cab was parked where he'd left it a few blocks away—with three tickets waiting on the windshield. He stuffed them into the glove compartment, hoping the girl hadn't reported the car stolen, which she would be entirely justified in doing. He'd taken her livelihood, after all.

Traffic was heavy on the main avenues, but he knew every back alley and short cut through the city. The road to Kvengard was on the western side of the river. Once he sorted out his Marks, he'd try to find Misha even if it meant venturing alone into the Void. Thirty thousand square kilometers of jungle, all of it Black Zone. At least his brother was with Lezarius. The old man could protect them both.

The shocks on the cab were nonexistent and he was slowly navigating the cobblestones of Armourer's Alley when a car pulled up and blocked the intersection. Alexei threw the gears into reverse, but another Curia vehicle boxed him in from behind. He killed the engine and waited.

A tall, slender form approached the car. Gloved knuckles rapped on the glass. Alexei rolled down his window.

"Fra Bryce?" Sharp black eyes, lined heavily with kohl, peered at him from inside the raised cowl. "I am Sor Tessaria Foy. May we speak?"

He leaned over and unlocked the passenger door. She slid into the car and lowered her hood. Graying dreadlocks fell down her back. The vestal had a face that could have been anywhere from fifty to seventy and he reckoned she had been a great beauty once. Still was, even as she stared at him with barely suppressed fury.

"If I had my way, Bryce, I'd have rooted you out of my god-daughter's bed days ago. But since you have a knack for sticking your nose into business that doesn't concern you, we decided to let you be."

The Conclave. And now it was concluded with Falke triumphant. Well, if the axe was going to fall, he'd as soon get it over with. "Am I under arrest?"

"No," Foy said sourly. "The charges against you have been dropped."

He blinked. "All of them?"

"All of them."

"Why?"

"Lack of evidence. The main witness cannot be located."

"Oto Valek."

She didn't react to the name, but Alexei knew it had to be the orderly. "Your partner now denies that he saw you attack Massot. He claims he was pressured by the investigating officers and has retracted his statement. It's a serious accusation. Normally, OGD would launch an inquiry, but both agents were killed by Invertido during the riots at the Batavia Institute."

"And the knife that was planted in my chamber?" he said pleasantly. "Let me guess. It's disappeared from the evidence room and no one is looking very hard."

Tessaria studied him without expression.

"So I'm free to go?"

"Don't be a fool. The Reverend Father requests an audience and you will grant it to him without delay."

"What does he want?"

"That is for him to say." Sor Foy's gaze swept Alexei from head to toe. "I've been told the Bryce brothers are legendary, but you don't look very impressive to me. What Kasia sees in you, I'll never know."

He smiled lazily. "Nor do I, but that doesn't seem to have stopped anyone."

"Watch your tongue, boy. You think you know what's going on, but you haven't a clue."

He scrubbed his jaw. "Am I allowed to shave first?"

"Oh, do be quiet, Bryce. Leave the car here." She glanced at the sparkly unicorn air freshener hanging from the rearview mirror. "It will be returned to whatever teenager you stole it from. Now, get a move on."

Crowds surged around the Dacian Gate, contained by lines of traffic police in yellow rain slickers. The crush of bodies continued all the way up the Via Fortuna and spilled into the plaza before the Pontifex's Palace, packing it from edge to edge.

Heavy clouds promised another downpour, but so far it had held to a drizzle. The sea of black umbrellas pressed against barricades lining the main thoroughfares. According to custom, the Reverend Mother's body would be laid out in the basilica for veneration of the faithful. After a six-day mourning period, she'd be interred in the crypts with her predecessors. There was supposed to be a pontifical interregnum in which the Curia was without a spiritual leader, but Falke's faction had circumvented it by invoking emergency wartime powers.

The car wound its way at a snail's pace, joining a long line of black vehicles. Tessaria gazed out the window. She did not speak to him again until they reached the parking lot at the rear of the Pontifex's Palace and an aide came out to collect him.

"Good luck, Bryce," she said crisply.

"Sor Foy. It's been a pleasure."

"No, it hasn't." She scowled. "But I won't have my god-daughter heartbroken so for the Saints' sake, behave yourself. I think you're capable if you try."

The aide, an elderly bishop named Ustinov, escorted him through the palace, past hurrying chars in mourning black and knights in the blue and gold tunics of the Pontifex's personal guard. They were all men, which Alexei found disconcerting.

At last, Bishop Ustinov paused before an ornate door. He knocked and received a summons. The door was opened by yet another aide who met his eye and stood aside in silent invitation.

Alexei put on his lawyer face and strode inside with the same energetic zest he felt on the first day of a major court case, ready to charm or dismember as the situation required. It was not the formal audience chamber, but rather a more intimate study. They were on the third floor and he could see the ocean of black umbrellas stretching across the plaza.

"Reverend Father," Alexei said, bowing his head.

Chapter Thirty-Four

D mitry Falke looked like he hadn't slept in days.
　　Dark pouches hung under his eyes and deep lines framed his mouth. Yet standing before the window, resplendent in a pure white robe and without a silver hair out of place, Falke appeared every inch the most powerful man in the Eastern Curia. He dismissed his aide with a nod. She retreated, the door silently swinging shut.

"You must be worried about your brother," Falke said. "We've managed to find all the patients except for Captain Bryce and one other. His name is confidential, but I believe you know him. Patient 9."

Alexei gave a cautious nod. "They were friends."

"Do you have any idea where they might be?"

"None. Is that why you've summoned me here instead of throwing me back in a cell?"

Falke sat down behind a rosewood desk. It held a handsome copy of the *Meliora* bound in embossed leather and a collection of his own books, with FALKE stamped in large block letters along the spines. He must have been in the midst of writing missives for there were a dozen brass cylinders of the sort Curia messengers carried for high-level diplomatic communications.

"Our interests coincide to a much greater degree than you imagine." He gestured to a chair. "Please, at least hear me out before you pass judgment."

Alexei saw no point in antagonizing him, not until he knew what Falke wanted. He sat down.

"You view me as an adversary." Falke tilted his head. "You think it was I who ordered your death. An understandable but erroneous assumption."

Alexei said nothing.

"You overreached so I reined you back in. But if you know anything about me, you'll realize the great esteem I hold for the knights of the Beatus Laqueo. I would never condone the extrajudicial execution of one of my own. Unfortunately, I was not consulted on the matter. The party involved has been reprimanded."

Kireyev. Unless Falke was shifting the blame, but why would he care? He could do whatever he liked now. Alexei's gaze drifted across a rectangular space above the desk, lighter than the surrounding woodwork, where he guessed Feizah's portrait used to hang. Across the city, people would be peeling down her picture and replacing it with one of Dmitry Falke.

"Did you order the charges to be dropped?"

A faint smile. "Domina Novak demanded to know why I was punishing you. She was quite forceful in her argument. At this point, I agree. Arresting you again would be counterproductive."

"I'm innocent, Reverend Father," Alexei said. "We both know it."

Falke regarded him blandly. "I believe you are, Bryce. So let us move on to other matters. I'm aware of your personal motivation to locate Malach, just as you must be aware that I knew your brother quite well before his accident."

"It was no accident," Alexei said coldly.

357

"Of course not." Falke gazed out the window. "I am not usually a man who shelters behind euphemisms. The last days have been . . . trying."

The Conclave. Alexei could well imagine the hostile factions jockeying for power in the hours after Feizah's death. But the Curia never did anything quickly and Falke must have expended a vast amount of mental energy to force a binding vote within two days.

"Your brother was a fine man. I cannot compare my loss to your own, but I mourned him deeply."

"May I ask you something, Reverend Father?"

"Go ahead."

"What happened when he went with you to Kvengard?"

Falke nodded slowly. "I won't conceal the truth from you any longer. Captain Bryce volunteered to infiltrate the mages by taking a Mark."

Alexei could easily see his brother doing such a stupid, courageous thing—but only if he had something tangible to gain from it.

"But why? We'd already won the war!"

"Not exactly, as you well know. And there were other reasons. Substantial ones. We needed to broker a deal, but he didn't trust them. Nor did I. There was no other way."

"Do you know what he asked for in return?"

"Yes. He asked for your life. I should have told you before, but I'd promised him I wouldn't. He didn't want you to carry the burden."

Alexei looked away, unable to bear the sympathy in Falke's eyes. "That sounds like my brother."

"I can only assume Malach learned of his treachery and decided to turn his Mark as punishment. He must have done the same to Ferran Massot."

It was time to test the waters. Alexei still didn't know why he'd been summoned to Falke's study, but he knew where the whole mess had started.

"It was you who had the doctor eliminated."

"That's a rash statement, Bryce."

"I'm just trying to get all this straight in my mind, Reverend Father. I have no sympathy for the man. He got what he deserved."

Falke eyed him stonily.

"However, in light of the evidence that Dr. Massot abused his patients in the most vile fashion, I must wonder if the Curia was aware of his predilections prior to last week?"

"The Curia was not aware. And I resent the insinuation."

"Forgive me, Reverend Father. I merely find it disturbing—"

"Enough." His voice hardened and Alexei caught a glimpse of the most feared and admired officer of the last half century. "I will not be cross-examined by you. Massot was corrupted by his association with Malach, of which I was entirely ignorant. I regret ever using him, but I had my reasons. And that's why you're sitting here, Bryce."

Falke rose and went to a cabinet, returning with a glass cube that resembled a paperweight. He handed it to Alexei. The glass encased a heavy gold signet ring, trapped like a fly in amber. It was identical to the ring Falke wore on the third finger of his left hand, but instead of the Raven, it had a different emblem.

"Do you know what that is?" Falke asked.

Alexei studied the circle with twelve jagged rays resembling lightning bolts. "The Black Sun of Bal Agnar."

"It was Balaur's ring. I cut it from his hand the day Bal Agnar fell. I keep it as a lesson, Bryce. The nihilim lost because their power, both political and military, relied entirely on mastery of the ley. When it was taken from them, they failed to adapt." He set the cube on his desk. Alexei stared at it in fascination. The Pontifex of Bal Agnar had been the worst of them, a monster now used to frighten children.

"I'll be blunt," Falke said. "The Curia is in crisis, one of our own making. My predecessor had good intentions, but she was unwilling to face the truth and thus left the problem to fester."

"Crisis?" Alexei asked warily.

Falke steepled his hands. "What do you know about the events that led to the civil war?"

"The Pontifexes of Bal Agnar and Bal Kirith broke with the Via Sancta, issuing their own doctrine which they called the *Via Libertas*. They were excommunicated from the Church in the year 945. In response, they declared war on us."

"But what was the exact nature of the schism?"

Alexei felt like a pupil summoned to recite before the class. "The essential moral nature of humanity. According to the *Via Libertas*, the only path to utopia is absolute freedom, allowing the strong to dominate the weak in a perverse form of natural selection. The Shadow Side is an inevitable aspect of human consciousness and the impulses it represents are beneficial to the evolution of the species. The role of the Church should be to allow nature to take its course, which would ultimately lead to a superior race. That was the true meaning of the Black Sun and Broken Chain. Of course, it was nonsense. They actively encouraged the worst and punished the best, while pretending to be above it all.

"Eventually, the ley itself grew corrupted and this taint spread through the cities until anarchy reigned. Most of the cardinals and bishops went along with it. Those who didn't were martyred. The ringleaders wore red. The symbol of abyssal ley."

A color that had since been banned for clergy throughout the Curia.

"But before the schism, nihilim were called by another name, yes?" Falke prompted.

It was in the *Meliora*. "Light-bringers." Lucifers, in the old tongue. "They were our saviors after the Second Dark Age. They built the six Arxes and founded the Via Sancta."

"Indeed. Some theorize that inbreeding led to the madness that seized them. Did you know that we share ninety-nine percent of our genetic code? The one percent deviation is related exclusively to the structures of the brain."

Alexei did, in fact, know that. "It lets the nihilim manipulate the abyssal ley."

"Among other things. There's something else I want to show you, Bryce."

They left the study, trailed at a distance by guards, and walked to a cloistered passageway overlooking an interior courtyard. Six children in blue robes were playing a game of tag among the columned archways. None were younger than eight nor older than twelve.

"This," Falke said, leaning his forearms on the marble balustrade, "is the next generation of the Eastern Curia."

Alexei stared at him. "What do you mean?"

"They can bestow a Mark, but the ability will die with them. There's no chance it will be inherited by the offspring."

"Why so few?"

"Why indeed, Bryce? You graduated at the top of your class. You must have an analytical mind. What changed in the last generation? What have we lost?"

He thought of the blood-soaked earth of the Void. "There were thousands of casualties. Knights, mostly."

"And that's the winning side," Falke said dryly. "What about our enemies?"

"Annihilated."

Falke watched the children laugh and run about. "Almost," he said softly. "But not quite. Which turns out to be rather fortunate since we need their blood to bestow a Mark."

The words hung in the air. "That's heresy," Alexei blurted before he thought better of it.

"Yes," Falke said mildly. "It's also the truth. I know what you've been taught. That only the most highly evolved among us have the ability. That bestowing Marks is a consequence of enlightenment. But it is not so. We use Sublimin to induce a state of openness, but the act itself requires the abyssal ley. I myself carry Light-bringer traits—enough to Mark others, but not enough to create offspring with the ability. Believe me, Bryce, I've tried. Of the ten children I've fathered, not one has the ability."

"Saints," Alexei muttered, deeply shaken. "But the abyssal ley is inherently tainted. How could it be used in the service of the Church?"

A vestal called the children to lunch. They fell into a line and left, chattering voices fading into the distance. Falke's soft exhalation broke the vacuum of silence that remained. "The human psyche is analogous to an iceberg, *da*? The visible portion is the conscious mind. Thoughts, memories and feelings of which we are fully aware at any given moment, the mental processes we can discuss in rational terms. But the vast underbelly remains submerged."

Alexei had shelves of books on the subject. "The unconscious and subconscious."

"Precisely. They are far more powerful in governing our behavior—all the more so because we are blissfully unaware of their existence. So it is with the ley. The abyssal is deeper and stronger, yet it is neither inherently good nor evil. Merely transformative. One day, we will not need Marks anymore. The human race will have evolved beyond our base instincts. But that day is not yet here and we will never reach it without the nihilim."

"So they were always using it?"

"Only to bestow Marks," Falke said. "Until Balaur and Beleth codified its use in other areas. Their predecessors understood the dangers and managed to avoid temptation for nearly a thousand years. Few know it anymore, but the white of the Pontifex's robe signifies the unity of all colors of ley." He sighed. "We lost a third of the Church hierarchy in this miserable conflict. A third! There are still some among us who can bestow Marks, but we are all old."

"You have mage blood," Alexei said flatly.

"Yes. So did the Pontifex Feizah."

"Yet the Wards don't react to you."

"Genetics don't matter." Falke's voice held a touch of impatience. "Blood doesn't matter." He tapped his forehead. "It is the mind that matters. The Wards reject those fully given over to the abyssal ley. I, obviously, am not in that category, nor was my predecessor."

"Who else knows about this?"

"I'm getting to that, Bryce." The cardinal turned away from the courtyard and walked slowly back to the study, Alexei at his side. "I imagine you have other questions first. Let's hear them."

Only a thousand. "How can you be certain there aren't any more children? Have you tested every single one in Novostopol?"

"We always have. When a Mark is given, there's a resonance in the ley. You must know the process intimately since you have even more than I do. The Mark is always tested afterward. The child pulls first at the surface ley, then the liminal ley."

Alexei nodded.

"If they have nihilim blood, they will reach for the abyss without even being aware of it. The Mark will flare red for an instant. The one who bestowed the Mark feels an echo, a backwash." They reached the study. Falke resumed his seat behind the desk. "Civil Marks will not permit an individual to use the abyssal ley, and even if a child has the innate ability, they will never touch it again. But in the moment of transference, we know."

"And Holy Marks?"

"Make it extremely unpleasant to touch the abyssal ley but

not impossible. However, touching it does not equal the ability to Mark another. Do you see the difference?"

"Yes."

"Ferran Massot had a theory that Invertido might be able to access the abyssal ley in the way we needed. I agreed to let him conduct experiments, all within the guidelines of accepted medical practice. The intention was to gain insights into the mechanism." Falke's face darkened. "But his ideas proved to be unfounded, as was my trust in him. I cannot tell you how sorely I regret our association."

"I am relieved to hear that, Reverend Father."

"Your absolution is a salve to my conscience, Bryce," Falke said dryly. "In any event, I'm a man who learns from his mistakes. There will be no more outside actors. This is the Church's predicament and we will solve it ourselves."

Here it comes, Alexei thought.

"Some years ago, when I first grasped the nature of the threat, I founded an Order called the Praesidia ex Divina Sanguis."

"Protectors of the Divine Blood," he murmured, thinking of the coraxes Kasia had shown him.

"Just so. Our mission is nothing less than the preservation of the Via Sancta through any means necessary. We need lucifers, Fra Bryce. As distasteful as it may be, that requires nihilim blood. And we must at least consider the idea that their race can be returned to a state of innocence. Properly raised, I believe they can be redeemed."

The words, coming from a man who was the mages' most implacable enemy, sounded utterly surreal. Rage quietly built inside Alexei. Was the last ten years all for nothing? He might be alive, but he wasn't the same. He never would be. And he was one of the lucky ones.

"The Beatus Laqueo will be reformed and deployed to the Void. I would promote you to captain. We'll capture Malach together. Get justice for your brother."

"He was Praesidia, wasn't he?" Alexei managed to keep his voice neutral, though his thoughts spun like tires in the mud.

"One of my first recruits." Falke studied him. "I've lost six men in the last week, every one of them irreplaceable. The Order is weakened at the very moment we need it most." He leaned forward. "Your war record is outstanding. You're smart and persistent. Perhaps not quite as strategically minded as your brother, but that will come in time. This is a chance to save the Church and redeem your family name. Think carefully, Bryce."

Alexei held his gaze. "Did you have a deal with Malach? Is that what the meeting Kvengard was about? Is that why he came here now?"

"Saints, no. I'm not under the illusion that any of the ones who fought against us can be saved. That meeting was another dead end. Feizah wouldn't permit further negotiations." His gloved fist clenched. "But I will not allow everything our faith has built over the last millennia to be destroyed in a single generation."

Alexei nodded in agreement, his eyes unfocused.

Natalya Anderle?

It had never stopped nagging at him.

Why did Malach mistake Kasia for her flatmate? Where did he get the name in the first place?

There were various possibilities. Kireyev. The orderly who found the card in Massot's pocket. Even Spassov himself, though Alexei didn't believe it for a moment. But the most likely was the man who had arranged the liaison with Massot in the first place.

The confession comes first, laqueus. Let's start with your first tour of duty in Bal Agnar.

Again, how did Malach know it was Alexei's first tour of duty? They hadn't met yet, and wouldn't for five more years. Could Misha have told him? Or was the truth far worse?

I didn't want to turn your brother that day. I wanted to kill him. Call it a favor for an enemy.

"How are you feeling, Bryce?"

He raised his head and met Falke's mild gaze. "Fine."

"It's been two days since the Reverend Mother died. Mark sickness is different for everyone, but it often begins quite innocuously. You might even feel better than usual, *da*? But this will not last."

"I'm aware, Reverend Father."

"I'll take over your Marks, Bryce. All of them. I've already done it for the others Feizah Marked." Falke looked unspeakably weary and Alexei understood it wasn't just the Conclave that had drained him. "The early symptoms are mild compared to the end stage, but with so many Marks, it would be suicide to refuse my offer. A pointless sacrifice, and for what? A grudge that I interfered in your attempt to capture Malach? I'm offering you the chance to do exactly that, with the blessing of the Pontifex and a cadre of knights at your command. Bring me Malach. When your brother is found, we will restore him to sanity."

Another win-win for the Pontifex.

If I kill Malach, he wins, Alexei thought. If Malach kills me, he wins.

A favor for an enemy.

"What about Domina Novak?"

Falke arched an eyebrow.

"Will you expose her?"

"She is in no danger from me." Falke touched the Raven on his neck. "Does that set your mind at ease?"

Not at all. "Is she in danger from someone else? Archbishop Kireyev, perhaps?"

"Always thinking like a lawyer. I did not intend for the statement to imply loopholes. Kasia Novak is under my protection. I'm not interested in ruining a young woman's life." He leaned back. "She may have shortcomings, but her patron is a friend of mine. And Natalya Anderle is practically a daughter. You needn't fear for either of them." He smiled. "I am not a mindless zealot. The Via Sancta must allow for latitude regarding the Unmarked when they have led blameless lives."

"That is wise of you, Reverend Father." Alexei bowed his head. When he looked up, Falke was staring at him.

"Flattery and false humility do not serve you, Bryce," he said gruffly. "When you're a captain, I expect the unvarnished truth, not what you think I wish to hear. My ego is not so fragile. If you believe I'm making a mistake, I want to hear your arguments why. I might overrule you, but you are to speak freely, always."

"I understand."

"Good." Falke rose. "However, tradition demands certain rituals." He extended a gloved hand across the desk. "I'm delighted to have you on board, son."

Redeployment to the Void. Even with the knowledge of Falke's lies and treachery, he was close to accepting. Part of him, the part he hated, would do anything to find his brother. Torture and kill. Get down in the mud, as Malach put it. And who would he be when it was done?

Alexei touched his lips to the gold signet ring.

As he stood erect, his elbow struck Falke's war souvenir, knocking it to the floor. Falke bent to retrieve the glass cube and Alexei grabbed one of the courier cylinders, stuffing it into his robe just as Falke stood up.

"I'm sorry," he said, raising a hand to his forehead. "I am feeling a little peculiar."

The Pontifex eyed him with concern. "We ought to transfer your Marks right away."

"Would you permit me to pay my respects to the Reverend Mother first? It's something I need to do."

Falke could hardly refuse. He nodded brusquely. "Return within the hour. I'll make time on my schedule."

Alexei bowed his head and withdrew, leaving the new Pontifex to resume his correspondence. How soon would he notice the cylinder was gone? With luck, not before the hour was up.

An aide escorted him to a rear door of the palace. The mourning crowds were contained within the plaza and along the Via Fortuna. Except for the lines of black cars, half with plates from Nantwich and Kvengard, the rest of the Arx was almost unnaturally quiet. Alexei went to the Tower of Saint Dima and found Spassov at his desk wearing a pair of half-moon glasses, pecking at the typewriter. The room was a wreck, books strewn everywhere, sheets torn from the bed. OGD had displayed their usual enthusiasm when they tossed the place.

"Alyosha!" He looked up, an expression of wonderment on his bluff face. An instant later, huge arms swallowed Alexei in an embrace that lifted his feet from the ground. Spassov had been drinking, but he didn't seem drunk. Or not excessively drunk.

"No one would tell me anything," he grumbled. "I figured they'd arrested you again. I finally told Kireyev I'd quit if they didn't let me see you." He glanced at the sheet of paper in the typewriter, which Alexei saw was a poorly spelled letter of resignation. "I don't think he cared, but it was something."

Alexei's chest tightened as he regarded this bleary-eyed mountain of a man. "They've dropped the charges for lack of evidence."

Patryk gazed at him shrewdly. "Why?"

"Oto Valek disappeared. He was their chief witness." Alexei smiled. "I understand you retracted your statement."

A rumble as Patryk cleared his throat. "They must have written it down wrong. We both know you never touched a hair on Massot's ugly head. Did Kasia Novak have anything to do with this remarkable reversal of fortune?"

Alexei hesitated. "I think so, yes."

"I wasn't sure about her, but I'm glad. Listen, you can help me finish the Massot report now." He started rummaging through the papers on Alexei's desk. "It'll be a load of horse-shit, but we have to file something."

"I'm leaving, Patryk."

"What?"

"My brother is missing. I have to find him."

"What about your Marks? None of mine are from the Reverend Mother, I'll be fine, but she was your patron." He looked worried. "You can't put this off."

"Falke offered to take them, but I can't do it."

Spassov pushed the glasses to his forehead. "Tell me why, Alyosha."

"He wants to send me back to the Void. I think we're going to war again."

Spassov didn't appear as shocked as he would have been a week before. "What will you do?"

"Go to Kvengard."

Patryk nodded slowly. His face was bleak. "Then I'll finish this letter of resignation after all. I'm too old for a new partner."

"You're forty-five," Alexei pointed out gently.

"I can't do it without you."

"Yes, you can." His voice was urgent. "You must. The others are . . . you know how they are."

Spassov sighed. He picked up a pint bottle of cheap Grodsky vodka and regarded it, but didn't drink. "I'm sad, Alyosha. I'll miss you."

"I don't even know if they'll take me in Kvengard." Alexei dug an exorason from the mess and threw it across his shoulders. The outer cloak would conceal the inverted trident of the Interfectorum on his cassock. "I've never dealt with matters of extradition. So I might be back."

Spassov regarded him steadily. They both knew that if

Kvengard didn't take him, he wouldn't live long enough to return. "How do you plan to get through the checkpoints?"

Alexei showed him the Raven-marked cylinder. "With this."

"You'll still need courier plates." He sighed. "Saints, you're trouble, Alyosha. Come on, there's a screwdriver in the trunk."

They went down the winding stairs. Alexei had spent most of his time as a priest either deployed or holed up in the Tower of Saint Dima. While not especially large, the Arx contained hundreds of buildings from the very grand to the highly obscure, and Patryk knew them all. The Order of Couriers turned out to be not far off. It was a nondescript brick heap next to the Tomb of the Martyrs, with just a few cars in the lot. Alexei stood watch while Spassov removed one of the license plates.

"I finally slept," he said.

"I'm relieved to hear it."

"For a day and a half."

Patryk glanced up at him. "That's all?"

"So what's the word? How did Kvengard react to everything?"

"Luk withdrew his nuncio after the Reverend Mother was murdered." Spassov handed him the plate and replaced it with one from the Interfectorem. "He's expressed condolences, of course, but it's hard to tell which way the political winds are blowing, Alyosha. Luk is close to the Conservative faction. I don't think he's pleased that Falke took the ring."

"That's good," Alexei said. "Shit, someone's coming."

Spassov dropped the last screw and they scrambled into the bushes, jogging back to the Tower of Saint Dima until Spassov ran out of breath and insisted on lighting a cigarette to calm his nerves. Alexei attached the courier plate to their car. The men embraced.

"What time is it, Patryk?"

Spassov took out his father's watch. "Two-forty. You taking anything with you?"

Alexei looked up at the moss-covered tower. He'd buried his own corax in the dirt outside the basilica at Bal Kirith. Whatever happened, this chapter of his life was irrevocably closed. "No."

"Write me a letter, Alyosha." Patryk held out the car keys.

"I'll do better than that. Expect a shipment of Kvengard whiskey."

Spassov grinned, but he looked heartbroken.

"And listen, keep an eye on Domina Novak, will you? If she ever needs your help . . . ."

"Of course." Spassov looked away, his eyes watery. "I'd better go. Take care, old friend."

Alexei watched him climb heavily up the stairs and vanish into the darkness. He almost called out, but what would he say? Not the truth. Alexei half wished he didn't know, either. And if Spassov lost his faith, Alexei wasn't sure what would become of him.

No, he did know. Patryk would drown himself in a bottle within five years.

The kennels were cool and musky. The Markhounds greeted him with desultory sniffs, but only Alice stuck around, leaning against his leg. Alexei scratched her ears. "Watch over Patryk, *da*? He needs you even more than I did."

She looked up at him alertly. Alexei gave her a pat and went back outside. He started the car and looked up to find the hound standing in the middle of the road. Alexei rolled down the window and stuck his head out.

"Ire!" he commanded. *Go!*

Alice didn't budge.

Alexei sighed and got out of the car. He walked toward her. Alice danced away, a gleam in her eyes.

"Ire!" he said again, pointing firmly at the kennels.

She yawned.

He picked up a pebble and threw it. Alice flinched and backed up a little. The hot lump in his throat grew tighter as he picked up another and pretended to throw it. "Ire!"

Alice shot him an inscrutable look and turned tail, her body blurring into dark motes that dissipated like a handful of dust.

"Fogging dog," he muttered savagely, slamming the car door.

He joined the line leaving the Arx, two fingers tapping impatiently on the wheel. Traffic moved at a crawl. The faces beyond the barriers scrutinized each car, hoping for a glimpse of someone famous, and Alexei was glad for the tinted glass.

His hour was almost up. Even if Falke hadn't noticed the missing cylinder, he would put two and two together when Alexei didn't return to pledge allegiance.

"*Suka blyat*," he muttered, his front bumper practically nudging the next car. "Hurry it up."

Bells tolled the hour as he reached the Dacian Gate. The guards barely glanced at him before waving the car through. Once out of the gridlock, he floored the pedal, taking the shortest route to the river. The mood was either somber or exuberant depending on the political leanings of the neighborhood. Falke was a liberal, Feizah a conservative. In the younger, hipper areas, block parties were in full swing. In others, including Ash Court, every shop was shuttered and old women in black headscarves gathered on the fire escapes, wailing over cheap lithos of the Reverend Mother.

The skies had darkened to pitch by the time he reached the checkpoint on the west bank. Four Oprichniki in yellow slickers manned the glass guardhouse. Their lieutenant approached before the car had even stopped. He was about Alexei's age, with calm gray eyes and an aura of competence.

"You are not permitted to leave the city, Fra Bryce," he said firmly.

The road to Kvengard began just beyond the iron gates.

Stelae lined the route, but the inscriptions were dark. No ley was being released into the Void.

"By whose authority?" Alexei stalled.

"The Reverend Father." The Oprichnik's voice hardened. "Get out of the car."

He lifted his hands from the wheel, moving slowly. "I think you're mistaken——"

"Get out!"

The lieutenant backed up a step and aimed a crossbow through the open window.

"Easy," Alexei said, raising his hands. "I'm just lifting the handle, *da*?"

The man gave a short nod, his eyes on Alexei's gloves.

Alexei opened the door just as the skies split wide. In one blurring motion, he slammed the heel of his hand into the Oprichnik's face and yanked the crossbow away. A bolt whistled past his ear. They were shooting from the guardhouse. Alexei dropped to one knee, taking cover behind the open car door. He tore his gloves off and drew deeply. Straight down to the abyss.

It's the last time. The very last time . . . .

Crimson ley seeped into his palm, sluggish like thick tar. There was no sensation of pain this time. No sensation of anything. He tried to give it purpose, to bend it to his will so he didn't have to hurt anyone else, but the power simmered in his veins, immobile. Cold sweat broke on his forehead. Something heavy hit him from behind, dragging him down. More bodies piled on.

"Cuff him, you idiots," someone yelled. "OGD wants him alive."

His cheek pressed against wet asphalt. Alexei gritted his teeth and managed to free a hand, but nothing happened when he grabbed one of the yellow slickers. He couldn't think beyond the pain in his head and the fear of ending up back in a cell. Through heavy curtains of rain, the lieutenant strode towards him. He had a bloody nose and looked irate.

"They said you were dangerous, some kind of special forces shit, but I don't see——" A dark blur streaked through the rain. It hit the lieutenant and carried him to the ground, snarling viciously. The Oprichnik screamed and rolled away, clutching one arm. Alice slowly turned to regard the men who pinned her master. Her head lowered, hackles bristling down her muscular spine. The hound's eyes reflected the greenish light of the storm. Powerful jaws opened wide, snapping and barking and spraying saliva.

"Saints, what the——"

"It's a fogging Markhound!"

Alexei managed to roll over and knee someone in the balls. Alice leapt forward. The Oprichniki swiftly abandoned him for the safety of the guardhouse.

Alexei gained his feet and ran through the deluge to the gate. He slammed a palm down on the stelae. The Key Ward had a circle enclosing a Raven just above the words *Kilometer Zero*.

Just the surface ley. Please, just give me a trickle . . . .

A single Mark lit up. His very first, bestowed when he was nine years old by Bishop Bartolomes. After law school, Alexei had clerked for the judge, a kindly and fair man. The Mark was a simple quill pen on his right forearm. So small he'd almost forgotten about it, overshadowed as it was by the Marks Feizah had given him as a knight.

Blue fire traced the Key Ward. The iron gates swung open. Lines of ley leapt from stelae to stelae along the road to Kvengard, unfurling in a shining ribbon. Alexei jumped into the car. A sharp whistle and Alice manifested in the passenger seat, panting. The smell of wet dog immediately filled the confined space.

He gunned the engine and stuck a hand out the window, waving goodbye as they leapt forward with a squeal of rubber.

Chapter Thirty-Five

The surging whitewater of the Traiana River ran below a narrow suspension bridge joining the Eastern and Southern Curiae. A deep gorge marked the border, with the Fort of Saint Ludolf on the far bank. A wolf banner flew from the garrison's tower.

Alexei hadn't passed a single car in five hours. The road cut through dense forest, but it was the only major artery between Novostopol and Kvengard. There should have been a fair amount of traffic.

He'd driven at a steady one-twenty, with a single stop to retrieve a fresh pair of gloves from the trunk, and seen nothing in the mirrors. If he could cross the border, he might stand a chance of actually pulling this off.

Alexei slowed as he approached the fort, an ancient, sprawling structure with meter-thick walls. The road ran straight through it starting at an archway flanked by two squat towers. He'd managed to convey to Alice that she needed to conceal herself. Also that she shouldn't attack the knights in the garrison, though he wasn't sure the lesson had been absorbed. The whole drive, she would periodically sniff him and whine. The hound knew something was wrong and it put her on edge.

Cool mountain air hit his face as he got out of the car. The knights of Kvengard wore chainmail hauberks beneath blue and white tabards bearing the Running Wolf. They'd watched him cross the bridge and a group of three rode out to greet him. The mounts had glossy black coats and luminous eyes that shone like a cat's in the gloaming. They faded to insubstantial shadows when Alexei didn't look at them directly, but that was typical of all creatures bred with the ley.

"Guten tag," he said to the officer, holding up the cylinder. "I have documents for the Nuncio Morvana."

"Leave zem here." His accent was clipped. "A party is going to Kvengard tomorrow. Zey can take it."

"The Reverend Father expects me to deliver it personally."

"I have not seen you before. What is your name?" *Vat iz your name?*

"I'm not with the couriers. I'm one of the new Pontifex's personal aides."

The knight's blue eyes narrowed. "Zis road is closed. Identification, please."

"If I could just speak with your officer—"

"Identification." He held out a gloved hand.

Alexei gave him Misha's corax. The knight stared at the inscription, brow furrowing. He looked up, his expression unreadable. Alexei wondered if he'd just made a bad mistake. Kvengard maintained neutrality in the war.

"You are a Laqueo." The officer turned to his knights. "Ey, boys!" He drew a finger across his throat and laughed. They eyed Alexei with new respect. "Our kommandant will want to meet you. He served as an advisor with the Laqueos, back in the day. Perhaps you know him."

Alexei smiled, inwardly cursing. "Of course."

They went inside the garrison. The knight brought him to a mess hall where men and women ate at long trestle tables.

Tall, pointed windows overlooked the gorge. Kommandant Rademacher sat with a handful of other officers, drinking wine and eating some kind of stew. The hall smelled of cabbage and paprika.

"Mikhail Semyon Bryce, sir. He carries a message for Bishop Morvana."

Rademacher set his cup down. His shrewd gaze took in Alexei's scruffy beard and wrinkled exorason. The drone of conversation suddenly got louder. Sweat trickled down Alexei's spine. He smelled something else under the food. A note of rot and stagnant water.

"Flay me, old friend! Is it really you?" Rademacher's accent was softer, more fluent.

Alexei held up his palms with a grin. "It's me."

Rademacher studied him, gray eyes narrowing slightly. "You look different without a beard." Alexei tensed. "Even younger and it's been what, five years?" He chuckled. "Sit down, Captain Bryce. Have some wine."

Alexei couldn't refuse. The other officers nodded politely as he took a chair next to the kommandant.

"My condolences for the loss of your Reverend Mother," Rademacher said, pouring him a cup.

"Thank you."

"We felt the ley surge," he said. "All the way out here in the boondocks. A bad flood season, yes?"

Alexei sipped his wine. It tasted peculiar. Flat and almost saline, like the swill that came out of the water purifiers in the Void.

"So you've been promoted? Well, you hitched your cart to the right horse, Captain Bryce." He slurped some stew. "Do you remember the time we had a few days of leave in Nantwich and went to that little hole-in-the wall dive bar down by the docks—"

Alexei smiled at what he hoped were the appropriate points of the story, but it was hard to focus on anything but the small black spiders crawling out of Rademacher's mouth.

"—and she said, I'll have to work it out with a paper and pencil, *ja?*" The table erupted in raucous laughter.

"Those were the days." Alexei drained his wine in one long gulp.

"Do you ever miss it?" Rademacher asked, brushing at one of the spiders. It skittered away from his gloved hand and crawled into his left nostril. "I mean, we did some things I don't like to remember, you understand, but I felt alive." His eyes grew distant. "Not much happens out here, Captain Bryce."

A sudden sharp scream came from just outside the mess hall. No one reacted. It lengthened, raw and full-throated, then cut off abruptly.

"I don't miss it," Alexei said.

"Well, you've done well for yourself. An aide to the Pontifex. More wine?" He held up the bottle.

"Not if I'm driving." Alexei forced himself to meet Rademacher's eyes. A beetle clung to the left one, six segmented legs braced on the upper and lower lids. "Will you let me through, kommandant?"

Rademacher hesitated. Alexei's gaze skittered across his neatly parted blond hair, his smooth pink cheeks and fussy mouth. The beetle started to feed.

"It's my first commission for the Reverend Father." Was that his own voice, so calm, so steady? "I don't want to disappoint him."

Rademacher smiled. His right eye sparkled with good humor. The other was being slowly devoured. "Naturally, Captain. Our own Reverend Father left it to my discretion, though officially the road is closed in respect for the mourning period."

Thank all the Saints. "I'd better be on my way then." The muscles of Alexei's face rearranged themselves in a broad smile. "Thank you again for your hospitality, kommandant."

"Anything for an old comrade, *ja?*"

Rademacher walked him back to the car and raised a hand in farewell. It was a profound relief to put him in the rearview.

Alexei drove slowly through the fort, accelerating once he passed through the second arch. The setting sun cast long shadows through the firs. *Mox nox.* Soon, nightfall. He switched on the high beams. Alice watched him from the passenger seat with a worried expression.

"Want to drive for a while?" he said. "I feel kind of weird."

She yawned nervously.

"Here's something good, little sister," he said, leaning back against the headrest. "There's no telephone service beyond the western checkpoint. I think we're clear for a while."

He glanced over to find Malach in the passenger seat, a knife sticking out of his stomach. A rising tide of blood filled the footwell.

Alexei blinked rapidly three times and turned back to the road. Kilometer 502 flew past. He was more than halfway there and making good time.

"Miss me?"

Alexei rolled down the window. Cold air rushed inside the car. He fumbled for the knob on the heater.

"I've been doing some thinking, priest. Here's my theory. You're obsessed with fixing your brother because deep down, you're secretly glad he went mad and the guilt is eating you up. Mikhail Semyon Bryce, the golden boy! You're a pale shadow of him, Alyosha." A mocking laugh. "Only your mother could love a lawyer."

Alexei braked into a sharp curve. Malach braced a hand on the dashboard.

"You think you're afraid of ending up Invertido like your

brother, but that's not it. You're afraid of failing to live up to his memory."

Alexei looked over at him. "Know what?"

Malach tilted his head.

"I'm an insomniac. I'm used to seeing shit that isn't there. So go ahead and psychoanalyze me." He turned back to the road. "Makes the drive less boring."

He could smell the blood now, like rusting iron. It brought him back to those endless nights in the Void. The interrogations . . . .

"Why do you think they gave you so many Marks, priest? Because you're tainted. You have a cancer inside that just keeps growing and growing no matter how hard your masters try to cure it. That's why you can't sleep." Malach laughed. "You pray for salvation, but no one's listening. The shadow will consume you in the end. You tell yourself you only did what you had to, but the laqueus is the real you, Alyosha. Falke knows it. You should have accepted his offer." He tapped his forehead with a grin. "Free your mind. Accept the truth. We're the same and there's no way out but down into the abyss."

The center line glowed in the high beams, unfurling in a serpentine red ribbon. It bathed Malach's handsome features in scarlet flame. "Take pains to waken the dead," he whispered, solemn now. "Dig deep mines and throw in sacrificial gifts, so that they reach the dead."

A quote from the *Via Libertas*.

Alexei didn't respond. Malach's voice hardened. "How about this. When I find them, I'll make Lezarius break the grid and I'll give Misha to Beleth. She'll find good uses for him, I'm sure——"

Alexei reached over and twisted the dagger. Malach's face melted and became his brother. Not as he was now, but in the prime of life. He wore a full suit of armor, polished to a high gleam. The helm rested in his lap. He smiled, faint lines deepening at the corners of his blue eyes.

"Don't listen to him, brother. Nihilim lie."

Alexei gripped the wheel. *Not this.*

"You're angry at me," Misha said. "Of course you are. I betrayed everything I ever taught you. I left you to clean up my mess."

Alexei checked the power gauge. The battery only had a quarter charge left. Stupid not to plug it in at the garrison. He tried to do the math. Four hundred kilometers divided by sixty . . . or was it the other way around?

"You should have been a rising star in the Curia. Maybe you'd be a nuncio by now. Instead, you wasted the last three years chasing down lunatics in the vain hope of finding Malach. I'm so sorry, Alyosha. Forget about me. I don't deserve your pity."

The road began to descend again, winding through the conifer forest to the rugged, windswept plains below. Kvengard lay at the tip of a peninsula dividing the Northern and Southern Oceans. The sea would not be far off now.

"That day in the basilica? I didn't care what happened to any of you. I only wanted to kill Malach. I was tired of being his pawn." Misha laughed hollowly. "But all I do is trade one master for another. First it was Falke. Then the mage. Now I serve a mad Pontifex. A soldier is all I am, Alyosha. All I'll ever be."

He started taking his armor off, piece by piece. The breastplate, vambrace and gantlets were adorned with silver embossing and intricate etchings. It had cost a fortune, but their father was happy to pay for it when Mikhail Bryce was promoted to captain. When he was still a source of pride rather than shame. The Raven motif featured prominently, of course, but Misha's armor also had images of Saint Jule and other icons.

Alexei didn't want to look, but something compelled him.

The images were wrong, all wrong. Instead of kneeling in attitudes of piety, the saints were performing lewd acts upon each other. Misha's Marks were also different from the ones he remembered. Sinuous animals with golden scales and teeth glistening with venom. Women with pale, bloated faces and staring eyes.

"Stop," he said brokenly. "Please, stop."

"What do you think of this one, brother?"

He'd only seen the Nightmark once, when six knights had pinned his brother down and stripped him to confirm the cause of his distress. A blindfolded man with a blade to his throat and a disturbing expression of ecstasy on his face. It was on his chest, inverted, so the blade sliced across his nipples.

"Why?" Alexei demanded. "I didn't need your help! I can take care of myself. If you'd only believed in me, none of this would have happened, none of it!"

"No. If I hadn't made the bargain, you would be dead now. We both would be." Misha's face turned to the window and the towering dark pines. "Remember when we stole Papa's keys and took his new convertible for a joy ride? You backed it into the rock wall and we thought he'd kill us, but he just laughed and said he did the same thing when he was a kid."

Alexei's eyes burned. The road blurred. "I remember."

His brother smiled sadly. "Let me go, Alyosha. I don't belong to you anymore."

"Yes, you do." He reached for Misha's hand. "Don't be stupid. We'll always have each other—"

Savage barking.

Alexei looked up. He was going too fast, foot pressing the accelerator to the boards, and the car had drifted across the road into the opposite lane. Something crouched there thirty meters ahead. A squat, misshapen shadow in the moonlight. He jerked the wheel hard to the right. The car skidded off the road and down a steep embankment. A feeling of peace came over him as it headed straight for a spruce tree. The next thing he knew, the world flipped over. He floated, weightless, for an endless moment. The seatbelt jerked tight. He smelled burning metal. Heard explosive crunching and scraping above his head. Time sped up in the final seconds and he had the peculiar sensation that the car was stationary and that big tree was speeding towards him.

He must have passed out for a bit because everything blurred until Alice shoved her wet nose in his face. It was very quiet. Alexei's eyes opened. She barked in his ear and he pushed her away, suddenly hyperalert. He hung suspended upside down in the seatbelt. Cracks webbed the windshield. Every other window was blown out.

Alexei found the release and tried to pop it open. It wouldn't budge. He remembered that seatbelts don't release under tension, so he braced a hand on the roof and pushed up to get his weight off the belt while he unlatched it with his free hand. That worked and he eased himself down and crawled out the back window.

His hands shook from adrenaline as he surveyed the wreck. The car had rolled down the embankment and come to rest right in front of the big spruce. If it hadn't rolled, he would have hit the tree at high speed and not even the seatbelt would have saved him.

Alice had wisely dematerialized when the car went off the road. Now she nudged his leg, gazing up with liquid brown eyes. He dropped a hand to her head, drawing comfort from her warmth and realness. A sudden fear rose that he was imagining her, too, but it was too terrible to contemplate.

"What was that?" he asked softly. "That thing?"

She trotted up the embankment with the slightly hitching gait caused by the scar tissue on her haunch. Alexei followed, stiff but otherwise unhurt. The road was empty in both directions. He watched the Markhound closely, but her hackles were flat, her ears relaxed. She sniffed at a patch of grass on the verge and then peed on it.

The car was barely visible from the road. Even if someone passed by, it was doubtful they'd notice it until morning. Alexei started walking. The next stela put him at kilometer 857, which was impossible. He'd only been a few minutes outside the garrison, hadn't he?

Or had he driven three hundred and fifty kilometers arguing with ghosts? If so, it was a miracle he hadn't crashed sooner.

The night was cold and clear, the road marked by a ribbon of stars above. Alexei shivered inside his cloak. Whenever he stopped, Alice would growl and nip at his heels until he started walking again. The sun was rising at his back when he saw the towers of Kvengard, black silhouettes against the rose-streaked sky. Alexei sank to his knees before the gates. His mouth was so dry, it took him a minute to form the ancient words. They dated to the Second Dark Age, when the citadels of the Via Sancta were the last refuge in a world convulsed with madness.

"I beg sanctuary," he whispered.

Wolf-Marked men came out.

The gates of Kvengard swung open.

Chapter Thirty-Six

Alexei lay in a stone chamber, naked and dying. The ley burned like acid inside him. *So thirsty.* He reached for a clay pitcher and knocked it to the floor. The crash brought a vestal, who fetched others. They wrangled him into a wheelchair, covered him with a sheet, and rolled him down a long corridor into a dim audience chamber.

A hazy figure sat on a dais. His white robe was sleeveless, revealing heavily Marked arms. Alexei bowed his head, which came easily since he could barely hold it up. "Reverend Father."

"I know who you are, Alexei Vladimir Bryce." A rich baritone. "Why did you flee Novostopol?"

"I still have my faith."

"That was not the question."

Alexei leaned over to retch. Nothing came out. He was empty except for the ley.

Luk leaned over to consult with a tall figure to the left of his chair. They didn't speak long and he guessed his fate had already been decided.

"Archbishop Morvana will take custody of your Marks. Do you accept her as your patron?"

He knew nothing about Morvana beyond the five seconds he'd seen her outside Kireyev's office. Which didn't bode well for him. The OGD had agents everywhere.

"I accept," he managed.

Walls blurred past and he found himself in an airy, light-filled chamber with a stone slab in the center. Hands lifted him up and whisked away the sheet. The sensation of air on his skin brought fresh agonies. He felt the sting of a needle in the muscle of his thigh.

"You must be well-acquainted with the procedure of receiving a Mark, Fra Bryce," said a crisp female voice. "Transference is slightly different so I will explain as I go. With each step, consent must be explicit. I have given you fifty milligrams of Sublimen. It will dissolve the walls in your psyche, temporarily, of course. You will remain awake and aware. Do you understand?"

He nodded, eyes sliding shut. An image appeared in the darkness. The Maiden.

"Tu aperi ostium mihi?" Morvana asked. When she spoke the old tongue, her Kven accent grew softer.

Will you open the door to me?

"Verum," he murmured.

Yes.

"Quaeque tua est pietas, ut te pignus Ecclesia?"

Do you pledge your loyalty to the Church?

"Verum."

"Uti tu pe ley in ministerio Ecclesiae sunt optimum illud exemplar?"

Will you use the ley only in service to the ideals of the Church?

"Verum."

Every muscle cramped. He thrashed and a cool hand pressed against his chest. "Perhaps I should have warned you that it will hurt like a hellbitch. Forgive me, Fra Bryce."

Now that he knew the truth, he ought to have been repulsed that she was using the abyssal ley on him. Morvana had mage blood. But he was just pathetically grateful to purge the decaying ley from his body. He could feel it seeping from the Maiden like bad humors from an infected wound.

A second image floated in the black mindspace. The Towers.

"Tu aperi ostium mihi?"

"Verum," he slurred.

"Quaeque tua est pietas, ut te pignus Ecclesia?"

"Verum."

Alexei braced himself this time, biting back a scream.

Again and again they recited the litany until Morvana had taken charge of all eighteen Marks. He was drowning in a puddle of sweat by the end.

"It is done." She lifted his head and gave him a sip of water. "You must sleep until the drug wears off."

"My dog," he whispered. "Where is she?"

The terror resurfaced—that he was alone in this strange place, that Alice had never followed him, that he'd imagined it all. Alexei gripped the damp sheets. He wasn't sure he could withstand the blow if she gave him a pitying or quizzical look.

"The Reverend Father has a fondness for Markhounds. She is being well cared for."

A tight lump loosened in his chest. He had one friend, at least. Someone who loved him no matter what he did. "I want to see her."

Bishop Morvana leaned over him, green eyes intent. "I just saved your life. When you're fit to speak, I want to know what the fuck is going on in Novo, *ja?*"

Alexei pretended to pass out. Her footsteps receded and vestals came, wheeling him back to the infirmary. He slept well despite some extremely vivid Sublimin-induced dreams about Kasia Novak.

The next day, he woke to find a new cassock neatly folded on a chair next to his bed. The *Meliora* rested atop it, along with a pair of gloves. Alexei stumbled from the bed naked and was rooting through the pockets when one of the vestals bustled in with a pitcher of water.

"My old cassock," he said, hastily grabbing the sheet and wrapping it around his waist. "Where is it?"

"Sent to the laundry."

"There was something in the pocket." He held up the *Meliora*, heart pounding. His chest felt too tight. It was hard to breathe. "Along with this. A corax."

She shrugged. "I don't know. I will ask."

"Please. I need it back!"

She looked at him warily. "Yes, I will try right away."

But she didn't return.

For the next two days, he was confined to the infirmary. Every time a vestal came, he asked about his corax and was given a vague reply. Alexei ate everything they brought him and did endless pushups and situps to burn off nervous energy. He could not shake the certainty that if the corax was lost, Misha was lost, too. His rational mind understood that it was just superstition, a transference of all his hopes and guilt to a material object that was not his brother, but this didn't ease the panic attacks when he reached into his pocket and found it empty.

Morvana did not come to see him. He still knew nothing about her except that she hadn't sounded very sorry when she told him it would hurt like a hellbitch. There was no psychic connection between them. But his life was in her hands now and he'd do almost anything to protect her so he never had to go through that again.

Perhaps most remarkably of all, he still had his faith.

Alexei took out the *Meliora* and read the first Sutra.

Nonviolence is one of the most consistent and reasonable doctrines ever taught to humanity. She who aggressively injures another fosters hatred, the root of all evil.

Falke and Kireyev had tested his devotion, but they were just men. The Via Sancta was larger than two scheming officials in Novostopol. It had lasted a thousand years and would last a thousand more if he had a say in it. The alternative was frankly terrifying.

The problem of Marks would be dealt with somehow. A more immediate threat was Lezarius and what the old man might do. Alexei didn't know the exact number of mages in the Void, but one was too many if the ley lines broke.

He arranged the bare facts in chronological order, as he would if he were preparing for a major court case.

Someone in Jalghuth had hidden Lezarius in an asylum. For the last three years, an imposter had worn the Lion ring, but his intentions remained unknown. Falke and Kireyev learned the truth through Ferran Massot. They sent priests from the Praesidia to eliminate Lezarius, but Gerlach and Brodzsky failed in their mission. Enraged, Lezarius went after the Reverend Mother Feizah, whom he blamed for his predicament.

So far, Alexei felt on solid ground.

Malach had some association with both Massot and Falke, and was playing them both. He went to the Arx that night to get Massot's message and took the blame for Feizah's death because only Kasia Novak had seen Mikhail and Lezarius, and she'd told no one but Alexei. Now his brother and the old man were gone.

The next bit was speculative, but Alexei felt confident he knew Falke well enough to predict his behavior. Misha had spoken of him often and Alexei read several of his books during downtime in the Black Zone. Falke would do everything he could to find Lezarius, but he was a pragmatic man. He would plan for the worst. And he would act preemptively, not waiting for the mages to strike. He'd told Alexei as much himself.

In short, war was coming, and possibly a return to continent-wide anarchy.

Did he have a moral obligation to tell Luk?

And what would the Pontifex of Kvengard do with the knowledge?

The biography he'd been reading the fateful night the hounds started howling painted a portrait of a man who was highly intelligent and deplored bloodshed. He'd kept Kvengard neutral throughout the conflict, only permitting observers into the field to embed with knights from the other Curiae. They were supposed to discourage human rights abuses, but as Komandant Rademacher had intimated, some became active participants once they saw the atrocities of the mages. Luk had been a vocal opponent of the rendition of captives to black sites in Nantwich, the most militant of the cities. He argued that the *Meliora* forbade extreme interrogation methods, which Alexei privately agreed with.

Yet Luk was also close to Lezarius. Was it conceivable he didn't know about the switch? Or was he part of the conspiracy? If Alexei guessed wrong, he would end up dead very quickly.

He sifted through the facts again and again, playing out various scenarios. Everything felt too big and messy, beyond his abilities. Despite Falke's many flaws, he was a ruthless master of strategy, which is what they needed. Falke would handle it.

The summons came on the afternoon of his third day in Kvengard, conveyed by two vestal knights in Wolf tabards with the faces of peasants and the burning eyes of zealots.

"The Reverend Father desires your presence."

Alexei rose and followed them out the door.

. . .

"DMITRY FALKE IS CONSPIRING to capture and breed nihilim because he thinks it's the only way to save the Curia. Is that about right, Fra Bryce?"

Luk stared down at him from the dais. Their first encounter had been a blur, and Alexei was getting his first real look at the Southern Pontifex. He was in his early sixties and very thin, with piercing eyes and a small, severe mouth.

"Yes, Reverend Father."

"He told you this himself?"

"He wanted me to join a secret order devoted to preserving the light-bringer bloodlines. I served under him previously so he had reason to believe I would be a willing candidate."

Luk eyed him with distaste. "One of the cardinal's killers. And yet you supposedly said no. Was this before or after he was raised to Pontifex?"

"Just after, Reverend Father."

"He allowed you to leave Novostopol?"

"Not exactly."

"So if I harbor you, I will draw his wrath?"

"Yes."

Bishop Morvana leaned over and whispered something in Luk's ear.

"To be clear, are you accusing him of collusion in the Reverend Mother's death?"

"No, I'm certain he wasn't involved." Not directly, at least.

"Why did you refuse the offer to join this . . . what did you call it?"

"The Praesidia ex Divina Sanguis." Alexei kept his voice calm and detached. "A nihilim turned my brother. I have no desire for revenge, but I think a truce would be unwise."

They already had the corax. He couldn't keep Mikhail a secret and the story was more credible that way.

"I'll take your information under advisement, Fra Bryce."

Luk waved a hand in dismissal. "You will report to Bishop Morvana's office at five bells."

Alexei bowed his head and strode from the audience chamber, trailed by the vestal knights. "May I see my dog?" he asked once they'd reached the corridor.

The women glanced at each other. "This way."

The six Arxes were built from nearly identical plans, yet Kvengard had subtle differences that made him feel like he was losing his mind again. The basilica faced north instead of south. The Pontifex's Palace was four stories rather than three. And the kennels were on the far side of the necropolis, adjacent to a structure that looked much like the Tower of Saint Dima except that it was circular instead of square.

The instant he entered, Alice came bounding up with a joyful bark. Alexei was relieved to see the Kvens were meticulous about caring for their packs. Each had a small house with fresh straw and access to a large outdoor enclosure. The fence wouldn't keep the Markhounds inside—only their training could do that—but it reassured casual visitors.

"May I have a few minutes alone?" he asked his escorts.

They nodded brusquely and left to wait outside. Alexei took out the *Meliora*. Misha had handled the book every day for years. His scent would be imbued in the leather. Alice gave it a thorough sniff. Then she barked once, spun around, and sat down, tongue lolling.

"Venari," he commanded. *Hunt.*

She looked away and whined. There was no trail to follow, but if his brother came anywhere near, he knew she would alert him. Alexei rubbed the twisting scar on her haunch. She seemed well-adjusted in her new surroundings and studied him with a pleased air, as if she knew she'd saved his life yet again.

"I won't leave you, *da?*" he told her softly. "Never, I promise."

Alice yawned.

"I'll be back tomorrow." He stroked her pointed ears. "If they haven't locked me up."

He ate a quiet meal in the infirmary, a mushroom and leek pie that was quite good, and a bowl of red grapes. At five bells, his minders escorted him to Morvana's office in the east wing of the palace. Dossiers covered her desk, along with dirty coffee cups, unopened correspondence and scribbled notes on scrap paper. The overall impression was one of chaos, but she wouldn't be Luk's ambassador and chief legal advisor if she didn't run a tight ship.

"Bryce," she said coolly, looking up. Her short blonde hair was parted to the side and combed back. The nose ring he remembered from Kireyev's office had been replaced with a tiny gem. She was about his age, maybe a few years older but still young for a bishop. Her cassock was dark blue silk with gold embroidery on the sleeves.

"Your Grace."

"Sit down."

He looked around. Every chair was serving double duty as a file cabinet. Alexei moved a stack of accordion folders and sat. Morvana stared at him for a long moment. Then she slid Misha's corax across the desk. He stared at it, resisting the urge to snatch it away.

"Which Bryce am I talking to? Is this your real name?"

He could tell from her face that she knew exactly who he was but couldn't resist tweaking him a little.

"It was my brother's. I told you, he's a patient at the Batavia Institute."

"So you are Alexei. The younger one."

"May I have it back? It means a great deal to me."

She made no move to return the corax. "The Reverend Father thinks Falke sent you here to spy on us."

"But you saw me," he protested. "I was near death."

"You're also Beatus Laqueo. A fanatic who would follow any order, no matter how demented."

The description was all too accurate. He met her level gaze. "That was a long time ago, Your Grace."

"You may dispense with the honorific for the purposes of this conversation." Her voice was clipped and precise. "Three years is not a long time by any standard."

"I left that behind."

"Falke didn't seem to think so, if your story is to be believed."

"I'm telling you the truth."

She picked up a coffee cup, gazed at the dregs, and set it down. "I'll be forthright. I don't like you, Bryce. Those of us who follow the orthodox version of the *Meliora* renounce all violence, and particularly the extreme brand of it promoted by Falke and his allies. You represent everything I despise. In many ways, you are worse than the mages because you pretend to know better."

He looked away and noticed that half the books on her shelves were related to humanitarian law. A principled woman —on the surface, at least. "So you're sending me back?" he asked.

"No. You will be a given a position as my aide."

Alexei looked at her dubiously. "Why?"

"Luk would rather Falke believes his little scheme succeeded. But you will report what we tell you to report, *ja?*"

He almost laughed aloud. Of all scenarios, this was the only one he hadn't foreseen. But it might be useful to let them think he was a spy after all. "I understand."

She sorted through the papers on her desk, drawing one from the stack. "You have legal training."

"Who told you that?"

Morvana shot him an icy look. "I have contacts. You think the Bryce name is unknown here? You also worked with the Interfectorem, which leads me to believe you have investigative skills."

"I've handled a number of difficult cases."

She leaned forward, resting her arms on the desk. "You are here at my discretion, Bryce. I concurred with the Reverend Father's decision, but he usually heeds my counsel and I could suggest a different course at any time, *ja?*"

"*Ja,*" Alexei said dryly. "You want something."

"Yes, I want something." She handed him a thick file. "I do not trust you, and you do not trust me. This much is clear. However, I trust others even less. You are an outsider. Whatever your intentions, I do not believe they are related to this case."

He accepted the folder, curiosity sparking.

"Over the last year, there has been a rash of disappearances." Her voice hardened. "Children. This sort of crime is unheard of. The Polizei are useless. We have no equivalent of your OGD here. No domestic surveillance apparatus." She smiled. "It is illegal, *ja,* but I know what Kireyev does. Spare me the denials."

"What do you want me to do about it?"

"Read the file. Then you will give me your opinion on an investigative approach. It should keep you out of trouble for a while."

He scanned the file. "I don't speak much Kven."

"You'll find a translation at the back. There is an empty office across the hall. You may work out of it while the arrangement lasts." By her tone, she didn't expect that to be very long.

"These children, are they light-bringers?"

Her gaze narrowed.

"I'm just wondering if you have the same problem regarding bloodlines and if there might be a connection."

"The children are regular children. As to the question of Marks, that is the Reverend Father's concern. The last time I checked, he had not taken you into his confidence."

Her light green eyes gave little away, but Alexei took that

as a *yes*. So the Curia was in crisis. He wondered what Luk was doing about it.

"Do you plan to monitor my every move?"

"No. You've been given apartments in the Wohnturm and will enjoy the freedom to go where you please. You would be of no use to me otherwise. But this latitude will be withdrawn at the first sign of misbehavior. I might be a pacifist, but you would not like to annoy me, Fra Bryce."

Bishop Morvana tossed him the corax without a word and returned to her paperwork.

He bowed his head. "Thank you, Your Grace."

"We will meet again at nine bells tomorrow morning." She did not look up.

His new accommodations were in a tower house not far from the Markhound kennels. The architectural style was unique to Kvengard and found throughout the city. The bottom half comprised a windowless tower with thick walls, whilst the upper half looked like a miniature castle complete with turrets and battlements. They were originally built for defensive purposes, but after climbing a gloomy, cramped staircase, Alexei discovered rooms that were surprisingly bright and comfortable.

He had a sleigh bed made of old mellow wood and a desk with rows of little drawers and cubbyholes that contained pens, a supply of ink and parchment. The window overlooked a garden in the Kven tradition, with straight, orderly paths bordered in white stones and shrubs pruned into geometric shapes. Alexei lit a candle and set the file aside. He'd have to read it before morning, but he had no intention of staying here long.

Mikhail was out there somewhere.

In the Black Zone.

With a mentally ill pontifex who was using him to carry out a murderous vendetta against the Church.

There was nothing Alexei could do about the mages, or

the mess in Jalghuth, but he could find his brother. What they would do then, Alexei didn't know, but he wouldn't abandon Misha. Never again.

He sank into a chair carved with a Running Wolf, selected a pen, and dipped the nib into the ink pot.

Dear Father,

I have gone to Kvengard to work in their legal office for a while. I have no word of Mikhail. Have you learned anything? Please write to me at the Arx, in care of Archbishop Morvana at the Office of the Nuncio, if he is found, or if you hear anything at all . . . ."

Alexei stared at the letter for a long minute. Then he tore it into pieces and threw them into the wastebasket. Contacting his father would only bring him trouble. The same went for Kasia Novak. And he very much doubted he would be here long enough to receive a response anyway. He would have left that very night, but he still felt weak. A few more days would likely make no difference and he needed to be fit when he entered the Morho if he ever hoped to leave the forest alive.

Alexei eyed the large bed, with its goosedown pillows and soft wool blanket. His eyelids drooped. He covered a yawn. *Just a quick nap.*

He lay down, stared at the ceiling for an hour or so, then got up and lit more candles. Night had fallen and the sky was alive with stars—another peculiarity. Kvengard's peninsula shared the same latitude as Novostopol, but was rocky and windswept, with hot, dry summers.

Alexei dragged an armchair near the window to catch the faint breeze. Then he opened the file on the missing children and started to read.

Chapter Thirty-Seven

❧❀❧

T he pills swam out of focus, hazy blobs in his palm.
One pink. One white.

Malach couldn't remember which did what, but it didn't matter since they were the last ones anyway. He tipped his head back and swallowed them dry. His gut was a throbbing white-hot coal.

The silver sports car sat at a fork in the road. The left side went to Bal Kirith. The right side went to the coast. A town had stood nearby once. Malach didn't know what it was called, but after Lezarius made the Void and the shells started falling, everyone fled. It was summertime and a traveling carnival had been camped next to the crossroads. They left the carousel rusting in a field of high grass. It might have been pretty once, but the paint was peeling and the lips of the horses pulled back from their big square teeth in agonized grimaces, wooden bodies frozen in mid-gallop, and the whole thing looked frankly demonic, which is how, even in his disoriented state, Malach knew exactly where they were.

He'd woken up long enough to guide Nikola through back roads around the Fort of Saint Jule and take some pills, then passed out again. Three things kept him going now.

Finding Lezarius.

Killing Falke.

And convincing Nikola to help him.

He'd made her a promise and meant to keep it, but he wasn't willing to die for it. Not yet.

She'd gotten out to pee. Now she came back.

"Better do a tick check," he mumbled. "That grass is infested."

The pain started to fade and he sagged against the seat. Malach mourned the lack of more pills, then realized she was snapping her fingers to get his attention.

"We have two hundred k's left on the battery. How far is the coast?"

"About that, give or take." Things were getting slippery and he forced himself to focus. "But I need you to take me to Bal Kirith first. If I don't get medical treatment in the next few hours, maybe less, I'm going to die."

She didn't look very sorry for him. "You told me Beleth would kill me."

"Only if she knows you're pregnant."

"Oh. Well, that's reassuring. I'm fine with going to see your batshit crazy aunt, who may or may not try to murder me."

"Please, Nikola."

"I thought the city was a ruin."

He blinked, slowly. "We have a vet."

"You have a vet." She shook her head. "Like an animal doctor?"

"He's my only chance."

He glanced down at the gauze bandage around his abdomen. The Wards at the edge of the city had undone most of Ani's work. It was stiff with foul fluids. He felt nauseous and feverish. His heart was beating too fast.

Nikola kicked the tire and swore. "The City of the

Damned? I'd rather be back at the Arx, scrubbing floors. One of you is bad enough, but a whole . . . ."

A tiny spider rappelled down from the sun visor above the passenger seat, hovering in front of his face. The silken strand spun and whirled. Malach watched its progress with rapt fascination.

" . . . you even listening?"

"What?"

She stared at him, her expression unreadable. "Just before we stopped, you said something about dead babies. What were you talking about?"

He must have been rambling in his sleep. "Oh, that," he said, still watching the spider. "I had a deal with Falke to give him a child."

"Why?"

"He said he wanted to redeem our race."

"And why would you cooperate with that horseshit? You're not an idiot. Well, not all of the time."

"He stopped shelling. Pulled out the knights and left us alone. He called it the Cold Truce."

She frowned. "So it was a few years ago?"

A faint warning bell was going off in his head somewhere, but it seemed like too much effort to determine the source. He felt very, very good now.

"I'm not the first, am I? There must be other women you've made this deal with."

He gently blew at the silk, sending the spider swinging to and fro.

"Seven."

A hiss of indrawn breath. "Where are the kids?"

"Stillborn."

"And the women?"

"They survived. Two are sterile though."

"Saints! Why didn't you offer Falke this one?"

"Because I want it myself. I want you, too—"

"Oh, don't you even dare. Conniving, selfish son of a bitch! I ought to leave you here."

Nikola stalked down the cracked asphalt and stood with her back to him. He heard muttered arguing and more curses. A minute later, she stomped back. Tears stood in her eyes. "You're going to keep your end of our deal." She stabbed a finger at him. "I need you alive for that. Which means you get to see a veterinarian, you heartless bastard."

The curtain was falling. He fought to stay awake. "I don't deny that I am those things, and worse. But I promise I'll do better. I promise—"

"Shut up, Malach." Nikola threw the car into gear and started down the lefthand fork.

THE TRACK WAS SO OVERGROWN, Nikola could hardly make it out in the thickening twilight. She flipped on the high beams. Clouds of insects swarmed in the headlights, along with larger fluttering things that might have been bats. Every few kilometers, she passed the skeleton of a vehicle being slowly devoured by the jungle.

The needle for the battery hovered near zero. Malach slumped against the window, muttering. A dozen times she almost turned around and drove back to that fork in the road, but it wasn't as if there were towns along the coast. No taverns you could swagger into, thump a purse down on the bar, and ask the barkeep to point out some mercenary smugglers drinking in the corner. The eastern side of the continent was wild and largely uninhabited. It could take days—weeks—to make contact. Malach had hours at best.

Of course, she could just let him die.

In many ways, it would be in her best interests. She had her own currency to negotiate the passage to Dur-Athaara. And she could always give the infant away to someone else, if it survived. Malach was self-absorbed, manipulative and callous. True, he had a crude animal magnetism and displayed occasional wit. He had courage. He despised the Curia, which went into the plus column. Nikola knew she could be callous, too. The child, for example. She felt nothing for it other than a desire to be rid of it as fast as possible.

But Malach was a murderer. He admitted it himself. Who knew what else he had done? What crimes he had committed to seal his vile bargains? An argument could be made that leaving him behind was for the greater good.

So why was she risking everything to bring him home?

She shook her head. It would be a moot point if she didn't get *somewhere* before dark. Maybe she'd taken a wrong turn. Other faint tracks crossed this one at regular intervals. Without Malach to guide her, she'd chosen randomly. Bal Kirith could still be a day away for all she knew.

Exhaustion washed over her. She blotted moisture from her forehead. The Morho was like being stuck in someone's sweaty armpit. And the trees . . . Nikola had never imagined such trees. Their trunks were nearly a hundred meters high and thrust out of a bulging mass of aboveground roots like the buttressed walls of a fortress. Umbrella-shaped crowns blocked out the sky, making it impossible to gauge the direction she'd been driving in.

A few kilometers later, the forest thinned. Fading daylight penetrated the thick canopy and she started seeing stone houses. Most lacked roofs and were tumbling down, but they clumped together in groups of a dozen or so. She turned a bend and the jungle opened up to a wide, serpentine river. The Ascalon. It began in the snowmelt of the foothills at Bal Agnar, meandering south until it divided at Bal Kirith, one branch emptying into the Southern Ocean, the other turning east to join a myriad of smaller waterways that fed into the Parnassian Sea and its hundred thousand islands.

On the opposite bank was a pitted wasteland. Almost no structures still stood, but it was undeniably the remains of a city, and in the distance, burnished gold by the setting sun, she saw the fractured dome of a basilica.

The river was spanned by a slender bridge and Nikola wondered why it hadn't been shelled. Perhaps because the knights wanted to preserve their access to the Arx. Either way, the bridge looked sketchy. The iron supports were all right, but the wood struck her as distinctly rotten.

She turned to Malach. His eyes were closed, dark lashes fanned across his cheeks. He looked helpless, vulnerable, not like his asshole self at all. "I ought to throw you in," she said. "Let the Ascalon take you."

He mumbled something incoherent.

She stared at the bridge for another long minute, then eased her foot off the brake. Planks creaked under the tires. At several points, she could see the river below through splintered gaps. It was not quite as high as the bridge over the Mont-moray, but it was high enough.

She drove very, very slowly.

The road on the other side was more weeds than asphalt, but it ran straight and true to the walls of the Arx. Nikola stepped on the pedal. The car leapt forward, bumping over potholes and fallen branches. At last she came to the broken, twisted gates of the inner citadel.

Nikola braked and sat with the engine running. A mosquito whined in her ear. She swiped at it and rolled up the window. Beside her, Malach had stopped muttering. His breathing was rapid and shallow.

"Well," she said. "Here we are."

Nikola Thorn drove through the gates of the Arx.

She knew a good deal about all six cities of the Via Sancta, not because she had any interest in history but because it would take a special effort to work in the Arx for a decade and not let anything trickle into your brain. Bal Kirith and Bal Agnar were the first cities built by the Praefators, and reputedly the most beautiful. The Morho had mines and quarries that produced unique building materials, as well as hardwoods not found anyplace else. The Pontifex's Palace in Bal Kirith was made of astrum, an igneous rock containing mineral chips that glimmered in moonlight, and leystone, whose veins glowed bright blue in the presence of the power.

Even in their neglected state, the buildings had a grandeur that made the Arx she knew seem a cheap imitation. Every bit of stone was carved with vines and flowers so it looked like part of the jungle. Gilded spires thrust toward the heavens in corkscrews like twists of barley sugar. Even the encroaching decay failed to detract from the beauty of the place—and occasionally enhanced it. Carpets of pink and white wild-flowers grew inside an oval structure where the roof had fallen in and exposed the interior to sun and sky. Verdigris oxidized copper statues, moss overran walls and fountains, lily pads floated on still pools, all merging with the jungle in a hundred subtle shades of green.

While the outer city of Bal Kirith had been reduced to rubble, the damage was far less inside the walls. Nikola under-stood that the Arx had been deliberately spared. Despite the crimes of the nihilim, someone had decided that destroying this place would be a greater one.

It was unsettling not to see a single Ward anywhere.

The battery died in the middle of an empty field. It had a few trees and the vague suggestion of pathways. Maybe it had been a park before the war. The dome of the basilica was visible not far ahead. Nikola got out and looked around, hands on hips. A chorus of insects hummed in the lengthening shadows.

"Hello?" She reached down and leaned on the horn. A flock of birds exploded from a tree, wings beating for the sky. Somewhere, a bullfrog emitted a lonely foghorn blast.

Movement in the corner of her eye made her turn. A lavish, baroque structure sat to the east, surely the Pontifex's Palace, with a long reflecting pool whose waters were thick with weeds and algae. The surface looked placid . . . and then a surge of ripples moved swiftly along the length of the pool. Something big lived in there. Nikola got back inside the car.

"Malach," she said firmly, patting his cheek. His head lolled to the side. His skin felt clammy, and his chest rose and fell too fast. She'd seen it once before in Ash Court, when an ambulance came for an elderly neighbor. The onset of septic shock. His system was going into overdrive.

Nikola bit her lip and looked around. She could drag him to one of the empty buildings, but what would she do with him then? Where the hell *was* everybody?

The hair on her neck rose up. Funny how one knows when another person is close even if they don't make a sound. Nikola turned to the driver's side window. A woman stood outside the car, not a meter away. She had large, dark, intent eyes. Her arms were bare and dirty and covered in Marks. Ugly, crude ones that conveyed anger and suffering merely in the brief instant that Nikola glanced at them. She did not wear gloves. Her nails were long and sharp.

"Are you nihilim?"

The woman stared. She had a patient, unblinking gaze that was almost lizard-like. There was something hungry in that gaze. And something else very wrong, though Nikola wasn't sure what. She rolled up the window and locked the door. She reached across Malach and slammed his lock down, too. When she looked back, the woman was gone.

There was nowhere she could have run to, not so fast. Had she crawled under the car? Nikola released a slow breath and turned the key, hoping to squeeze a little more life from the battery. It gave the classic quiet *click* that signaled zero juice.

"Malach," Nikola said desperately, shaking him. "You have to wake up."

His eyes fluttered open. There was no recognition. Nothing but pain and confusion. Glass smashed. Nikola screamed as hands dragged her from the car. Three of them together now and she saw what it was that had tripped a wire in her brain. The pupils of their eyes had vertical slits like goats. She punched and kicked. Somehow she fought free and ran into the field. From the dusky hollows under the trees, more appeared, swift and silent. They'd probably been following the car like hyenas on the trail of a wounded animal, waiting for it to give up so they could close in.

In the distance, the last molten bit of sun sank behind the basilica.

The world tilted. Nikola was swept by a powerful sense of deja vu. Her field of vision—the basilica, the palace to the east, the grassy bowl-shaped cavity in the middle of the park where a shell had exploded a long time ago—superimposed itself over a place she knew, a place Malach had shown her.

She sprinted left, tearing through thorny bushes that raked her skin, and there it was, partially hidden by dense foliage. She could just make out the Raven in a circle at the top. Another ten strides and she was able to read the words carved on the stone pillar.

Pax intrantibus salus exeuntibus.

Nikola heard Malach's sweet teenaged baritone giving the translation even as knives scraped the marrow from his bones.

Peace to those who enter, health to those who depart.

She tripped over a root and fell on her face, frantically crawling the last few meters. She pressed her back against the stela, praying to all the Saints and Martyrs that it would work.

Her pursuers stopped ten meters away as if they'd hit an invisible wall. They stared at her for a long moment, faces slack, then turned as one and started back for the car.

"Hey!" Nikola yelled, waving her arms. "Over here!"

They didn't slow. She swore loudly. Even if she could have carried him along, the stela wouldn't shelter Malach. It would finish him.

"Hey!" she screamed. "Come back!"

The female reached the car first. Nikola watched, gorge

rising, as she yanked Malach's door open. He tumbled out and she caught him by one arm, dragging his limp body from the vehicle. Her mouth opened, far too wide for a human mouth, more like a snake unhinging its jaws to swallow an overlarge meal. Nikola didn't even realize she'd picked up a rock until it was flying from her hand. She was too far away to do any damage, but the noise of it striking the ground made the female pause. Nikola moved a little way from the stela and waved her arms.

"Come on," she yelled. "Come get some!"

There were eight of the creatures. Not people, though from a distance it would be easy to mistake them for human. Three suddenly exploded into motion, sprinting for the stela. Nikola almost pissed herself. She waited, giving them hope, then dashed back to the Wardstone. Two stopped at the perimeter. A straw-haired boy kept coming, his eyes fixed on Nikola, until blood gushed from his nose and he finally gave up.

She realized that several of them were children. They even looked alike. Some kind of twisted family unit.

The female had paused to see what happened. She held Malach the way you might hold a leg of chicken, dangling from one hand. Nikola thought the things were stupid, brainless, but then the female caught her eye and gave a calculated, knowing smile. She seized Malach's hair in her free hand, bringing his face up as if she meant to kiss him . . . and then she stiffened and fell down, an arrow jutting from one eye. A woman in a red cloak stepped out from behind a tree. She drew fletching to her cheek and released another arrow in one fluid motion. She had two companions, both wearing clothes that blended with the jungle, and they were armed with crossbows.

The creatures died. Some died running and some died where they stood, but not one managed to escape.

When it was over, the woman hurried to Malach and knelt

down, then beckoned to her companions. They lifted him up and bore him towards the Pontifex's Palace, which was not far off, struggling a bit under his weight. The woman walked to the stela, pausing at roughly the same distance the attackers had. Wisps of auburn hair fell around her face. The rest was tied back in a high, bouncy ponytail. She looked like the university girls who jogged around the oval at Arkadia Park on Saturday mornings, except for the Broken Chain around her neck and the blood red cloak, which fell in rich folds to her feet.

"I am Bishop Dantarion." Her face was grave. "Did you do that to Cardinal Malach?"

Cardinal? "No! I just drove all night from Novostopol. I was trying to save his life when those things attacked us."

"Perditae. When the ley floods, they go mad. What is your name?"

"Nikola Thorn, Your Grace."

"You are safe now, Nikola Thorn." She held out a gloved hand. "Come with me before night falls. There are things in the forest that do not fear the stelae."

Nikola hesitated. She trusted the nihilim about as much as a rabid dog, but she couldn't stay there forever. A refusal would cause offense and this woman had saved their lives.

"Where did they take him?"

"To Tashtemir. If Malach can be saved, he will do his best." Her hand fell. "Remain at the Wardstone if you wish. But do not expect us to come out again."

Nikola slapped at a mosquito. Darkness cloaked the buildings now. She thought of the thing in the reflecting pool and wondered if it emerged at night to hunt. With a last glance at the Raven Ward, Nikola pushed off the stela and approached the nihilim. She halted a short distance away, ready to run again, but Dantarion made no move to threaten her.

"He was stabbed by a priest," Nikola said. "A laqueus."

Dantarion's eyes went flat. "I know the Order."

She'd practiced the tale in her head and thought it credible enough. "Cardinal Malach was looking for something inside the Arx. I'm a char there. Our paths crossed and I agreed to aid him."

Dantarion's clear blue eyes weighed her. "Why?"

"He said something to me when we met. That he would rather rule in the Void than serve the Via Sancta. I will never rule anyone, but nor do I wish to serve for the rest of my life. We made a bargain. I helped him get into the Arx, and he was supposed to help me escape Novostopol. I intend to leave the continent and built a new life elsewhere. But he was badly injured so I brought him directly here."

The young bishop smiled. She had rosy cheeks and a scattering of freckles across her upturned nose. "You have our heartfelt thanks, Nikola Thorn. Cardinal Malach is a favorite of the Pontifex. She will wish to meet you right away."

Dantarion turned to the palace across the field. It was an enormous building of pale stone with symmetrical wings that extended for a full city block in either direction. Lights shone in the windows—and glimmers of silver emanated from within the stone itself. *Astrum.* Despite her misgivings, Nikola felt she'd slipped into a land of dark enchantment. Her life in Novostopol was a blur of sameness. Work nights, sleep days, drink to dull the tedium. Bal Kirith was different. She could sense the danger here, lurking just below the pretty surface like the reflecting pool. The water had gone still again, but Dantarion gave it a wide berth.

"What's in there?" Nikola asked.

"Only a few crocodilians." Dantarion glanced over with a faint smile. "But they have excellent night vision."

The palace entrance was flanked by tall columns that twisted like horns. It appeared to be unguarded. "Aren't you afraid of the Perditae?" Nikola asked.

"Usually, they are afraid of us," Dantarion replied wryly.

"But the ley riled them up. My cousins and I were keeping an eye on that band."

"Lucky for us."

"Yes." She pressed an ungloved hand against one of the huge bronze doors. It swung open on silent hinges. "Lucky for you."

Small yellow birds swooped through the interior. The vaulted triple-height ceilings and insane amount of gilding indicated a place that had once been opulently furnished. Most of the windows were broken. The marble walls were bare. The niches and pedestals were empty. Every painting, tapestry and statue, every knick-knack, had been carted off to Novostopol and Nantwich, where it was on display in various museums. The result was a gorgeous shell, slowly going to seed.

"Will you take me to Cardinal Malach?" Nikola was always conscious of using proper titles with the clergy and doubted the mages would be any different.

"We shall see, Nikola Thorn." Dantarion threw open the door to a long hall where a banquet was in progress. Masked servants moved along the table, refilling goblets. The hall was lit by three enormous crystal candelabra that hung suspended over the table, but Nikola's first overwhelming impression was of the color red. Tablecloth, drapes, carpet, candles, even the stained glass windows—all were of the deepest crimson.

"Make an obeisance to the Pontifex Beleth," Dantarion said softly.

Conversation ceased at once. A dozen faces turned to the doorway. Nikola couldn't decide which was more disturbing—the porcelain masks of the servants or the people seated around the table. She curtsied deeply.

"Reverend Mother."

"You may rise," a melodic voice commanded.

Nikola had never seen anyone quite like the woman seated at the head of the table. She wore a low-cut red gown with a tight corset that thrust her breasts skyward. The skin of her face and bosom was powdered deathly white. It was hard to guess her age, or even speculate as to what she truly looked like, because her features were painted on—scarlet bow-shaped lips and two thin arching lines for eyebrows. A white wig threaded with black pearls towered above her head like a wedding cake, the sides trailing ringlets that tumbled across her exposed shoulders.

"Dante," Beleth said, her eyes still locked on Nikola, "come here."

The bishop hastily approached and bent down to whisper in her ear. Thick makeup made the Pontifex's reaction difficult to gauge, but one hand tightened around a folded fan, tapping it against the table. The fourth finger held a heavy gold signet ring.

"Malach has returned," Beleth announced. Her gaze settled on Nikola. "You bring me my nephew at the brink of death. I would hear what happened to him."

Nikola repeated the story she'd told Dantarion, sticking as close to the truth as possible. They'd first met a few months before. The only major lie was the terms of their bargain. Right now, she meant nothing to them. But if they discovered she carried Malach's child . . . .

"He entered the Arx?"

"Yes."

"What was he looking for?"

"He didn't tell me, Reverend Mother."

"Do you have Malach's Mark? If so, I would see it."

"He was stabbed before he could give it to me. But I kept my end. I helped him escape the city. He said nihilim always honor their bargains, Reverend Mother."

Beleth stared at her without speaking for a long moment. "I hope he tells the same tale when he wakes, Nikola Thorn." She used the fan to point to an empty chair near the head of the table. Scarlet lips curved in a perfunctory smile. "Join us."

Nikola curtsied again. She made her way down the table, feeling their eyes on her the whole way, and sat down. Immediately, a servant filled her goblet to the brim with dark wine. Another set a gold plate in front of her. It held a few withered tubers and some kind of fish swimming in a thick cream sauce.

"A toast," Dantarion said. "To the swift recovery of Cardinal Malach."

Everyone raised their goblets. Nikola touched the rim to her lips, but the fumes made her stomach roll. Through her lashes, she studied the other nihilim. Except for Dantarion, all appeared to be in their sixties or older—the last survivors of the generation that had been excommunicated. Nikola loathed the Curia, but her skin crawled as if she'd tumbled into a pit of vipers. Surely their faces must reflect some sign of corruption and cruelty, although as with the Pontifex, it was hard to see past the extravagant costumes. Both men and women were heavily painted, powdered and perfumed.

"She tried to draw the Perditae away from him," Dantarion said.

"How brave," Beleth said. "Do you dislike the vintage, Domina Thorn?"

Nikola looked at her untouched goblet. "Not at all, Reverend Mother."

"Then why did you not drink?" Her blue eyes were cold. "It is an ill omen to snub a toast to a dying man's health."

"My stomach is a bit rough from travel, Reverend Mother."

"Still, I find it distinctly peculiar. Let us try again." She raised her goblet. "To Malach."

"To Malach," the others echoed.

Nikola forced herself to swallow a mouthful of wine. It was cloyingly sweet. The moment it hit her stomach, she knew she wouldn't keep it down. She lurched to her feet. With a muttered apology, she ran from the hall, just making it to the corridor before violently retching. She'd drunk bad wine plenty of times before. Never had she felt so ill.

"Are you all right?"

She wiped her mouth and looked up. A boy and girl stood there, obviously siblings, both quite pretty. They had straight black chin-length hair and wore clothing in shades of green. Nikola realized it was the two young mages who had been with Dantarion. The ones who took Malach away.

"I'm afraid I've disgraced myself," she said.

"The servants will clean it up," the girl replied carelessly. She was taller and sturdier than her brother, who hovered behind her.

"I'm Nikola." She smiled. "I don't believe I've thanked you for saving us. What are your names?"

"Sydonie and Tristhus."

"Can you show me where you brought Cardinal Malach?"

"He's with Tashtemir. We must not disturb them."

"I promise I won't disturb anyone. In fact, I have some medical training. Perhaps I can help."

"Then why didn't you help him before?"

The girl was sharp. "I didn't have the supplies. Please, I would like very much to see him."

"Maybe you can do that tomorrow."

Nikola wanted to take her by the collar and shake her, but no doubt that would end badly. "Well," she said, looking at the door to the hall. "I suppose I'd better go apologize for my abrupt departure."

"They won't care if you go back in. The feasts last all night sometimes. They've probably forgotten about you already."

Nikola very much doubted that, but it was true that no one had come to look for her, not even one of the servants.

"Where did you come from?" Tristhus asked. He had plump cheeks and a high, sweet voice. Nikola placed him somewhere between eight and ten, while his sister was about twelve.

"Novostopol."

"Oh, that's a very long way. You must be tired. Maybe that's why you sicked up."

"Trist." Sydonie frowned. "Don't be rude."

"It's all right," Nikola said. "I don't mind. He's right, I'm quite tired."

"Would you like us to show you to a bedchamber?"

"That would be wonderful. But are you sure it won't cause offense if I retire without the Pontifex's permission?"

Sydonie gave a merry peal of laughter. "Beleth doesn't care about things like that."

"What does she care about?" It seemed a sensible question to ask.

"Her manifesto. She's always scribbling. And Malach. He's her favorite."

"And us," Sydonie said. "She loves us ever so much."

"Of course she does," Nikola said. "You're both charming."

Tristhus beamed, but Sydonie gave her a sly smile. "You say that, but you don't know us at all, Nikola."

"That's very true. And I must remedy the situation by getting to know you both better tomorrow."

"Oh yes, we would like that," the girl said, flashing even white teeth.

The children led her up a wide flight of stairs and along a gallery lined with mirrors that were miraculously intact, chattering all the way about the Perditae and how foolish they'd been to enter the city. Except the children didn't call them Perditae. They called them leeches.

"It's more fun to watch them fight each other," Tristhus said. "If you put the leeches in a pit and let them get hungry enough, they'll provide good sport. But we couldn't let them eat Malach, could we?"

Sydonie giggled. "Beleth would have gotten very angry with us."

"Shooting them is okay, too," Tristhus said, miming pulling the trigger on a crossbow. "Not much of a challenge, though."

"Why are the Perditae like that?" Nikola asked.

He shrugged. "They just are."

"Where do their Marks come from?"

"You ask a lot of questions," Sydonie said. The friendliness vanished like a switch had been flipped. "Are you a spy?"

"If I was a spy, why would I bring Malach back to you alive?"

"Barely alive," she pointed out.

"I'm not a spy." Nikola turned her head, exposing the side of her neck. "Do you see a Raven?"

Both children inspected her closely. "No."

"I hate the Curia. I've been little better than a slave since I was sixteen. When Malach wakes up, he'll tell you."

Sydonie took her brother's hand. They shared a long, intense look that made Nikola uneasy. "Give us the car keys," she said.

"The battery's dead."

"We don't care. We want to pretend to drive."

Oh." Nikola fished the keys from her pocket. "Keep them."

Sydonie flung her arms around Nikola's waist. "Thank you!"

"You're welcome." She gently disengaged. "Now, where shall I rest tonight?"

"They're all empty." Tristhus gestured down the corridor. "Choose any one you like. Sleep well, Nikola."

The children scampered off. Nikola opened a few random doors. The first chamber was empty. The next had a large rust-colored stain on the floor that looked like dried blood and probably was. The third was defaced with graffiti declaring

Lux, Veritas, Virtus! in meter-tall letters. Mildew speckled the feather mattress and damp mottled the plaster, but Nikola was too tired to search for better. She sat down on the bed and took her shoes off.

Malach had better wake up soon.

And if he didn't?

She pressed a hand to her stomach. It was flat—hollow, actually—but how long before it started to swell? Nikola thought of the seven women who had come before her. With any luck, she'd miscarry, too. She didn't care if it left her barren as long as she was free.

Happily, the door had a working lock. Nikola bolted it, then lay down on the musty mattress, using one arm as a pillow. If they came for her, at least she'd hear them breaking in.

She woke just before dawn to the cries of strange birds. Mist pressed against the windows. She used the chamber pot, then slipped into the corridor and made her way stealthily through the dark to the ground floor. No one seemed to be stirring, not even the servants. Once outside, she kept to the thickest patches of fog and made her way to the field. The sun was still behind the trees, but within an hour or so it would burn off the mist. She could feel the mercury rising already.

For a minute, she considered running away. The nihilim didn't seem to care much what happened to her. She was a light sleeper and she felt sure no one had come near her room in the night. Of course, there were the Perditae to worry about. And Beleth might send Dantarion or even the children to hunt her, in which case Nikola doubted she'd make it far.

But the thing that stopped her is that she didn't want to go without knowing if Malach was still alive. It was foolish, she knew. The chance might not come again. But she remembered the look in his eyes outside the Arx when he said that only death would keep him from returning to her. No one had ever said anything like that to her before. Her life was invisible. If she slipped in the bathtub and broke her neck, it would be days before anyone found her. Most likely, it would be her bosses at the Arx who notified the Oprichniki when she didn't show up for work. But when she was with Malach, narcissistic and volatile though he was, she felt like she mattered to someone. Just one person, but it was nice.

He deserved a proper goodbye.

The car was where she'd left it, keys dangling from the ignition, both doors wide open. The children had pulled all the paperwork from the glove compartment and gotten into the trunk, as well. Her suitcase sat open on the ground, clothes strewn around. Nikola was not surprised. It's why she had hidden her valuables in a place not even Sydonie and Tristhus would think to look.

Moving quickly, she took a screwdriver from beneath the footwell carpet and worked it around the rim of the front right tire. Her hands were stiff from the damp and it took several long minutes before the wheel cap finally popped off. A small drawstring bag nestled inside the cavity. She'd hidden it there after agreeing to go to Bal Kirith, assuming the mages would search her. They hadn't even bothered, but there were a million places inside the palace she could stash it. Nikola wanted to keep her nest egg somewhere she could grab it in a hurry. She tucked the bag into her pocket and sealed the wheel cap again. Then she bent to gather her belongings from the dewy grass.

"Hello, Nikola."

She looked up. Sydonie and Tristhus appeared out of the fog in their matching green jerkins. Caps of black hair gleamed in the soft dawn light.

"Good morning," she said cheerfully. "Did you enjoy your drive?"

"Yes, we went all the way to Bal Agnar," Tristhus replied.

"That sounds fun. You're up very early."

"We don't sleep much," Sydonie said. "What's in your pocket, Nikola?"

Her pulse spiked, then smoothed out again. She frowned. "What do you mean?"

"We saw you put something in your pocket." She pointed to the wheel. "You took it from there."

"You're mistaken. I just came for my things."

Sydonie smiled. "That's a lie. Show us, Nikola."

Nikola felt a flash of anger. "It's not your business."

The girl thrust her hand out. The edges of her mouth curled down. "*Show us.*"

"No."

Quick as a snake, Sydonie grabbed her arm. "Give it to me, Nikola."

Her voice held a note of command and utter confidence that she would be obeyed. When Nikola just stared down at her, the girl's face tightened to a furious glower. "How are you doing that? Give it to me now!"

"No." Nikola jerked her arm free. "Run off and play somewhere else, or I'll tell Dantarion about this."

Both children fell silent. As she had the night before, Nikola sensed some wordless communion between them. Suddenly, the boy grabbed her shirt, trying to force a chubby hand into her pocket while his sister twisted Nikola's arm behind her back. They were stronger than they looked— which shouldn't be surprising since they were sent out to kill Perditae and Saints only knew what else.

Nikola had dealt with bullies before. It was clear that Sydonie was the leader, Tristhus the follower. She kicked Sydonie hard in the shin, earning a cry of pain. The boy hesitated, looking to his sister, and Nikola seized the opportunity to run for the stela. She could hear the children behind, breathing heavily. A hand brushed the back of her shirt and then she was over the invisible line, the Wardstone a short distance ahead. Out of spite, she slowed and walked the last few meters. The whole thing felt like a twisted game of tag. Laughter bubbled up as she placed a hand on the stela. *Home safe!*

"Nikola Thorn," Sydonie howled. "Come back here this instant!"

Nikola smiled. "Fog off," she yelled back.

The children stared at her for a long minute, then ran to the palace. She sat down and rested her back against the stela. Her knees ached. The doctor had recommended she cease the activity that caused the inflammation—kneeling for hours with a horsehair brush in hand—but if she heeded the advice she'd be out of a job and as much as she hated being a char, the thought of sitting home doing nothing was worse.

"Well," she remarked aloud. "Whatever happens, at least I'll never scrub a fogging stone floor again."

The sun rose. The Morho stirred to life. Tiny white-faced monkeys with long ringed tails chattered in the trees and bright tropical birds darted overhead. The dew evaporated and the air grew hot and thick. She stood and paced. With little else to do, she spent some time examining the stela. It was slick and cool to the touch, much more so than the surrounding air. There were shallow pits all along the surface, almost like insects had been at it, which was impossible. Nothing ate stone. Nikola traced a fingertip along one of these needle-like depressions. Peculiar . . . . She knew the ley in the Morho was corrupted. Could it actually be rotting the stelae? It was an unpleasant thought.

No one came out until twilight, when the birds fell silent and clouds of bloodthirsty mosquitoes took the stage. Then Dantarion appeared in her red cloak. Auburn hair fell in waves across her shoulders.

"Nikola Thorn!" she called.

Nikola stood up, knees cracking.

"You are being foolish. Come away from the Wardstone."

"I want to see Malach," she called back.

"You have no right to ask for anything. You are only here at the pleasure of the Pontifex."

"Then my answer is no."

Dantarion shrugged. "Stay here if you prefer. We respect free will. And when I hear you screaming, I will choose to remain in my bed. So we will both do as we wish."

"Sounds fair to me," Nikola shouted.

Dantarion left. Night fell. Nikola wrapped her arms around herself. Her breasts were swollen and tender. Not even her body was her own anymore. Hunger made her light-headed, but part of her was glad because it meant the parasite inside her was starving, too.

She took out the drawstring bag and shook the gems into her palm. One or two should cover her passage to Dur-Athaara. The rest could set her up for life—if she ever escaped Bal Kirith.

"Wake up, Malach," she muttered, watching the lights come on inside the palace.

Chapter Thirty-Eight

Malach drifted in and out of consciousness. Needles pierced his arms. When the drugs hit his system, he floated on a warm sea of tranquillity, but the moment they started to wear off, his heart raced and he couldn't draw enough air.

Voices came and went. Patterns of light moved across the vaulted ceiling. Sometimes he was aware of people standing at his bedside, sponging the wound. That didn't hurt much, but his head ached like the devil.

Fever raged. He shook until his teeth chattered and the sheets were soaked with cold sweat.

He called for Nikola Thorn, but she didn't come.

Malach woke to a cloth pressing against his forehead. He felt weak but more fully aware than he had in . . . days? Weeks? Time was a blur. He knew he was in his own bedchamber at Bal Kirith because of the painted fresco on the ceiling, herons flying across a stormy sky.

Beleth leaned over him. He smelled a hint of her favorite soap. "Do you know me, Malach?"

"Reverend Mother," he whispered.

She smiled. Fine lines webbed her eyes and the corners of

her wide mouth. "You're lucky. The wound was shallow and the blade didn't penetrate the abdominal wall. Tashtemir says you're through the worst of it now. Another few days and you'll be on your feet again."

He tried to swallow, but his throat was too dry. "Where's Nikola Thorn?"

"Oh, she's around here somewhere," Beleth said casually, though her gaze went flat.

"Water," he rasped.

She held a cup to his lips and helped him drink.

"I want to see her."

"After you tell me what happened to you."

"What did she say?"

His aunt's voice hardened. "No games." She touched the fresh bandage around his wrist, a dangerous glint in her eye. "Who tried to sever you?"

"No one. It's a cut from a fight."

Beleth regarded him suspiciously. "Did you truly pass the Wards of the Arx as she claimed, Malach?"

If any aspect of their stories didn't match, Beleth would hone in on it. "Lezarius is no longer in Jalghuth," he said, knowing this revelation would erase any interest she had in Nikola Thorn.

"The Lion?" Beleth stared at him in disbelief. "He hasn't left the north in thirty years." She laid a hand on his forehead. "Are you sure you didn't dream it? You were raving, Malach."

"It was no dream." Malach drank a little more water. He eased himself up to sitting. "That's what Falke told me. He had no reason to lie. He thought he'd won and wanted to rub salt in the wound."

"Won?" Her eyes narrowed. "You were supposed to be pretending to collaborate. What happened?"

Malach related the events as succinctly as possible, omitting any mention of Nikola's pregnancy. He also didn't tell Beleth that Falke tried to cut his hands off because she would have flown into a screaming rage and he didn't have the energy to deal with it. The main thing was what Ferran Massot had discovered at the Batavia Institute.

"Falke tried to kill Lezarius, but I think he failed. That was no natural surge of the ley. I've seen it flood before. The level wasn't nearly high enough to shatter the Wards. And the timing fits."

She sat back, thinking. When the sun was up, Beleth wore her usual garb of a man's trousers and shirt with the sleeves rolled to the elbow, revealing heavily Marked muscular forearms. She was in her mid-sixties, but there was nothing soft about his aunt. She had a long nose, thin lips and wide-set blue eyes that saw everything. Silver hair rippled down her back. "Where is the Lion now?"

He shrugged. "If the Curia tried to assassinate me, I'd head for the Void before they caught me again."

"He could leave the city by sea."

"He's Invertido. How would he pay for passage? He has no friends in Novostopol. If he did, they wouldn't have left him to rot."

She nodded slowly. "What will Falke do next?"

Beleth was asking if they needed to evacuate Bal Kirith.

Malach recalled the cardinal's words just after he spat in Falke's face and just before the knights pinned him to the stone floor.

The Cold Truce is over.

"Given the choice, he would retaliate immediately, but Feizah has to approve military actions. She may not know about any of this. Falke's playing his own game. Either way, it'll take weeks for a decision to be made. Except for the outer forts, the knights are demobilized. Restarting the war machinery will take time."

"Then we'll stay in Bal Kirith and make the search for Lezarius the priority. You'd be my first choice to lead it, but it will be weeks before you're fit to ride."

"Send Dantarion." His cousin was more than capable.

"I mean to." Beleth took a bowl from the bedside table. Except for the gold signet ring on her left hand, she looked like a farmwife. "I have my own exciting news to share, Malach. Open up."

He turned his head away but she poked a spoon at his lips until he had no choice but to open his mouth or have it spill down his chin. Some kind of meaty broth, not too bad, actually—

"Dantarion is pregnant. It's yours."

Malach choked on the soup. The spastic coughing sent spears through his abdomen. Beleth patted his chin with a napkin.

"How do you know?" he managed. "She's not exactly the faithful type."

"She says she's sure. I'll admit, I was surprised. I thought she was barren."

"When's the baby due?" Malach desperately counted backwards to the last time they had sex. It was just before he left for Novostopol, which meant . . . .

"Two months." Beleth studied his face. "I know you don't love her, but this is a blessing. Other than Sydonie and her brother, we haven't had a child in far too long." Her gaze sharpened. "It will be a pure-blooded light-bringer, not like those aborted bastards you promised Falke. Just as well the attempts failed. Half-bloods are dangerous. Unpredictable." Her lip curled in contempt. "Human vessels are too fragile to contain our offspring. Dantarion is strong. She will give us a child to be reckoned with, Malach."

"Of course." He forced a smile. "I'll Mark it as soon as we have ley."

"If Dante lets you. The child is hers. Now, be a good boy." She tried to feed him more soup and he pushed her hand away, forcefully this time. Beleth clucked her tongue and set the bowl down.

"How long since I arrived?"

"Four days."

"I want Nikola Thorn brought to me," he said. "At once."

Beleth looked amused at the imperious tone. "You are not yet well enough to play with your toys, Malach."

"She can serve me until I'm better."

"You never had much use for servants before." A narrowing of the eyes. "What is she to you?"

"Nothing at all." He summoned a lazy smile. "But she worked inside the Arx. She might know something about Lezarius."

Beleth snorted. "She was a char. What could she possibly know?"

He wanted to ask where she was, what she'd been doing, and why Beleth was obviously playing games with him regarding Nikola's welfare, but those questions would only bring unwanted scrutiny.

"Nothing, I suppose." He lay back against the pillow. The smell of the Morho drifted through the open window. Decaying leaves, damp earth, the sweetness of flower-laden vines and a hint of the river. The smell of home.

Beleth studied his face. "How did it feel to enter the Arx?"

"Not as bad as I expected."

"Liar." She patted his cheek. "But I'm proud of you. If it's true . . . ." Her eyes glittered. "The Lion. To have him here in my custody. It would not be long before he was begging to shatter the stelae."

"Are you certain he can't work ley in the Void?"

"I am certain of nothing. But he can always be drugged and broken in other ways." The Broken Chain around her neck flared red for an instant. "You say he is mad. I wonder how that came to pass? Either way, it will make our task easier. How long can one old man hide in the forest? Let us hope it doesn't eat him up first."

"Find him quickly, Beleth."

A flash of rage crossed her face. "We will," she said softly.

Beleth strode out, bellowing for servants. Malach peeled the edge of the bandage back. Tashtemir had removed Ani's stitches and drained the wound, then sewed it up again himself. It was already scabbing over. Time in which Nikola had been completely on her own. Time in which anything might have happened to her.

He sat up and swung his legs over the edge of the bed. When the first wave of dizziness passed, he tested his legs. A bit wobbly, but they bore his weight. Pants were out of the question, so he summoned a servant and ordered a plain red cassock of the sort novices wore. Malach studied himself in the standing mirror. His face was gaunt and wasted. A four-day beard covered his cheeks. He looked almost as bad as the laqueus.

"You shouldn't be out of bed."

Malach turned at the door, long-faced man in the doorway. "And you do your job too well, Tashtemir. I feel fit as a butcher's dog."

"I doubt that," came the dry response. "Mending you emptied my dispensary. I have just enough to finish the course of antibiotics."

Tashtemir Kelavan always dressed impeccably, as if he were a noble in the court of the Golden Imperator rather than a middle-aged animal doctor. Lace spilled from the sleeves of a dark frock coat. A silk cravat was knotted around his neck, pinned in place with a large ruby. Wiry black hair sprung up from a wide, sloping forehead.

"Your aunt said you'd finally woken. She's in quite a state. What did you tell her?"

"That there's a conspiracy to install a puppet in the north because the real Pontifex went mad," Malach replied, testing a few steps from the bed to the window. "They tried to murder him but he got away and he's running loose in the Morho."

Silence greeted this statement. When Malach didn't laugh,

Tashtemir raised a thick eyebrow. "Oh, that's all? Yes, I can see why she might be interested. This is Lezarius we're talking about?"

"The Lion. The architect of the Void. The only man with power over the ley itself. *That* one."

Tash whistled through his teeth. "It's been awfully boring here since you left, but I imagine things will pick up now."

"The woman I came with," Malach said casually. "Have you seen her?"

Tashtemir cast him a wary look. He knew Malach's temper. "I've seen her."

"Where, Tashtemir?"

The doctor sighed. "At the stela in the park. She refuses to budge."

Malach's expression clouded. "How long has she been there?"

"Three days, I think." His voice lowered. "I brought her some water, but she threatened to cut my balls off if I came too close."

That sounded like Nikola Thorn. "What happened?"

"I'm not entirely sure. There was an altercation with Sydonie and Tristhus."

Malach scowled. Syd was behind it, then. She was the queen and Trist the loyal pawn. "Where are they?"

"Your aunt's gathering everyone in the Great Hall. I imagine they're there."

"Perfect." He opened a wardrobe and threw a crimson cloak around his shoulders.

Tashtemir looked alarmed. "Oh no, Malach. You mustn't leave this chamber. Not for a few more days at least. We need to take a conservative approach——"

"I won't have those little monsters running amok. No one ever disciplines them, that's the problem. When I was a child, Beleth regularly had my hide, but she's gotten soft in her old age."

Tashtemir glanced at the door. "Soft is a relative term. And she does discipline them. It has very little effect that I can discern."

Malach braced a hand against the wardrobe. "Do you have any painkillers?" he asked hopefully. "Somnium, maybe?"

"You're already on the highest dose I'll allow."

"Shit."

"Yes, shit. The pain is talking to you, Malach. It's telling you to stay in bed so you don't tear yourself open again."

"This is important. Please, Tash. I need your help."

The doctor shook his head. "I'd go fetch Domina Thorn for you myself, but I doubt she'll listen to me."

"She won't," Malach agreed. "She might not even listen to me. But I won't let her starve to death at the stela, do you understand?"

"No, I wasn't suggesting that. Don't be too angry at the children. They've taken turns guarding the Wardstone. Twice, Perditae came. They were hungry enough that they tried to break through. Syd and Trist held them off."

Malach gave a mirthless laugh. "I can promise you, they aren't doing it out of the goodness of their murderous little hearts. More like cats toying with a mouse before they bite its head off."

Tash eyed him skeptically. "Why did you bring her here? You know what it's like."

"She brought me here, if you'll recall. We had no choice." His pulse spiked from a toxic alchemy of anger, frustration and fear. Perditae? He knew how they fed. To think they'd come so close to her. "I didn't intend to pass out for four days!"

"Well, you still can't expect—"

"Enough," Malach growled. "It's time they realize I'm not dead."

He allowed Tashtemir to help him down the two flights of

marble stairs since he would have fallen on his face otherwise. He couldn't let the others know how bad off he was, that would be like tossing a chunk of raw meat into a leech pit, so once they reached the Great Hall he straightened his back and walked unaided through the doors.

Most of the nihilim hated him. He was Beleth's favorite and they were endlessly maneuvering for power, as if there was anything to fight over. They might be his elders, but Malach had no respect for any of them. Ever since he negotiated the Cold Truce with Falke, they'd been sitting on their bony arses in Bal Kirith, pretending nothing had changed. They played dress-up like the old days, eating and drinking too much, staging sad little orgies and lording it over a handful of Nightmarked servants who surely regretted their bargains but saw no way out of them and were just waiting for their bewigged masters to die of old age.

The younger ones shared his goal of destroying their enemies, but like him they spent most of their time away from Bal Kirith, ranging through the Morho.

Murmurs erupted at Malach's appearance in the Great Hall, cold eyes tracking him as he walked to his usual place at Beleth's right hand. She watched silently, waiting to see what he would do.

Malach's slow gaze took in the assembled nihilim, then settled on Tristhus and Sydonie. Trist looked away—not guilty, Malach was certain neither of them even had the emotional capacity for guilt, but wary at the wrath on Malach's face. His sister stared back, sullen and unafraid.

"I understand you interfered with my Marked," he said.

"She's not Marked yet," Sydonie muttered.

"She will be. Do you know what I'll do to you if you lay a hand on her again?"

Sydonie tucked chin-length black hair behind her ears and smiled. "What will you do, Malach?"

He'd thought about it on the way downstairs. Tash was

right. Simple beatings, and even more elaborate punishments, were shrugged off. "I'll Invert your Marks. All of them. How would you like that?"

The smile slipped.

"Let me be perfectly clear. The Thorn woman belongs to me. If you trifle with her, you trifle with me. And I don't like being trifled with. In fact, it's a capital fucking offense." His gaze swept the table. "That goes for all of you."

The hall was quiet. Then a chair scraped back. It was Dantarion.

"She's hiding something. They had every right—"

"Sit down," Beleth said.

She didn't raise her voice, but Dantarion subsided, a flush rising in her cheeks. Malach stared at the siblings. "I'm not done with you yet," he said.

They looked at him, guileless. "We're ever so sorry, Your Eminence," Sydonie said. She twisted in her seat, masterfully feigning remorse. "It was just a game."

Her answer to everything. "If you behave yourselves," he said, "I'll give you each another Mark. A very powerful one."

"Yes, Your Eminence!" This was said with far greater enthusiasm. Malach understood the children better than they knew. Punishment failed to deter, but the prospect of a reward set off little chimes in their reptile brains.

"I'm relieved that's settled," he said. "Bishop Dantarion, may we speak privately?"

Dantarion waited a heartbeat, then stood. "Of course, Cardinal Malach."

"Don't be long, Dante," Beleth said. "I need your counsel."

She bowed her head. "Of course, Reverend Mother."

They left the Great Hall and walked to the end of the corridor, where a loggia with open archways looked west over the Morho. The sun sat low in the sky, turning the clouds a blazing orange. Malach loved this time of the evening. The intense heat of the day was fading. A flock of white birds with long serpentine necks winged past on their way to the river. Soon, the night creatures would emerge. Owls and frogs, foxes and tawny cats. Crocodilians, too. He meant to have Nikola Thorn safely in his rooms before dark fell, but Dantarion had to be dealt with first.

"Do you truly believe Lezarius is out there somewhere?" Dantarion asked, studying the forest. They stood shoulder to shoulder at the balustrade. He wished there was somewhere to sit. Or better yet, to lie down and pass out cold.

"Yes, I do."

"Then I'll find him." Her voice was calm and sure.

Malach frowned. "You're still going on this hunt?"

"Did you imagine I'd sit idly by?" She glanced back at the Great Hall. "I don't trust them to manage it. If you're right, Lezarius cannot slip away from us. He's the only one who can unmake the grid."

"It might die with him."

"I don't believe that and neither do you. No, we need him alive. Some of our cousins are rash. Vengeful. I intend to handle him gently until he's given to Beleth."

"She told me about the child."

Dantarion reached out and touched his hair, then curled her fingers in it, painfully. "Don't think you'll claim it, Malach."

"I have no designs on your offspring." His lips twitched. "Fucking you generally ends in contusions, not babies. I prefer the former to the latter."

"Good." She released him. "Because he will be Pontifex someday. After Lezarius breaks the Void and we finish the conquest begun by our parents."

"He?"

"Or she. I don't care which. What else can you tell me? We leave tonight."

Malach just wanted to get away from her. "Very little. He's

Invertido so it may affect how he handles the ley, but I know he still has some of his powers because I felt the surge myself. He's dangerous, Dante. Be careful."

"Nikola Thorn didn't tell us any of this." She didn't look happy. "I'd be long gone if she had. We've already wasted four days."

"Nikola Thorn didn't know. I was gut-stabbed. We didn't have a long conversation in the car. I told her to drive me here and she did."

To her everlasting regret, no doubt.

"There's something strange about her." Dantarion gave him a searching look. "Syd tried to use compulsion. She said it didn't work. When she touched the Thorn woman, the ley seeped away like water in sand."

Compulsion? "Those little brats—"

"She was hiding something, Malach. Something she took from the car. They saw her do it." Dantarion fiddled with her ponytail, pulling off the band and twining her auburn hair into a bun. "I'll drown her in the river if you want. I don't like her creeping around while I'm gone."

Dante, Malach knew, was not so easily threatened. It was a test to see how he reacted. If he showed undue concern, she might dispose of Nikola just to spite him. "I'll get to the bottom of it," he said. "But she's just a char. She's not even Marked. Are we afraid of the Curia's castoffs now?"

"Not Marked?" Dantarion laughed. "Well, I like her better then." She grabbed Malach by the hair again and kissed him. "Let's stay friends, shall we? You're the only one around here I can talk to. Maybe I'll even let you name the baby."

The odd thing was, they *were* friends. He'd always felt the same way about her. She was whip smart and nothing frightened her. He didn't want to hurt her, but he also wouldn't let her hurt Nikola.

"Bring me the Lion," he said.

His cousin's eyes held an almost mystical fervor. "The end

of our exile nears, Malach," she said, her breath whispering against his cheek. "A new age is dawning."

Dantarion kissed him once more, hard enough to bruise. Then she strode away, red cloak sweeping the stone floor.

HE FOUND Nikola sitting against the stela from the sweven he'd given her. She jumped to her feet when she saw him. "You're here," she said. "I was afraid . . . ."

Even from a distance, he could see how thin she looked. Her almond eyes locked on him, but she didn't come closer. He could hardly blame her for not rushing into his arms. She'd been alone out here for days. Maybe she thought he'd abandoned her.

Malach held out a hand, pitching his voice low even though there was no one around. "Come to me. I'll get us out of here tonight. We'll take horses and ride for the coast."

"And have you die on me after I went to all this trouble?" she called back. "I doubt you could sit on a privy unaided, let alone a saddle."

She was right, but it still infuriated him. "I know I failed you, but I swear——"

"It's not your fault." She grinned suddenly, silver pirate tooth gleaming. "I'm glad you're alive."

Malach desperately wanted to hold her tight, to kiss her hair and hear her laugh. His chest felt tight. "There's another way. I can still feel some ley." He hesitated. "If you'd just let me Mark you, you'd be mine, they wouldn't dare——"

"No." Her voice hardened. "I already told you no."

"At least come back to my room. I promise to keep you safe."

Nikola stared at him, arms folded. "Don't make promises you can't keep."

"I'll keep this one."

"No offense, but you look terrible. I think I could kick your ass and I've barely eaten or slept in days."

He leaned against a young kapok tree, taking care to avoid the thumb-sized thorns along the trunk. "You're right," he sighed. "I can't get back to my room alone. If you don't help me, we'll both starve."

"Why," Nikola asked, "do you think I'd ever fall for your horseshit again?"

"Because I'm your type of metal."

"Bugger off, Malach."

"Please."

"No."

"Then I'll come to you." He started walking towards the stela. Cold sweat erupted on his brow. He took another step. And another. Malach pressed a hand to his side. It came away bloody. He was leaking straight through the cassock. Another step and the retching began, hot needles stabbing his guts—

"Stop, damn you!" Nikola strode from the Wardstone. She looked as angry as she had when she slapped him across the face in her flat. "You're a bloody psychopath, do you know that?"

He smiled with red teeth. "Thanks for coming out."

"Oh, you're welcome," she said crossly. Nikola slung an arm around his waist, careful of the bandage. Together they walked slowly back to the Pontifex's Palace. His knees gave out in the antechamber. Nikola shouted for the servants and followed as Malach was spirited up to his bedchamber.

"Fetch that animal doctor," she snapped. "And do it quick."

"Food for her, too," Malach rasped. "No wine. Just water."

Nikola drank cold broth while Tashtemir examined him, muttering oaths under his breath. He replaced the bandage and smeared Malach's abdomen with a foul-smelling unguent.

"Don't let him leave this bed," he told Nikola. "Shoot him if you have to. I'll bring up a crossbow."

She nodded seriously. "I'll aim for a bit that isn't already mangled, assuming I can find one."

"Excellent." They exchanged a look of mutual appraisal.

"I'm sorry I threatened you," Nikola said. "It was kind of you to throw me that waterskin."

"Think nothing of it." Tash stroked his mustache, keen black eyes scanning her quickly from head to toe. She wore a cheap flower print dress, the kind they sold for six fides at the central flea market in Novostopol. It was streaked with dirt and her collarbones poked from her thin chest, but she was still the most beautiful thing Malach had ever seen. "Do you have any injuries I should treat? I'm quite professional, I can assure you."

Nikola smiled, though Malach sensed her unease at being examined. "I'm well, thank you."

"Then I'll leave you two to rest. If I can't find a spare crossbow, just bludgeon him with something."

Tashtemir left. Malach ordered hot water for the claw-footed bath in the corner. Nikola perched on the edge of the bed, arms wrapped around herself. "I like him. What's he doing in this pisshole?"

"That's a long story." He studied her face. "Are you truly well, Nikola? I mean, as well as can be expected?"

"I haven't lost the child, if that's what you mean."

She didn't sound exactly happy about that.

"I'm glad, but I was asking about you."

"It's weird, but I stopped feeling hungry on the second day. I had this big boost of energy, like I could run all the way to the coast without stopping."

"Why didn't you?"

Nikola ignored the question, covering a yawn. "This is a monstrous bed."

Malach looked at the elaborate finial posts that mimicked the sharp spires of the basilica, the sea monsters frolicking across the carved triple-panels of the footboard. He barely noticed it anymore, especially since all the furniture at Bal Kirith was of similar style and proportions.

"You could fit six people in there," Nikola said.

"Plenty of room for you, then," he said with a wan smile.

"Bath first." She turned her back and undressed, then slipped into the steaming water. There was a curve to her belly, so slight he wouldn't have noticed if he didn't know her body so well. Back in Novostopol, he'd wondered how he would feel when she started to show. Now he knew the answer. Malach was seized by an intense, consuming possessiveness. He didn't only want the child. He wanted her. And he could never let her know it or she'd fight him tooth and nail.

"I can't stay here, Malach," she said, soaping a lean brown arm.

He scowled. "Why not?"

Nikola gave him a level look. "Besides the two demon spawn? Because I'm knocked up, obviously."

"Beleth doesn't know it's mine."

"And she won't guess when the fetus grows four times as fast as a human?" There was a tremor in her voice and Malach realized she wasn't only afraid of Beleth. She was afraid of what was happening to her.

Their eyes locked. "I'll deal with it."

"You're the one who warned me about her. In fact, I seem to recall you saying she might kill me. Please, Malach. Be reasonable. We both know I can't stay. So you can help me or not, but I'm leaving tomorrow."

He stared at the frescoed ceiling, where storm clouds surrounded a lone patch of blue sky. "You still owe me the child."

"And you're welcome to it! But I'm not giving birth in this place. Can't you see it's madness to think otherwise?" Her voice rose and Malach raised a placating hand.

"Fine. Do you know how to ride?"

"No."

"Well, I won't let you go on foot. That would be suicide."

"How hard is it?"

"Not very. But you should practice. I'll teach you, if you'll only wait a little bit—"

"How long, Malach?"

"It'll be at least two weeks before I'm riding," he admitted. "But I could give you lessons in a day or two. I won't stay in this bed every hour of the day. It would leave me weak. Even Tash will have to let me take walks. You can cover yourself with a cloak."

She submerged under the water for a long time. Malach was just starting to worry when she surfaced. "What about Dantarion? I think she's angry at me, too."

"Dantarion is leaving, along with some of the others. We'll have a reprieve."

"Three days," she said, grudgingly. "Teach me how to ride and make me a map." Nikola stood up from the tub and looked around. "No towels."

"Take one of my cloaks from the wardrobe."

She wrapped herself in crimson. "Your chamber is much nicer than mine."

"Most of them are shit." He propped up on an elbow. "I've had three years to make mine decent. Come on, get under here. You look cold."

"Hang on." She went to the chair where she'd piled her dress and shoes and took something from a pocket. "I need a good hiding place, Malach."

"Is that what the children tried to take from you?"

She nodded.

"What is it?"

"Kaldurite."

His brows rose. "Really?"

"Really."

"May I see?"

She came to the bed and gently tipped a velvet drawstring

bag open on his lap. It held six gems shaped like teardrops. Malach picked one up. The gem appeared blue like a sapphire, but when he angled it to the candlelight, the color shifted to ruby red. Another facet sparkled violet like an amethyst.

The gems were very rare, found only on the barren Plain of Kalduria. They repelled all three currents of the ley, though they wouldn't have worked against the Wards at the Arx. The pain stelae induced was not inflicted through the ley because it worked even when there was no ley present. But Kaldurite could protect an individual from someone else using the ley against them, making it quite valuable in certain quarters.

"I did my research," Nikola said. "The witches practice lithomancy. They prize Kaldurite. I imagine it protects them against your sort, and the Curia, too. There's a black market dealer in Ash Court who converted my fides. Those six little stones are ten years' worth of scrubbing floors." She lifted one to the light. "I wasn't about to let two ill-mannered children steal my life savings."

"They wouldn't want the Kaldurite anyway," Malach said. "It not only blocks the ley from being used on you, it blocks you from using the ley. That's why mages shun it."

"Well, good, because they're mine." She gathered the stones and tied them up in the velvet bag. "Does it bother you if I sleep with this under the pillow?"

"Not in the least." His eyes felt very heavy. "Kiss me, Nikola."

Warm lips pressed to his. It wasn't anything like the brutal, violent kiss he'd gotten from Dante. Once he'd enjoyed being his cousin's chew toy. It held a certain novel attraction. But he'd never felt anything for her beyond a sort of rough affection. If it had been Dantarion at the wheel and he'd begged her to take him somewhere very dangerous for her because it would save his life, she would laugh and take the other fork in the road.

"If they do find Lezarius," Nikola murmured, "I hope I'm gone before he breaks open the ley. No offense."

"None taken."

He'd told her everything in the car between blackouts. And he would tell her about Dantarion's child, too. No more secrets. But not now. Malach could see she was on her last legs.

"It was good you didn't tell Beleth," he said. "The less you know, the less interested she'll be."

"Um-hmmm." Nikola curled on her side, wiry hair brushing his shoulder. He pulled the blanket over them both. "Promise me you won't let our child end up like Sydonie and Tristhus. Raise it right, Malach."

He kissed her forehead. "I promise."

Nikola fell into a deep slumber. Malach was a heartbeat from joining her when he heard the ring of hooves echoing in the courtyard. He dragged himself out of bed and watched through the window as Dantarion and a dozen other nihilim emerged from the palace. Servants waited with the bridles of laden horses. Dante looked up, sensing his presence, and he raised a hand in farewell. She gave him a mock salute, then sank to one knee. The others joined her, pressing their palms to the earth where a weak current still flowed. Malach watched it darken as they drew the abyssal ley to the surface. He didn't need to be part of the circle to decipher the urgent message they were sending to the Morho.

Find Lezarius. Twist the threads of chance and lead him to us.

He looked out at the thick canopy, a green sea stretching to the horizon. The forest was a sentient thing, an extension of the mages' psyche. Nothing would escape without their permission.

Malach went back to bed. He touched Nikola's cheek.

Then he laid a hand on her belly. She was right. It was madness. Pure madness. Yet it could be no other way. He understood that now.

"I won't let you go, Nikola," he vowed softly. "Not without me."

Chapter Thirty-Nine

For the first time in recent memory, Novostopol enjoyed two successive days of blue skies and bright sunshine. Children played outside at recess, birds twittered in the trees, and raincoats were left at home. The only ones who complained were the cab drivers, who found themselves suddenly without fares.

By Saturday morning, the skies grew dark again. The reprieve was over.

Kasia and Natalya huddled under umbrellas for Falke's first public audience as the Pontifex Dmitry. He stood on a balcony of the palace, waving at the cheering multitudes. From behind the barricade, she could hardly make out his face, but it didn't matter. Everyone was focused on the white robe. How simple it would be to substitute someone who vaguely resembled Falke. If the cardinals and bishops played along, the masses would never know.

Is that what had happened with Lezarius? But how on earth did the conspirators manage to alter his face to look like someone else? Surely not everyone at the Arx in Jalghuth was in on it, which meant the imposter must be very close to a twin or the ruse would have been discovered long before.

Kasia's eyes moved across the various Orders gathered in the plaza below. With a little squinting, she made out the trident of the Probatio, the Golden Bough of General Directorate, the knights of Saint Jule, many others.

"Which is that one?" she asked.

"The Sheaf of Wheat? That's the Order of Saint Marcius. The ones who enforce the *Meliora*. Arch-conservatives. If they had their way, we'd be living like the Kvens." Natalya jerked her chin. "Bishop Maria Karolo. Tessaria said she came within two votes of being Pontifex herself. Doesn't look well pleased, does she?"

Kasia studied the slender, dark-haired woman with a severe bob that just touched the corners of her unsmiling mouth. Her gaze swept the crowd like a teacher about to send the whole class off to detention.

"Thank the Saints she didn't win," Kasia murmured. "I don't fancy losing indoor plumbing."

It was as if she'd shouted the words at the top of her lungs. Bishop Karolo's eyes caught on Kasia—and held for a long moment. There was a personal hostility in the bishop's expression, though Kasia felt sure they'd never met. Then Falke blew a kiss and a scream went up among the women in the crowd. He was already insanely popular because of his rugged looks and, as Nashka had phrased it, badass war record. Bishop Karolo turned away, whispering in the ear of an aide.

"Let's get out of here," Kasia said, suddenly claustrophobic amid the tight press of bodies.

Natalya's brow notched. They'd both dressed to the nines for the occasion and arrived hours early so they could get as close as possible. Natalya still adored Falke, insisting he was blameless in the Massot affair, and Kasia only knew she needed to be here. The cards had told her so.

"What's up, kitten? The chorus hasn't even performed yet."

"Karolo just stared at us." Kasia shot her a meaningful look. "In a way I didn't much like."

Natalya knew Kasia had been in the Pontifex's Palace the night Feizah was killed. She knew about the lost Six of Storms. She did not know any of the rest. Kasia had made it seem she never managed to gain an audience and simply snuck out the way she came when all hell broke loose. She didn't like lying to her best friend, but she'd promised Alexei she would protect Mikhail Bryce. And Kasia kept her promises, whatever the cost. Tess had taught her that doing so was morally correct.

"But if they thought you were a witness, wouldn't they have come for you already?" Natalya asked in a low voice.

"Perhaps. I don't know. But I want to go home."

"Yeah, okay. My feet are killing me anyway. How on earth do you wear spiked heels every day?"

"Glutton for punishment," Kasia muttered.

They were only two rows back from the first barricade facing the palace. She put on an apologetic smile and turned to the man behind her. "Excuse me, but there's been an emergency and I'm afraid we have to get through. . . ."

It took almost half an hour of squeezing, pushing, and incessant apologies to escape the plaza. Once they reached the Via Fortuna, the crowds thinned enough to walk at a normal pace. Kasia held her head down, hiding beneath her umbrella as she passed through the Dacian Gate, but none of the Oprichniki standing outside gave the women a second glance.

It was the eve of Den Spasitelya, Saviors' Day. On Sunday, people would visit each other's homes, bringing sweets and cordials, to commemorate the building of the Arxes. But the night before had a wilder, grimmer theme. Young people donned masks and costumes evoking the evils of the Second Dark Age, while the Oprichniki deployed in force to fill up the drunk tanks. The fun was generally harmless. Kasia and

Natalya went to a party or two, and perhaps a cafe for a night-cap, before staggering home singing old pop songs.

"The kids start earlier every year," Natalya observed as they cut through the lush, hilly north end of Arkadia Park, where a group of teens in sinister face paint lounged in the shelter of a gazebo with kicked-up skateboards. Pungent Keef smoke filled the air. "It won't be dark for hours."

"Yeah, but can't you feel it? There's a weird energy, Nashka. I'm not going out tonight."

"What? Oh, no. You can't make me go to Club Dumas alone."

"You're staying home, too," Kasia said firmly. "We'll play board games and order in."

"Saints, is this what it's like to get old? Soon you'll be putting a second chain on the door."

"You'll survive a single night at home." Kasia's gaze probed the scattered clumps of trees. She had the distinct feeling of being watched. "Besides, it's unseemly to get drunk on the night of the Pontifex's official inauguration."

Natalya laughed. "Unseemly? I think you've been spending too much time with Tessaria."

"Then here's your opportunity to properly corrupt me again."

Her friend grinned. "When you put it like that. No curry though. I'm sick of curry. How about we buy some food and cook it over a . . . you know, what's it called?"

"Stove?"

"Yeah, that."

Kasia nodded slowly. "Sounds dangerous. Count me in."

They topped a rise. Some way ahead, four figures approached along the brick pathway. They wore white masks with smooth, empty features and black eyeholes. Each carried a red umbrella.

"Fogging creepy," Natalya muttered. "You're right. I'm not in the mood for this shit."

Kasia hooked her arm, steering her along another path. When she glanced back, the men were gone. "Let's get a taxi."

A dozen occupied cabs passed them by in the financial district south of the Arx. The only vacant one was snagged by a well-dressed couple with their two equally well-dressed children.

"I should have driven," Kasia muttered.

"And parked where, exactly?" Natalya gestured at the yellow cordons and NO STANDING signs. "I'd even consider taking a tram, but they must be running on a holiday schedule. I haven't seen a single one."

The sidewalks grew emptier as they neared Ash Court, but the traffic evaporated, too. Natalya thought she saw an empty taxi four blocks away and waved her arms to flag it down, but the driver turned a corner.

"Fog it," she grumped. "These shoes are *torture*."

"Let's try over by the river," Kasia suggested. "There are some fancy houses and it's on the way home anyway."

She glanced across the Boulevard of Saint Ruda, a wide commercial thoroughfare that divided the haves from the have-nots. The men in white masks were back. They weren't laughing or singing like any of the other merrymakers in costume. They stood in a line waiting for the light to change, holding the red umbrellas. Kasia couldn't see behind those blank eyeholes, but she sensed they were staring.

"Oh, fog it," she said, grabbing Natalya's hand. They hurried down the boulevard and cut into the warren of narrow cobbled streets that signaled the edge of Ash Court. Kasia never came through the Unmarked district even if it meant walking kilometers out of the way. It reminded her of how close she was to anonymous poverty. No doubt she'd end up living here when she refused Kireyev's demand to continue spying and he made her true status known. She eyed the trash littering the curbs, the peeling paint and lack of street lamps. Nikola Thorn lived in Ash Court. She said it was a neighborly place. Kasia supposed she'd get used to it. One could get used to anything if there was no choice—

"Any idea where we are?" Natalya paused in a gloomy alley. Not a single lamp shone through the grimy windows of the buildings to either side.

"Not a clue."

"If only the sun would come out—"

"As well wish for a magic carpet or Dark Age aero-plane," Kasia interrupted savagely. "Any sign of those ghouls?"

The street was empty, but that didn't mean the men were gone. They wore long cloaks, black gloves, and heavy boots. Could there be cassocks under the cloaks? It was impossible to tell.

"Are you sure it wasn't a coincidence?" Natalya asked hopefully.

"They were looking right at us."

"There's no crime in this city. You know that. It's probably just a prank."

"Let them prank someone else," Kasia muttered.

Natalya pulled off a pump and rubbed her toes. "You think everyone's looking at you," she murmured.

"What does that mean?"

"It means you seem a bit paranoid. First, a bishop is giving you the eye. Now we're being tailed by strange men. I don't blame you after the lunacy of the last week, but I think you might be seeing things that aren't . . . ." Natalya trailed off, eyes widening.

"They're behind me, aren't they?"

"*Shit!*"

The four men strode at a relaxed but steady pace down the alley. Two of them used the red umbrellas like walking sticks. One was whistling an upbeat tune. Kasia could see their identical masks clearly now. The nose was a shapeless nub, but the corners of the mouth curved upward in a faint smile.

This time, it was Natalya who grabbed her hand. They

broke into a run. Kasia heard the men's footsteps just behind. "Help!" she screamed.

But Ash Court, it seemed, was not a neighborly place—or at least not towards strangers. The curtains stayed closed, the doors securely locked. If anyone was about, she saw no sign of it. Then Nashka's heel caught on a broken cobblestone and she stumbled, skinning her knee. She kicked off the pumps with a sailor's oath that would have struck Tessaria Foy deaf and perhaps blind, as well.

Kasia moved to stand between Nashka and their assailants. She slipped a hand into her pocket and gave the men a level stare. Fear would only incite them more. "What do you want?" she demanded. "Who are you?"

The one in the middle of the pack stepped forward, head slightly tilted. His voice was a hoarse rasp. "The Black Sun rises again. We bathe in its radiance."

Natalya got to her feet, blood flowing from her shredded stocking. "You've had a few too many," she said curtly. "But it's not funny anymore. Leave us alone or you'll end up in the dock."

The man twirled his red umbrella. The point on the end had been sharpened to a wicked spike. Kasia's fingers closed around the cards in her pocket as she exchanged a worried look with Natalya. This sort of thing didn't happen in Novostopol. People were friendly. Helpful and polite. Even on Saviors' Day, they only dressed up for a lark. They certainly didn't assault each other in alleys.

The one who'd spoken drew a slow finger across his throat. "Caput corvi. The dragon consumes itself, dying to rise again. One must be at home in the darkness of suffering, Kasia."

She stiffened. "How do you know my name?"

He held out a gloved hand. "Our master wants you. The suffering will be greater if you resist."

"And who is your master?"

"He is the devouring black fire."

The sky above them darkened, as though a great wing had fallen across the tenements of Ash Court. Kasia knew she should be afraid, but tightly compressed fury made her temples pound.

"Tell your master," she said, "that I am the hunter, not the hunted."

She drew the top card from the deck in her pocket and threw it down between them. Four masks angled to follow its progress. The card landed in a dirty puddle and floated there. The Bridge. One of the Major Arcana, it spanned a raging river. One bank was lush and green, the other barren and rocky. A figure stood trapped at the center of the span, which had broken in half, leaving a wide gap.

"That's not right," Natalya muttered, staring at the card. "I didn't paint it that way."

The first man laughed softly. "*Mortificatio* is experienced as defeat and failure. It is the essence of hell. Now you writhe and twist in the purifying flames—"

He paused as a bright flash of violet light traced the design. Metal groaned somewhere above. Kasia looked up, her eyes widening. She dragged Natalya out of the way just as the rusted fire escape tore loose from the side of the building and tumbled down in a cloud of plaster dust and bricks. The men scrambled back. She heard a hoarse scream but didn't pause to see what had happened.

"Run!" she urged.

Natalya limped at high speed to the end of the alley, Kasia half supporting her. As they reached the street, a black car screeched to a stop, blocking the way out. Kasia glanced behind. Three of the men were climbing over the downed fire escape. The first one across sprinted towards her, moving with a swift, loping stride that was more apelike than human. Within seconds, he'd halved the distance. She had another card ready in her hand when the car window rolled down.

"Get in!" Tessaria barked.

The women dove into the backseat. The engine roared and the car rocketed forward down the empty street. Through the window Kasia watched a cloaked man burst out of the alley, his chest heaving. That eerie blank mask stared after them until the car screeched around a corner.

"Saints, who were they?" Tessaria asked, glancing at Kasia in the rearview mirror.

"No . . . clue," Natalya replied breathlessly.

Tessaria looked troubled. "Saviors' Eve gets worse every year. It ought to be banned."

"Those men were no—" Kasia began, but Tessaria cut her off.

"We have bigger problems than a few hoodlums," she snapped. "If you'd told me the truth about what happened on Monday night, I would have dealt with the problem before it became unmanageable." Brakes squealed as she sped around a traffic circle. "One of Feizah's knights regained consciousness an hour ago. She had a very interesting story to tell."

Kasia watched her in the mirror. *Loose ends. One hard tug and they could unravel a whole story.* "I thought the guards were dead."

"All but one. She was badly injured, but she pulled through. She said they tried to detain a young woman who was discovered roaming the palace shortly before Feizah died. It didn't take long to connect that same young woman with the three guests who'd been staying at the Castel Saint Agathe."

Kasia licked her lips. "What else did she say?"

"She wasn't very clear on how you got away, but they'll get it out of her eventually. The truly unfortunate part is that she told all this to Bishop Maria Karolo rather than the OGD. Karolo and Feizah were thick as thieves. This guard is sympathetic to the Conservatives and made sure Karolo got the information first. Have you any idea of the damage this will do to Dmitry's office?"

Kasia shared a look with Natalya. "They're lying about the Reverend Mother being murdered so I don't see how the bishop can make it public anyway."

"Oh, you callow child," Tessaria exclaimed. "I'm talking about damage to his allies within the Curia, which is what counts! Then there's the matter of a certain card you dropped outside the Pontifex's bedchamber. I might have explained it away, but combined with the guard's testimony . . . we're in deep!"

"So Bishop Karolo sent those men?" Natalya asked with a frown. "Why not her own priests? Or the Oprichniki? Everyone knows the Conservatives hate Saviors' Eve. They think it's decadent. Why would she—"

"Saints, stop yammering, I have no idea who those men were." Tessaria steered the car down a lumpy, potholed street that reeked of fish. "You two seem to have a knack for acquiring enemies."

"We've laid low for the last two days," Kasia protested.

"Well, good for you. It's still too little, too late."

A pair of gulls swooped over the car, clever eyes scanning the ground for scraps. Kasia stared up at a huge blue and green sign declaring, "Welcome to Novoport!"

"Where are you taking me, Auntie?" she asked with a sinking feeling.

"Far away, that's where."

The waterfront was a mix of warehouses and a few dock-side restaurants serving raw oysters and half-priced happy hour drinks. Two dozen steamers and double-masted barques rested at anchor alongside stone piers. Cranes and colorful shipping containers lined the wharf, ready to be loaded onto tramways leading to the central market where one could buy everything from carpets to cherry peppers.

Ninety percent of trade in the Via Sancta was conducted by sea. The land routes were shorter but vulnerable to attack and sabotage. Normally, the docks would be teeming with activity. On this dreary Saturday afternoon, sandwiched between the inauguration of a new Pontifex and a major holiday, the place was deserted.

"You can't just kidnap her," Nashka said indignantly. "Don't I get a say?"

"You're going, too." Tessaria gave her a grim smile.

"*What?*"

"Guilt by association. You know far too much, Natalya Anderle. The new Pontifex agrees with me. He wants you both spirited away until he's dealt with this mess. Honestly, you're lucky he isn't throwing you both to the devilfish!"

"He can't though, can he?" Kasia said shrewdly. "Or he'd be thrown to the devilfish right along with us."

Tessaria didn't reply.

"What about all my stuff?" Natalya demanded.

"I'll buy you new charcoals and . . . " Tess made a fluttery gesture. "Underthings. Whatever you want. But it's not worth your lives to go home and pack, is it?"

"Shit," Nashka whispered under her breath.

Tessaria must have read her lips in the rearview mirror because she scowled mightily. "Be grateful I found you."

"How did you?" Kasia wondered.

"I used the ley and my need was great." Her tone softened. "I love you both, despite your foolishness, and will not allow a single mistake to ruin both your lives. Trust me, this is the best way."

Natalya stared disconsolately out the window. She had the most to lose—friends, family, a budding career as an artist. Kasia had only casual acquaintances. She felt no great sorrow at leaving Novostopol. The abruptness was inconvenient, but all she cared about now was determining the limits of her newfound power and mastering it better. If she knew how to make the cards work every time, she would never be running for her life again.

Those men would have been the ones to run.

"At least tell us where," Kasia said. "We have a right to know where we're being dragged off to."

"Nantwich. That ought to be far enough. The Reverend Mother Clavis is a longtime friend. She'll help." Tessaria parked next to a small pleasure boat with a striped awning. She took out a pair of binoculars and swept the lenses slowly across the piers. "Ah, there she is."

The ship was a merchant freighter called the *Moonbeam*. It was scheduled to sail at dawn, but Tessaria had a hastily penned writ with the Pontifex's seal giving them safe passage from the city and commanding any subject of the Via Sancta to obey the bearer without question. Tessaria drove to the end of the pier and shut off the engine. She tucked the keys in a pocket.

"Don't move," she said. "I'll roust the captain."

"Planning to stuff us into the cargo hold?" Natalya said sourly.

"Keep complaining and I just might." She applied dark purple lipstick in the rearview and blotted it with a tissue.

"What about our clients?"

"Your clients will be told you're working on a very important commission for the Church. And I already paid the rent on your flat for the next six months." Tess caught her long dreadlocks in a silver clasp at the nape, exposing the Raven Mark on her neck. "There will be an inquiry to satisfy the Conservatives, but by then we'll have several witnesses who saw you in the Castel Saint Agathe at the same time the guard claims you were in the Pontifex's Palace. With luck, you won't be charged."

"Won't it make me look guiltier to run away?" Kasia asked.

Tessaria opened the car door. She wore stylish low-heeled black boots beneath the cassock. "You didn't run away." A small smile touched her lips. "As I just explained, the Reverend Mother Clavis heard of your talent and summoned you both to Nantwich. Now sit tight, darlings, I'll be back in a jiffy."

The *Moonbeam* was an iron-strapped steamer with twin funnels and four masts to hoist auxiliary sails. Kasia watched Tess march up the railed gangway. She spoke to a crewman on watch and he hurried to a hatch and down a ladder.

"I'm sorry," she said to Natalya. "It was so stupid of me to lose that card."

"What about the knights?" She slid down in the seat, bleached curls floating in a cloud around her head. "What did you do to them?"

"Just made them sleep. I didn't even mean to. They grabbed me and a card fell out of the deck."

"Which one?"

"The Knight of Wards."

"Ah, the Dreamer." Nashka sat up straighter. Kasia could see she was intrigued despite everything.

"So it fell out and lit with ley and the knights just dropped." She snapped her fingers. "Like that. I checked to make sure they were still alive and then I ran away."

"The mage killed them all except for one?"

"It seems so, yes. But when I tried the card again later, it didn't work."

"Each card must do something different. Perhaps more than one thing, depending on the circumstances, since there are layers of meaning."

"Yes, that's what I was thinking, too," Kasia said in excitement. "It only seems to work when they're drawn randomly, but maybe there's a way to choose. I think it must use the liminal ley since that twists chance." She took Nashka's hand. "Maybe we can design a new deck together. Think of the possibilities!"

Natalya's eyes shone. "Nantwich won't be so bad. We were talking about visiting there anyhow. And it's not forever, is it? We can come back someday?"

"Of course. This will all blow over." She peered out the window. "What's taking so long?"

Natalya opened the door and got out, testing her skinned knee.

"How is it?" Kasia asked.

"Just a bit stiff. I've done worse tripping on the dance floor." Natalya gave her neck a loud crack in each direction. She'd lost her shoes in the alley and stood on the worn planks of the dock in stocking feet. "Looks like the general's invasion has met with resistance."

Kasia joined her, leaning on the still-warm hood. Tessaria was arguing with a white-haired man in a captain's uniform. Or not arguing, exactly. Tess was going on at length while he stood there quietly shaking his head. Then the purr of an engine whipped the vestal's head around. She stalked down the gangway just as two Curia cars sped up to the dock.

"This can't be good," Natalya murmured.

Tess gestured sharply and they hurried to join her at the foot of the gangway. The cars stopped a short distance away. Nashka gave a soft groan as Bishop Maria Karolo and five priests from the Order of Saint Marcius got out. They had the look of former knights, with broad shoulders, closely shaved heads, and flinty eyes. They wore cassocks with a sheaf of wheat embroidered on the breast. Kasia wondered if any of them had been wearing cloaks and masks half an hour ago.

"You have no authority here," Tessaria said, lifting her chin.

"I have all the authority I need." Bishop Karolo's voice was thin and arrogant, much like the woman herself. She held up a piece of paper. "This is an arrest warrant—"

Tess's arm moved in a blur. The paper tore from the bishop's hand and plastered itself to a wooden piling, stuck there by a small bone-handled dagger. Kasia and Natalya looked at their benefactor with stunned awe.

"Get back in your car, Maria, and be on your way," Tessaria said calmly.

The bishop stared. Her face was bloodless except for two crimson splotches on her cheeks. "Do you really believe your *association* with Falke will protect you when the truth comes out? Come quietly and there's a chance you'll only be charged as an accessory. But if you interfere with me, I'll make sure you're destroyed, Tessaria. The Foy name will be reviled throughout the Curia." She eyed Kasia and Natalya with loathing. "And your two little pets will go to prison for the rest of their lives."

"We're ready to depart immediately," Tessaria called to the captain, who was watching from the rail with his first mate and half a dozen crew. He opened his mouth, then closed it again.

"Take them," Karolo snapped at her priests.

One strode towards Kasia, another beelined for Natalya, and three headed for Tessaria Foy, who was clearly deemed the most dangerous of the bunch.

"Get up the gangway!" Tess shouted.

Kasia made it four steps before a hand yanked her back by the hair. She struggled wildly, but the muscled body behind her was solid as an ironbound door. Bishop Karolo approached with a satisfied expression.

"I only allowed you to leave the Arx so I could take you without injuring innocent people," she said with quiet venom. "I know what you are." Her lip curled. "A Nightmarked sorceress. You were part of the plot to murder the Reverend Mother! Falke knew about it. I'll see him ruined for this, but not before you confess your guilt to the tribunal." Spittle flew from her thin lips. "I don't know how you passed the Wards, but interrogation will loosen your tongue, witch."

Blue light leaked from her sleeves as her Marks soothed the bishop's rage. Karolo's face went eerily blank. "Throw her in the trunk," she said.

A roughspun hood came down over Kasia's head, cutting off light and air. Her arms were twisted behind her back. She struggled to breathe, gasping through the scratchy material. Strong arms lifted her off her feet and dragged her down the pier. She kicked and screamed, to no avail. Then she heard an *oof*, followed by a thud. The hood was yanked off. Kasia stared at the hulking man before her, disoriented and disbelieving.

"Fra Spassov?" she gasped.

One of the priests swung a length of rebar at his head. He ducked and hammered the man with a giant fist. The priest dropped like an anchor and didn't get up. Bishop Karolo stepped forward, Marks flaring. The sharp points of her bob framed a mouth set in lines of livid fury. "What do you think you—"

Spassov grabbed her like a sack of rice and threw her over the edge of the pier into the water.

"Hurry!" he urged Kasia. "Go aboard!"

Before she could reply, he stomped over to Tessaria Foy, who was fending off three priests with a pair of daggers and acrobatic moves that Kasia never suspected she possessed. Within a minute, one of the priests had joined Bishop Karolo in the water and a second lay unconscious on the planks. The third launched himself at Spassov's broad back, then screamed as Tessaria's knife flew into his thigh.

Natalya stood over another priest of Saint Marcius. He writhed on the dock, croaking soundlessly and clutching his crotch. Kasia dragged her up the gangway. Tessaria and Spassov hurried behind. A line of blood ran from Spassov's nose. He looked ready to pound any comers into the ground like tent pegs. The captain watched them approach with alarm.

"I can't have any part of this," he stammered. "I'm an honest trader. I don't take passengers, especially ones in trouble with the Curia."

"Are you blind?" Tessaria demanded, waving the paper in

his face. "This is from the Pontifex himself! He rewards those who heed his writ just as he punishes those who don't. Which category do you prefer to be in, Captain?"

The man eyed her uneasily. "With all due respect, Domina, I think I'd better call the gendarmes and let them sort it out—"

"Start the boiler or I'll summon the hounds," Spassov snarled, boots thumping on the deck. "They're hungry and ill-tempered and they hate hearing the word *no*."

The captain blanched at the inverted trident on Spassov's cassock. He started shouting orders at the bewildered crew. Within minutes, the lower furnaces were lit and the anchor weighed. Smoke trailed from the twin funnels. "Call the harbor master," the captain said to his first mate. "Get us a pilot boat." A quick glance at Tessaria. "Tell him it's the Pontifex's orders."

Sailors leapt to the pier to untie the heavy mooring lines from the iron bollards. Tessaria grabbed Spassov's meaty arm and dragged him aside. "What do you think you're doing?"

As usual, Patryk Spassov looked the worse for wear—and not just from brawling. He needed a shave, his eyes were bloodshot, and there was a bit of dried egg yolk on his sleeve. "Helping you, Sor Foy," he replied.

"Who sent you?"

"No one." He sounded indignant. "I came on my own."

"Why on earth would you do that?"

"Domina Novak tried to help Fra Bryce, so now I return the favor."

"Well, that's lovely, but you can go now."

He hunched his shoulders. "I resigned my post today. I thought I'd leave the city anyway—"

She chuckled. "Oh no, you don't. I appreciate your aid, but you can go retire elsewhere, Fra Spassov."

"What if more people come after you?"

"I'll handle them myself."

"And if you can't?" he asked mildly.

Her lips thinned. "I already told you, we don't need your help—"

"Yes," Kasia said firmly, walking up. "We do."

Tessaria's eyes narrowed.

"He comes or I swear by all the Saints and Martyrs I'll run at the first chance. You know I always keep my word."

The older woman looked ready to argue, but two of the priests on the pier were stirring. She tossed her head and gave an angry nod. "Only to the next port. And you'll do as I say, Fra Spassov, or you'll be swimming next to that foolish bishop."

His lips twitched, but he kept a straight face. Patryk touched the Raven on his neck. "I'm yours to command, Sor Foy."

Maria Karolo and her minion had been forced to dog-paddle all the way to the end of the pier to find a ladder leading up. They stood dripping on the dock as the *Moonbeam* drifted free and the great screw thrummed to life. A long blast claimed right of way in the harbor.

"I thought she'd shake her fist at us," Nashka said dryly, leaning on the rail. "Shout some villainous curses and vow revenge."

Kasia didn't laugh. "Without us, she's got nothing. But I don't think we've seen the last of that woman." She turned to Spassov. "Thank you. I have no idea why you're here, but I'd be in the trunk of a car heading for the Arx if you weren't."

"I promised Alexei I'd keep an eye on you." Spassov rubbed his scalp. "I hear whispers, *da*? Your name in connection with some serious trouble. I wanted to warn you, but I lost you in the crowds so I followed Sor Foy instead."

They all looked at Tessaria, who stood in the pilothouse vigorously negotiating with the captain.

"We never noticed a car behind," Natalya said with a frown.

"Because I'm good. Anyway, there is nothing left for me in Novo. But I think you need a bodyguard, *da*? Who was that fellow back at Ash Court?"

Kasia shot Natalya a quelling look. "You know Saviors' Eve," she said lightly. "All the freaks crawl out of the woodwork."

Spassov cast her a shrewd look. "Hmmm. If I hadn't been following, I would have stopped to teach him a lesson."

Natalya flashed her thousand-watt smile. "Well, I'm glad you're here, Father. It makes it a proper adventure to have a mysterious priest from the Interfectorem in our party."

Spassov flushed. "I hope Sor Foy comes to see it that way."

"I'm sure she will. Now, what did you hear on the dock?"

He gazed at her blandly. "Only the bit about Domina Novak being a sorceress and conspiring to kill the Pontifex. Of course it was all lies."

"Vile lies," Natalya agreed.

His chin jerked to Tessaria. "Does she really have a letter from the new Pontifex?"

"Yes."

He nodded slowly. "Then in helping you, I've kept my vows to serve the Via Sancta. Maybe the Reverend Mother Clavis will allow me to stay at the Arx in Nantwich. Alyosha said war is coming—" Spassov cut off.

"You saw him?" Kasia asked.

Patryk looked around and lowered his voice. "He came to say goodbye. I'm pretty sure he got out of the city safely. I would have heard otherwise."

Kasia wanted to ask him more questions, but not in front of Tess, who walked back with a look of contentment. "I've just negotiated a cabin for you two. Fra Spassov, you will sleep on the deck. It's only a five-day journey to Nantwich, I'm sure you can make do."

He shrugged. "I've slept rougher."

"The captain generously offered me his cabin." Her gaze

speared the two younger women. "Come along, I'll show you your quarters."

Spassov lit a cigarette and rested his forearms on the rail as they followed Tessaria to a hatch, down a steep flight of metal stairs and along a narrow corridor that smelled of iron and wood smoke. The cabin was small and spare, with two bunks on either side of a round window that had a bench between, its legs bolted to the floor. Natalya started poking around, opening the built-in cupboards and drawers.

Kasia turned to Tess. "Have you ever heard the phrase *Caput corvi?*" she asked in a low voice.

Tess stiffened. "It means the head of the raven—more precisely, decapitation. In alchemy, it is the first step of the *nigredo*. Putrefaction of the soul to its darkest essence." Her voice grew sharp. "Where did you hear that?"

"Hey, look what I found!"

Natalya brandished a bottle of rum with a happy expression. Tess smiled, though it didn't quite reach her eyes. "Settle in, darlings. I'll see about some supper."

LATER, after Natalya fell asleep, Kasia went up to the deck and found a quiet place to sit. The lights of Novostopol were long gone. Not a glimmer could be seen along the entire southern coast. A thousand kilometers of Black Zone stretched between Novo and Kvengard. She closed her eyes, enjoying the fresh breeze and salt spray flung up across the bow.

She'd been waiting for something to happen that tipped the scales one way or another. Normally, Kasia wasn't the passive type, but the cards had been so muddled she knew certain threads had to untangle themselves first. If the guard had never regained consciousness, she might have explained away the Six of Storms. If Malach had not escaped, the wrath of the Curia would be focused on him rather than

Kasia. If Spassov had not decided to follow them, Bishop Karolo would be interrogating her in some dank cell right now.

Yet all of those pieces had slid into place, forcing her path. She hadn't expected Natalya to be dragged along, but that was fated, too. Whatever channel she had discovered to the ley, Nashka was a part of it.

"I hope you're not feeling ill, darling." Tessaria sank gracefully to the deck next to her. "You've never been aboard ship before. It takes some getting used to."

"I don't mind the motion. It is a bit peculiar, but mainly I disliked the stuffiness of the cabin. The windows don't open."

"Portholes," Tess said absently. "Well, you'll get a reprieve tomorrow night. The captain refuses to sail straight to Nantwich. He has cargo for the Arx in Kvengard and insists he won't bow to one Pontifex just to aggravate another. It won't be a long stop, just a day or so. We need supplies anyway."

Kasia wiggled her toes. Both she and Natalya had lost their shoes in the fray. "Clean clothes would be nice. Do you plan to requisition those, too?"

A faint smile. "I have money. Better not to wave that letter around too often. People will remember seeing it."

Kasia glanced down the deck at a large snoring form curled up near the bridge. "What about Fra Spassov?"

"I find his presence highly suspicious and painfully awkward."

"I think he means well."

"What do you know about him?"

"Very little," Kasia admitted. "He's Alexei's partner at the Interfectorem. He came to our flat once when they first tracked me down. I didn't see him again until we came to the Arx."

"About that." Tessaria's dark eyes held her. "You lied when you claimed you never saw Feizah. Let's have the truth."

"Fine." She rubbed her arms. It was getting chilly. "I did manage to get inside the palace. But I never spoke to her."

Tessaria sighed. "Give them to me," she said, extending a gloved hand.

"Give you what?"

"The cards."

"I don't have them."

"Of course you do. You carry them everywhere and they allow you to use the ley. Don't attempt to prevaricate. It's far too late for that." She leaned closer. "You turned Ferran Massot."

Kasia shook her head. "No—"

"He touched you with his gloves off and you were rightfully furious. You didn't mean to do it. You didn't even realize you had, perhaps not until much later, but it's the only thing that makes sense. His Marks inverted at that moment and you were alone together."

Kasia was stunned to silence. Not at the accusation—she'd suspected the same herself—but at Tessaria's shrewdness.

"I think you've always had the ability and it was only a matter of time before it manifested openly. The ley got you inside the Pontifex's Palace and past those hapless guards. What happened next?"

Tessaria's sharp eyes demanded answers. But it wasn't just a contest of wills. Kasia loved and trusted her guardian. Perhaps there was a way to tell part of the truth and keep her promise to Alexei.

"Okay, yes. I did get inside the Reverend Mother's bedchamber. I told her everything. She believed me. She was going to help Fra Bryce." Kasia met her gaze steadily. "I swear, I'm not lying now, though it sounds mad—"

"Lezarius," Feizah whispered. "Was it?"

"You know?"

"I guessed. You think I didn't read those letters, too?"

"I didn't—"

"Of course you did. He's gone now, I suppose."

Kasia nodded, still struggling to accept that none of her secrets were in fact secret at all.

"I must send a message to Dmitry the moment we reach Kvengard. He wondered, but he wasn't certain."

So now Falke was *Dmitry?* Kasia resisted the urge to lift an eyebrow. "Lezarius only killed Feizah because he believed she sent assassins for him. Do you know anything about that?"

Tessaria stared at her for a long minute. "Let's move on. Those men back at Ash Court. Did they speak to you? Is that where you heard the phrase—" Tess paused and looked around, her voice a bare whisper. "Caput corvi?"

Other than the slumbering Spassov and a few sailors inside the bridge, they were alone on deck, but Kasia dropped her voice to match. "I tried to tell you, they weren't just revelers. They were after me, personally."

"I assumed as much, but it's better Natalya doesn't know all of it yet, darling. Now, what happened?"

Kasia recalled every detail of the encounter with perfect clarity. "One said, 'The Black Sun rises again. We bathe in its radiance.'"

"Saints."

"What does it mean?"

"The Black Sun of Bal Agnar. Followers of Balaur."

"Isn't he dead?"

"Yes, but there are still some who worship him like a god. What else?"

"Then he said, 'Caput corvi. The dragon consumes itself, dying to rise again. One must be at home in the darkness of suffering, Kasia.'"

Tessaria's hand grasped hers, too tight. There was a hint of fear in her eyes—the first time Kasia had ever seen her patron afraid of anyone or anything.

"I asked, 'How do you know my name?' And he said, 'Our master wants to meet you. The suffering will be greater if you resist.' I asked who his master was, and he said, 'He is the devouring black fire.'"

"Another reference to alchemy," Tessaria said softly, her gaze distant and troubled. "Perhaps it is well that we have Fra Spassov with us after all. He might prove useful. The Order of the Black Sun is not spoken of in polite circles, but it exists and not only in Novostopol. There are members in every city, in positions both high and low. We do our best to root them out, but they hide well, often in plain sight."

Kasia let out a slow breath. "I had no idea. Is that what Kireyev was using me for?"

"Partly, yes."

"Were any of my clients . . . .?"

"No." Tess squeezed her hand and let go. "Not that we know of."

Kasia shifted as Feizah's words echoed in her thoughts. She'd dismissed them at the time, but now they took on an ominous portent.

I don't know who you really are, girl, but I intend to find out.

"Why does the Order of the Black Sun want me, Auntie?"

"They must be aware of what you can do." Tessaria looked away. "Sister Chernov was found with her throat slit this morning. I didn't want to upset you so I didn't tell you before. But someone got to her. The body showed signs of torture."

Sister Chernov was the vestal who'd shown Kasia to her chamber at the Castel Saint Agathe. "The poor woman," she murmured.

"It's not your fault, darling. But I fear we got out of the city just in time. And we must be very careful until we reach the Arx in Nantwich. Even then. When we stop, false names would be prudent."

"Will you teach me to throw knives?"

An amused smile played across her face. "I'd be delighted. Now, I haven't forgotten that cartomancy deck in your pocket.

How many cards are there? Seventy-eight? That's the equivalent of seventy-eight Marks capable of wreaking untold havoc. It's like a toddler with a machine gun!"

Kasia frowned. "What's a machine gun?"

"Never mind. I won't have it! Give me the deck for safekeeping."

Kasia looked her square in the eye. "No."

The tension stretched near to breaking. Then Tessaria laughed softly. "I knew you'd refuse. You're pigheaded and rash. But also brave and occasionally noble. I suppose you must learn to control this power before it devours us all. I only ask that you wait until we're on dry land to experiment."

"Agreed," Kasia said immediately.

"Well, then." Tessaria drew her hands into the sleeves of the cassock. "It's getting a bit cold, eh? Should we cover that oaf with a blanket?"

"I'll fetch one from my cabin."

"Good girl." She eyed Spassov's sleeping form. "It might come in handy to have him around. He dispatched Maria's thugs rather neatly."

"So did you. Where did you learn to fight like that?"

Tessaria stared out to sea. "I ran some of the Curia's underground intelligence networks for Archbishop Kireyev during the war."

"In Novo?"

She shook her head. "Bal Agnar."

"Saints! I had no idea you were there."

"It was a long time ago." She sighed. "And not a time I think of often. We did good work, but not all of us came back. Not even most of us." Her smiled looked forced. "My skills are decidedly rusty, but not gone entirely it seems. Goodnight, darling."

Kasia kissed her velvety cheek. "I'll come along and get that blanket."

Five minutes later, she was tucking it around Patryk

Spassov's broad shoulders. He never stirred and she suspected he'd done some damage to the bottle she saw him nipping at when he thought no one was looking.

She stood for a minute longer at the rail. If she possessed a latent ability to touch the ley, did other Unmarked have it, too? Had she stumbled over something huge? If there were ways to use the ley besides Marks, it would change everything. The Curia would no longer hold a monopoly over the power, and Kasia doubted they'd take kindly to that fact.

The problem—one she would never admit to Tessaria— was that she had little control over her newfound abilities. She'd spent the last two days trying and most of the time when she drew a card, nothing happened. The harder she consciously tried to make the ley do what she wanted, the more it resisted. It was pure luck her gambit with the masked men had worked, and she and Natalya had nearly been crushed by the falling fire escape, too.

Tessaria was right. Best not to meddle while they were on board the *Moonbeam*. The captain didn't trust them and a mistake could prove disastrous. When they reached Kvengard, she would try again.

She tugged off her gloves. It was a moonless night, but the skies had cleared and a scattering of stars cast a faint illumination, augmented by the ship's running lights.

Just one card. For a quick weathervane reading only.

She reached blindly into her pocket. Two came out, stuck together.

The Martyr and the Knight of Storms.

The origins of the Martyr dated back to the war. It was what the nihilim did to clergy who resisted the new order. They would be strung up by one ankle in a public square, their hands cut off so they couldn't touch the ley, and left to bleed to death. The Tomb of the Martyrs at the Arx was a monument to their suffering and sacrifice.

The card she'd drawn was reversed, so the figure appeared

to be standing upright on one leg, the other bent at an angle. Instead of being severed, his hands were clasped in prayer, a halo surrounding his wild white hair.

Lezarius had found solid ground again, yet the background troubled her. That, too, had changed. A city lay on the far horizon, lightning forking down to strike a jagged tower. Although it was only a vague outline, something about the place was deeply unsettling.

The next card was worse. The Knight of Storms was one of just three cards with a figure whose face was angled to show only one eye (the others were all Jacks). It meant an individual who concealed a hidden side, potentially someone dangerous. The Knight of Storms was an archetype so driven by his own obsessions that he was blind to the consequences of his actions. A powerful figure who needed to balance his fiery ambition with compassion and responsibility.

In Natalya's deck, the Knight leaned forward on a white charger, sword raised as he galloped into the teeth of a gale. The horse symbolized intellectual purity, but red light gleamed along the edge of the blade. Trees bent and swayed in the stormy darkness around him. His helm was open, his face turned at three quarters. The visible eye was electric blue. It seemed to be staring directly at her.

Kasia shuddered and flung the two cards over the rail. The wind took them, buffeting them this way and that until they finally alit on the choppy surface and were swallowed by the sea. She rubbed her arms, suddenly in dire need of Natalya's laughter.

"The Saints shelter you both," she muttered, turning from the rail and heading back to the warmth and light below.

Chapter Forty

S moke trailed from a small fire, over which a copper kettle
steamed merrily. They camped at the edge of a lake in a
clearing carpeted with fragrant pine needles. Lezarius had
chosen the spot because of the stela that stood there. The
motto carved beneath the Raven proclaimed, "Libertas
perfundet omnia luce." *Freedom will flood all things with light.*

He dangled a bit of string over the little cat. It growled
and leapt, swiping with needle-tipped paws. Across from him,
Mikhail ate black bread and soft yellow cheese packaged in
waxy red rounds. They had broken into a market on the way
out of Novostopol. The knight carried the largest duffel bag,
but Lezarius managed his own blanket roll and a small ruck-
sack. Now he tore the wrapping from a package of Keefs and
stretched his bare feet toward the fire.

"Take the cat," Lezarius said. "I want to have a smoke."

Mikhail held out a hand, tucked the kitten into his shirt,
and returned to his meal. He ate with quiet, methodical intensity, as if it were a task he was determined to complete.

Lezarius lit one of the Keefs with a twig from the fire. The
brand was unfamiliar, but he liked the logo, a spiky seven-
pointed leaf, so he'd taken several cartons from the store. The

cigarettes tasted funny, both sweeter and harsher on the throat than the ones he bummed from staff at the Institute, but they had a pleasant calming effect.

"I am happy to see you eating again," he remarked. "You must get your strength back." He gestured with the cigarette. "It is not the madness that kills us, it is the captivity."

Mikhail lifted the wooden-handled kettle, pouring out two cups. He was still too thin and he slept in a tight ball with the blanket covering his head. He didn't like being outside the walls of the Batavia Institute, but Lezarius hoped he would get used to it in time.

They sat on logs arranged near the fire. Lezarius blew on his tea and watched the sun sink behind blue-gray hills. The only way across the Traiana River ran through the Fort of Saint Ludolf, so they had been forced to veer northwest into the rolling fields and sparse woodlands bordering the southern reaches of the Morho Sarpanitum. Lezarius was a geographer by training and knew the continent well. In another day or two, the river would grow shallow enough to ford. The route took them uncomfortably close to Bal Kirith, but there was no other way.

The cat used its claws to escape from Mikhail's shirt and leapt down with an arched back to prowl around the campsite. The knight's gaze followed until he was satisfied that it stayed away from the fire, then he began to sharpen his sword with a whetstone. Lezarius had been observing him closely but saw no sign of Mark sickness. It was peculiar because he had heard Feizah say she held twelve of Mikhail's Marks and Feizah had been dead for three days now. Mikhail should be in the final stages of ley poisoning, seeing terrible visions, his organs rupturing like so much overripe fruit, yet he appeared the same as ever.

The only explanation was that the Inverted Nightmark was protecting him. It was entirely possible. The combination of an Inverted Nightmark with a dozen Holy Marks was so rare as to be unheard of. In such cases, Lezarius suspected the outcome would depend on the individual. Mikhail Bryce was a priest of the Via Sancta. Lezarius sometimes eavesdropped when the brother came to visit and he knew Mikhail had been a forceful and formidable man, devoted to his beliefs. The Nightmark had undoubtedly corrupted him and its reversal left him mute and nearly catatonic save for their occasional chess matches. But the events at the Institute, the surge of the ley and breaking of the Wards, had awoken someone else. Not Captain Mikhail Semyon Bryce and not Patient 26, either. This was someone new.

At the Pontifex's Palace, he'd been a tornado of death, killing with no remorse or hesitation. If Mikhail had been militant before, now he was a fanatic, and Lezarius, having recruited him, was responsible for keeping him in line. Beneath the stony exterior lurked a worrisome fragility. Strike Mikhail in exactly the right place and his psyche might shatter into a thousand pieces.

"I know you were betrayed," Lezarius said quietly.

The rasping of the whetstone paused. Mikhail did not look up, but he was listening.

"I don't know who it was, or how you came to be Marked by a nihilim, but that is all in the past. I was betrayed, too. Betrayed by those I trusted the most. I remember little besides my own name, but it must be so. Yes, I see from your face that you know what I'm talking about." He drew deeply on the cigarette, then fell into a minor coughing fit. Mikhail laid the sword aside and handed him a cup of tea. Lezarius took a sip. The tightness in his chest eased.

"There is a great darkness on the horizon, Mikhail. As the nihilim say, night is falling. It is falling on the Via Sancta, on all we have built. This long night begins in the north, but make no mistake, it will work its way southward until it covers the land." He took a last drag from the Keef and tossed the twist of paper into the flames. "You might be thinking I'm mad, what do I know, but it is all true."

Mikhail touched the Raven Mark on his neck.

"Ah, you believe me, that is good. So the next question is, what can we do about it? Two escaped lunatics and a cat." He smiled. "I am suddenly rather hungry, Mikhail, can you find something sweet in your pack?"

Lezarius watched the reflection of the clouds moving across the lake for a while. Then he heard the rustle of foil. Mikhail gave him a chocolate bar. He took a bite. It tasted extraordinary.

"What was I saying?"

Mikhail pointed to the west, where the first stars were coming out. Lezarius stared at him, puzzled, then broke into a gap-toothed grin. "Darkness, yes. It has already gained a stronghold in Jalghuth. If they deposed me and locked me in an institution, it is safe to assume their intentions are not benign. But all is not lost. Not yet. There is still a chance. I must ask you to do something for me, Mikhail. I want you to become a soldier again. I cannot do this alone."

His companion's dark brows drew together.

"I know it is a great deal to ask. Everything was taken from you, the last time you trusted. But I am not like them. I will never betray you. I want only light and law. *Lux et lex.* That has always been my motto, Mikhail. Light and law. I am a martyr now. So are you. We have sacrificed, yes? We have paid the price for our convictions. Over and over, we have paid it. They buried us, but we are not dead yet, are we? Together, we climbed out of the grave." His mouth quirked in a humorless smile. "And won't they be surprised when they see us again?"

Something sparked in Mikhail's gaze. Very slowly and deliberately, he touched the Raven Mark again.

"Give me your sword," Lezarius said.

With ritual grace, Mikhail offered it to him, hilt first. Then he sank to one knee in the sandy soil at the edge of the water, head bowed. Lezarius took up the blade and tapped him once on each shoulder.

"You are the first knight of the Order of Saint Lezarius," he said. "The Order of the Invertido. Rise and be reborn."

Mikhail climbed to his feet. He was tall and fierce, yet there was also a childlike innocence about him that touched Lezarius's heart.

"We will make our way to Kvengard," he said solemnly. "Saints willing, we will find sanctuary there, and perhaps some answers. But since we are comrades now, there is something else I must tell you. Something no one knows. The Pontifex Balaur . . . he is not dead."

The knight stared at him, shock in his azure eyes.

"I know what you were told. It is what the world believes. That Balaur was executed for his crimes." Lezarius swallowed. His voice was barely a whisper. "After all the death, the destruction, I could stomach no more. I tried to be merciful. But I think I made a very bad mistake, Mikhail. I am afraid—"

A long, wavering howl broke the silence. A moment later, the unified baying of a pack came from the south. The Markhounds were still far off, but they would close the distance fast. Mikhail leapt into action, kicking the fire and scattering the embers, while Lezarius found the kitten. It was in the midst of stalking a grasshopper and mewed in protest. He pressed trembling lips to its head and placed it in the shoebox, which Mikhail had pierced with air holes. They quickly gathered their belongings. Mikhail slung the duffel bag across his shoulders and belted on the sword.

It was not the first pack to find them, and Lezarius doubted it would be the last. The conspiracy against him was vast. He wondered if he could trust anyone besides Mikhail, if the poison had already spread too far and they were all doomed. It was a terrifying thought.

The dogs howled again. The sound grew louder until Lezarius pressed his hands to his ears. He squeezed his eyes shut, trying to force it down, but his Inverted Marks flared with ley and he knew there was no stopping it.

Wind shrieked around a tower so high it pierced the heavy, roiling clouds. Through ragged shreds of mist, snow-wreathed mountains marched into the distance. His white robes whipped around him. He stood on an ice-slick stone platform, his back to the chasm beyond. Ahead were two cloaked figures, eyes burning from the depths of their hoods. He heard laughter, colder than the glacial wind that flayed the exposed skin of his face and hands, and the figures advanced, driving him backwards to the very edge. Wards shone along the octagonal walls of the tower, but they were not the blue of the surface ley, the pure blue of the Flame of the North, no, these flickered with a sickly red light that weakened his knees. Betrayed!

Lezarius screamed as a steel net closed around him, snaring his limbs so he couldn't move, but then the starry sky returned overhead and he realized it was only Mikhail carrying him from the clearing.

It had happened the first time with Doctor Massot. In his panic, he'd broken several of the Wards before the doctor jabbed him with a needle. Massot never brought him back to the little examining room after that, but the vision had returned several more times. At first he thought it was a waking nightmare induced by the Sublimin, but now Lezarius suspected it was a true memory.

"I can walk," he managed. "We will never outrun them if you must bear me in your arms the whole way."

Mikhail frowned down at him.

"I promise, I am well now. It was just a spell."

The knight set him on his feet. He cast a worried glance to the south. The hounds had gone quiet. If they were like the last pack, they would not utter another sound until they materialized like smoky shadows beneath the trees.

Lezarius clutched the shoebox with his little black cat. Mikhail had saved them before, but it was a close thing. They'd been walking for three days, pausing only to eat and snatch a few hours of sleep. The knight might have the strength to fend off the dogs once again, but he might not. And Lezarius could see it had pained him deeply to kill the creatures. They hunted at their masters' command, but they were not the true enemies.

Lezarius dropped down, ignoring the ache in his knees, and pressed a palm to the earth. There was very little ley left in the Void, but he found enough to push their trail a few kilometers west. It would not fool the Markhounds forever, but it would buy a little time.

The effort cost him dearly, but Lezarius hid his weariness. He stood and patted Mikhail's shoulder. "Let us make haste to the Traiana," he said. "Fate will find a way across, my friend."

Mikhail nodded. His blue eyes were resigned, the look of a soldier who had seen many tours of duty. He would live or he would die, but either way he would go down fighting. Lezarius wiggled a finger in front of one of the holes in the shoebox. A paw playfully batted out. He touched it, then tucked the box under his arm.

A pale crescent moon rose over the lake as the two men set off for the heart of the Morho.

Afterword

Read on for a sneak peek of the next book, *City of Wolves*. The complete series is now available at most major booksellers.

Sign up at www.katrossbooks.com/newsletter so you don't miss new releases, as well as sales and exclusive freebies, like a copy of *The Thirteenth Gate* from my Gaslamp Gothic series. Probably some cat pictures, as well.

In the meantime . . . Cave ab homine unius libri.

Beware of anyone who has just one book.

Cheers, Kat

City of Wolves

PROLOGUE

First came darkness.

A night so long and deep there could be no end to it.

A black sun rose in the fire-streaked heavens, but it gave no warmth or light. A terrible melancholy seized him. He was worth nothing. A crude lump of matter scorched in the black flames. How it stank, that fire! Like the earthy, putrid mould of the grave.

He confessed his sins, throat choked with bile. Was that a hooded figure in the shadows? Watching, listening? If so, it offered no absolution.

Listless misery turned to terror as he felt his very essence dissolving, pulverized to a bitter dust swept away by the wind.

Then, visions. A headless raven, dull feathers the color of tar. It took flight from his pale, bloated corpse.

He saw a boy lying with one arm flung wide on a rocky shore, hair washed by the outgoing tide.

He saw a white peacock in a garden. A two-headed lion spewing darkness.

The Black Sun again, devouring the world.

He tried to scream but had no voice.

Light.

The faintest glimmer at first, yet growing brighter with every arduous step. A journey of a thousand years through the blasted landscape of his own private hell.

Slowly, slowly, the foul vapors faded.

Sight returned.

His first thought was, *I am dead.*

The Light was all around him, flowing in whorls and eddies. He remembered the long night, but it was distant now. The Light warmed him. Made him safe and whole.

He turned his head, shocked to find he could.

Thick iron bars framed a window set high in a brick wall. Beyond it, the rolling thunder of the ocean.

Am I dead?

Was it all a dream?

He felt no hunger or thirst. No pain. If he had a name, he could not recall it.

But when footsteps sounded outside the door, he discovered that he could still feel fear.

City of Wolves

CHAPTER ONE

"This is it. Number 26."

Alexei reined up before a white house with mullioned windows and decorative timbers in a crosshatched pattern. Low shrubs, pruned at precise angles, flanked a flagstone walk leading to the front door. The curtains were all drawn, giving the place a grim, shuttered air.

Bishop Morvana Ziegler shot him a hard look. "They speak only Kven. I'll do the talking, Bryce."

He nodded. She delivered the same lecture each time.

"You will not mention anything about Marks, is that clear?"

"I thought you just said they wouldn't understand."

Her pale blonde brows flattened in displeasure.

"*Ja, ja*, I won't bring it up," Alexei said, turning his attention back to the house.

The boy lived in a respectable, well-to-do neighborhood east of the Arx. He was the fifth child to vanish without a trace in the last year. Willem wasn't the most recent. They'd just come from that house, a thatched cottage on the other side of the city. A girl of seven who'd been taken a little over a month before. But Alexei had asked to reinterview each and every family himself. It was his habit when he took on a new case to reassemble the pieces of the puzzle from scratch and see how they fit together. The Polizei might have missed something. Since they had no leads, Morvana had agreed, although she insisted on accompanying him.

He swung down from the saddle. Most of the horses in Kvengard were regular stock, but the Arx used Marksteeds. Creatures bred with ley. Their eyes shone like burnished gold and they faded to shadow when you didn't look at them directly. Riding them took getting used to, not because their gait was any different, but because he had the strange sensation that the tall, blond woman at his side was floating on thin air.

Alexei looked around, the ever-present salt breeze tugging at his cassock. Willem had vanished on this very street at some point between the corner where his school chums said goodbye and the front door of his home. In broad daylight, yet not a single witness had come forward.

Had it been Novostopol, Alexei would have guessed the boy got into a car, most likely driven by someone he knew. But there were no cars in Kvengard. No electricity or telephone service. It could have been a carriage, though his friends hadn't seen one, nor did the neighbors.

A servant admitted them to a dark, stuffy parlor. Solidly middle-class. A portrait of the Pontifex Luk, robed in white, hung over the fireplace. In person, he was thin bordering on cadaverous, but the artist had softened his harsh features and added color to his ashen cheeks. Luk looked almost grandfatherly, if not as hale and benevolent as Dmitry Falke. Luk thought Alexei was Falke's spy, but he seemed to believe the old axiom about keeping friends close and enemies closer. Instead of sending Alexei back to Novostopol in disgrace, he'd been assigned as aide to Bishop Morvana Ziegler.

She'd made it abundantly clear that she disapproved of his service during the war. He still wasn't sure why she'd given him this case. Perhaps just to see him fail—though that wasn't entirely fair. Morvana had agreed to his every request and seemed determined to catch the culprit.

"It's an old family in Kvengard," she said, watching the door. "We must tread carefully."

"Their only son is gone. Surely they understand the need to follow every line of inquiry."

She gave a reluctant nod. "*Ja,* I know."

"What did you tell them about me?"

"The same as the rest. That you're a special investigator from Novo." A small smile. "Most Kvens think your city is a den of iniquity. It makes sense you would have expertise on crimes like these."

Willem's parents appeared, the mother red-eyed, the father stoic and gruff. They showed him a smaller portrait of a handsome boy, dark-haired and blue-eyed. He stood stiffly next to a small white dog, gazing off to the side. It had been painted less than a year ago for his thirteenth birthday.

Alexei ran through his questions. He ordered them deliberately, posing the easiest first and the most uncomfortable last.

Had he made any new friends lately? What about girl-friends? How did he get on at school?

Did he seem unhappy before he disappeared? Nervous or different in any way?

Had any workers come to the house in the last few months? Tradesmen or peddlers?

Did they notice any strangers hanging about the street?

Did they have any enemies? Anyone at all who might want to harm their child?

What about relatives? Were there any falling-outs in the family recently? Old grudges?

Had he ever run away before? Did they have an argument?

It was useful to watch their faces while Morvana translated. The father stiffened most at the part about running away, angrily responding that Willem was a good boy who did well at school and was happy at home. Such a denial was to be expected, but Alexei sensed no anxiety from the mother—not towards her husband, at least. Only grief.

The interview unearthed nothing new. The Polizei had already been through the house, but Alexei wanted to look for himself. He signaled to Morvana.

"May we see his room?" she asked.

They were ushered upstairs to a bedroom overlooking the street. Single bed, neatly made. No posters of starlets or sports heroes like he'd expect to find in Novo. Just a desk with school books and half-finished homework assignments. A chest of old wooden toys that he'd probably outgrown but wasn't ready to part with. Three pairs of polished leather shoes sat lined up under the wardrobe. And a muddy pair of sneakers.

Willem was a runner. He had three first-place trophies from races at school. A fit, athletic boy. It wouldn't have been easy to take him against his will.

"It is just as he left it," the mother said from the doorway. Her face held both bleakness and a terrible hope. "Will took good care of his things."

The room reminded Alexei uncomfortably of his brother, Misha. A dusty shrine to a boy—now a man—who would never return. He prayed it would not be the same with Willem.

Alexei ran a hand beneath the feather mattress, hoping he might find a diary or some other hidden clue indicating that the boy knew his abductor. He lifted the carpet and tested for loose floorboards. Nothing. The forensic team had been thorough. If Willem had something to hide, it wasn't here.

Afterwards, they interviewed the two servants. They were sisters and both had worked for the family for many years. On the day Willem went missing, one was in the kitchen chopping vegetables for supper. The younger was polishing the silver. They swore Willem never arrived home.

"Where's the dog?" Alexei asked. "The one in the painting?"

Morvana conveyed the question. The older sister, a woman of about forty with thick blond braids, answered. "She says it ran away."

He felt a small jolt. This was new. "When?"

Morvana spoke with the woman in Kven for a minute. "Two days after Willem went missing."

That's why it wasn't in the Polizei report.

"She'd taken the carpets outside to beat them. The back door must not have closed properly. The dog got out."

"Did they look for it?"

Alexei waited impatiently through a longish exchange in Kven. Finally, Morvana shook her head. "Not really. She called a few times, hoping it hadn't gone far. She expected it would just show up."

"But it didn't."

"No."

"She feared her masters would be angry, but with their son missing . . . well, they were too frantic about Willem to worry about the dog."

It made sense. "Was it the boy's pet?"

The servant must have understood for she nodded before Morvana translated. "He love very much," she said in thickly accented Osterlish, wiping away a tear with the edge of her apron.

Alexei could think of nothing more to ask. The parents met them at the front door.

"Will you find him?" the mother asked. Pleading. "Do you think he's alive?"

Alexei was far from fluent in Kven, but he understood those questions. He'd heard them at each house they'd visited.

They didn't want the truth. What parent would?

"I'm sure he is," Morvana said firmly. "We're doing everything we can."

She'd repeated the same empty words again and again in the last week.

On his way out, Alexei paused. There was a peculiar smell in the hall. Almost putrid, but with an overlay of sweetness. A row of cloaks hung on pegs. It seemed to be emanating from the wool.

"Did you smell that?" he asked softly, as they stepped outside.

Morvana wrinkled her nose, diamond stud glinting. "It's the tannery. The father owns several in the city. They make gloves."

Kvengard followed a strict interpretation of the Meliora that forbade the slaughter of animals for food, but leather remained the most effective medium to block accidental use of the ley. Dairy cows that were old or diseased were humanely killed after an injection of tranquilizer and used at the tanneries. They'd passed near one yesterday. The stench was brutal.

"What did you make of the dog?" she asked.

"I'm not sure. It could be a coincidence."

Morvana had questioned the parents about their whereabouts on the afternoon of the disappearance, and both repeated the stories in the file. The mother had been out shopping with a friend all afternoon. They returned to the house together and discovered Willem hadn't come home from school. The father was at work all day. Both accounts had been confirmed.

"We should see if any other pets are missing," Alexei said.

She nodded. "I'll send some officers, but we have an audience with the Reverend Father at six bells. He wants an update on the investigation."

Outside, the pair of glossy black steeds waited patiently for their masters to return. Just as the hounds were bred to sniff out particular Marks, the horses were bred for docility and speed. Alexei had heard they could outrun an automobile at full gallop, though he'd never had the chance to test it.

Dusk had fallen and the lamp-lighters were out with their ladders. The clatter of iron-rimmed wheels on cobblestones and cries of hawkers seeking a last sale echoed through the narrow, canyon-like streets. Kvengard was a port city, sitting on a rocky promontory above the Southern Ocean. A steady breeze kept the air relatively fresh, though the smell of manure was pervasive. Alexei didn't find it unpleasant. Yet as he rode toward the Arx, his blue eyes swept each carriage that passed, lingering on the expensive lacquered ones with enclosed benches.

If it was just one child, he would suspect the parents or someone else in the household, regardless of their alibis.

But there had been nine.

And whoever was taking them, he didn't think they intended to stop.

Alexei left his mount at the stables and climbed the stairs to his apartment in the Wohnturm, a tower house on the grounds of the Arx. He slept in a chair near the window and used the large sleigh bed for his timeline. After hanging up his exorason, the loose outer garment worn over the cassock, he studied the files laid out in two rows on the quilt.

The children all lived in different parts of the city. They attended different schools. Some were wealthy, some not. Some had siblings, others didn't. They ranged in age from eight to fifteen. The older ones had all received their first Marks after the testing.

The first was Noach Beitz, the last little Sofie Arneth.

He could find no pattern, nothing they had in common, except for two things.

First, there was never any sign of violence. Some were taken from their beds in the night without raising an alarm. Others, like Willem, vanished into thin air within sight of their homes. As if they knew and trusted their abductor.

The second was the dates. Nine children over the last year. One every forty days, precisely.

He'd spent hours staring at a calendar, ruling out any connection to lunar cycles or holidays. Yet there must be a reason for it.

How was he choosing them?

Of course, it could be a woman, but Alexei felt that possibility to be remote.

There had been a case in Novo when he was still in law school. An Unmarked man who raped and murdered four women, all strangers, before he was finally arrested. Debate raged over whether this was proof that denying the deviants Marks was correct, or whether it was better to do something to restrain their impulses.

But those were crimes of opportunity. Impulsive and messy. The man was caught when a neighbor saw him entering his flat covered in blood.

This perpetrator was different. Methodical and intelligent.

He would not make a careless mistake.

If not for the children, Alexei would have been gone. It was his tenth day in Kvengard. In the long nights when sleep refused to come, Alexei dwelt on Mikhail and Lezarius, imagining various scenarios, each worse than the last. They must be in the Void somewhere. Lezarius had told Kasia that he planned to raise an army. But who would follow a madman— other than Alexei's mad brother?

Each night, he would vow to slip away on the morrow and search for them. Then he would wake and look at the timeline spread across the bed and think, *one more day*.

He'd grown obsessed with the case.

Kvengard had no newspapers. People knew because of the

missing flyers on every street corner and they were keeping a close watch over their offspring. He wasn't sure it would do any good. It hadn't for Sofie Arneth.

He picked up Willem's file and jotted: *Dog?*

Then he reviewed the other dossiers again, even though he felt certain they hadn't mentioned pets. He'd glimpsed a cat in the Keller house, a fat orange tabby that fled when he'd entered the home. And the dog had disappeared *after* Willem did, making it unlikely that the creature had been disposed of to prevent it from protecting its master or making noise.

The surge of excitement at finding something new faded to a dull ache in his temples, but Alexei kept reading. There had to be *something*.

Shortly after five bells, he made his way to the kennels to see Alice.

She trotted over and licked his hand. As he did every day, Alexei let her sniff Misha's copy of the *Meliora*, the foundational doctrine of the Via Sancta. His brother had read the book so many times the binding was coming loose from the seams. Alexei kept it wrapped in oilcloth so it would hold his brother's scent.

"Venari," he commanded. *Hunt.*

She gave it a snuffle and looked at him—a touch regretfully, he thought.

He didn't really expect Misha to turn up in Kvengard, but it made him feel like he was doing something useful.

"Are you happy here?" he asked, scratching the base of her nubby tail where a scar intersected her muscular haunch.

Alice wriggled and barked.

"You can come sleep with me tonight," he said in a low voice.

Sleep being a euphemism for curling up at his feet while he stared at the ceiling—or, as he'd done the last two nights, re-read the case files, hoping he'd overlooked some critical clue.

The other Markhounds watched with slitted eyes from

their little straw-filled houses. Alexei hadn't heard them howl and the Wohnturm was close enough that he couldn't have missed it. He felt sure no one's Marks had inverted since he'd arrived in Kvengard.

He set off through the wooded grounds for the Pontifex's Palace, a colossal limestone rectangle with blue Wolf Wards glowing above the windows and doors. The captain of the knights guarding the brass doors demanded to see his new corax identifying him as a member of the Nuncio's office. The man's chilly light blue eyes, so like Alexei's father's, kept flicking to the Raven on his neck. At last, the knights brusquely waved him through the doors. He strode through the corridors to the audience chamber, reaching it just as the bells tolled six. More knights in green surcoats stood guard outside.

Bishop Morvana waited for him beneath a faded tapestry, having changed into her robe of dark blue silk with gold embroidery along the sleeves.

"You've been to the kennels," she said, eying the short brown hairs clinging to his woolen cassock.

"Just visiting the hound I brought with me."

An appraising look. "I've never met a priest of the Interfectorem who treated them as anything other than working dogs."

"We share a history," he admitted.

Morvana's emerald eyes cooled. "In the war, you mean."

She didn't wait for a response, striding past the knights and pushing through the tall doors to the audience chamber.

Luk sat on a raised dais. His white robes were sleeveless, which Alexei still found faintly shocking. Running Wolves wound down both spindly arms. For all that the Kvens were arch-conservatives, they seemed to find nothing wrong with displaying their Marks for public view.

Alexei lowered his head in deference. "Reverend Father."

"Reverend Father," Morvana echoed, stepping forward to kneel and kiss his offered ring.

The Pontifex of the Southern Curia had a soft, mellow voice, nearly unaccented when he spoke Osterlish.

"So," he said. "How are you getting on?"

"We're finishing up the interviews," Morvana said. "The Polizei were thorough, but Fra Bryce thought it would be worthwhile to reexamine all the evidence."

Alexei suppressed a sardonic smile. He knew what she thought of the Polizei.

"Any theories?" Luk asked, propping his sharp chin on one hand. The heavy gold signet ring gleamed in the standing lamps to either side of the dais.

"It has to be an Unmarked." Morvana glanced at Alexei. He nodded, though he felt a twinge of guilt. Kasia Novak had failed the tests and she was a good person regardless. But it *had* to be. Anything else was impossible. Marks would not allow an individual to commit such evil. They'd already ruled out an Invertido by the simple fact that none of the hounds had barked on any of the days in question.

"What do you recommend?" Luk asked.

"A door-to-door search of the Burwald."

The Burwald was Kvengard's equivalent of Ash Court, a community designated for deviants. Alexei had ridden through it several times in his trips around the city. It was cleaner than the one in Novo, though solidly working class.

"That's a violation of civil rights," Luk pointed out.

"I see no other course." Morvana's jaw set. "We have six days before the next one."

"You're certain of the timetable?"

"It's the *only* thing I'm certain of," she admitted grimly.

"Perhaps we can ask for written permission to enter the premises," Alexei ventured. "That's perfectly legal."

Morvana cast him an appraising look. "And if they refuse, at least we have a shorter list of suspects. Clever."

"You have my permission to do so," Luk said, his gaze piercing. "This *must* be stopped."

The pontifex was bald as an egg, which only enhanced the impression of a skeleton draped in skin. Alexei didn't know what was wrong with him and hadn't dared to ask. But he wondered how much longer Luk would wear the white robe.

"I would also suggest an official announcement, Reverend Father," he said. "People should be warned."

Morvana stared at him, though her expression gave little away.

"And what would you have me say? That an Unmarked maniac is loose in our city?" Luk leaned forward. "Tell me, Fra Bryce, what will happen if the Arx issues such a message?"

Alexei remained silent.

"The days of lynch mobs are thankfully over," Luk continued. "But I imagine life would become very unpleasant for the poor souls who failed the tests, most of whom are blameless. I understand the gravity of the situation, but I will not condemn an entire class of human beings to poverty because they lose their livelihoods."

"You needn't say it's an Unmarked—"

"Everyone knows there is no other possibility. I imagine the whispers have already spread and I refuse to give them weight." The mild tone vanished. "Find this person and arrest them. That is the only solution."

"Yes, Reverend Father."

"Now, on to other matters. I've received word from the garrison that the Knights of Saint Jule are marching on the Morho Sarpanitum." He watched Alexei's reaction closely. "They're heading towards Bal Kirith."

"Falke . . . the Reverend Father implied as much when he spoke to me," Alexei said carefully.

"I assume the action is intended to inflict retribution for the Reverend Mother Feizah's murder at the hands of the Nightmage Malach." Luk's thin mouth tightened in a grimace. "He should be brought to justice, but I wonder how many will die in this operation. Morvana, what say you?"

"It is to be expected," she replied crisply. "Dmitry Falke would seize any pretense to invade. We will continue to monitor the situation."

Pretense? A Pontifex was dead. True, Malach hadn't done it, but only Alexei knew that.

"Very good." Luk flicked a finger. "Keep me informed. You're both dismissed."

Two cardinals passed on the way out of the audience chamber. Both eyed Alexei with open hostility. Morvana earned a cold nod.

"Does everyone think I'm a spy?" he wondered.

"I do not know what they think, Fra Bryce."

Morvana's long legs carried her ahead down the stone gallery, hands tucked into her sleeves and a preoccupied expression on her face. He hurried to catch up.

"They don't seem to like you much, either," he observed.

She glanced at him. "I've spent the last five years in Novo. The Arx here is much the same as yours. Some thought I was too young to be nuncio and their opinion has not changed."

"When will we start the search?"

"I must coordinate it with the Polizei and community leaders."

"We have no time for red tape. Why not start tonight?"

"Because we need to do this properly or else any evidence we find might be deemed inadmissible. Surely you know that."

He gave a reluctant nod.

They parted ways outside the palace. The phalanx of heavily armed knights guarding the doors didn't even glance at him as he passed, but his back itched as he walked towards his rooms in the Wohnturm. Kvengard was a peculiar place. Calling it insular would be a laughable understatement. They walled themselves away, renouncing all technology or contact with the outside, but he wondered how long it could endure.

Falke had moved at last. The Curia was headed for war again, whether Luk liked it or not.

The man was a puzzle. Brilliant and difficult, with a tendency to go his own way regardless of what the Pontifical Council decided. From the talk Alexei had overheard in the mess hall, Luk commanded absolute loyalty among the clergy. More than that—an almost divine authority, which was a heretical notion. There was no God but the ley. No heaven or hell but those we create ourselves.

What would the Kvens do when he was gone? Oh, there were always cardinals waiting in the wings. Someone would take the ring. Yet Luk had been Pontifex when Alexei's *father* was still an infant. It was his hand that guided Kvengard in all things. Would he still cling to neutrality if he knew what had happened in Jalghuth?

Luk wouldn't believe me even I told him, Alexei thought. He'd think it was some scheme by Falke to force his hand.

Saints! Intrigues within intrigues. He almost longed for the days when all he had to do was chase down Invertidos. When Lezarius was not a threat to the known world, but just an old man in pajamas bumming cigarettes from the orderlies.

Alexei rubbed his temples. One problem at a time. Something had to break in the case. It *had* to.

He climbed the stairs, lit a candle, and sat down in a chair with the files. By the time he finally nodded off hours later, Alexei had a softly snoring dog at his feet.

Glossary

OF PEOPLE, PLACES AND THINGS

Alexei Vladimir Bryce. A priest with the Interfectorem and former knight of Saint Jule. Suffers from severe insomnia. Marks include the Two Towers, the Maiden and the Armored Wasp. Enjoyed a successful law career before joining the Beatus Lacqueo. Wears a midnight blue ankle-length cassock with an inverted trident on the breast.

Alice. A Markhound and loyal friend to Alexei. Has a scar on her haunch from Beleth and harbors a special hatred for nihilim.

Arx. The inner citadels of the Via Sancta, they're akin to small cities and sit atop deep, churning pools of ley power. The Arxes in the two rebel cities were largely spared by the Curia's bombing campaigns, but they've fallen into ruin. Now the walls of the citadels in Nantwich, Novostopol, Jalghuth and Kvengard are Warded against anyone steeped in the use of abyssal ley, i.e., nihilim.

Bal Agnar. Situated in the northern reaches of the Morho Sarpanitum, amid the foothills of the saw-toothed Sundar

Kush mountains, the city was abandoned after Balaur's defeat. Emblem is the Black Sun, a circle with twelve jagged rays. Before the war, the city was controlled by a small, vicious oligarchy with the blessing of the Church.

Bal Kirith. Twin city to Bal Agnar, located in the central Morho Sarpanitum on the Ascalon River. Once considered the most beautiful of all the Arxes, its emblem is a Broken Chain symbolizing free will.

Beatus Laqueo. A specialized Order of the Knights of Saint Jule whose name means *Holy Noose* in the old tongue. Notorious for using extreme tactics against the mages. Motto is Foras admonitio. *Without warning.*

Beleth. Malach's aunt and the former pontifex of Bal Kirith. Fond of wigs, powder and decadent parties, she's spent the last three decades writing books of poetry and philosophy that are banned throughout the Curia, as well as a manifesto on the *Via Libertas*, a counter ideology to the Via Sancta that embraces the Shadow Side as inevitable and argues for social Darwinism in its purest form. Despite Beleth's eccentricities, she's cunning and formidable with a sword. Dotes on Malach, whom she raised as her own.

Balaur. The former pontifex of Bal Agnar. His sign is the Black Sun. Believed dead since the war, he still has secret followers in every city.

Cartomancy. Divination using cards. Kasia uses it to foretell the future with oracle decks made by her best friend, Natalya Anderle. In Novostopol, it's fairly lighthearted entertainment, often done at parties, but also for certain wealthy men and women who are devotees of the occult.

Casimir Kireyev. The archbishop of Novostopol, head of the Office of the General Directorate. Widely believed to be the Pontifex's spymaster. Gnomelike and bespectacled, he is one of the most feared men in the Church.

Clavis. The Pontifex of the Eastern Curia in Nantwich. The youngest ever to wear the ring, Clavis's special powers encompass doors, boundaries, and crossroads. A keeper of knowledge and technology from the past.

Corax. The word for *raven* in the old tongue. Symbolizes Fate's Messenger, a bridge between the material and spiritual realms. In common parlance, coraxes are copper coins given to knights in the field and used to identify bodies burned or mutilated beyond recognition. One side is engraved with the owner's name, while the other side indicates the Order within the Curia.

Dantarion. A bishop of Bal Kirith, she is Malach's cousin and daughter of Balaur and Beleth.

Dark Age (second). A cataclysmic period a thousand years before in which the world devolved into violent anarchy. Led to the founding of the Via Sancta and the abolition of most technology.

Dmitry Falke. A cardinal of Novostopol and member of the liberal Neoteric faction of the Church. Patron of Natalya Anderle and close associate of Archbishop Kireyev. He led the knights of Saint Jule to victory against the Nightmages and defeated Balaur in single combat, severing three of his fingers. Balaur's signet ring is now encased in a glass paperweight on Falke's desk.

Dur-Athaara. Capital city of the island of Tenethe, part of the witches' realm across the sea in the far east.

Feizah. The Pontifex of the Eastern Curia in Novostopol. A Conservative with the power to exhale wind and fog. Also called Feizah the Bold.

Ferran Massot. The chief doctor at the Batavia Institute. Marked by Malach. Conducted illicit experiments on his patients, in the course of which he discovered Patient 9's true identity.

Interfectorem. The Order tasked with hunting and detaining Invertido. Emblem is an inverted trident. The name means *murder* in the old tongue.

Invertido. Unfortunates whose Marks suddenly reverse, causing insanity. Symptoms include narcissism, paranoia, lack of remorse and severely impaired empathy. A genetic component is suspected as it often runs in families, although the condition can be deliberately inflicted using abyssal ley. Generally believed to be incurable.

Jalghuth. The capital of the Northern Curia, it's located in the far north, in the shadow of the Torquemites. Surrounded by glacial fields with hundreds of stelae to repel nihilim. Its emblem is the Blue Flame. Motto is Lux et lex, *Light and law*.

Kasia Novak. A cartomancer with a rare ability to work the ley through her tarot deck. Classified as a sociopath by the Curia, although she adheres to her own moral code and doesn't always act selfishly.

Kvengard. The capital of the Southern Curia, it sits on a rocky, windswept peninsula between the Northern and

Southern Oceans. Emblem is the Wolf, often depicted running in profile.

Ley. Psychoactive power that upwells from the core of the planet. Neither good nor evil, it's altered by interaction with the mind. Divided into three currents that correspond with the layers of consciousness: surface (blue), liminal (violet) and abyssal (red). These opposing currents flow in counterpoint to each other. The ley itself can become corrupted when thousands of people behave in selfish, wicked ways. Twice a year, it floods the artificial grid of stelae, temporarily bringing ley to the Void.

Lezarius. The Pontifex of the Northern Curia in Jalghuth. Also called Lezarius the Righteous. He alone controls the ley in a physical sense. Creator of the Void and the stelae. A geographer by training.

Liberation Day. A holiday commemorating the surrender of the mage cities and the end of the civil war, marked with parades and celebrations in the streets.

Light-bringers. Also, **lucifers**. What nihilim were called before Beleth and Balaur led their fellow clergy to disgrace and excommunication from the Via Sancta, they are a species distinct from humans, although the differences all involve the structures of the brain. Light-bringers learned to use the ley and offered refuge to those fleeing the Second Dark Age.

Lithomancy. Divination/magic using gems and minerals. Practiced by the witches in Dur-Athaara. Kaldurite, for example, absorbs the ley and prevents it from being used against you.

Luk. The Pontifex of the Southern Curia in Kvengard. His unique talent is wielding the ley as an evolutionary force. Luk created the Markhounds and the shadow mounts used by Kven knights.

Mage trap. Four interconnected Wards that form a box with no ley power inside the boundary. Can only be activated by someone with Holy Marks. During the war, it was one of the few effective defenses against the nihilim.

Malach. A nightmage from Bal Kirith. Nephew of Beleth. Malach struck a Cold Truce with Cardinal Falke to spare Bal Kirith from destruction, but his failure to deliver on the promise of a child leaves them mortal enemies.

Markhounds. Creatures of the ley, bred to detect specific Marks. Invaluable during the war to hunt nihilim in the ruins. Now the hounds are mainly used by the Interfectorem because they sense it when someone's Marks invert and start to howl.

Maria Karolo. A bishop at the Arx in Novostopol and head of the Order of Saint Maricus, which enforces the *Meliora*.

Marks. Intricate pictures on the skin bestowed by someone with mage blood. Civil Marks suppress anger, greed and aggression and enhance creative talents. They primarily use surface ley. Holy Marks are only given to the clergy. They can use the deeper liminal ley and twist chance to manifest a narrow range of outcomes. People with Marks must wear gloves to prevent accidental use of the ley, which is drawn through the palms of the hands. Each Mark is as unique as a fingerprint. The first one is generally given before the age of eleven.

Meliora. The foundational text of the Via Sancta. Written by the Praefators, it has forty-four sutras dealing with the human condition. Its title means "for the pursuit of the better." The *Meliora* argues that form of government is irrelevant and the root of all evil is violence against Nature and ourselves. Technology is a false panacea that creates social disharmony. According to the *Meliora*, the Church itself will eventually become obsolete when society reaches a state of utopia.

Mikhail Semyon Bryce. Alexei's older brother. A former captain of the Beatus Laqueo and a patient at the Batavia Institute. Marked by Malach.

Morho Sarpanitum. The primeval jungle at the heart of the continent.

Morvana Ziegler. A Kven bishop who takes on Alexei's Marks. Formerly Luk's ambassador in Novostopol.

Nantwich. The capital of the Western Curia, it sits on the shore of the Mare Borealis. Emblem is Crossed Keys.

Natalya Anderle. A free-spirited artist and unrepentant rake. Kasia's best friend and flatmate.

Nightmage. Also called **Nihilim**. A somewhat derogatory term to describe light-bringers after their fall from grace. They wear blood-red robes and maintain a church in exile called the *Via Libertas* that espouses a version of extreme free will. In Bal Kirith, they have human servants who've been promised wealth and status when the mages regain power. Motto is Mox nox: *Soon, nightfall.*

Nightmark. A Mark bestowed by a mage, distinguished from the Civil and Holy Marks given by the Curia in both form and function. First practiced by Beleth and Balaur, it allows the Marked to tap abyssal ley and to twist chance in their favor more directly and violently. In return, they are beholden to the mage. Nightmarks morally corrupt over time and the images are much darker in tone than regular Marks.

Nikola Thorn. An Unmarked char at the Arx in Novostopol who becomes Malach's lover. Her dream is to leave the Via Sancta and live among the witches of Dur-Athaara.

Novostopol. Capital of the Eastern Curia. Humid, warm and rainy. A port city, it sits amid two branches of the Montmoray where the river empties into the Southern Ocean. Despite the dreary climate, Novostopol is a lively place, with bustling cafes and nightlife. Thanks to the system of Civil Marks, crime is virtually nonexistent.

Office of the General Directorate. The most powerful organ of the Curia, headed in Novostopol by Archbishop Kireyev. Ostensibly, it oversees the other offices and reports directly to the Pontifex. Has a vast intelligence network and used to run covert operations in the mage cities. Emblem is the Golden Bough.

Oprichniki. A regular force of civilian gendarmes in Novostopol. Uniform is a yellow rain jacket and stylish cap. They carry only batons.

Order of Saint Marcius. Tasked with enforcing adherence to the philosophy laid out in the *Meliora*, in particular, the tight restrictions on technology. Emblem is a sheaf of wheat.

Oto Valek. An orderly at the Batavia Institute. On the payroll of Archbishop Kireyev and the OGD, Oto is a shady mercenary—and a bad penny who just keeps turning up.

Patryk Spassov. Alexei's partner at the Interfectorem. Also served as a knight during the war. A functional alcoholic and all-around bruiser with a heart of gold.

Perditum (pl., perditae). Feral humans who live in the Void. Once residents of Bal Agnar and Bal Kirith, they were warped by the psychic degradation of the ley before Lezarius created the grid. Some are more intelligent than others, but all succumb to bloodlust when the ley floods. Smart enough to fear and avoid Nightmages (whom they recognize by scent), but anyone else is fair game. Also called leeches.

Praefators. Founders of the Via Sancta, they were visionaries who discovered how to use the ley through Marks. The name means *wizard* in the old tongue. Most now comprise the canon of Saints, but due to the tumultuous upheavals of the Second Dark Age, little is known about the first Praefators beyond their names. It is assumed they were all light-bringers.

Praesidia ex Divina Sanguis. Protectors of the Divine Blood, in the old tongue. Founded by Cardinal Falke, this secret Order strives to ensure the continuation of lucifer bloodlines in service to the Via Sancta. Motto is Hoc ego defendam. *This I will protect.*

Probatio. The office of the Curia that administers morality tests. Emblem is a trident, indicating all three layers of mind.

Saviors' Eve. The night before Den Spasitelya (Saviors' Day), a holiday commemorating the building of the Arxes, it has a grimmer theme, with young people donning masks and costumes evoking the evils of the Second Dark Age.

Sweven. A memory, vision or fantasy shared directly with another person through the ley, as if they're experiencing it firsthand.

Stelae. Also called **wardstones**. Pillars engraved with Wards to repel nihilim. Found in the Void at the junctures of the ley lines. Most stelae are emblazoned with an emblem of the Curia (Raven, Crossed Keys, Flame, or Wolf, depending on the location) and a pithy maxim such as *Ad altiora tendo* (I strive toward higher things), *Fiat iustitia et pereat mundus* (Let justice be done though the world shall perish) and Vincit qui se vincit (He conquers who conquers himself).

Sublimin. A psychotropic drug used to bestow or transfer Marks, it temporarily dissolves the barrier between the conscious and unconscious.

Sydonie. A young Nightmage at Bal Kirith, sister to Tristhus.

Tabularium. A vast archive, it's one of the few buildings in the Arx to have electricity. The Tabularium holds files on every citizen of Novostopol, as well as a separate register for members of the clergy. An even larger Tabularium exists in Nantwich, with records dating back to the Second Dark Age.

Tashtemir Kelavan. A veterinarian who serves as the only doctor at Bal Kirith.

Tessaria Foy. A retired Vestal and godmother of Kasia Novak. Close to Cardinal Falke and Archbishop Kireyev. In her mid-seventies, Tess is an elegant and enigmatic figure.

Comes from a moneyed family in Arbot Hills, not far from the Bryce family mansion.

Tristhus. A young Nightmage, brother to Sydonie, whose lead he follows without question.

Unmarked. Individuals who fail the morality tests administered by the Probatio and are denied Marks. The lowest caste of society, they live by the charity of the Curia since few will employ them. All the chars at the Arx are Unmarked, as proclaimed by their gray uniforms. Unmarked comprise about one percent of the population. In Novostopol, they're relegated to a slum district called Ash Court.

Via Sancta. The Blessed Way. A social, scientific and spiritual experiment to improve humanity. Teaches non-violence and beauty in all things.

The Void. Also called the **Black Zone**. The region where the ley has been banished. Encompasses the cities of Bal Agnar and Bal Kirith and most of the Morho Sarpanitum.

Wards. Symbols imbued with emotional power that concentrate the ley for a specific purpose. Some repel nihilim, others force the ley from a particular area (see mage trap). A surge can cause them to short for minutes to days, but they self-repair. Most use surface ley and thus glow bright blue. Activated by touch.

Acknowledgments

The concept of the ley owes a huge debt to Carl Jung, the Swiss psychiatrist who coined the term *shadow side*. It represents the hidden aspects of the personality—the parts of ourselves that we find intolerable and can't acknowledge. Jung also explored the collective unconscious and the significance of archetypes in the human psyche. When Malach tells Alexei, "Take pains to waken the dead. Dig deep mines and throw in sacrificial gifts, so that they reach the dead," that's a direct quote from Jung's *Red Book*. It still gives me chills! A fascinating source I came across in my research was *Jung and Tarot: An Archetypal Journey* by Sallie Nichols for anyone interested in going deeper down that particular rabbit hole. Other books I (and Malach) eagerly devoured were Robert Greene's *The 33 Strategies of War* and *The Art of Seduction*.

Heartfelt thanks to first readers Laura Pilli and Leonie Henderson, whose feedback always makes my stories a hundred times better.

To the wonderful, talented team at Acorn, for making dreams come true and being the best publishing family an author could ever ask for.

Last but never least, to Mom and Nick, my darlings.

About the Author

Kat Ross worked as a journalist at the United Nations for ten years before happily falling back into what she likes best: making stuff up. She's the author of the Nightmarked series, the Lingua Magika trilogy, the Fourth Element and Fourth Talisman fantasy series, the Gaslamp Gothic mysteries, and the dystopian thriller *Some Fine Day*. She loves myths, monsters and doomsday scenarios.

www.katrossbooks.com
kat@katrossbooks.com

facebook.com/KatRossAuthor
instagram.com/katross2014
bookbub.com/authors/kat-ross
pinterest.com/katrosswriter

Also by Kat Ross

Nightmarked
City of Storms
City of Wolves
City of Keys
City of Dawn

The Fourth Element Trilogy
The Midnight Sea
Blood of the Prophet
Queen of Chaos

The Fourth Talisman
Nocturne
Solis
Monstrum
Nemesis
Inferno

The Lingua Magika Trilogy
A Feast of Phantoms
All Down But Nine
Devil of the North